PENANCE OF BLOOD

PENANCE OF BLOOD

PENANCE OF BLOOD

OATHBREAKER BOOK ONE

A. J. DRUMMOND

Podium

Podium

PENANCE OF BLOOD

CHAPTER ONE

HEADSMAN

Angels are good at wielding guilt. Devils are sometimes better, but you'd need a priest to explain the difference between the two. As far as I can tell, it's mostly a matter of aesthetics.

A crowd gathered in a storm-shadowed square. The slick cobblestones, weathered by long centuries of rain and trodding feet, ran with tiny rivers. Water rolled across the steepled roofs of the surrounding buildings, fell from the mouths of snarling gargoyles, and formed endless tears down the faces of stone seraphs.

The crowd stood silent, their eyes fixed on a raised wooden platform where several figures stood and one knelt. Armored guards with tall poleaxes, their eyes shadowed by the brims of their elegant helms, held the rain-slick blades of their weapons to the throat of a kneeling man. The town's earl watched with grim silence, his shoulders draped with a black cloak as though in mourning.

At the Earl's side stood a thickset man in a crude leather vest, a hood shadowing his face almost in mockery of the elegant helms of the guardsmen, a long hafted axe in his hands. He stood over the kneeling prisoner, waiting for the order to bring his weapon down, a grim shadow in the rain.

I don't know what the kneeling man had been condemned for. A beheading was usually the punishment for treason. From the mutters of the crowd I caught beneath the storm, I gathered he had been a knight. He glared up from the block they'd pressed him to, eyes piercing through the haze of rain without even a hint of pleading. A brave man. I could almost taste his pride in the damp air.

Regardless, I wasn't there for him.

Another man stood on the platform. A priest, clad in white robes draped in a grand crimson cloak, its edges stitched with patterns of gold. He called out to God and Her Choir in a brassy orator's voice, speaking between rumbling peals of thunder.

He was good at his job, I will give him that. He used the storm to advantage in his speech. The rain falling down his cheeks made it seem like he wept, and indeed his speech on behalf of the soul of the man they were about to execute seemed genuinely remorseful.

The storm picked up. I'm not sure if it was that or the impatient expression on the Earl's face that spurred the Bishop to end his speech. The nobleman nodded to the Headsman, who wasted no more time. The axe came down, its wide blade splitting rain to form a blurring arc of motion so even the untrained eye could follow its path. Some in the crowd gasped.

I noted the skill of the swing with a professional eye. The executioner was good, too. The head came free on the first blow, as surely as if they'd used a guillotine. The sharp crack as the axe split bone and sank into the wooden block could be heard even over the rain, echoing across the square.

There came no more ceremony once the condemned man's blood mixed with rain on the stone beneath the scaffolding. The Earl provided no words of his own. At a signal the crowd began to part. The headless corpse was left where it lay, bleeding over the wooden platform. The soldiers escorted the nobles back to the fortress.

The Bishop, along with some guards and attendants, moved to the looming cathedral rising up over the surrounding township.

I adjusted the wrapped bundle resting on my shoulder and melted into the alleyways, following the Bishop like a distant shadow. He had claimed a life on behalf of the divine today, or so he'd convinced himself.

Little did he know that I would claim his.

Leonis Chancer, the Bishop of Vinhithe, always performed a private prayer in the cathedral's main chapel after executions. It was a cavernous room, ostentatious, with towering pillars carved in exquisite detail and a vaulted ceiling rising overhead like a brooding night sky.

The chapel stood empty save for the Bishop. He knelt beneath a towering statue of the Heir. The God-Queen was represented in Her classical form as a saintly woman with heavily lidded eyes, arms fallen to her sides with palms open and forward facing. A horned crown, fashioned from gilt vines, enwrapped Her brow.

God looked down, silent, as the clericon murmured his prayers, head bowed and arms crossed to enfold his shoulders. His red cloak, still damp from the rain, pooled around him, almost mimicking how the blood had spread from the condemned man's body.

I waited until near the end to walk out into the central aisle, stopping between the rows of pews where, on another day, the townsfolk would sit to listen to this man preach. I was his only audience now, and I let him reach the final invocation.

When he gave those final words, "In faith we wait for the gates to open," I let my voice mingle with the Bishop's.

Leonis startled, turning. When he saw me standing in the aisle, his graying brows knit in confusion. He seemed young for his position, not yet fifty. Though his hair was hidden by a deep cowl bound close to his skull by a golden band, I could still make out dark hairs peeking through.

His dark blue eyes, almost black in the poor lighting, studied me without fear. They took in my red cloak, closer to brown than his rich scarlet one, soaked from the rain, and the pointed cowl shadowing my face. I said nothing as his eyes noticed other details; the wrapped bundle resting on my left shoulder, the poor quality of my cloth, the ring set on my right forefinger.

That last detail, his eyes rested on. The ring was a smooth band of ivory set with a black stone. I didn't bother hiding it.

Leonis Chancer swallowed. "I am sorry, my son, but the chapel is closed at the moment . . . I am certain I can make time for you another day, but I am in private prayer."

I said nothing, and began to walk forward at an unhurried pace. The sound of my boots striking the floor made soft echoes through the chapel, a space built to make sound carry.

The Bishop rose to his full height. The confusion writ in his regal features quickly shadowed with anger.

"The cathedral is closed!" he said, his voice lashing across the room very much like the thunder still rumbling above. He had used aura in that. I felt its pressure against my senses.

"Remove yourself or . . ." He gave up on command then, seeing that my pace wasn't faltering. "Guards!" he called.

No guard would be coming. I hadn't killed the men standing watch in the room's connected passages—they had done me no wrong, and I wasn't there for them—but they would be indisposed for a while. It was just me and the priest.

"Who are you?" The Bishop's skin ran with sweat now. He backed away as I approached the short flight of stairs leading up to the dais. "W-what do you want?"

"It's not what I want that matters right now," I said.

My voice is hoarse and low, but it carried well enough in that room. "You weave a good sermon, preoster. Did you cry at Llynspring, too?"

I saw his face go pale as he recognized the name. "Is this revenge, then?" he asked, taking a step back. God, wrought in stone and wood and gold, towered over him.

I had never been at Llynspring, but I'd heard the rumors of the witch trials that had flared like a killing flame across the west, ending in the deaths of more than five hundred—either through accusations of apostasy or the accident of inhuman birth.

Accused by this man, before he'd become the archclericon of a little earl-dom far from those regions. Not the worst of the atrocities committed during the war, not by far, and most had forgotten the blood spilled in the rural west thanks to the seas of red washing the east.

The Bishop's expression confirmed the truth of it.

"Llynspring, Kilcast, House Wake . . ." I muttered, just loud enough for him to hear as I continued to approach, ascending the steps. "How do you say our God's name without your throat bleeding?"

"Guards!" the Bishop cried out for help again, his voice cracking. He'd backed all the way to the towering effigy of the Heir again, and as he felt it at his back he flinched and stopped.

I had reached the top of the steps. I let the cover fall away from the object I held as I loosened the rope binding it. It was an axe. Not so big as the one the executioner out in the square had used, but the design did have similarities, particularly in the dramatic curve of the long blade.

Most comparison ended there. The handle of the weapon had been fash-ioned from a single branch of uncarved oak, almost like a poor vagabond's walk-ing stick, gnarled, twisted, and burnt. I felt its familiar roughness in my hand, the sharp imperfections brushing my calloused fingers.

The branch entwined around the head, from which a hooked blade emerged, glinting with a brassy sheen. Intricate whorls had been inlaid in gold into the metal, and the cutting edge had many scars.

If the Bishop had not guessed by the ring, he knew well enough who stood before him now.

"The Headsman," he breathed, all the remaining color draining from his face. He began to incite a prayer of banishment. I felt a shiver of power ripple out from the priest, and had to suppress a laugh. He was trying to cant at me.

"Sorry, preoster, but I'm not a revenant. Or a demon, before you try that too. We have the same masters, you and I."

"But why you!?" the Bishop cried out. He tried to skirt around me, probably to make for one of the passages behind the altar. I tensed, ready to spring for-ward if he attempted to escape, but his own desperation for an answer kept him in place.

"If they were so displeased, why not smite me down? Why send a . . . a—"

"Ask them yourself," I snapped. I wanted this over.

"I deserve more than that!" the Bishop snarled, stopping in his tracks and taking a sudden step forward, surprising me. "Have I not served them faithfully?"

His fingers formed claws as he dragged them down the front of his mantled cloak, clutching at the fabric so the smooth material bunched in his hand. "Heresy. Greed. Hate. This land was so full of poison, and anyone is surprised it burst forth like pus from a wound?" A cold pride entered his voice. "I drew that poison forth and cleansed it. I have *served*."

"Is that what you think?" I took another step forward, cautious of him bolting, or trying something else. He'd already demonstrated he could wield aura, and it always paid to be cautious of that. "You think you served Her," I gestured at the statue with my axe, "by slaughtering innocents while the rest of Urn burned?"

"Innocents!?" The Bishop laughed, a manic edge in his voice. "Necromancers, pagans, cultists, trollkin, escapees from Draubard . . . apostates all. Urn burned because we turned our backs on the teachings of the Onsolain, on the promise of Heaven!"

I glared, silent. There was no getting through to this man. I don't know why I even bothered trying. I hadn't been sent to reform him, just to kill him.

Even still I spoke, the words coming unbidden to my lips. "Urn burned because men like you turned power mad."

The Bishop pointed a trembling finger at me. "Devil! Crowfriar! You were sent to test my faith."

"Afraid not," I said, and took my axe in both hands. Maybe he was right, I mused. But I wouldn't be the one to tell him whether he passed that test or not.

The Bishop shook in terror, then steeled himself and drew a dagger from within his robes. If he thought this was a test of faith, then it seemed he wasn't willing to leave his fate fully in its hands. I couldn't blame him. I suppose the real difference between me and the priest was that he had murdered for faith, and I had lost mine a long time ago.

I killed for something far less easy to define.

The rest happened swiftly. The Bishop didn't bring any powers to bear, either divine or dark. Instead, he lunged at me with the dagger, a prayer on his lips. Stupid, but I guess he didn't want to die fleeing for his life.

For my part, I tried to make it quick. I sidestepped his strike, but he attacked with a speed and fervor I hadn't expected. His blade put a shallow cut on the side of my neck. Baring my teeth I smashed a fist into his nose, sending him sprawling down the stairs of the dais. His golden headband came loose and clattered across the floor.

Of all the things he might have done in that moment, he reached for the band. He missed it by inches, his fingers clutching at empty air.

When my shadow fell over him, he closed his eyes and muttered something under his breath. A prayer? An apology? An admonition? I didn't catch the words.

Then he met my eyes and his face set in cold stone.

"Your judgment will come soon enough, traitor." He bared bloody teeth at me, his face masked with red deeper than his clerical vestments. "I know who you are! What your order did."

He spat out a glob of red. "We will see which of us is truly damned when all is said and done."

I hesitated only a moment. It was brief, perhaps forgivable to an onlooker as the pause one takes to gather their breath or muster a thought. But in that moment, I didn't see the monster who'd condemned hundreds to iron and flame on the mosaic floor where Leonis Chancer sprawled. I didn't see the dangerous zealot who could push the Faith into a dark new age. I knew that creature *was* there, beneath the mask.

All I saw was a frightened old man who did not wish to die.

He *was* that monster, though, and had chosen to be it over and over throughout his life. His actions had consequences.

I was that consequence. I adjusted my stance. "I already know where I'm bound, Your Holiness. I am sure we'll see each other there."

My swing mirrored that of the Earl's executioner. A long arc, high over my head, before the axe fell in a hiss of parting air. The crack of bone, and the sharper impact of magicked steel on smooth marble.

As the body, now headless, stilled, the winglike folds of the Heir's stone-carved sleeves seemed to enfold it from above. Red cloth darkened further with blood until it seemed a pool of it was all that remained of the priest. The head rolled unbelievably far. I followed its movement with my eyes. It seemed to keep rolling forever, until its path finally came to an end in the shadows of a pillar.

Where it came to rest near the foot of a young acolyte, who stared at the scene in wide-eyed horror.

CHAPTER TWO

RED RAIN

I cannot say how long that moment lasted, as the novice and I stared at one another. It can't have been longer than seconds, but it felt like time froze.

The acolyte was young. A boy, I think, though it could be hard to tell with priests. His white robes weren't yet darkened by red dye, and a band of copper encircled his head rather than gold. His pale face, made sheet-white by horror, stared at me in frozen shock.

I should have killed him. I tensed to do it, fingers tightening around the shallow bend in my weapon's haft. A sudden dash, or even a throw of the axe, and the acolyte would be silenced. He wouldn't be faster than me in those layered robes. I could stop him with a spellcant, just long enough to cut him down.

The words formed on my lips. If I spoke, I knew I'd have to do the rest. Who was I to worry over scruples? To care about mercy?

I hesitated, and like a spell breaking the acolyte ran.

I watched him run, telling myself all the while to stop him. Then, cursing myself for a fool, I ran the opposite way.

The bells began to toll before I made it even a block from the cathedral.

I crouched in an alley as armored soldiers poured through the street beyond, rain pattering off their armor. Vinhithe had come alive like a kicked beehive, armored guardsmen emerging from barracks and towers across the settlement to scour the streets for whoever had beheaded their bishop. They had emptied the streets of townsfolk, leaving the cobblestone paths of every block clear for ranks of poleaxe-bearing foot troops or mounted cavalry.

As the one who'd done the beheading, I felt inclined not to satisfy them. The gates would be closed, and every wall and tower manned, which left me a rat scurrying in a maze riddled with packs of vengeful cats.

High above, the bells of the cathedral struck mournful tones across the streets. The sky rumbled forth an echoing peal of thunder. I turned my eyes up to the clouds, sullen.

"Didn't you want this?" I muttered. The sky didn't answer, and I hadn't expected it to.

When the patrol had moved down the street and vanished into another block, I dashed across to the opposite alley, boots splattering through puddles with every step. I poised my axe on my shoulder, held in a tense grip.

A flash of light drew my attention. Not lightning. A shimmering emblem had appeared in the sky, silver chased with something the color of sun rays, formed into the shape of a snarling wolf with a single horn, the mark of the Earl of Vinhithe.

A phantasmal banner. I cursed. If they'd put some Art in it to hem me in . . .

"There!" someone called from a window. Distracted by the sorcery blazing over the city, I flinched, half expecting an archer. But it turned out to be an old man peering out of a high window, pointing with a gnarled finger.

"He's there!" the citizen said, his eyes wide with fear.

Even the citizenry were against me. I'd botched this badly.

Why hadn't I just killed the boy?

I knew why. Even still . . .

Fool, I called myself, and moved.

I didn't know if any guards were near enough to hear, and didn't wait to find out. I reached the mouth of the alley and moved into the relative shadow between craftsmen shops and townhomes. Vinhithe was a big town, built along a major river winding through the fertile heartlands of the subcontinent. Its streets merged and twisted with little order, buildings packed tight together to take advantage of what high ground could be claimed over the wetlands.

Some of the alleys were narrow enough that even a small man might struggle to move quickly through them. I am not a small man. I had to turn sideways deeper down the alley as it dipped into a lower side street, my weapon and cloak becoming obstacles as I moved cautiously on the slick ground. The rain cascaded down off the roofs above, running in a shallow stream down the alley as though it were a miniature canal. It surged around my ankles, dragged at the tattered hem of my worn cloak.

I reached the end of the alley and stopped, listening through the rain. Water dripped off the edge of my cowl, the dull roar of the storm making it difficult to tell if the next street was empty or not. There could be soldiers waiting for me to emerge, hidden in a hundred places.

The town was a maze, and as much a danger to me as an advantage. The guards would know these streets, know how to head off an intruder. No doubt they were already putting up barricades and checkpoints.

I should have killed the damn acolyte. Why hadn't I?

Because the war is over, I reminded myself, *and you want to keep it that way.*

Well, my softness would end in either my death or the deaths of more than a few members of the Vinhithe garrison. I glanced up, recognizing the belfry tower of another church, not the main cathedral.

I had an escape plan already. All I had to do was reach the river.

Something tore past my head, missing an ear by a finger's width, and clattered across a nearby wall. It broke drops of rain in its path, the sound oddly muffled. I turned and saw figures at the mouth of the alley. The townsfolk had alerted the guard, and they had crossbows.

I ran.

If not for the rain and the wind, I doubt they would have missed me.

More crossbow bolts whipped past, clattering off stonework and splitting rain. I emerged from the alley into a small square, a fountain in the center fashioned in the likeness of three elf-maids pouring water from ewers into a basin. One of their pointy-eared heads erupted as a bolt went through it. I snarled out a bitter curse.

Figures moved through the rain as I passed the fountain. There were guards waiting for me, as I'd feared. Or I was just unlucky. I counted six through the haze of rain, not counting the marksmen approaching from behind.

I didn't wait for them to encircle me or bring up reinforcements. I went forward like a battering ram, and closed on the first soldier within seconds of their entry into the square. He was a big man, his breastplate bearing the horned wolf emblem of the local earl. His gauntlet wrapped around the handle of a flanged mace.

His eyes widened beneath the brim of his helm at my speed, but he didn't hesitate to grip his bludgeon in both hands and bring it up for a swing.

Too slow. Still resting on my shoulder, my axe levered back as I took it in both hands, kicked off the slick stone to give myself a burst of speed, and then swung.

The Earl's executioner had been good. I am better. Raindrops parted as the fine-honed edge of the axe's cleaving edge came down, driving through the big soldier's peaked helm. Bone split beneath layers of metal and leather. One of the man's eyes rolled up into his skull, the other popped loose, and he fell in a steely clatter.

I went over him. The second guard died in two cuts, losing a hand at the wrist before I took his jugular on the backswing. The third took more doing, managing to parry my first swing in a flash of sparks before I slammed the butt of the axe's haft into his jaw.

Their helms were open-faced, made for sentry duty and not war, and his face broke in a splatter of blood and teeth.

The thrill of combat, an old companion, rose up in me. My limbs sang with tension, and a beast's snarl, very like a grin, tugged at my lips. I could hear my blood beating through my veins.

This was not the time. I was not that man anymore. I fought that part of me down, buried it deep, and made myself cold.

I turned as a fourth soldier jabbed at my neck with the tip of a halberd. He caught the edge of my neck, drawing blood, but I leapt aside before he could use the curved hook beneath the spear's point to catch me. He tried to turn, to get his weapon between us, but I was faster.

Chain mail split as easily as flesh beneath my weapon's alloy mortal steel and fey bronze. I took the halberdier's left arm at the shoulder, dropping low to duck under the wild swing of his cumbersome weapon as he turned in a death spiral, blood spraying in an artist's mark across the rain-slick square to form a near complete circle.

Eight seconds.

I'd made my gap, and turned toward another alley to escape the patrol. But the crossbowmen had arrived now, four of them. They fanned out on the far side of the square to take their aims, killing darts loaded.

I dove. They fired. I'm not sure which happened first. Two bolts missed, sinking into stone and the whitewashed wood of nearby buildings with sharp cracks of impact. One broke off the fountain statues, shattering a slender elfin arm.

The fourth found my shoulder. It punched deep, going through layers of cloth, then meat. I didn't wear armor. I had not come for war, but it had found me anyway.

It always found me.

I hit the stone rolling. The bolt in my shoulder snapped, leaving half of its length still jammed in. I let out a gasp of pain, even as my mind took stock of the injury. Left shoulder, close to the bicep.

I came to my feet, using the fountain as cover, and tried to take my axe in two hands. As muscle and bone brushed against the embedded dart, agony erupted like a detonating cannonball.

Bad. Very bad.

I glared through a gap in the statues. The crossbowmen were already reloading. I could kill them now, get them off my back, but it would heighten the risk of being penned into this square if more of the garrison were converging. Not to mention I'd be just as likely to get shot down the moment I stepped out of cover.

High above, another wolf's head burned itself into reality. The Earl's knights were getting closer, and they had adepts.

I ran instead, making the decision instinctively. I wasn't here to wage war on the garrison. I'd completed my task. Now I needed to escape. I'd planned for this, in a loose fashion—I had an escape.

But I needed to reach the river.

One of the surviving guards from the group that had tried to head me off moved into my path. Young, his face tight with fear beneath his helm, he lifted his poleaxe in shaking hands and prepared to die bravely.

Brave lad. I lifted my axe and saw him flinch.

I'd spilled enough blood already today. Instead of cutting the boy down, I gathered my aura and shaped it. To the naked eye, it would look as though a soft ray of golden sunlight pale as an autumn dusk illuminated my form for a single moment. I knew my eyes shone brighter also, that gilt fire flickered from between my teeth.

I brought the power to my lips and cast it forth with a word.

"Stop."

The guardsman froze, lips parting in a breath he didn't draw in. I'd put very little power into the cant, so it would only last a few seconds. Otherwise the boy might suffocate or die from a stopped heart.

I dashed past the immobile soldier and continued on, the crossbowmen hesitating as their comrade got in their line of fire.

The bolt in my shoulder screamed with every step, but I ignored it. I'd been trained to focus through pain, and I could tolerate much of it. Still, a lethal injury would kill me.

As the sky darkened with the setting of the sun and the worsening storm, I made my way to the river. Behind me, blood ran with rain in the street.

I avoided further encounters with the guard. My goal was not to leave a bloodbath in my wake. Truly, my goal had been to be gone from the city before anyone had known I'd been there. I made an effort not to kill more of the garrison as I navigated the winding alleys and streets until I reached the river.

By then night had drawn very near. The already overcast sky left my flight in darkness broken only by the flare of lanterns and torches as the Earl's men continued their hunt. That, and the frequent flashes of lightning forking half-seen through roiling black clouds.

And sorcery. The horned wolf howled in a dozen places over the sprawl of the township, marking where the guard had secured the area.

Hemming me in.

The storm grew worse, and that did not bode well for my planned method of escape. The Earl sent his knights out in force to reinforce the garrison, and more than once I found myself sinking into the shadows as armored riders tore across my path, arms shining with odlight to pierce the veil of rain and storm-cast dusk, their war chimera made into nightmare shapes by the deepening gloom.

I'd hidden a raft beneath one of the river docks, having intended to let the current sweep me miles from the township before a proper manhunt could get underway. Half of that plan was well botched, but I wasn't about to try fleeing into the wilderness on foot from chimera-mounted knights.

I ghosted through alleyways, flinching at every distant shout and beat of claw or hoof that reached me through the storm. The wound in my shoulder burned with each step. I'd removed the bolt, and already the magic in me would be healing the injury.

But not immediately, and not soon enough. The wound throbbed with pain.

I'd lost too much blood.

It was in this state I finally reached the docks.

There I found three figures waiting for me, starkly visible from arms and armor shining softly silver in the gloom.

Knights.

CHAPTER THREE

STEEL AND ART

They were knights, more of the Earl's regulars. I could tell at a glance, from the visible enchantments on their gear to the artistry apparent in the fashion of their weapons and armor.

Two held swords, and one a warhammer with a cruel backspike. That last stepped forward. I couldn't see their face; the same magic illuminating their helm made the interior of the visor impenetrably dark, granting the illusion that there might have been nothing at all inside.

The armor the knight wore seemed of a new fashion, more complex in design than anything I'd seen in the war. Possibly even made outside the sub-continent—it lacked any House emblem I knew, and had no motifs of tree or familiar beast.

The guilds were bringing all sorts of interesting new toys across the Riven Sea. I suspected it to be alchemy, and not elf craft, that had fashioned the arms for these.

I didn't bother hiding. I could tell they were waiting for me, arrayed on the narrow street between the last block of homes and the river docks. I stepped forward, forcing my breath to steady from my long flight, and rested my blood-stained axe on my shoulder. Already, the rain had begun to wash the residue of my kills away.

"So it's true," the knight with the hammer said. Their armor made their voice androgynous, caused it to emerge brassy and inhuman through the slits in their visor. I couldn't guess at gender. I could hear the voice clear through the storm, but couldn't tell if that was their own aura or some property of the foreign armor.

I took another step, getting well clear of the alleyway, and waited. I'd played this game before. The game of naming oneself, of delivering fair challenge. I'd once lived for it.

"The Headsman himself, come out of hiding to plague us. What have you to say for yourself, blackguard?"

Despite the inhuman quality the ensorcelled armor gave the knight's words, I could hear the anger in them.

I shrugged, and let a bit of aura leak into my voice so it would carry as clear as the knight's. I needed no continental alchemy to do it for me. "I say you're in my way, and you should move aside. We've no quarrel, and I'd rather not kill you."

The wound in my shoulder thrummed. Hopefully, they wouldn't see it.

The other two knights shifted at my words, agitated. One of them growled something I didn't catch. The one with the hammer gave a sharp nod, causing the faint light around them to shimmer like a mirage.

"But we've quarrel with you, O' Headsman. Two, in fact. The Earl holds our service at present, so that one is professional. The other . . ."

They shrugged, making their asymmetrical pauldrons rise and fall. "My brothers and I are eager to test the legend. Are you man or devil? You will let us see your blood so we may be sure."

Mercenaries, then. Glorysworn. I knew the type, and knew there'd be no negotiating my way out of this.

Glorysworn Knights, nobleborn fighters with little prospect for inheritance, drift from liege to liege, going wherever hospitality and excitement take them. Adventurers of a fashion, though they tended to form their own fraternities and were disdained partying with more common Fellowships.

They weren't paladins—I'd heard no hint of an Oath in that little speech. But they would be skilled, and their magical arms could be trouble. I wore no armor, so they had the advantage in war gear as well as number.

This wouldn't be as one-sided as the guardsmen from before. And if they stalled me long enough, I'd have those to contend with as well.

I pointed my axe at the leader, showing them the blood splattered across the bearded blade. The hammer-wielder knew a challenge when they saw one. They stepped forward, harness clattering, and took a stance. A metallic silver sheen encased their hammer, drowning out the paler light from before.

I raised an eyebrow. "No introductions?"

They might have snorted beneath the helm. "I would normally be honored, but I hear you are no knight."

I admit, the retort bothered me a little. Not least of all because it was true.

I took my own stance, axe held low to the ground at an angle. My gloved hand slid down the curve of the gnarled haft, until it hovered near where the blade fused with wood. The weapon began to emit a dour amber light touched with the faintest red, like gilt copper.

There was little drama in our first meeting, me and that nameless knight. We waited ten beats of a heart, and then we were both running forward. I don't know who moved first. My leather boots slapped the rain-slick stone, and the knight's sabatons struck a piercing note with each step.

Axe met hammer, elfbronze and alchesteel sliding together, and then we went past one another in a brief flash of sparks quickly dead in the rain.

The other two knights watched, silent, their features unreadable beneath their helms.

I turned, and then twisted to avoid a chasing blow following within an instant of the first. The next I parried, and this time our weapons tolled like twin bells striking as they met. Silver and amber magic collided along with physical steel—

And the silver sliced through the amber, sharp as a blade through cheese. The bell toll of our meeting weapons continued, a keening note, and I felt a rippling force pass through my weapon and into my hands, my bones—

The knight's magic ripped through me with what felt like a hundred hammers striking every major bone and organ in my body at once. The force carried on, rippling through rain and stone, until what seemed like an invisible fist struck the street.

Stone cracked. Water scattered. I leaped back on pure instinct, parting from the knight, and drew my aura back into an aegis. It is difficult to describe, the wielding of one's soul. With thought and will and hard-earned experience I shaped mine, focusing on defense rather than attack.

But damage was done.

I stayed on my feet, barely, reeling. When bile rose in my throat and I coughed up blood, I knew I'd been badly hurt.

What was that? I thought, on the verge of panic. *Their Art?* I'd never felt sorcery like it. It had cut through my own defenses with ease.

The Glorysworn didn't give me the chance to recover. They advanced, relentless, and I dodged their hammer's downswing rather than try to parry again, fearing a repeat of that tremorous magic. It became something of a dance then, as the knight advanced and I fell back, narrowly avoiding an endless series of blows. The knight's stamina seemed inexhaustible.

I, on the other hand, already shaken and wounded, started to labor. My bones seemed to ring continuously, adding disorientation to my woes. The Glorysworn's magic had literally rung me like a thin bar of metal struck hard, causing my entire being to vibrate violently.

I suspected it hadn't just hurt my body. I was having difficulty shaping my aura into a coherent form. I had no way of knowing for certain whether what I'd been hit with had been the martial sorcery of the knight's Soul Art, or some quirk of their weapon.

I had a suspicion, though, from the unfamiliar sensation of it.

When two fighters with wakened auras clash, it's not just their bodies at odds with one another. The wielding of Art is not the whole of sorcerous combat, only a specific application of it. Various phenomena can manifest in such duels, some of which can be unique and unpredictable.

But a common one is the exchange of emotion, emanations of the mind and spirit bridging between two opponents as they become lost in the fury of combat. It's not mind reading, not quite. Thoughts are trickier.

But rage, fear, excitement—these things you can give away to an enemy.

It is not too different from playing cards, really. The difference is that the plays happen more instantly, and the results are more lethal. It's common to train to quell this flow, so you don't give away your intentions.

The Glorysworn knight was not nearly as well trained in this aspect of combat as I. That's why when they stepped in close with hammer lifted for a killing blow, sabaton sliding across the ground so water sprayed around my ankles, I knew they were frustrated with my endless evasion.

They overcommitted, and I punished them for it. I stopped, legs braced, and spun my axe like a quarterstaff, knocking the hammer off balance without letting my own weapon touch its head. The Glorysworn stumbled and I got the hooked blade of my axe around the haft of their weapon.

I jerked hard, twisting. The hammer flew free of their grip and the knight stumbled past me several steps. The hammer clattered to the ground, which shuddered slightly around it.

As I'd thought. Their weapon had been imbued with a sorcerous technique, one that acted automatically when it struck something.

Without it . . .

I didn't smile. No time for gloating. I swung, merciless, and caught the knight with the shining amber bit of my axe between pauldron and neck. Steel crumpled. Bone broke. The Glorysworn went down with a sharp cry.

They wouldn't be getting up again soon.

I faced the other two, who still stood between me and the docks.

"Move." I infused my words with aura so they rang through the storm. **"Aside."**

This time, the command did not prove so effective as it had on the young guardsman earlier. One of the Glorysworn jerked, nearly obeying, but the other simply stepped forward with *claymos* raised.

The sight of the war sword, a two-hander and beautifully made, made my jaw clench. This time, I didn't suppress the surge of angry bloodlust. I had lost interest in keeping calm, in staying *patient*.

I lifted my axe to meet their challenge. Wisps of amber fire danced around its edge. I squeezed, and the small burs on the branch handle bit into my palm.

The sound of crackling wood passed through the rain. Above, a tongue of lightning flickered across the sky.

The two knights, brothers by their leader's earlier speech, spread out to flank me. They wouldn't be dueling me one on one like the hammer wielder, then.

Fine. I kept my eyes on both, backing away from the fallen Glorysworn in case they weren't so incapacitated as I'd hoped.

They both held swords. The one on the left a tall claymos, a weighty greatsword, and the one on the right a shorter, but hardly less heavy, broadsword.

Like the first, their faces were hidden behind ornate helms of strange design, alien visages made eerie by the storm. The one with the smaller blade had a helm crafted in the likeness of a snarling gargoyle, while the larger brother resembled a deep sea fish, the crest of the helm even fashioned into a sort of antenna.

The weapons of both were etched from pommel to blade tip with complex geometric patterns and emitted a faint light in the rain. Like the first, then, their weapons were ensorcelled.

That didn't necessarily mean they would do exactly the same thing. I took a defensive stance, cautious of tricks.

I considered using my own Art. I thought better of it, and settled for maintaining the aegis I'd made before. My left shoulder burned, and I still felt nauseous from that magicked hammer, but I ignored the discomfort.

The Glorysworn with the broadsword attacked first, bringing his wide-bladed armament up to rest on a vambrace and advancing with heavy, plodding steps. When he drew near he lunged, weapon driving forward in a powerful thrust.

I parried, axe scraping against sword as I brought my weapon up in a rising motion across my left side. I would have riposted, but the knight ducked and his brother was there at his back, fish helm comically quizzical, greatsword cleaving rain as it sought my head.

I'd come in stealth, not for war, and wore no helm. I reeled back, letting the tip of the claymos miss me by a hand's width, but the Glorysworn with the gargoyle helm chopped at my legs even as Fishhead recovered from his mighty swing. I blocked Gargoyle's sword, causing metal to scream tortuously as our weapons clashed.

No bone quaking Art this time. But the weapons moved fast, and produced an eerie whine. Whatever strange alchemy had mixed that metal, it made them wasp quick and terribly sharp.

Worse, the two knights fought as a single body, two swords and four arms moving in concert, so I could barely avoid both and was left no time to retaliate.

They used no Art, but they were fast for their size and took no risks like the hammer-wielder. I might have taken either alone, but together they matched me step for step. My wound screamed, restricting my full range of movement. Sweat mixed with rain as I avoided death by the space of heartbeats, struggling for every moment of life.

They were good. But, I thought, also inexperienced. And they'd followed the one with the hammer's lead. An elder brother, I thought, and had a grim idea.

They had said it themselves. They had called me a blackguard, and guessed I wasn't a knight. I saw no reason to disappoint their assumptions.

Gargoyle advanced with an artful downward stroke, almost a fencer's technique despite his heavy weapon. I saw Fishhead through the rain, a step behind, bringing up his tall blade to follow his sibling in a two-pronged attack. They were content to keep this going, advancing and retreating in turn, Gargoyle harrying me while Fishhead focused on killing strikes.

Eventually, one would land. But I was done with this game, and batted the broadsword away almost negligently as I leaped back, opening my guard. Fishhead hesitated, likely sensing a trap. But his brother had less caution and turned his blade into a thrust, positioning it again atop his vambrace, intending to stab forward into my exposed chest.

Which was when I used the hooked blade of my axe to jerk the hammer wielder in front of me from where he'd been lying stunned on the ground. The inner curve of the axe blade was not sharp, so I didn't cut his neck as I lifted him, hooking the blade under his chin beneath the helm.

Lucky for us both Gargoyle froze. I used the opportunity to adjust my grip, twisting the captive knight's head sharply to one side. He let out a cry of pain that came ethereal through the helm.

The threat was clear enough without words. If either of the other two came at me, I'd break their sibling's neck.

"I'll ask again," I said, breathing hard. "Fucking *move*."

Somehow, the bastards had kept themselves between me and the water. I could hear it churning, hear the docks creaking and the boats grinding against their tethers.

Fishhead stood stock still, a titan in steel with a sword nearly as tall as he was, and remained silent. Gargoyle drew up, and even through all the armor I practically felt his rage.

"Blackguard!" he snarled through his monstrous helm. "She has already fallen. Let her *go*."

A sister, then. I didn't comply, instead meeting the shadowed gaze of the Glorysworn evenly. "She said it herself—I'm no knight. I won't ask again."

To make my point, I gave the axe a slight twist. Through the helm's mask, I could hear the hammer wielder begin to choke. I knew her brothers heard it too.

I don't know what expression the two Glorysworn wore beneath their eerie helms, but I could guess well enough. Gargoyle gestured sharply with his sword at his brother.

"Let him," he said, voice strained.

To my relief, Fishhead complied. They both moved, clearing a path toward the edge of the river. I moved, cautious, never taking my eyes from the two knights. I kept their sibling in custody, hearing her occasionally give out a pained sound as the movement disturbed her broken collarbone.

I didn't feel much sympathy, considering she'd been trying to kill me only minutes before. Or so I convinced myself in the moment, heart pounding from the tension of battle.

I *had* been a knight, once. I will not pretend like I felt aright with how I'd handled this. But I also wanted to live, so I hardened my heart and kept moving until I reached the river.

The town met the river as a stone wharf, with docks extending over the churning waters. The River Vin flowed fast and deep, and in some places more than half a mile wide. Not so wide here, but enough that I couldn't make out the far shore through the night and the rain, even with the lightning and the phantasmal banners.

I came to a sheer drop, seeing black waters running swiftly below. The storm had sped the current, and made it deeper too. I swallowed, but knew this to be my only escape. I'd steal a boat, and trust myself to the current. At least they wouldn't follow me in this weather.

I caught shouting from across the wharf and looked up to see guardsmen moving into position. Many had crossbows. With them rode a towering figure in armor of nearly black iron, filigreed with scenes of chivalrous glories and odes of prayer. Another knight, and no Glorysworn. Possibly the Earl himself.

The noble warrior rode a chimera, some local breed that looked like some cross between an ancient equine and a wolf, covered in shaggy fur but long limbed and long necked, with predator teeth and glinting white-green eyes.

The knight lifted his spear, and a silver light bloomed high above it. The emblem of the Earl blazed in the sky, wrought from pure aura. It illuminated the whole wharf.

Then, the rider pointed his weapon at me.

I cursed. Unhooking my axe from around the Glorysworn's neck, I placed a boot on her backplate to shove her toward her brothers. I didn't think the hostage would be as effective against the Earl's men.

Which was when she drove a dagger into my leg.

The blade went deep. A rondel with a long spike of a blade, made to punch through gaps in armor. I wasn't wearing any, and all it found was muscle and meat. I shouted, more in surprise than pain, and slammed the butt end of my axe into the back of the Glorysworn's helm. She went down flat on the stone, leaving the dagger embedded in my leg.

The crossbowmen fired. Their lord's sorcery made me very visible. Likely, it also made their movements more keen and their eyes sharper, enhancing their natural abilities as they bathed in that silver light.

A volley of bolts slapped through the rain. Most missed. Not all. I felt an impact in my hip, jerking me back. That one saved my life, for the next bolt scraped across my scalp rather than going through my skull.

Red flashed through my mind. Shock. Pain. I jerked my arm up only for another bolt to go right through the muscle, stopping a hair's width from my eye.

I fell backward.

Into the raging river.

CHAPTER FOUR

MEMORY OF A DREAM'S END

In my dream, I see fire raining from the sky.

Not a dream. A memory. But in the manner of dreams, visions flash before my eyes without order or sense. I relive fragmented moments of time, become lost in them until I feel as though I am descending into an ever-deepening whirlpool.

Spinning, spinning, and all the while I see—

A regal figure pierced by a dozen blades, made to kneel as his crown slips from silver hair to shatter on a floor carved from living crystal—

Flame raining from a tortured sky to fall on a dream-wrought city, white towers crashing down as armies clash in the burning fields beyond—

Golden forests blackening as fire sweeps across them, trees twisting into nightmare shapes as a great shadow strides through the destruction, winged in cinders and crowned by a smoldering sky—

Columns of ash-masked figures trailing across the land, fleeing the destruction, beginning to scream as the sky darkens moments before arrows and worse begin to fall—

A man in beautiful gilded armor, his eyes burning with golden fire, blood-soaked and suffering, stumbling toward me with an uplifted sword—

A woman reaching for me as I back away. I raise a sword between us. Her eyes melt into red tears as fire bursts from them and she lunges, clawed fingers stretching, her form coming undone to reveal what lies beneath—

I can't stop seeing it. Any of it. It is all burnt into my eyes, just as permanent as the golden fire in them. The flow of images is unceasing, until I fear my mind will come apart with them, that I will become nothing but fragments of moments, shards of mistakes.

And, as death draws near at hand . . .

I know this is just the beginning.

"—And so it is the judgment of this court that you are to be stripped of your titles and any inheritance they may allow. Your knighthood is hereby revoked, your name stricken from canon. You may not bear your own mark or wear the mark of any member of the peerage, either in this or any other land, under pain of death."

Murmuring voices echo through these words. Beams of sunlight filter through gray clouds, too cold to wash away the gray pallor of fallen ash across the shattered city. It shines through the collapsed roof of the temple, but it does not fall on me.

"You are declared anathema to all divisions of the Church, whose servants will not grant you aid or succor so long as you are bound by the terms of your excommunication. Do you understand these terms as I have read them to you, Lord Alken?"

He still called me lord. I might have laughed at that, though it would have been a dry ghost of humor. It would be the last time, in any case. Perhaps he meant it to soften this blow.

But nothing could do that.

I looked up from where I knelt in the center of the hall. I met the eyes of the man—the king—who stood foremost amid a ring of stern faces.

He dressed for war still, as did most of those who stood in the hall, even though it had been months since the last battle. An iron crown rested on his charcoal hair and his scarred face may as well have been wrought from the same.

He was not the only monarch who stood within the remnants of that blasted city. Dale kings, earls from the heartlands and the northern coasts, counts, barons, chieftains—a hundred or more great nobles formed large portions of the ring in which I knelt.

But it wasn't just nobles in that court. I met the eyes of Wildedale rangers, militia captains, clericons, and adventurer fellowships. Towering dwarf giants glowered at me alongside furtive irks, the latter group's eyes gleaming eerily from their dim nooks.

Some elves were there too, their beautiful faces made wolfish from years of war and grief.

There were so few of them left.

The war had brought together the peoples of Urn like nothing had in half a millennium. Among them were faces I knew well. Friends, once. Benefactors. Comrades.

Now they seemed barely more than strangers.

I saw Maerlys standing with her people, face hooded to hide her wounds. Lias stood with her, face shrouded in a midnight blue cowl so only his mouth and chin were visible, hand gripping a twisted blackwood staff. Donnelly, or his shade, slouched in half-solid form in the shadow of a pillar. Karledaler knights who'd once been my brothers and sisters watched me with pity, or anger.

I made myself look at Rosanna. She stood by the king who passed my sentence. She would not meet my eyes.

Damn her, then. She had put me here, and she would say nothing?

I don't know what I'd been looking for in their faces. Hate? Disgust? Pity? Whatever it was, all I saw were dour masks caught fast by years of struggle.

I turned back to the king acting as the voice of the court. "I understand, lord." Grander titles were inappropriate here. As far as this new Accord was concerned, all here were equal, save for me.

The iron-crowned king nodded once, slow and thoughtful. "In light of your service in the war, we are prepared to offer you clemency. You will face no incarceration or censure. You may travel to whatever land you will so long as whatever power governs it is willing to accept you, and you may bear arms insofar as it is necessary to protect yourself."

So they would not leave me a wretch.

"You may find work as you will, but may not hold any official office with connection to the Accorded Realms or their representatives."

I would never again be a knight. I'd dedicated my life to it, and now . . .

All gone. Didn't matter anyway.

It went on for some time. I heard it all, though seemingly at a distance. I had withdrawn deep into myself, aware the whole while of the ring of eyes fixed on me, some of whom I'd once called friends, rivals, comrades in arms. They may as well have been a council of statues.

When movement in the gathering caught my eye, I followed it without lifting my head. I thought I caught sight of a dark shape drifting through the assembly, black-and-white cloth shifting as though in an unseen wind. I could almost see a hint of gray eyes in the bands of daylight cutting through the chamber's high windows.

When I blinked the phantom image had vanished. She wasn't there. It was just a trick of my mind, not a ghost like poor Donnelly.

Or perhaps, I thought, it was the beginning of a curse.

They say fire rained from the sky the day Golden Seydis fell.

This is true. I can say as much because I had been there, and I could have stopped it.

I deserved far worse than mere disgrace.

I woke in the mud.

There came a terrible moment where I believed I was back in the war, lying in the mud of a trampled battlefield surrounded by terror and death. I could almost hear the roars of chimera, the shouts of combatants, the clash of swords, and the eerie music of sorcery.

But those sounds faded and it was just birdsong and wind through leaves.

It took me a while to stir. Even then, rising did not come easy. I was methodical about it, testing fingers and toes before trying to shift my limbs. Nothing seemed paralyzed, at least. I managed to get hands under me, sliding them through damp mud, then one knee. I rose.

Regretted it. Pain shot through my body from so many sources I couldn't guess where each ache originated. I groaned. Froze.

I didn't fall back down, though that's all I wanted to do. I made myself keep moving, ignoring the pain, until I reached my knees. I opened my eyes and saw only darkness.

I began to panic. Had I been blinded? Had I lost my sight?

Would that be a mercy, or just a new kind of hell?

I brought my hands up to my face, feeling tentatively, and realized it was just mud. I wiped as much of it as I could away—my hands were just as filthy— then blinked at my surroundings.

I knelt in a forest. An almost profanely cheery bright day claimed the sky above, which I found nearly as disorienting as the temporary blindness had been. The sun pierced through the canopy as so many golden blades to dapple the woods in light. I could hear the river at my back.

It all came back to me in a rush. Vinhithe. The Bishop. My flight through the streets, the garrison, the knights. The storm. Getting shot and falling into the river.

I reached down, winced, and found the crossbow bolt still embedded in my hip. The one in my left forearm remained as well, though it seemed to have missed the bone. A small mercy.

Still alive. Though, judging by the bruising and myriad other injuries I felt beneath all the mud, I was in a bad way. The river hadn't been gentle.

How far had it taken me?

Judging by the sun it was near midday. Night had just fallen when I'd been taken by the river. I had brief memories of being in the water, being swept along its current, unable to do anything. Terror, helplessness . . .

I shuddered at the memory. I couldn't remember if I'd pulled myself onto the shore by some stroke of luck or if I'd just washed ashore and fallen unconscious then. It was all a jumble.

In a surge of sudden panic I checked for my ring. When I found it still where it always lay on my right forefinger, I breathed a sigh of relief. I took the time to brush mud away from it to reveal the ivory band.

I ran a thumb along the smooth black stone set in the ring, and felt calmer.

Only then did I flex the fingers of my right hand and, finding them empty, looked around for my weapon. I found it quickly enough, stuck in some driftwood near the edge of the water. It had been jammed into a broken segment of a small tree.

Another memory flashed through my thoughts. Tumbling through the river along with bits of wreckage. I'd kept hold of the axe and sunk it into a broken segment of tree, using it to keep aloft and keep hold of my weapon.

I'd like to call it quick thinking, but it had been little more than dumb luck.

Wincing, I stood and limped over to the axe. Every step disturbed the bolt stuck into my hip and I collapsed halfway, breathing hard and sweating. I stood after several minutes and reached the axe what felt like an eternity later. I pried it from the driftwood where, of course, it had gotten stuck. I finally had it free with a shout of effort and pain that echoed through the forest.

When done, I collapsed on the dead tree, gasping for breath. I lifted the axe up to the sunlight.

As my heart calmed I found myself glowering at the weapon. Beautiful. I hated it as much as I ever had, then.

"Can't get rid of you, can I?" I said to the axe. "You bastard thing."

I don't know what I'd expected. It was my burden, and one I'd chosen willingly enough. Not that the alternative had been more appealing.

I'd come close to that this time. *I botched that one badly,* I thought, thinking of Vinhithe. And now I was in the woods, possibly miles downriver from the town, with two bolts stuck in me and the whole earldom probably out for my blood.

Perhaps they'd assume me dead, but I wouldn't count on it. Then, when the sun went down, things would get worse. I needed to find shelter and get my injuries treated, or . . .

Or nothing. There was no use considering the alternative. I would survive. I *had* to.

I had not yet done enough.

CHAPTER FIVE

THE FALLEN

I stumbled through the woods, every step an agony. I knew, subconsciously, that I wasn't going to last. My wound—wounds—were bad.

The bolt in my hip had lodged in bone, which I discovered when I tried pulling it out the first time and nearly passed out. Not long after that, I started coughing up blood, possibly from whatever the Glorysworn with the hammer had done to me with her unfamiliar magic.

The power in me seemed fractured, almost withered. I couldn't concentrate on it, did not feel the normally constant warmth in me from its presence. Without it . . .

These wounds would kill me. The one in my shoulder burned, and I might have had a fractured rib or three.

I wouldn't last. Yet still, stubbornly, implacably, I put one foot in front of the other. Again and again, each step celebrated by the crunching of leaves.

Step. Crunch.

Step. Crunch.

Step . . .

I stumbled and caught myself on the rotten trunk of an ivy-coated tree, gasping for breath. Sweat poured down my face to trickle into the undergrowth below. I vomited, wiped my mouth, and continued on my way.

Step. Crunch.

"Look how the mighty have fallen."

The voice whispered from the shadows, so faint I believed I only heard my own thought at first.

But then more voices answered it, drifting from the gloom of the wild like whispering insects.

"He killed him! The old man. Cut off his head and left him there to rot on holy ground."

"Almost killed the boy, too. Should have done it. Who's he kidding?"

"Thinks he's still on the side of the angels."

"He is! That's just the trouble, isn't it?"

"Do his oaths warm him?"

I clenched my teeth against the tide of evil whispers. I shouldn't have reacted. The trees filled with trilling laughter.

Damn shades. Even in daytime . . .

Step. Crunch.

"This is not what you were meant for."

I took several labored breaths before I could speak. "I know that."

Perhaps another fifty steps passed before another presence drifted into the forest. A shadow seemed to fall over the trees like a cloud moving overhead and the air grew noticeably cooler. Only, the sky remained clear.

The wind died. The birds ended their singing and even the distant music of the river died. The ground beneath me began to reverberate with what felt like the beating of an enormous, subterranean heart, the sensation traveling up through my legs.

I steeled myself and felt a shudder of fear anyway.

An iron-shod hoof stamped the grass within the sudden darkness of the deeper forest, so heavy I could feel the *thud* in my chest. A horse snorted—a real one—the sound somehow evoking a deep, guttural growl.

Leather creaked and a towering shape seemed to form amid the shadowed trees. I took a deep breath, schooling my face and forcing my pounding heart to still. I did not stop walking, though I wanted nothing more than to turn and flee to the nearest patch of brightest light I could.

Still that great heartbeat, warning me of danger.

Warning me that something not of this world had come.

The horse, a great destrier, emerged from the darkened woods at an unhurried walk. It had been clad in the remnants of war barding, rotten chain mail and scraps of rusted plates covering most of its leathery hide, its equine head crowned by a cruelly designed helm set with a long blade so the beast resembled a fiendish unicorn. Its hide sported rusted iron thorns and protruding hilts from blades sheathed into its flesh.

Its many wounds wept blood with every movement of its ever-shifting muscles. It twitched and flexed, never for even a moment still. Its bloodshot eyes were disturbingly human and full of an insane malice as it regarded me.

The rider of the fell warhorse, on the other hand, could not have been more mismatched to the steed. She was beautiful, with a heart-shaped face and slender build, riding sidesaddle to accommodate a flowing gown seemingly spun from foam and starlight. Her hair was raven dark and so long it seemed a cloak.

A gentle smile formed on her lips even as she looked down at me, letting her nightmare steed match my unsteady pace as she drew alongside.

I took all of this in with a sideways glance and kept walking. "Nath," I greeted the rider.

Nath's berry red lips curled into a frown. She leaned forward over her steed's head to inspect me. Her eyes told the lie to her beauty. They were twin hollow pits, like the empty sockets of a porcelain mask. Nothing but shadow lay within.

When she spoke, she did so with a voice that made the forest shiver.

"Alken, my dear, what have you done to yourself? You are covered in mud and bruises like a little boy."

I spoke through gritted teeth, "Just a small . . . disagreement. It's really not as bad as it looks."

It was getting harder to breathe.

Nath snorted, placing her fingers over her lips. "Even so close to death—indeed, in the very *presence* of death—you haven't lost that wry touch to you, my dear little knightling. I do adore a man who can jest in such times."

She propped an elbow on the devil steed's head, which stilled at her touch even as its mad eyes rolled hatefully. One of her fingers uncurled lazily in my direction. "I would give you six hours, twelve at most, and then you're done. Your aura is all a mess. You won't be able to rely on the fire those faeries alloyed into you to save your life."

She leaned down, breathing in and shuddering as though catching the most enticing of scents. Her lips curled back from small teeth.

"I suppose you wish to bargain with me?" she asked sweetly.

I turned a sullen glare on the Onsolain. "I'm not desperate enough to make deals with a Fallen. Piss off."

"Pah." Looking bored, Nath propped her chin on her fist. The movement of her arm seemed to irritate the horse further, which stamped its iron hoof restlessly. "Your word. Men call *you* a devil, do they not? So many fun names you've earned since we last spoke. Headsman. Blackbough. *Bloody* Al. I feel as though I should take issue with that last."

"I didn't coin that one myself," I replied. "If I find out who did, I'll let you know."

I didn't mention that the "Bloody" epithet was about as common in Urn as apple trees. Not every poet can be original.

The being known to many as Bloody Nath smiled, pleased. "So sweet. I will take that as an oath and call it binding. But I digress. As much as I enjoy flirting with you, knightling, I'm rather busy of late. What are you willing to offer so I might save you?"

"I already told you." I had to pause and catch my breath, leaning against another tree. "I'm not willing to offer you a damn thing. Up to and including . . ." I took several more deep breaths. "My soul."

"So dramatic."

Nath scoffed and spurred her monstrous steed forward, turning it to block my path. The beast was enormous, as large as most war chimera I had seen, and its bloodshot eyes rolled hatefully toward me. If not for the pale hand holding it at bay, I suspected it would gladly stomp me into a gory paste.

Nath tilted her head as she spoke to me. "You have *already* sold your soul to my brothers and sisters, Alken Hewer, and they hold it in penance until they deem you worthy of salvation. If you die today, where do you think you will go, hm?"

She arched a perfect eyebrow at me, waiting for my answer. It didn't seem a rhetorical question.

Forced to stop my agonizing march, I glared up at her. "I know where I'm bound," I said, repeating the words I'd said to Leonis Chancer.

"Do you?" Nath asked, propping her chin on the other fist, shifting that arm to dig a bony elbow into the fiend steed's scarred neck. Its mad eye rolled up in insane, impotent hate, and the Fallen continued speaking as though she didn't notice. Perhaps she didn't.

"Your order allowed the Gilded City to fall. Your own captains betrayed the elf king and *you* . . ."

Her lips curled into a lazy smile, her empty eyes narrowing coyly. "You, Alken Hewer, Knight of the Alder Table, failed in your duties to safeguard that realm and all others that fell under its shadow. You have betrayed, lied, murdered, even become outcast by the mortal priesthood and the lords who were once your peers."

Her grin widened into something macabre. "Your sad tale will have a *fiery* end, I think."

I could barely stand, much less muster up some witty riposte. I glared for a long while before I could gather the strength to answer.

She was right. Not just about how close I drew to death, but also about where I could expect my soul to go once that end came. Images of crumbling towers and bloody fields scorched my mind. I closed my eyes against the flood of images. Of memories.

"What do you want?" I finally asked when I felt able to speak. My voice was hoarse, weak, and without much fight. I had been fighting a long time. I had to admit part of me wanted it to be over.

But it *wouldn't* be over. I knew that better than most. In the surrounding forest, the dead watched me with mad eyes and whispered among themselves.

"In return for saving you?" Nath's smile widened and she lifted herself up, regarding me thoughtfully. She seemed to be the only thing in the world that produced light, as though she'd drunk it all into her. Even the sky seemed dimmer.

Despite my weak show of defiance, I was very afraid of her. I would be a fool not to be. She *was* Onsolain. Or she had been.

"Hm . . ." Nath tapped a long fingernail against her red lips. "How about that pretty ring and the name of the woman who gave it to you?" She smiled winningly down at me.

I glanced at the ring on my right hand. "No," I said without hesitation.

"Poo. The axe, mayhap?"

"It's not mine to give." Though, I felt tempted. Maybe she could actually free me from the cursed thing.

Nath hummed quietly, unperturbed. She tapped a finger against her chin, running her eyeless gaze across the sun-dappled canopy as though looking for inspiration there.

She was *enjoying* this, I realized, even as I stood there bleeding out.

Damn immortals and their games.

"Why are you even bothering?" I asked, exasperated. "You know you can't make me a pawn easily, Nath, not with your brethren looking over my shoulder. They will take issue with any attempts to turn me to your own ends."

"True enough," Nath agreed, her smile fading as her empty eyes turned skyward. "But favors owed . . . *that* I am allowed. I may not be able to lay claim to your soul, knightling, but that holds less interest to me than you might think, Alder touched though it is."

She turned her regard back on me, and I felt the weight of that void stare like the pull of a bottomless chasm. "This land is *broken*. The Fall culminated in the deaths of kingdoms, and there are power vacuums that have yet to be filled. I have already made some progress in this, but I need agents. *Allies*."

She smiled again and placed a delicate hand on the head of the fiend horse, which rolled its veined eyes hatefully. It seemed as though the beast longed to buck her, but wouldn't dare. "I am refashioning myself as a warlord, you see."

"Allies," I said, making the word a surly growl. "You and me? Is this the part where I laugh in your face?"

"Do it," Nath said, her voice quiet and cold as glacial ice. "See what results."

I had to suppress a shiver of quiet, primal horror and remind myself that there *were* worse things than death, even the one that awaited me.

I chose to forgo laughter.

"Point is," I continued, "my soul isn't for sale, metaphorically or literally. I'll help you about as soon as the stars freeze over. Now, are you going to move?"

I tightened my grip on the axe, feeling its sharp imperfections press into my skin. "Or am I going to have to move you?"

It was an idle threat, and we both knew it. Even at the top of my form, taking on a being of Nath's caliber would be tantamount to suicide. In my experience, however, it never paid to let the world's monsters see you sweat.

Nath snorted in disdainful amusement. "Oh, knightling. If vapid bravado wasn't part and parcel of your ilk, I might weep for you. But hear me; you *will* die. Soon. There is no one else who can save you, no one else who *cares* to. Your old allies have long since dismissed you from their thoughts. My brethren think of you as a disposable tool. Many of the lords of Urn would happily see you dead as a murderer and a renegade."

A touch of what might have been genuine emotion laced her next two words, had I not known better. "Be *reasonable*. You need help, Alder Knight. You and I are not so different, after all. We were both outcast. We both long for a home we can never return to."

I opened my mouth for an angry retort, and then closed it as her words settled on me. Perhaps there was a touch of aura in the Fallen's voice, but . . .

But she was *right*, damn it. For the rest of Urn, the violence of the Fall of Seydis was years gone now. The Accord had instituted something like peace across the land, though its authority varied from region to region.

But for me, the fighting had never truly ended. Vinhithe had just been the most recent in a long parade of bloody, terrifying tasks.

I had done things. Could I really scruple at this? Better men than me had fallen to the Briar's wiles.

I had served. I had bled. Would it be so wrong to accept an offer of aid, even from a being so untrustworthy as Bloody Nath?

I did not know. Doubt gnawed at me, as it often did. The Church of Urn taught that those who lived outside the light of the Heir were not to be trusted or heeded under any circumstances. But I had just killed a bishop. *I* lived outside that light as an excommunicate. I had refused to heed the words of another such, long ago, and a kingdom had burned.

Several minutes passed before I spoke. When I did, it was in a quiet, tired voice. I could muster no anger, no righteous fire. Just hard-earned weariness and bitter resignation.

"The difference," I said, "is that I didn't spend the last four centuries trying to conquer this land, or make friends with the Briar. You've left *mountains* of corpses in your wake."

I took a steadying breath and spoke as calmly as I could, making certain my words left no room for doubt. "The answer is no, Nath. I don't want your help. Get thee behind me."

"Fool," Nath said with no particular feeling. "You will die."

I began to walk, not caring that the enormous fiend horse blocked my path. "So be it. But I'll die *me,* not as one of your monsters."

Nath did not move her steed. "They already see you as one of the monsters."

I stopped and stared pointedly forward, standing nearly underneath her now. Her bare feet and the hem of her white gown were coated in blood, I noted.

I began to gather my will, focusing my aura until it thrummed within my chest. It did respond, though weakly and in fits. Could I muster enough to smite the horse? Not the dark spirit who rode it, but just this one petty victory I could claim, even if it were my last?

"I don't care how they see me," I said. "I swore oaths to protect the realms from things like *you.* I fight monsters."

Nath lifted her narrow chin. "And yet you kill your fellow men."

"I fight monsters," I repeated. "Even human ones. Now are you going to move, or am I going to have to axe your pet?"

A faint flicker of amber flames stuttered around my weapon. They were short lived, but the threat was clear enough. We stood there awhile, in that still forest where even the wind held its breath. I counted each of my own, wondering which would be my last.

After what seemed an eternity, Nath inclined her head and tightened her grip on the horse's reins, spurring it to move aside. I moved past her.

Step. Crunch. Step. Crunch.

Step—

My vision went blurry, and at a remove I realized I'd lost too much blood. The world began to spin.

Damn it. Not now. Not in front of *her.*

I fell. I didn't really feel myself hitting the ground. I lost my grip on my weapon and my fingers stretched for it.

I have an old nightmare, of dark things catching me before my hand can grasp a weapon.

The nightmare came true. A monstrous hoof slammed into the ground near my head. I could *feel* the world shudder beneath me with that impact. Nath's power thrummed through the rotten soil, and her voice caught me in a low, soothing murmur from what seemed like a world above.

"Such a shame. You had potential, Goldeye, but your stubborn pride has proved your bane. As it has so often been for the True Knights. Farewell. I would wish you peace in death, but I assure you there will be none."

I expected that hellborn creature to bring an iron-shod hoof down and flatten my skull.

It did not. Instead, cruelly, it began to move away. Nath left me there to die slowly.

CHAPTER SIX

KINDNESS OF STRANGERS

The first thought I had, when I had any again, was that Hell wasn't as warm as I had thought it would be.

Hearing came after thought. I could hear the crackling of fire, and that seemed appropriate. Insects chirped and wind whispered through leaves, which seemed a bit out of place. The surface beneath me was hard and uneven, but I rested on a rough cloak or blanket. My hands searched and I found grass.

Alive. I was still alive. The thought gave me more worry than relief. Where was—

"I wouldn't suggest moving too much," a scratchy, mellow voice said. "You're in a bad way, son, and I put a lot of effort into those stitches."

I opened my eyes and ran them over my surroundings. I lay in the forest still, and stars glowed overhead. A campfire crackled nearby.

I had been stripped naked. Layers of bandaging covered my body beneath the blanket. Though sore, I noted I no longer bled my life out into the woodland undergrowth.

I was not alone. A figure sat opposite the fire, watching me. He was an old man, somewhere in the uncertain years beyond fifty, with a fringe of gray hair around a wide, leathery face tanned by sun. He wore a thick brown robe, and watched me with deep set, patient eyes the color of a lake on a cloudy day, gray and blue. A pair of spectacles covered those eyes, making them appear huge and owlish.

"You," the old man said, "should not be awake. I gave you some very strong poultices." He frowned as though annoyed at me.

I didn't reply, instead testing my own body. I wiggled my toes, then my fingers, making sure everything worked. Everything *hurt*, but that wasn't necessarily a bad sign. I felt a curious numbness throughout my whole body, and something in the back of my mind muttered a panicked warning at that.

I tried to speak and my voice emerged as a dull, faint croak.

The man—a monk I thought, by his woolen robes—stood to hand me a skin I found to be full of water. He helped me drink it, and I was familiar enough with being wounded to let him.

When I could speak, I did so in a hoarse whisper. "You're a healer?" I swallowed, trying to better wet my throat. "A priest?"

The old man's thin lips twitched. "A doctor, actually. Olliard of Kell, at your service." His eyelids lowered and he inclined his head in something approximating a bow.

A potion brewer, I thought. *An herbalist.* He'd mentioned poultices, which explained the numbness in my limbs and my blurry thoughts. "How . . ." I tried to sit up and nearly blacked out as a lance of agony went through my hip.

Olliard of Kell laid a hand on my shoulder and pushed me back down. He was gentle, but surprisingly strong for his age and size. When he'd set me back in position he nodded and said, "You've been down for nearly a day. I found you not far from the road. Or, Brume did."

I saw no one else in the camp.

Olliard chuckled at my confusion. "My chimera. She and my apprentice are collecting water at the stream nearby. They should return shortly." He gestured toward one edge of the clearing.

"Ah." I settled back, feeling myself relax a bit. A part of me wanted to leap up and grab the nearest weapon, but I sensed I wasn't in any danger.

Stay calm, Al. If this man wanted you dead, you'd be dead.

The kindness of strangers. It seemed something more than a miracle, in the post-Fall world.

Olliard shuffled off and began to sort through the contents of a large pack. The fire crackled, and the wind played lazily through the leaves. I took the opportunity while the doctor turned his back to search for my equipment. I saw a suspicious cloth bundle nearby, the right size for my weapon, but no sign of my clothes.

"My apprentice has your clothes drying near the stream," Olliard said without turning. "They are quite ruined, but I'm afraid I have nothing to fit a man your size. Your weapon is there." A long, calloused finger pointed toward the bundle I'd noticed.

I idly ran a thumb along my ring, checking it was still there. *He's not a thief, then,* I thought, and relaxed more.

"Then I owe you thanks," I mumbled, still struggling to get much volume.

"You owe me nothing," Olliard said. "This is my profession. We should both thank the Heir that I found you when I did. Another few hours, and there wouldn't have been anything I could do."

Good thing his back was turned and he couldn't see me go still. A man of piety, then. I quelled the surge of wariness and shame I felt and settled back on the blanket, closing my eyes.

I lost time. When I became aware of the world again, Olliard spoke with someone else in a low tone, his scratchy voice tinged with frustration.

"What would you have me do? Leave him there to die?"

"No, of course not." The second voice had a higher pitch, younger. A young woman's, I thought, or even a girl. "But you don't know who he is. He *looks* like some kind of brigand, and—"

"And that matters?" Olliard's voice held an arched impatience. "We do not pick and choose who we help, Lisette. We are healers, not judges."

"And if he were one of the men who attacked the monastery?"

Lisette's voice tightened with barely suppressed anger. "Who murdered my sisters and put my home to the torch? Would you heal him even then?"

A weighty silence passed before the doctor replied. When he did, he sounded tired. "That is not fair. He is not one of those men."

Lisette's voice became calmer, more reasonable. "The bells in Vinhithe were ringing for hours the other day. *Something* happened in the town, and there have been more patrols on the roads since. What if he had something to do with the commotion there? What if the Earl's soldiers are trying to find him?"

"That is not our concern," Olliard said, and his voice seemed more solid than it had been before, unbending. "We will not leave him to die or turn him over to the ill mercies of the Earl of Vinhithe on suspicion. We will give him the chance to show us his quality before we damn him."

"But—"

"That is the end of the discussion, Lisette." Olliard sighed and spoke more kindly. "What would the abbess tell you?"

A pause, then Lisette answered in a sullen tone only lightly tinged with shame. "She would tell me to cleanse my heart of hate and let Her pass judgment."

"Yes. This man has done nothing to earn it, other than carry arms. Perhaps he is a man of violence, but there are many such in the world and not all are monsters. Now, Brume is hungry. See to her, then get some rest."

". . . Yes, master."

If more conversation came after that, I didn't hear it. Darkness took me again.

When I came to again, morning blue had washed out the starry black of night. I needed to piss something fierce, and my mouth felt full of scuttling dung beetles.

Groaning, I shifted, winced, and managed to move a couple of inches.

"Be still," a familiar, impatient voice said. I felt a cool hand on my collarbone and opened my eyes. A girl a year or two shy of twenty knelt over me, her features tense with concentration. She had yellow hair, wore the same brown robes as Olliard, and watched me with wary, blue eyes brighter than the cloudless sky above her.

When she saw me looking at her, those blue eyes narrowed and her mouth twisted into a frown.

"You're the apprentice," I croaked. "Where's the old man?"

"Sleeping," Lisette said. "He has been tending you for nearly two days. Now be silent. I need to redo these stitches."

She worked at my collarbone, and only then did I start to actually feel what she busied herself with—restitching the crossbow wound I'd taken in the shoulder. Long, thin fingers moved with assured dexterity, pulling lengths of thread from swollen flesh.

"Not very polite for a nun," I mumbled, still half asleep.

The girl stiffened. I winced as her fingers tightened on the thread. Her blue eyes flashed with anger as they fixed on mine. "How did you know I was—"

"Heard you and the old man talking," I said, forcing myself to keep still so she didn't inadvertently make the hole in my shoulder wider. "He mentioned a monastery and an abbess."

I glanced at her. Judging her age, I made a guess. "You were a novice."

The girl sniffed and continued to work at my shoulder, somewhat less gently than she had before. "That's none of your business."

"Sure," I muttered. She was right, and I fell silent as she bound my wound. I closed my eyes and *felt* something more about the girl with my less worldly senses. A subtle thread of warmth ran from her fingers as she worked, weaving itself into the fabric of the fine string even as she wove it into my flesh.

Aura. She used magic, and a particularly delicate kind. The almost dreamy quality to her expression hid a tense concentration behind it, one that ran through many levels of awareness. By the faint shine in her blue eyes—I realized there were flecks of gold in them—I knew her to be an adept.

Not just a novice nun and a doctor's apprentice, but a genuine cleric. Was the old man one, too?

No, I decided. There had been no trace of aura in the pastes and medicinal teas he had given me. I could be wrong, but my instincts told me that the girl had power, and the old doctor was just a skilled, but mundane, healer.

I would have to be cautious, lest she sense my own magic. I didn't much feel like answering too many questions just then.

Almost as though sensing my guard going up, Lisette spoke without stopping her work. "We found you in a bad way. Your hip is broken, along with three ribs, and *this* wound practically went all the way to the other side." She nodded at my shoulder. "Bruises, internal bleeding, the onset of infection . . . one might think you'd just come out the wrong side of a battle."

I grunted noncommittally, trying to meditate through the tugging spikes of pain at my shoulder.

"Funny, though." The girl's voice remained level. "There haven't been any wars around here in years."

"I'm glad," I said mildly. "Wars are a bad business."

"If not a war, then how were you injured?" The question was mild, remote.

I suppressed a sigh. "I had a disagreement. Weapons were involved."

"I see." The young healer's fingers worked more stiffly, and I had to suppress another wince of pain as she tugged at my abused skin. "We also found tracks where we picked you up. A chimera, Olliard thinks, and a very large one. Yours?"

"Never much cared for them," I said, shrugging the shoulder that didn't have a hole in it.

"Then who did it belong to?"

I turned a sour look on the girl. She returned it without a hint of apology, lifting a golden eyebrow.

I showed the neophyte my teeth in a humorless smile. "An angel."

Lisette's cheeks reddened. I spat out an involuntary curse as she tugged on the threads and broke one, leaving the edges of my wound neatly stitched together. She stood, brushed down the skirts of her woolen robes, and stalked off without a backward glance.

A low chuckle drew my attention to another blanket nearby, where Olliard lay. His eyes followed his apprentice, his lips pursed. He glanced at me and rolled one shoulder in a shrug. "Try not to tease the girl. She has very little humor in her, I'm afraid, and for good reason."

I recalled another part of the conversation I had heard. "Her monastery was attacked?"

Olliard winced as he propped himself up on one elbow. There were shadows under his eyes despite the early hour, and his age showed, but he nodded in answer to my question. "Some years ago, not long after the end of the war. Bad business."

"You mentioned brigands."

"Of a kind," Olliard confirmed, his lips setting into a thin line. "It isn't a tale to sully a fine day like this."

". . . Fair enough." I leaned back and closed my eyes, sweating a bit from pain. I still needed to piss, but didn't think I'd be standing just then. Two days . . . probably the two physicians had already cleaned me more than once.

Still, I held it.

Olliard spoke again after a few minutes. "So what's your name, stranger?"

Sleep was approaching fast. Lisette must have given me more medicine. I mumbled a reply. "Alken."

"Shame we met under these circumstances, Alken." Dead leaves rustled as the doctor shifted again. "We'll be heading off soon, and intend to take you with us. The road will be rough, but you need a proper bed to recover in. There's a small village perhaps a day or more north of here where I know some people. It will be safe."

I opened my mouth to speak. Closed it. It *wouldn't* be safe, though my hazy brain struggled to come up with a reason why.

"Should leave me," I muttered.

"What was that?"

"You should leave me behind," I said.

"Nonsense. You can't even walk!" Olliard sounded offended at the suggestion.

"Could be trouble for you," I said. My thoughts were growing more distant, but some kernel of urgency kept me awake. *Hunted. Vinhithe. Bishop. Don't want them to get caught up in—*

"Should leave me," I whispered.

But he didn't hear, and I fell back into a dreamless blackness.

CHAPTER SEVEN

ILL-OMENED ROAD

We went northward, and though I had wanted to be left behind in my half-delirious state, I kept my mouth shut once I'd come to. I wasn't in much of a position to be turning down free care and a ride out of the demesne.

I rode on a small cart pulled by the itinerant doctor's chimera. It was an ugly beast, big, with a mottled gray hide covered in coarse fur and an enormous hog's head. It had a dense mop of hair hanging low over its four glassy eyes and huge curling horns hanging low to the ground, their weight bowing its head so it seemed to walk in a perpetual depressive fugue.

The creatures bred for nobles to use in war and travel were also molded for aesthetic. Chimera can come in strange and beautiful shapes.

Not this one. Its humped back blocked my view of the road. It smelled bad, shat a lot, and its brassy lows had me gritting my teeth halfway through the first day of the journey.

Olliard sat on the cart's bench, guiding the smelly beast with a grand-fatherly fondness that spoke of long familiarity. His gentle murmuring lulled me to sleep more than once despite the rough ride. His apprentice sat next to me in the cart, ignoring me.

Perhaps the angel comment had been in poor taste, even if it had been true.

The landscape drifted by in a surreal blur of images. First dense woodland, then rolling hills, then a gentler patchwork of lighter woods and wide, culti-vated fields. The weather stayed clear, pleasantly warm, the recent storms hav-ing washed the land in an emerald sheen. Shallow lakes had formed here and there from rainfall.

At one point I saw brooding clouds and flickering lightning in the distant horizon, and felt a tug in my chest. Instinctively, I knew that direction to be east.

Not long after, clouds rolled over the land to cast that shining, emerald world in gloom. A gentle snow of pale gray flecks began to fall in a lazy dance from on high.

"Ash rain," Olliard commented darkly. "Been a few months since the last one. Thought we were done with these."

"There are parts of the land still burning," I said, shifting to find a more comfortable position in the cart and failing.

Olliard shook his head, grimacing. "It's been years now since the fighting ended. A decade since the old capital burned."

I didn't reply. It wouldn't do my traveling companions any good to know that much of the destruction wrought by the death of Elfhome was supernatural in nature, and that some of those wounds might never heal. Nor did I want to explain that there were demons still loose, keeping the storms of choking smog and ever burning flames lit even after ten years.

We hadn't managed to hunt down all of them. We'd been too few, the realms too battered. And I'd had other duties. My hand lingered near the axe, lying in its own wrapped bundle at my side.

Lisette pulled something from beneath the collar of her woolen robes and clutched it tightly. It was a medallion worked of pale rose gold, fashioned into the image of an arc pierced by three converging lines. She closed her eyes and muttered a prayer over the auremark, and I felt a gentle tug in that direction. I closed my eyes and tried not to show my discomfort.

"This is a fertile land," Olliard continued, his eyes roaming the green countryside. "But there are fewer like it every year. I hear the famine has become so bad in the Dale Kingdoms that the Accord had to intervene." He glanced back at me and casually asked, "You from the Dales, Alken?"

I glanced at him. "How did you know?"

"You talk like a Gyldener," the doctor noted, "but there's a subtle accent you've not quite hidden. My mother was from Bryndale originally." He tapped one ear. "I've still got the sense for it."

I settled back. The old physik was fishing for more information about me, and not very subtly. Well, I could humor him.

"I was born in the Herding, but I've lived most of half my life elsewhere."

"Oh?" Olliard was all innocent interest. His apprentice, however, seemed a bit too intent on the conversation, her idle gaze too stiff as it lingered on the distant hills.

Her master adjusted his grip on the chimera's reins and said, "I know the life of the itinerant well. I've traveled all over, from the foggy shores of the Linden to the sunlit cities of Cymrinor. I've even been outside the subcontinent. Made the crossing over the Riven Sea more than once in my time."

He chuckled, a low and throaty sound. "They call me Olliard of Kell. You know where Kell is? Little duchy in the continent where I studied for a time, and now folk see me as a foreigner." He shook his head in amusement. "Wasn't there longer than two years."

"Funny where life can take us," I said, staring at the falling gray flecks. So much like snow.

"Yes." Olliard kept his gaze on the road as he spoke, so I couldn't see his expression. "Funny indeed. I imagine our travels have been quite different though, you and I. You're a mercenary?"

The question was abrupt, and it took me a moment to muster a response. "Of a sort."

Lisette finally stopped pretending to ignore the conversation. Her nose scrunched in annoyance. "There's only one sort of sellsword."

"That a fact?" I arched an eyebrow at her. The girl's expression turned sour and she averted her gaze.

"As you can imagine," Olliard said with wry amusement, "us healers don't tend to have much fondness for men, or women, who've taken on violent lives. Yet the two often find themselves joined at the hip. Ironic, isn't it?"

"You get good business from us," I said, "and we need you to keep fighting. Makes sense."

"It's not about business," Lisette said acidly.

"Peace, Lisette." Olliard's voice was gentle, but firm. His apprentice glared at me a moment longer, then snorted and propped her chin in one palm, returning her attention to the countryside.

There wasn't much conversation after that. The land rolled by, and the sky grew steadily darker.

The ash rain wasn't the last dark omen on that journey.

"We're getting close now," Olliard announced with forced cheer. His mood had improved once the ash had stopped falling in midafternoon. The rolling fields beyond Vinhithe had steadily become more forested as the doctor's chimera plodded along. The placid beast had stamina, and we ate through the miles at a speed that surprised me.

Lisette leaned forward, her dour mood and annoyance at me momentarily forgotten. "Is *he* near, master?"

Olliard flashed yellow teeth in a knowing smile. "Indeed! Ah, Alken, I nearly forgot to warn you. There's a troll bridge ahead. Harmless fellow, but we'll need to pay his toll to get on. Just don't panic when you see him. Shy fellow, blessed big as he is."

I shifted in the cart until I could get an arm up on the edge, trying to look beyond Brume's mountainous back. The country trail had become a woodland road, carrying us through a dense growth of forest that shrouded the gray sky. The woods were deep, and old—I could feel a weight pressing in on my senses not unlike the pressure of deep water. The more distant parts of the forest were lost in a deep darkness, as though the daylight did not touch them. The trees grew close, their canopies intermingling in a twisted labyrinth.

Damn healer's brought us into an irkwood, I thought. I settled back, letting my hand rest on the bundle at my side.

"Something the matter?" Olliard glanced back again worriedly. "I promise you, the Troll of Caelfall is harmless. Most of them are, really, at least this far from Trollwood." He paused and added, "You're not some eld hunter, are you?"

Lisette glanced at me and narrowed her blue eyes.

"Not exactly, doctor." I winced as I tried to find a comfortable position in the bumpy cart, then suppressed a hiss of pain as the goring chimera took us over a rut. When I could speak again, my voice was strained. "I've had dealings with the eld before. You don't need to worry about me."

Olliard nodded, looking relieved. "Good, good."

I felt some surprise at the old physik's concern. Few people in recent times distinguished between the benign and malignant elements of the Fae.

Not just an educated man, but knowledgeable in old lore too. I would need to be even more careful of Olliard of Kell.

It would be best to part ways soon. Still, I needed more time to fully recover.

Another half hour passed before we came upon the bridge. I knew immediately something was wrong. I smelled it before I saw it, and the other two noticed not long after. Lisette's expression went pale as she placed the sleeve of her woolen robe over her mouth.

"What is . . ." Her words drifted off as we all heard something else.

Buzzing flies.

Olliard stopped the cart, his hands tight on the chimera's reins. A moment later, we all began to hear the buzzing ambience more clearly. It confirmed what I'd already suspected, and I knew the smell too well.

The scent and song of death.

Olliard spoke to Lisette in a calm, quiet voice. "Remain here. I will go ahead and take a look."

The apprentice clutched at her master's sleeve. "But—"

"No time to argue," Olliard said, patting the girl's hand. "I'll be quick. Perhaps my old friend just didn't clean up after a meal, eh? Gluttonous fellow. Besides," he added with forced cheer. "I should warn him about you two before we all approach. It's been many years, and I don't wish to startle him."

I closed my eyes, considered for a moment, and then heaved myself out of the cart. Both of the healers let out cries of alarm. Olliard all but lunged for me.

"What are you doing, man! You're—"

He paused as he watched me stretch. I rolled my shoulders first, grimacing as I felt my skin pull at Lisette's stitch-work. I placed one hand against the side of the cart and tested my hip. It twinged with pain, but the bone seemed to have set well.

Olliard's dark eyes widened in disbelief. "Your hip was cracked. There's no way you should be able to move."

I blew out a breath and turned my attention forward. "Must not have been as bad as you thought," I said lightly, knowing it to be a weak excuse.

Olliard just shook his head slowly, lips turning into a deep frown. "No, you were near dead when I found you, and it hasn't been three days. Even with Lisette's Art, you shouldn't have been moving under your own power for another two weeks at least."

I would have given myself another four days, maybe five, but the girl's magic had improved even my quick healing. I began to rummage around in the cart until I found my axe. When I pulled it out, both of the healers recoiled from me.

"Stay here," I said, jabbing a finger down at the road. "Try to keep quiet. I'll be right back."

I didn't wait for them to argue or ask me questions. I moved past the cart and went forward, heading toward the sickly-sweet smell and the sound of buzzing flies. Every step sent a lance of pain through my side, but I tried to keep my movement steady while I knew Olliard and his apprentice were watching.

If danger lay ahead, I wasn't certain I'd actually be fit to deal with it. But those two had saved my life. I didn't want to return the favor by sitting in a cart while the old man got himself killed.

So, resting my axe on my shoulder, I ignored the worried eyes on my back and pressed forward. There was a bend in the road ahead, the trees obscuring my view of what lay beyond it. I moved until I reached the corner of the bend. Only then did I see the bridge.

It was an ancient structure, as most troll bridges are. Three arches twenty feet tall each framed the stonework, every inch of it engraved in intricate geometric runes. Moss and ivy grew over the green-gray stone. The plant life had taken on a subtle glow from the magic bleeding off the bridge, giving the whole scene a starkly unreal quality, like some scene right out of a dream.

I suppose it was, in a way. It always is when the Sidhe were involved, and trolls are as much Fae as elves.

Someone had taken steps to turn the scene into a nightmare.

They had cut the bridge's builder into ten pieces, and left each on a separate spear on either side of the structure's entrance. Its head, like an enormous toad's, had been displayed on the tallest of the pikes, the eyes already eaten away by the cloud of buzzing insects to leave two sightless, accusing pits.

Other parts of the dismembered body were harder to tell apart. Both arms and both legs had been displayed, but the rest looked like little more than dripping chunks of green-hued meat, much of it covered in warty protrusions and growths of horn sprouting like keratin tumors from the troll's flesh.

The spears were wood and steel, modern make. This had been human work. Or something predisposed to using human weaponry.

"Forsaken Throne," Olliard swore from behind me. I sighed.

"I told you to stay with the cart." I glanced back and saw the old doctor staring at the butchered carcass. He'd left the cart, chimera, and his apprentice behind, at least.

He didn't seem to hear me and began to move closer. I held out an arm to stop him.

"Don't," I said. "Trolls lay curses on their gates."

Olliard blinked at me through his spectacles. "Curses?"

I nodded. "Hold on a moment."

Then I stepped forward, concentrated, and reached for the golden fire resting within me.

It is difficult to describe, using one's aura. The way I understand it—and understand I am no magus—it is different for every individual being. This I believe, for every soul is different and unique, each marked by its own scars and hopes.

As I burned my magic, it emerged from my eyes as a pale, golden light. The shadows of the forest did not fall away so much as they shifted, like everything in my vision, into abstraction and allegory.

I saw the world not as it seemed to mortal eyes, but as it truly was. Past, present, the lingering echoes of all who'd crossed this place, the perceptions and beliefs of every mind who'd directed its attention to this haunted wood. I could see it all, and make sense of very little of it.

But I only needed to understand one thing, and that was what had happened to this guardian. Trolls are sacred beings, feared by mortals for good reason but respected by us too, at least if we are wise. To elves, they are honored cousins and occasionally rivals.

To me—to the man I'd once been—this death was profane. I focused on its echo.

I regretted it as a wave front of sensation passed into me. For a moment, I was no longer Alken. I was—

Fear. Pain. Rage. Betrayal. A collection of nerves and sinew bursting with stars of agony as cold steel punched into me, over and over. The sleeping forest alive with the sound of laughing, shouting men, of weaponry, and of my own guttural howls. Huge, blocky yellow teeth appear huge in my vision, set in macabre grins beneath eyes that glint like those of beasts.

Even cautious and knowing what to expect, the wave front of psychic trauma hit me hard. I realized, dimly, that Olliard was speaking to me.

"I'm fine," I gasped. I had fallen to one knee, and cold sweat covered my face. I wiped some of it away and stood on unsteady legs.

"What just happened?" Olliard's expression was tense with worry and confusion. "One moment you stepped forward, and the next you fell. You really shouldn't be standing with your injuries. Let's get back to the cart."

I waved the doctor off. "I'm fine. It's not that. I just . . ." I wasn't sure how to explain, and before I had the chance to say anything more I felt a sudden queasiness rise up through my gut. I barely made it to the edge of the road before vomiting.

When I could speak again, my voice emerged hoarse. "This bridge might not be usable for months." I grimaced. "Maybe years."

"Who would do this?" Olliard pressed a sleeve to his nose against the smell, his attention wandering back to the dead troll. "Why? He's been living here peacefully for generations."

"Maybe someone didn't want to pay his toll," I suggested, studying the scene. I wiped my mouth and nodded toward the head.

"See that? Its horns were removed. Elfhorn is a valuable commodity in a lot of places. They didn't take the buds," I noted, studying the smaller growths of pale, slightly shimmering horn on other parts of the troll's corpse. "It grows even after death. Probably they intended to come back and harvest it in a few weeks."

Olliard's face twisted with horror and disgust. "Barbaric."

I hummed softly, keeping my own thoughts to myself. I looked for more clues as to the identity of the eld's murderers.

"They took trophies," I noted as I paced through the scene, "but left this as a warning. Those weapons are good quality, but I'm not seeing any House signet or knight's mark."

I tapped my axe against a shoulder, thinking. "Mercenaries, I'm guessing, or bandits."

Or something else, I thought, remembering the huge yellow teeth in my vision, the too-pale eyes. That could have just been the troll's perception, panicked and afraid, coloring the event over. Even still . . .

I glanced at the doctor and waited until he returned my attention. "The village nearby." I jerked my chin toward the remains of the troll. "You think they hired some sellswords to chop up your friend here?"

Olliard looked affronted at the suggestion. "He's practically a member of the community! Defended them during the Fall, and was living here near two centuries before that. They would never."

I sighed and turned back toward the cart. "World's changed these past ten years, doc, and not for the better. Not the first time I've seen the friendly local monster getting torn apart because the crops turned bad or a kid got dragged into the woods by something nasty."

Olliard just shook his head, eyes hard. "They wouldn't. I know the preoster who counsels the villagers well, and he would not condone this."

I didn't much feel like arguing with the old man. "In any case," I said, "we need to find a way through. You know another path?"

Olliard's expression fell as he shook his head. "No. More than thirty miles of wilderness in either direction, and no path I know of that we could get Brume and the cart through. Caelfall is an isolated country."

I ran my eyes over the darkening forest. "I'm not about to suggest going through those trees. The beings who dwell in these woods aren't going to be happy about the troll's death. We need to get moving, and quickly."

Olliard followed my eyes nervously. "What do you suggest?"

I directed his attention back to the carcass. "We bury your friend there and hope that appeases his spirit. It won't lift the curses placed on his bridge, but it might give us a chance to get through them safely."

I met the doctor's eyes and held up a finger. "That's not a guarantee. It'd be safer to turn back the way we came."

I didn't much like suggesting it, since *back the way we came* was a hostile demesne where I'd be executed if caught.

"No," Olliard said firmly. "I must press on."

He didn't elaborate, even when I lifted a questioning eyebrow.

"Who are you, to know so much about curses and troll ways?" Olliard's eyes had narrowed as he regarded me.

Smooth, I thought. Old man wasn't quick to give an excuse as to why he wouldn't turn back. It seemed like we were both hiding things from one another.

"Do you care?" I asked.

Olliard's lips twitched in a small smile. "I *am* curious. But I digress, and we are wasting what little light we have left. So we should bury the troll?"

I nodded, inwardly grimacing at the task ahead. "We'll need to make a grave of river stones and make sure it's in sight of the bridge. Does your apprentice know any wards against disease? Troll corpses rot fast."

Olliard shrugged and sighed. "I have no idea. I suppose we will find out."

"Then let's get to work."

CHAPTER EIGHT

NIGHTFALL

The clouds had cleared by the time we finished burying the troll, and red bled across the sky. A thin gray silt had been left across scores of miles by the ashfall earlier in the day, giving the irkwood a dour, surreal quality. A gray winter in the last days of spring.

Lisette stood from the last of the markers we'd made from river stone and shattered pieces of the old bridge, murmuring a *preosta*—a song of prayer. She had a soft, halting voice I felt suited the scene better than anything more dramatic or beautiful.

Nothing beautiful about that poor creature's death.

When done, the young cleric moved to Olliard and pressed her auremark against his chest, continuing her prayers, her eyes narrowed in concentration. I could feel warmth emanating from her as she worked her aura, cleansing him of both disease and malignant od that might have clung to him from handling the troll's carcass.

The physiker breathed a sigh of relief at the touch of her magic and smiled, murmuring thanks. Even those without awakened aura can still feel it if it's tangible enough.

When the girl moved to me to do the same, I held up a hand to stop her. "No need," I said. "I'm covered."

The doctor's apprentice frowned, studying me. When I didn't elaborate, she huffed in frustration. "You're the one who told me I should do this," she remarked pointedly.

I didn't want to tell her I was largely immune to disease and had my own protections against curses, and I especially didn't want the cleric to make contact with my own essence. She'd probably sense something was off with it, and that wasn't a conversation I felt interested in having.

She used her power to stitch up your wounds, I reminded myself. *If she was going to notice anything, she'd have done so already.*

Maybe so, but it was still a risk I wasn't interested in taking. I'd get myself cleansed later if I needed to. There were other ways besides the services of a priest.

"We need to get moving," I said. I nodded toward the bridge. "Now we've buried the poor bastard who built that, it should be safe enough to cross it. *Should* be, mind. Your chimera warded?"

Olliard nodded. "Of course. I had her protections renewed only a few weeks ago by a warder in Isengotta."

With that, there wasn't much more to say. Olliard took another ten minutes to fuss over his beast, and I watched him add a few more small baubles to the array of charms tied either to the hog-headed creature's harness or woven into her coarse fur. Surreptitiously, I closed my eyes and inspected the wards with my own senses. They weren't the best work, but they were professionally done. They'd serve.

Lisette watched me the entire time Olliard tended to Brume. I grew annoyed with the attention and glared at her. "What?"

Burying the troll had been foul work, and between that and my taste of the creature's dying trauma I wasn't in the best of moods. My ordinary mood didn't tend toward gregarious most times.

"You're an adept," she said. "You've been trained to wield your soul."

I lifted one shoulder in a shrug. "Common enough."

Lisette shook her head slowly, more in thought than denial. "Yours isn't some layman's talent. You knew about curses and burial rites, and a moment ago . . . you were *feeling* Brume's wards. I sensed you doing it."

I shifted, uncomfortable. *Damn clerics,* I thought. "Surprised?"

"Yes," the novice said honestly. "You don't look the type. Sorcerer or warlock?"

I carefully set my face into a mask and averted my eyes, not wanting to give anything away. True enough, I didn't much look like your typical magicker.

I am tall, more than two meters, and broadly built, much of my weight a swordsman's hard-earned muscle. I keep my copper hair long to help hide the glint of gold in my eyes, as well as my scars, and life on the move doesn't lend to regular grooming. My skin is calloused and abused by a life of violence. I've got a long face with a heavy chin, deep set eyes, and a nose many times broken.

I'd once been told I look something like a brooding lion. I'd hated that comparison. I hate lions.

I didn't often get a look at myself, but I knew well enough what I must look like to these gentle healers. A brute. A killer. Hard-edged.

There were plenty of words for it, but it all boiled down to the same thing—I didn't much look like the type to know my way around an arcane conundrum. Or the type who'd even know words like *conundrum*.

Lisette's inquiry was a dangerous question. Sorcerers are common enough, and anyone with even a passing talent at magic could be described as such, usually if they're untrained or gained their power from some natural source. Warlocks are another matter entirely. Not all are evil or draw their power from diabolical sources—the only prerequisite is to have gained power through some sort of ritualized pact or bargain—but the word still carried a certain stigma.

Especially when talking to someone trained among the clergy.

I decided for a half truth. "I knew a magician back before the war. A proper wizard. He taught me some tricks."

Lisette's frown deepened. "A magus taught you Sidhe burial rites?"

I folded my arms. "The Magi are said to be all-knowing."

I could tell the girl wasn't convinced, but Olliard, bless him, chose that moment to approach and clap his hands together, startling Lisette out of her suspicion. "I think we should be set! I put a few of the charms I bought last time I had the chance on the cart, too. I've heard that wild magic can stick to objects as well as people."

I nodded. "Good idea. Cart's made of wood, and dead matter collects od like you wouldn't believe."

Olliard blinked in interest, his owlish eyes widening behind his foggy lenses. "Is that so? I'd never heard of this."

"It's true," Lisette said, a note of scholarly interest trickling into her voice. She noticed her master's interested gaze and her cheeks turned slightly pink. She adjusted a lock of yellow hair and elaborated. "It's why you find so many ghosts and fey spirits in dead trees and the like."

"Fascinating." Olliard's eyes glittered, and Lisette gave the old man a shy smile.

"Much as I love class time," I drawled, "we don't have much light left. Time to be on. I'd like to get as far from this bridge as we can before we camp."

Lisette's mood darkened again, and she pointedly turned her back to me.

We all piled onto the cart. With the sun quickly sinking beneath the distant horizon beyond the forest, we crossed the ancient, now masterless bridge.

Night fell, drowning the forest in a deep, impenetrable darkness.

We made camp. Resting in an irkwood is dangerous and foolish, but we had no other recourse and at the very least the wards and Lisette's unique skill set made it about as safe as it could be.

Olliard lit a lantern and attached it to a long pole, which he hung over the cart to light the forest after we brought it into a small clearing off the path. The doctor lit two more lanterns and attached them to the sides of the cart, making the vehicle a little island of somber orange light within a sea of shadowy wilderness. I made the campfire.

"No insects singing," Lisette noted. Her eyes blinked sleepily and she suppressed a yawn as she wrapped herself in a blanket against the night's chill. "No owls. It's just . . . silent."

"Hm." Olliard patted his ugly chimera, cleaning her fur with a bristly brush as his eyes wandered the depthless black beyond the light. "Should be out of this before noon tomorrow, unless the path has been altered. Be a terrible time for elf mischief."

I closed my eyes, though I was careful not to let exhaustion whisk me away into dreams. I didn't sense any tampering with the road or the woods here. There were no illusions, no phantasms, no subtle enchantments that might cause us to lose days of time or walk off a cliff.

Even still, I didn't dare let myself sleep just yet.

I wanted to, very badly. Despite my bravado earlier, my injuries were *not* healed and burying the dead troll had been exhausting, painful work. Every bump and jostle of the cart after had made me feel like my hip bone was about to burst out of my skin, and my ribs ached with a dull, constant agony.

Part of me wanted to take my leave of the healers and vanish into the night, foolish as the thought was. Lisette was already suspicious of me, and there might be every chance we'd run into a patrol from Vinhithe. We weren't so far from the city still, and I would be hunted.

Would they send messengers into this other domain, this Caelfall? I hadn't heard of it before, but Urn has many small realms and little dominions tucked away in its mountains and river valleys. Would the Earl's men hunt me there?

I had more immediate concerns than knights and bounty hunters, though. My eyes wandered into the dark.

Something looked back. I couldn't see it, but I felt it. I knew it well.

Knew them well.

More than my desire to get far away from the city, however, was another vexing issue. Olliard of Kell and his apprentice had saved my life. I didn't want to repay that favor by dragging them into my affairs. But Olliard's wards also helped protect me in my vulnerable state, and his ministrations helped me heal faster.

Further, parting company might not keep them safe from the dark things in these woods, both what I'd brought with me and what I knew would already dwell here.

Those Glorysworn had called me a blackguard. Perhaps they were right. What claim did I have to honor anymore?

Yet . . .

I owed them. And I wasn't in any condition to wander off alone, in any case. So instead I took out my axe, ignoring the discomforted looks the healers cast my way. When I freed the arm from its cloth bundle, Brume stirred and let out an uneasy grumble.

I took out my dagger—a long, curved piece with pale inlays near the mesh-wrapped hilt—and began to run it along the gnarled branch that formed the axe's handle. I sliced off small twigs and sharp burs, then began to shorten it down. It had grown in the days I'd been injured and unable to tend it.

"That is a very strange thing," Olliard said, swallowing. "I admit, I've never seen anything quite like it."

"It's elf make," Lisette said. She worked at a length of cloth, one of the doctor's shirts, and busied herself resewing some of its tears.

Olliard leaned forward with interest. "Ah! Is that why the handle seems . . . alive?"

"It is alive," I muttered, slicing a length off the branch.

"And the metal?" Olliard asked, rubbing at the wiry growth on his chin.

"Hithlenic Bronze," I said. "Alloyed with ordinary steel."

I lifted the axe, letting the light from the campfire and the lanterns glint along the crescent-moon shape of the blade. It had a dramatic hook, leaving a circular hollow between the sharp point of the lower blade and the grip. The light seemed to set the spiraling inlays to burning. Those had gold worked into them.

"It's profane," Lisette muttered, glaring at the weapon sidelong. "Something made to kill people shouldn't look so beautiful."

I couldn't disagree. We sat in silence for a long while, listening to the fire and the silence of the woods.

"You should sleep," Lisette said to me after some time. She didn't meet my eyes. The apprentice healer sat with her back to one of the cart wheels, hugging her knees to her chest. She looked very tired, and very young. Younger than I'd first thought.

She was a tall girl, gangly, with a narrow face splattered in freckles and eyes just a bit too large for it. With her straw-colored hair, she looked more like some scrawny farmer's daughter than a neophyte of the Aureate Church.

My mind flashed back to the boy in the Vinhithe cathedral. He'd been even younger.

"Dangerous to sleep in an irkwood," I noted mildly. "Dangerous to dream in one."

Idly, I rubbed at the ring on my right hand with my thumb. My axe tended to, I'd returned it to its wrappings.

"Master Olliard's wards are good," Lisette assured me. "And I've blessed them myself. You should be safe."

I didn't reply, and the girl shrugged the conversation off, indifferent. Her attention wandered. My gaze fell down to my ring. The black stone swam with eddies of red, and I grimaced at the sight.

"That's a beautiful ring," Lisette said.

She didn't seem upset at it as she had with the axe. I glanced at her, then frowned and held it up, inspecting it. The ivory band was a very pale yellow, nearly white, with tiny claws—evoking nothing so much as a splayed rib cage—holding the black stone. I'd always thought it had a rather fell look to it.

"It is?" I asked skeptically.

The apprentice nodded, tucking her chin on her knees. "It's the detail. Whoever made it had an exquisite hand. Who gave it to you?"

None of your business. I bit down on the thought before it became words. The girl hadn't done anything to deserve my anger, or create it.

"An ally," I said. "One who knows curses."

Lisette frowned. "Curses?"

Olliard spoke up from where he tended his chimera. "That's enough, Lisette. Leave the man in peace."

The apprentice blushed and cast an apologetic look at her master. The three of us fell into silence, and listened for a time to the crackling fire.

Perhaps ill at ease with the eerie silence of the woods, Olliard changed the subject. "Once you're healed, Alken, what's next for you? Not that I'd mind having a strong arm keeping me and the girl safe, but I imagine you have your own roads to walk."

His voice held a questioning note. I sensed an offer there, and almost laughed at it.

I closed my eyes, though I hadn't decided to accept sleep. "Suppose I'll cross that bridge when I come to it. How about you? What's your business in this village we're heading to?"

"I'm a traveling physician!" Olliard explained brightly. "I wander here and there, offering my services where they are needed. I have a few places I visit every once in a while. Caelfall is one such. I haven't been there since before the war, given, but I've known the people there, oh . . ."

He rubbed at his wiry gray beard. "Well. A long time. The preoster there is a good man."

More priests, I thought sourly. Aloud I said, "And if they did have something to do with what happened to the troll?"

Olliard fell quite a while. When he finally spoke, his words were nearly a whisper. "Sometimes, good people do terrible things to protect the ones they love. Even when the way in which they do so is misguided."

I shifted against the packs I'd stacked to lean on. No matter how I sat or lay down, no position wasn't a torture on my injuries. "You think the troll went fell? It happens, sometimes."

Olliard shrugged and let out a tired sigh. "I don't know. I try not to act without facts. Misunderstandings sometimes create the saddest of tragedies."

I arched an eyebrow. "That why you didn't just leave me to die, like your apprentice wanted?"

Olliard glanced at me over one shoulder, and there was slight reprimand in that look. "Lisette did *not* advocate to leave you to die. She is a kindhearted girl, for all the horror she's seen. She may growl, but she could no more leave another soul to suffer than the moons could fail to rise."

By the cart, the girl in question snored softly. She'd fallen asleep only a few minutes before.

"And what if she was right?" I asked, keeping my tone casual. "What if I *am* dangerous, and I go on to hurt someone after you've helped me?"

Olliard turned his eyes back to the fire and didn't reply for a while. Finally he said, "Then it would be my responsibility to stop you, and make amends for my sin."

"And you'd do it?" I asked. "Try to stop me?"

I tried not to put any special emphasis on the word *try*. I was curious, not trying to intimidate the man.

"I would stop you," Olliard said, very quiet. He spoke calmly, without bravado or conceit. I noted the way the firelight reflected on his glasses, obscuring the eyes behind them.

I waited, but the doctor didn't elaborate. Finally, in a lighter tone, he said, "Time to get some rest. Don't want you catching a fever now. Sleep. Doctor's orders." He turned to me and flashed a grin. "Trust me, these wards are professionally done. No mischief will find you in your dreams."

I rubbed at my ring idly as a faint smile touched the corner of my lip. "That so?"

"Well." Olliard rubbed his hands together. "If any of us are possessed or stark-raving mad come morning, we will simply have to trust whoever managed to keep sane will put us out of our misery. I imagine it will be Lisette. She's far too sensible to succumb to such things."

I didn't answer, my eyes wandering back to the fire. I *did* need sleep. I could go longer than most without it, but one needs to dream to replenish their body and their spirit.

Only . . .

I feared my dreams.

CHAPTER NINE

HE WHO WIELDS GOLDEN FIRE

Alken! Wake up, damn it!"

I shot awake, and the shaking hand on my shoulder flinched away as I reached for my dagger.

It took me a moment to realize where I was. The irkwood still. The heady stench of Olliard's chimera and the cold night air were like ice water over my head.

My sleep had been deep and black. The ring on my right hand felt warm against my skin, and the black stone swam with red eddies. *Another dream.* One I wouldn't remember.

I forced myself back to reality, turning to meet the panicked eyes of Olliard. His fringe of gray hair stuck out wildly in all directions, and a bead of sweat formed on his brow. Night still clung tightly to the forest. All was silent, and the campfire had burned down.

Why had they let the fire burn down?

Then I realized it as I looked around. "Where is Lisette?" I demanded.

"Gone," Olliard said, his voice tight with fear. In the background, the chimera Brume rested on her haunches, fearful breaths snorting out of her huge nostrils in misting plumes. It had become intensely cold, despite the late spring warmth we'd enjoyed for the journey so far.

I stood, on guard, and Olliard rose with me.

"I woke just a few minutes ago, and the fire had gone out." Olliard swallowed and adjusted his spectacles. "She wasn't here. I thought, perhaps, she might have had a call of nature, but . . ."

"But she's too sensible to wander off into an irkwood," I finished for him.

I worked quickly, redoing the laces on my boots, grabbing my belt and dagger, freeing my axe from the bundle I'd been keeping it in for the comfort of the healers. Last, I threw on my cloak against the unseasonable chill.

All the while, I focused my senses on the forest around me. Clouds had moved across the sky, casting everything in an impenetrable black only broken in our camp by the lanterns Olliard had kept lit. He had one in hand now as he paced at the edge of the camp, agitated and impatient.

I focused on the sense of cold. It wasn't natural. I felt *anger* in it.

"You stay here," I told the doctor. "I'll find her."

"To hell with that!" Olliard rummaged around in his cart. When he turned, he held a cumbersome object in his hands, the lantern tied at his belt. A crossbow.

It was a beautiful piece, a work of art. The brown wood had a smooth, almost shiny finish, and the metal had been worked with detailed inlays. It seemed almost too hefty for the thin man, but he held it with a familiar ease.

Odd thing for a physiker to have.

Seeing my questioning look, Olliard's lips formed a tight line. "Pays to be careful."

He had already loaded a bolt into the device. It had little in common with the simple yew pieces the guard in Vinhithe had used. The crossbow had a complex loading mechanism, and parts I wasn't familiar with, including two levers in addition to the iron trigger.

I couldn't say whether I made the decision because I didn't want to waste time, or because of the wicked-looking crossbow, but I nodded. "Fine. Keep behind me, and don't point that thing where I'm standing."

Besides, Lisette was his companion. He had a right to go.

"Stay, Brume." Olliard patted the chimera's boar head. "That's a good girl."

Brume let out a distressed grunt and snuffled at the doctor, then shrank her enormous bulk against the cart. The wooden vehicle creaked at the beast's weight. She wouldn't be going anywhere, I suspected.

"How are we going to find her?" Olliard asked me. "Can you track?"

"In a way," I said. "I'll lead. You just keep close, and keep that lantern up."

He didn't question it. We moved into the forest. I led, following the eerie sensation I felt in the air. We ducked under the curse wards Lisette had placed at dusk.

"Why in all the world would she leave the safety of the wards?" Olliard asked, perplexed.

"She might have been made to," I said, my eyes wandering the dark. I'd taken a lantern too, and its pale light gave ominous definition to the trees.

"I thought spirits couldn't get through barriers like that," the doctor muttered. "Not to mention, I thought they couldn't approach a campfire without permission."

"The Law of Draubard," I agreed. "That's just for the dead. Will-o'-the-wisps and other fae things don't play by the same rules. Still, you're right about the wards."

I glanced back at him. "Likely, nothing came in. She was probably lured *out*."

And I'd been too deep in my sleep to notice. My jaw clenched in frustration. What had called the young cleric out into this darkness? The denizens of this ancient wood, or . . .

Was this *my* fault?

I forged into the dark.

We found Lisette in a small clearing. She hadn't strayed terribly far from the camp, all told.

I spotted a distant light at first, and thought perhaps it belonged to one of the lanterns Olliard kept. They were alchemical pieces, of the sort becoming more popular across the subcontinent in recent years. They produced a light closer to greenish white than yellow, and could burn far longer than any torch.

I realized soon enough that the light I saw belonged to nothing fashioned by human hands.

Approaching the edge of the clearing, I got a better look at what lay ahead. Towering trees, some older than kingdoms, rose high into the black sky, their twisted canopies intermingling into an oppressive barrier. Within that ring, the young adept stood still.

She didn't wear her brown robes and apron. The girl had gone out barefoot, wearing just a thin shift suitable only as an undergarment, which couldn't have provided any warmth in this bitter air. Her pale blond hair hung loose around her shoulders, and she had her head upturned.

Mist coiled through the trees. It seemed to grow thickest around Lisette. It glowed as though reflecting strong moonlight.

Yet, no moon shone through the overcast sky.

Seeing the same thing I did, Olliard began to rush forward, his apprentice's name on his lips. I stopped him with an upraised arm.

"What?" he asked, almost growling. He looked afraid, and relieved to see the girl alive.

"Don't approach her," I told him. "She's ensorcelled."

I could make out shapes in the mist. Gaunt, sharp, hollow eyed.

"Forest spirits?" Olliard asked, his throat bobbing as he swallowed.

"Worse." I took a steadying breath and stepped into the clearing, letting the mist part around my legs. "Stay back. Do *not* fire that thing. It won't do any of us any good."

Olliard obeyed me, and I focused my attention on the girl. She swayed slightly from side to side, as though moving to some slow tune. The near-invisible shapes moving in the mist swirled around her, circling like predatory fish.

"Lisette," I said. "Look at me."

She didn't seem to hear me. I could hear her voice—she muttered something, an unceasing torrent of words too low for me to make out. The mist writhed. It spilled out of the surrounding trees, like blood pouring into a hollow. There was no wind, no stars, no moon, no ambience of night.

Yet all within the clearing shone stark, illuminated by witch light. It made everything look unreal, as though we stood in an endless abyss, a sea of black.

"Lisette," I tried again in a firmer voice. "Do not heed them."

I could hear sounds emerging from the glowing fog. Whispers, which grew more agitated as they took note of me. They *knew* me.

Lisette suddenly spoke louder, so I could hear her words. "But I didn't—"

She wasn't speaking to me. Her voice cut off with a choked sob. Hugging her own arms, she spoke again. "I was scared. I didn't want them to die. I was just scared."

I narrowed my eyes, focusing on the presence in the mist as I moved forward at a slow, steady pace. I could hear it better now, too.

"You abandoned them."

"Left your sisters to die."

"The ones who brought you out of war, out of hunger . . ."

"They made you family, and you just watched them DIE."

Lisette sobbed openly now. "I'm sorry! I didn't want to die. I'm *sorry.*"

"Those soldiers butchered them."

"Hunted them like beasts."

"Laughed while they did it!"

"They killed them. Raped them."

"You just watched!"

"Coward. USELESS."

"Should have died in the mud with your parents."

"Just another dead peasant. No one would have missed you."

Lisette sank to her knees, pleading for the voices to stop. I knew well enough they wouldn't.

I drew in a deep breath of freezing night air, pulled from the warmth within me, and poured aura into my voice.

"Lisette."

"Look. At. Me."

Lisette stiffened. Slowly, as though pulling against a tight grip, she turned to face me. Her eyes were haunted, deeply shadowed as though she hadn't slept in many days, and her white face beaded with sweat despite the cold.

Again, the mist writhed. Ghastly faces formed in it, their eyes empty pits, their silent screams forming like melting wax.

"Leave her," I snarled at the dead. "You have no quarrel with this cleric. She had nothing to do with your deaths."

I stopped when I'd reached the girl, standing over her and facing the writhing fog. As I'd intended, it directed its attention at me.

"*You.*"

"*Murderer!*"

"*Failure.*"

"*Deceiver!*"

"*TRAITOR.*"

"I've earned your curses," I told them, standing firm. "She hasn't."

More distinct shapes began to form in the deepening mist. Ungainly crawling things, long limbed and emaciated, all bone and ghostly sinew, with bestial heads and hair like writhing tendrils. They skulked and crawled, the light in the damp air condensing until they became near-solid phantasms, potent as the spells the knights of Vinhithe had cast into their air.

Real enough to be dangerous.

"*Playacting the knight again?*" They laughed at me in a score of voices.

"*Do you think she'll be grateful?*"

"*Do you expect she'll let you have her as reward?*"

"*We know what lurks in that heart of yours, you wanting beast.*"

"*Does she not remind you of* her?"

My jaw clenched with fury. Even still, I kept my voice low and calm as I could. "I know you are all in terrible pain, but remember what you were. You've suffered enough. I do *not* want to hurt you."

Hate boiled from the spirits. They had become like forms of silver fire, sharp as glass and bright as slivers of a baleful moon.

"*Hurt us!?*" they hissed.

"*We have become this because of* YOU!"

"*We will never give you peace.*"

"*Never let you rest!*"

"*Your sins will follow you into damnation, oathbreaker.*"

I bit down hard on the bitter emotion I felt then. I swallowed my shame, and lifted the axe. The brassy sheen of its alloy reflected their lambent forms. When I spoke, pale fire flickered between my teeth.

"Your quarrel is with me, *Seydii*, and there will be plenty of other nights to settle it."

"*Perhaps this will be the last?*"

A silver form burned itself into reality almost within my reach, lashing out with crooked talons. Flinching, I caught the blow on the edge of the axe, ripped it aside in a shower of sparks both real and phantasmal, then swung with a roar.

The axe cleaved through the spirit, and it erupted. Amber fire ate away at silver, and the wraith loped into the forest as it burned, wailing with agony.

Regret settled in me, very much like the onset of great weariness. Even still, I brandished the axe, sweeping it to one side as a trail of golden fire—the *aureflame*—traced its cut. My voice echoed with power when I spoke.

"I do not want this fight. This fire will hurt you. *Go.*"

I put a pleading note into my voice. "Please."

But their hate had reached a crescendo. Wailing in voices like shrieking metal, the wraiths surged forward. Lisette let out a cry of fear, and Olliard shouted something from the clearing's edge.

I closed my eyes, breathed in deep, and spoke the words of an Oath.

"I am the sword in the darkness. I am gold and iron. I am the sentinel flame."

The power alloyed into my soul surged like a roaring fire. It scorched me, angry and broken in its own way as these silver ghosts.

But it heeded my command, and I shaped my aura into an Art.

A ring of pale light, chased with images of branches and leaves in an autumnal wood, burst to life around me and the girl. It scattered the mist, brightened the night, cast away the cold. All for a moment.

Then the phantasms faded, leaving faint impressions of themselves in the air that lingered for several moments, and the amber light condensed into a faintly shining circle around me, so I became like one of Olliard's lamps.

Lisette looked up at me, her blue eyes reflecting the pale golden light as though she looked directly into the sun. Her mouth fell agape.

I ignored her, keeping my attention on the wraiths. They had recoiled from my magic, but remained at its edge, their bestial faces snarling. I held my axe in both hands, the head poised under my chin, the oak handle parallel to my chest.

"You would turn our own gifts against us!?"

The wraiths hissed at me.

"Blasphemer!"

"This was *his* gift," I reminded them. "And Hers. And you've become the very thing it was made to repel. It doesn't *have* to be this way."

The light around me had already begun to fade. My forehead beaded with sweat, and the aureflame . . .

It hurt. I could feel it crawling through my veins. My skin began to blister here and there, and my mouth felt terribly dry. I clenched my jaw, ignoring the pain.

The wraiths laughed.

"The Alder's fire is withered. It turns against you!"

"You will go like the rest."

"I will take you all with me," I promised them. **"Be gone."**

I made the word an auratic command, spiking it with energy. Suggestion and compulsion is far more effective on spirits than living mortals. They scattered, screeching in rage.

"This is not over! We will haunt you to your death, Headsman!"

"But not tonight," I said. "And not them."

"*You are no protector.*" The darkness writhed with the scorn of the dead. "*You already failed this land, and now its wounds fester.*"

"*GO!*" I roared.

And they went, scattering into the black woods. As sudden as an ending dream, the forms of silver fire faded away. The glowing mist went next, leaving all the irkwood in an impenetrable veil of shadow.

The light around me remained. It rippled, growing brighter. I grit my teeth, fighting against the violent surge of power flaring out of me. Lisette winced at the brightness, casting a hand up over her eyes.

No. Not here. Not where others would be hurt. I focused on the words of vows emblazoned into my memory, into my *soul*. As familiar to me as my own skin, my own heartbeat.

My flesh peeled. My lips blistered. The ends of my copper hair flickered with fire, emitting a burnt smell. It caught at the edges of my cloak, already singed from past times, and ruined it further.

I forced myself to calm. I focused on my breathing, let my racing heart steady. The tension in my muscles, with effort, relaxed. I lowered the axe.

The fire withered, and the amber light faded. Soon enough, the girl and I were left in total darkness. I heard a hollow *thump*, and only then realized my right hand had gone limp so the head of the axe had fallen down to the grass. I managed to keep hold of it, barely.

"Lisette!"

Olliard raced forward, illuminating us again with lantern light. He held one in hand, his crossbow in the other, a second lantern tied at his belt—I'd given him mine before moving into the clearing.

Shaking with fear and shock, Lisette clung tightly to the old man as he knelt next to her. I let them be, clenching my teeth against the scalding pain racing across my skin, and *within* it.

I'd been badly burned. My flesh had peeled along my arms and neck, leaving angry red marks. I couldn't get moisture into my mouth to swallow, and my throat felt dry as a desert. Smoke trailed into the cold air around my shoulders.

Olliard blinked up at me, afraid and awed at once. "What *are* you?" he asked.

I couldn't answer, couldn't even draw in half a breath to speak. Lisette answered for me, her blue eyes calm and wary as she lifted her head from the doctor's shoulder.

"He's a paladin."

CHAPTER TEN

A SUNKEN LAND

When I'd managed to catch my breath and get a bit of moisture into my scalded throat, I felt a very different heat rise up in me.

Anger.

Olliard had helped his apprentice up. She stood on shaky legs, her face still drained of color, her eyes red from crying.

I stepped forward, pushed the doctor aside, and grabbed the girl by the collar of her shift. My lips peeled back from my teeth in a snarl.

"What were you *thinking*?" I snapped. "You should know better than to wander off after voices in the dark, idiot girl!"

She gaped at me, shocked at my anger and the nightmare she'd just experienced. She was covered in scratches and clinging leaves, the hem of her dress muddy. The wraiths had drained some vitality from her—the clear blue of her eyes had faded into something closer to gray, and her cheeks and eyes looked more sunken than they had even hours ago when we'd made camp. A single streak of white touched her blond hair.

The spirits had tormented her before I'd arrived. I had only seen one piece of the nightmare she had experienced. Had I been even a few minutes later, I suspected I'd be staring at an old, withered face aged far past its time.

"Fool," I called her. "Next time, I'll leave you to them."

"Leave her be!" Olliard stepped forward, his kindly face hardened into a mask of anger. "Hasn't she suffered enough?"

I turned my glare on him. When he saw my eyes, he flinched.

"Those were wraiths," I told them both. "They can rip your life right out of you, but they'll usually drive you mad first. That's just one of a legion of dangers in a wilderness like this."

I looked at Lisette again. "Do *not* leave the light of a campfire out here. *Ever*."

"Your eyes are glowing." Lisette's voice had a dreamy quality. I could see a shimmer of gold in the blue of her own eyes as they reflected mine.

I let her go. Olliard caught her as she stumbled back and glared up at me.

"Wraiths?" he asked. "Ghosts, you mean."

"Elves." I scanned the forest. With my aura still faintly burning, I could see through the darkness. I saw no sign of any threat, but knew it lay out there.

"Dead elves, you mean?" Olliard asked. "Their shades?"

I shook my head. "Elves are immortal. They don't die, not like we do. Their spirits are made of sterner stuff. Those you saw were Seydii from the Golden Country. They lost their bodies when Seydis burned, but they'll linger like that."

"They're still burning," Lisette muttered, still looking dazed and half aware of her surroundings.

I didn't disagree. I thought of the one I'd cut. I hadn't wanted to add to its pain, but it had left me no choice. Even still . . .

Damn them. I knew I couldn't reason with madness, but it still galled.

"Why did you leave camp?" I demanded, turning my frustration where it could find purchase.

Lisette blinked, frowning. She seemed to be slowly pulling herself out of the shock. "I thought I was dreaming. I didn't even realize when I'd left camp, then the mist came and . . ."

She shivered. "I couldn't find my way back. They showed me things."

"They blame us for the war." I watched the woods. "For the destruction of their realm."

"Us?" Olliard asked, furrowing his bushy brows.

"Humans," I said.

The doctor's frown deepened.

"Be grateful those were just spirits," I said darkly, turning my back on them. "I wouldn't have been able to banish them so easily otherwise. Let's get back to camp."

I'd taken five steps before Olliard called out. "Wait!"

I stopped.

"Who are you?" the doctor asked me.

"He's a knight of the old orders," Lisette said, her voice full of quiet awe. "I thought they'd all died during the Fall. Or gone mad."

I started walking again. "They did. And I am no knight."

We set out early, none of us well rested. As before, Olliard sat on the bench and drove, while Lisette and I remained in the cart's bed. For many hours, none of us spoke to one another.

I felt content with that. I knew they must have questions, could practically *feel* their dour curiosity. I just didn't know what I would tell them, if anything.

Those wraiths had been following me. They weren't the only dark things that did. I thought of the whispering shades who'd taunted me after I'd escaped the river, and Nath. Plenty of more common ghosts haunted my steps.

But those shapes of silver fire were deadly. Just one more reason to recover quickly, and part ways with this little company. I shifted in the cart, and bit down a growl of pain as my new burns let out cries of protest along with my other half-healed injuries.

"You should let me see to those burns," Lisette said. She'd been watching me.

"I heal quick." I folded my arms, ignoring the discomfort. "There's no need."

"I have a healing Art," the girl insisted. "It will at least ease your pain. You saved my life. Let me—"

"You saved mine already," I interrupted her. "No need to keep unbalancing the score."

"Stop being impossible," Lisette snapped, some of the thorns she'd lost in the previous night's horror reappearing. "There is no reason to sit there and grimace through it."

I caught Olliard's glance as he turned back, one of his gray eyebrows lifted. He shrugged, then tutted to his chimera. A moment later, the cart stopped. I sighed.

I let Lisette tend to my injuries. She checked the stitch work she'd already done, then began to run her fingers along the burns on my arms and neck. A subtle warmth passed from her touch into my skin, and I knew she wove something less tangible than gut string into me—aura.

She worked her power into my flesh like she would ordinary stitches. Half an hour later, much of the pain had faded.

I kept stoic throughout, but . . .

She had a talent. I'd rarely met any adept who could weave a healing Art more potent than the aureflame.

"I don't understand," Lisette said after she'd finished. "I can tell your magic is healing you, but last night it burned you."

I adjusted my shirt as I answered. "Depends on how hard I use it. Anything dramatic, and . . ." I waved at the burns.

"Has it always been like that?" Lisette asked, seeming disturbed at the thought.

I shook my head. "Not always, no."

"A flame that can heal as well as harm," Olliard pondered as he checked Brume's tack. "What a strange thing."

"Lots of strange magics in the world," I said dismissively.

Neither of them had a riposte for that, and soon enough we were moving again.

We cleared the irkwood not long after, and passed into the domain known as Caelfall.

My first impression of the country wasn't a kind one. Brooding gray clouds obscured the sky, casting a dull pallor over an already dour-looking land. Small lakes and marshland dotted dreary fields. Dead trees burst from murky, shallow water in many places, sometimes scattered and sometimes rising dense to form small, sunken woods, their bare limbs stretching toward the sky like the grasping fingers of the dead.

Hungry growth threatened to choke the narrow road, causing our journey to slow. Morning mist coiled sullenly beyond the path, shrouding the terrain in a jealous haze. It grew denser farther out, where the terrain seemed lower and more water-logged.

Lisette watched the mist-veiled country with quiet concern, and Olliard kept his calm gaze fixed firmly forward, his eyes unreadable behind the almost opaque lenses of his spectacles.

We came within sight of our destination in the late afternoon. I saw the bell tower first, rising like a mast over one of the very few tall hills in that sunken land, and soon recognized the structure as a church.

Olliard let out a breath of relief. "There it is. Somewhere beyond that rise is the Cael Village, the largest settlement in this country. You can see Castle Cael out on the lake when the weather is clear. That's where the Baron lives."

"The Baron?" I asked. "He's the lord of all this?" My eyes roamed the sickly landscape.

Olliard nodded. "Orson Falconer. Don't let the dire scenery fool you, Alken. House Falconer is an old line, prestigious and well respected by the folk in this country."

I hadn't heard of the family, though there were hundreds of noble clans scattered across the subcontinent, and I hardly knew all of them. I guessed it to be a Low House, isolated to this little dominion.

Brume climbed the winding path up the steep hill with dogged eagerness, perhaps sensing an end to the long journey. I half expected the brutish animal to try going into the marshlands and playing in the mud, but she kept her big snout forward and her legs moving along the road. Soon enough we pulled through the posts that marked the entrance to hallowed ground.

I recalled the words of a mighty lord from many years prior. *You are declared anathema to all divisions of the Church, whose servants will not grant you aid or succor—*

I had done far worse than intrude on holy ground. I said nothing as we crossed over.

Churches have many varied designs in my homeland. This one was old, with a circular central structure winged by two separate buildings. The holy auremark, the same symbol Lisette wore around her neck, had been engraved both into the front door of the chapel and into the bell above it.

A man in the pale brown robes of a preoster, a preacher of the Church, waited for us on the steps. He was young, round in body and face, with dark hair grown in unkempt rings around his head. Hard to tell from a distance, but he didn't look pleased.

As Olliard navigated the cart into the field before the chapel, the priest descended the steps to approach us. He had a haunted look about him, with an almost sickly pale face and bruised eyelids.

"Is that little Edgar?" Olliard smiled at the man, whom I placed in his mid-twenties. "My, you've grown!"

Edgar tilted his head, studying our small company for a moment that lasted uncomfortably long. Lisette and I had climbed out of the cart as well.

"Doctor Olliard," the priest finally replied to the physiker. I got the sense he hadn't recognized the older man at first. "It's been a very long time."

"Thirteen years, I think." Olliard hid his own unease behind a grandfatherly smile. "Is Micah in? It's been a long journey, and I would like to settle in. I got his letter!"

Edgar only stared, as though nonplussed.

The doctor frowned, scratching at his pockmarked cheek. "Dear me. Is he in one of the villages? My timing has always been terrible."

My own unease, growing steadily ever since we'd crossed the border into this country, spiked at the dead expression on the young priest's face. He wasn't wearing the plain robes of a monk or a junior member of the clergy, but of a senior preoster, the head of a chapel. His amber robes, though faded and well worn, had golden thread in them, and gold also was the auremark dangling from his neck.

I already knew what the young man would say before he said it. Even still, I watched the hammer strike Olliard hard.

"Preoster Micah is dead," Edgar told us. "I am the caretaker of this shrine, now."

"Dead?" Olliard asked, blinking. "How?"

"Illness." Edgar spoke with no particular emotion. "It happened three weeks ago. He passed in his sleep."

Preoster Edgar turned then, ushering us toward the chapel door. "He told me you were expected, doctor. I will prepare rooms for you and your companions, and meals. Come."

I traded a glance with Lisette, seeing my uncertainty mirrored in her eyes. I suspected she felt the same as me.

This sanctuary did not feel safe.

CHAPTER ELEVEN

SHADOWS OVER CAELFALL

It happened three weeks ago," Edgar explained. Frowning he added, "No, it started earlier than that."

We sat in a warm, simple room with chairs and benches set out before a hearth, tucked into one of the side buildings attached to the chapel for the priests and travelers to use for warmth and rest. Lisette tucked into a bowl of hot soup. I stood near the door with my back to the wall, toying at my own meal with a spoon idly.

Olliard paced before the fire. The unseasonable chill hadn't faded with the sunrise, and even inside the air had a bite.

"Micah was not so old," the doctor said, scowling. "Certainly younger than me! You say illness took him? He was an adept."

"Healing Art doesn't always work on oneself as well as it does others," Lisette said to her master in a soft voice. "Further, God's gifts are meant to be given, not used to extend one's own life. He would have been taught this just as I was."

Edgar said nothing. The holy symbol dangling from his neck seemed to weigh him down, I noted, giving him a hunched posture.

"Even still." Olliard rubbed at the bridge of his nose, pushing his glasses up. "The timing of this seems . . . uncanny."

"You said he sent you a letter?" Edgar turned curious eyes on the doctor. "What did it say?"

Olliard sat on a stool and propped his elbows on his knees, staring at the floor as he answered. "He didn't say much. Here." He fished in a fold of his robes and produced a folded scrap of parchment. "See for yourself. You're in charge here now, I see no reason to keep it from you."

Edgar studied the letter for several minutes. His brow had creased by the time he'd finished.

"As you can see," Olliard said dryly, "he didn't tell me much. Only that he needed my help, and to bring *all* my arts. Tell me, young man—did your mentor ever speak of my work?"

Edgar lifted his haunted eyes from the page. "He said you are a healer, and a worldly man. You've traveled to many places."

Olliard nodded. "That is one way of putting it."

Though I remained quiet by the door, my axe hidden in its wrappings and my dagger hidden beneath my dull red cloak, I recalled the fine crossbow the old man kept hidden in his cart. Olliard of Kell had some secrets of his own.

"And these two?" Edgar asked, glancing between me and Lisette.

"Ah, of course." Olliard gestured to the girl. "This is my apprentice, Lisette of the Bairns. She is a trained cleric with a very rare talent for healing."

Lisette bowed and murmured a respectful greeting to the priest, who would have been her senior had she still been with the clergy. Olliard indicated me then.

"And this is Alken, a mercenary I hired to keep us safe on the roads. He is a capable armsman."

I hid my surprise at the lie. Lisette turned a worried gaze on her master, while Edgar gave me a dubious look.

"They are trustworthy?" the priest asked.

Olliard nodded. "You may speak freely. Tell us, what is happening here? Why did your predecessor wish for me to make such a hasty journey?"

Edgar paced to the window, which was paned in foggy glass. He studied it a moment, his face an emotionless mask.

Not emotionless. I recognized the real feeling hidden behind that glassy stare.

Fear.

"Things in Caelfall have been . . . dark." Edgar swallowed and turned back to us, his fingers lacing together as though in prayer. "For many years now, but it has become much worse lately."

Olliard leaned forward, narrowing his eyes behind his spectacles. "Explain, please." He spoke patiently, but with a firm edge.

"Father Micah has always been well respected in the villages," Edgar said. "The Baron has been a recluse since before I was born, and while the people have always paid homage to the Falconers, it was the preoster who truly led the community."

Olliard nodded. "Indeed. He cared deeply for these people."

"Things started to become strange about two winters ago," Edgar continued. "The Baron started to have guests. They would stay in the old inn in Cael Village, or they would go into the castle. Sometimes they would stay for days, and sometimes for weeks."

"Not so odd for a country lord to have guests," I noted, drawing the young priest's attention.

"These were not ordinary guests," Edgar said darkly, his eyes drifting back to the window. "They would often come cloaked and disguised, and almost every time . . ."

He took a deep breath. "Something strange would happen. People would go missing, or the weather would turn foul, or strange things would be seen out on the lake, or in the marsh. It kept getting worse. Several months ago, he brought soldiers."

"Soldiers?" Olliard asked, perplexed.

"Mercenaries," Edgar explained. Once again his eyes flicked to me. "Foreigners, too. Some company of killers from the continent I think."

I met Olliard's eyes. I suspected he had the same thought I did, and saw images of the butchered troll displayed on spears behind his own eyes.

"How many?" I asked.

"Over a hundred strong," the young man said. "They are well armed, and have war chimera. Others have arrived too, most vanishing into the keep. Some of those guests who arrived some time ago never left, and joined the Baron's household."

"Bleeding Gates," Olliard cursed. "What, is the man preparing to start a war?"

That was a dark thought. "The Bairn Cities are to the south of us," I said. "Vinhithe is a great stronghold, and it's not far northeast . . . then you have Reynwell to the west, with the capital of the whole goring Accorded Realms at its heart. I don't see this marsh baron starting a war from here."

Not with an ordinary army, anyway. Just what had I wandered into?

"We passed the old troll bridge just last night on our way here," Olliard told the young priest. "The troll had been butchered, apparently by soldiers. Was that these mercenaries?"

His face draining of color, Edgar nodded. "That happened just a week ago. They bragged about it in the village. They are . . . terrible. I've never seen men so hungry for violence."

Edgar folded his arms, as though cold. "Before he died, the preoster went to the castle to demand answers. When he came back, he seemed different. Agitated. He wouldn't tell me what had happened, and then . . ."

The priest's voice trailed off. We all knew what had happened.

"You say he died of illness?" Olliard asked quietly.

"He started to become sick some weeks before it happened," Edgar said. "It took him quickly. Some ill humor, I suspect, probably strengthened by all the stress he was under. I doubt a trip over that fetid lake did his lungs much good."

Lisette stood suddenly. "I would like to pray."

Edgar nodded to the door. "You are welcome to use the chapel, sister."

Lisette thanked the man, then left the room. Edgar mumbled some excuse and departed as well. That left me and Olliard brooding in front of the fire, retreating into our own thoughts.

"You do not have to stay," Olliard told me after some time. "Once you are recovered, you may depart. I only spun that excuse about hiring you so he wouldn't question you."

"Lying to priests is a sin," I said, quirking an eyebrow at him.

Olliard shrugged. "It will not be my first."

I considered doing exactly as he suggested. This wasn't my problem. I had other roads to walk.

But none right now, I thought. *Not until I have new orders.*

"My wounds are pestering me," I told the doctor, though I actually felt quite good after Lisette's ministrations. "I'm going to go stretch. You?"

"It's been a very long road," Olliard said. "I think I will rest tonight and . . . consider everything young Edgar has told us."

"Micah was your friend." I didn't make it a question, and I kept my voice soft.

Olliard nodded. "Like my own brother. Do you have any brothers, Alken?"

I'd had a sister, but I had not seen her since childhood. She'd be a woman grown now, if she still lived, with a family. The thought, which I hadn't had for many years and hadn't expected to have just then, almost made me reel.

It had been so *long.* Another life. I couldn't even remember what she looked like, when I tried to picture her.

"I've had people who are like siblings to me," I admitted. "I have not seen them in some time. I've been wandering mostly, since the war."

"You were a soldier?" Olliard asked. "You fought in the war?" Then, laughing he said, "Of course you did! Lisette said it herself. You were a knight, right?"

". . . Once," I admitted. "I'm not sure what I am anymore."

"Alive." Olliard's voice was firm. "And you saved my apprentice's life. She is like a niece to me, Alken. I saved her from starvation in the wilderness after those beasts destroyed her cloister."

The old doctor's eyes, usually foggy with a sort of grandfatherly whimsy, seemed very sharp behind his wire-framed glasses in that moment. "You have power. I saw it. Will you not consider staying? These people clearly need help."

I narrowed my eyes without meeting his intense gaze. "I'm not the sort of man you want helping you, Olliard. Those spirits in the forest . . . you heard what they said. What they called me."

"Some of it," Olliard admitted. "But they were quite clearly mad. They wanted to hold my apprentice complicit for hiding from danger as a *child*. I think I will choose to trust, until you give me an excuse not to."

I wanted to laugh. Instead I said, "I'll think about it. Long walk out of here without your beast, anyway. For now, I'm going to stretch my legs."

I found Lisette in the chapel. She still wore her surgeon's garments, the brown robe and apron with all its pockets, but she looked very much the young priestess then as she knelt before the basin.

The chapel was of a very old design, circular, with pillars upholding a dome ceiling. An opening at the top of the dome allowed natural light in, and could be shuttered during bad weather, probably from the roof. Directly beneath the center of that ceiling, a raised stone bowl had been set. Here, water would be blessed and blood given in honor of the God-Queen.

On every stone support, images of the Faith's history had been etched. My eyes ran across them all, recognizing many. I'd heard these tales since childhood, and seen these same images in temples and castles across the long roads of my life.

There, I saw the Heir of Heaven descending in a beam of light, surrounded by Her Onsolain, her vassals and kindred. Edaean kings knelt at Her descent, or turned their faces if they were Recusant. I saw those same figures waging war during the Exodus, battling monsters and slave armies in fanged mountain passes. I saw them raising great strongholds in the sunlit east as the old west burned.

I passed by knights battling demons with darts of light and spears of lightning, wielding their Battle Art in defense of the realms. I saw images of trolls and dwarf giants and other relations to the Sidhe kneeling before kings, and kings kneeling before angels. I saw the same figures killing one another, ancient wars reenacted in stone. I saw riders on strange beasts, horned and many limbed, and elves riding in flying chariots lit by cold moons.

All the long history of Urn. There were so many wars.

I lingered by an image of a youthful figure with hair grown so long and thick it seemed a shrouding cloak, clad in long robes, arms uplifted before the severed trunk of a tree. An axe lay in those hands. More knights knelt around him, the points of their swords aimed at their hearts, the hilts offered to the elf lord.

I tore my eyes away from that last image, focusing on Lisette. She knelt at the base of the altar, murmuring prayers with her auremark clasped in tightly clenched hands.

I walked to the opposite side of the bowl, studying it. No water lay inside, though I could still make out old stains from offerings of blood.

I felt the urge to offer some of my own. I clenched my fist against the compulsion.

Lisette lifted her blue eyes to look at me. "Do you pray, Alken?"

I shrugged. "Sometimes. When I need to."

I could tell I'd confused her. She frowned, tilting her head to one side. "You seem to greatly enjoy wrapping yourself in mystery."

"Not sure it's about *enjoying* it," I muttered, rubbing at my chin. I hadn't shaved in some time, and my stubble had started to turn into the beginnings of a beard. I didn't grow a good beard. My hair, blond and red, came out wiry on my face.

"I should apologize for the forest," Lisette said, still kneeling with a troubled expression. "I fell asleep when it was my task to tend to the fire. It was careless."

"I was a bit harsh," I admitted, scratching at my cheek. "It was an unpleasant situation all around."

"You saved my life," Lisette said, her eyes stern and serious. "So I will not interrogate you on things you do not wish to speak of. However, while I never took my final vows before a matriarch of my order, I *am* a lay sister of the Abbey."

She hesitated, then continued in a kinder voice. "If you would like to give confession—"

"No."

I spoke more quickly, and more harshly, than I had intended. Lisette flinched.

Irritated at myself and her, I turned away from the altar. "No, I don't want to give confession."

I left her there in the chapel, feeling her blue eyes on my back.

I navigated the corridors, looking for the guest rooms. A country church like this would have places for travelers to stay. I stepped into a long, narrow hall lined in small cells.

This place was once tended to by more priests, I thought, wondering at the size of the structure. For a place of worship so isolated, it seemed rather impressive. There had also been a very large cemetery attached, one that had covered most of two sides of the hill, complete with sepulchers and mausoleums. I'd noted suspiciously empty segments on the outside of the building, which I suspected had once held gargoyles.

Gone away on their own, or . . .

Either way, it was just Brother Edgar now, alone in this eerie, isolated land of mist and marsh and darkened wood.

I wondered at what to do. Should I go? Or . . .

I wasn't that man anymore, if I'd ever been. This land's troubles weren't mine to hack at like some knight errant. I'd made a dramatic show in front of the healers, and that would bring trouble on me. Lisette knew, or suspected, what I was. Olliard seemed not to understand it, but if either of them said anything to the priest . . .

I was drawn from my thoughts by the creaking of bad hinges, of coarse cloth scratching across stone. I stopped, turned in a sudden motion, and reached through the ajar door at my side. There was a yelp, a flailing arm, then I had the one who'd been lurking there slammed against the far wall.

Edgar let out a whimper—I'd dashed his head against the stone, mostly by accident. He went still when he felt my dagger prodding his broad belly.

"Wait!" The priest let out a noise of protest. "Please, don't—"

"Why are you shadowing me?" I asked him, keeping my voice low. "You kept looking at me before like you recognized me. Explain."

I pressed the blade more firmly against his navel. The young priest swallowed, his eyes flitting in every direction without meeting my own.

"I do recognize you," he hissed, wincing at the touch of the steel. "I can explain."

"Do it quickly."

"I had a dream!"

I paused, tilting my head at the dark-haired man. "A dream?"

Edgar nodded quickly, his pale skin beading with sweat. "Many. Ever since the bridge troll died, I've had the same dream every night. Of a man with golden eyes, scars over the left, carrying an elven axe."

He looked at my left eye. Though partly hidden by the bangs of my long hair, his gaze fixed on the four long scars that ran from my left temple to my cheek.

I kept my forearm pressed to his throat, trapping him against the wall, while my heart quickened in my chest. "What else did you see in these dreams?"

"Only you," Edgar insisted, his eyes wide with fear. "You walked through the darkness, but you shone like a torch flame."

Not just fear in his eyes, but also conviction. *Hope.*

Sneering, I released him with a sharp motion. He collapsed against the wall, pressing a hand to his stomach. My dagger had left a cut in his preoster robes, and probably a bruise beneath.

"I prayed," the young preost said. "I prayed every day, sometimes every hour, not stopping until my throat became too dry to form words. I have been so afraid these last months, and after the preoster died . . ."

Edgar looked up at me, his mouth falling agape. "Did *they* send you? Are you here to save us?"

I turned, putting my red cloak between us. My jaw had clenched in anger, and the knuckles of my hand were white from the fist I made.

They didn't send me anywhere to *save* anyone. That wasn't my duty. Had it not been chance those healers had found me in the wilderness?

Of course not. Nothing to do with chance in my life. Even that goring storm that had struck Vinhithe. It had come so suddenly, and I would never have escaped that city in clearer weather. The distance the river had carried me, Nath's appearance, my rescue at the hands of a blessed healer . . . I cursed myself for not seeing the signs.

The Choir wanted me here.

CHAPTER TWELVE

COMMUNION

I waited until the doctor, the girl, and the priest were all abed. Then, in the deep hours of night when silence clung to the halls of Caelfall's lonely church, I entered the chapel.

The room held a very different aspect in the deep of night. The weather over the marshlands had remained clear, allowing bright moonlight to beam through the window above the altar. It formed a silver island within the chapel's darkness, illuminating the stone basin like some beckoning grail. Tiny motes of almost shining dust hovered around it, so much like faint stars around a cold moon.

I also doubted the picturesque night to be coincidence. I glared at the bowl as I circled it, the whisper of my worn cloak and the click of my boots overloud in the quiet.

Scenes of war, of the death and birth of kingdoms, surrounded me, all worked into quiet stone. I could almost *hear* them, echoing through the ages. The clash of metal, the music of Art, the weaving of ancient vows.

The prayers of those who'd lifted this temple, and who'd prayed within it over the centuries, had melted into the stone. Its history hummed through my aura.

I'd brought a ewer of water with me. I poured its contents into the bowl. It didn't come near to filling it, but I did not need to. The thin trickle of water reflected the moonlight, giving it an almost surreal quality.

Placing the ewer down, I drew my dagger, cut my palm, and squeezed my blood into the basin. Once that spreading shadow had curled its way through the water, I stepped back, took my axe in hand, and knelt. Propping the head of the weapon against the floor, I bowed my head.

One last step. I hesitated here, toying with the ring on my right hand. Then, steeling myself, I removed it.

"You brought me here," I muttered into the moonlit air. "Now tell me what I'm supposed to do."

I closed my eyes, and allowed my weariness—always present, always beckoning me—to have its due. Though I'd let my body rest some thanks to Olliard's cart, I had not dreamed in many months. It had taken its toll.

I slept. And I dreamt.

But I did not sink into my *own* dream.

I first became aware of the scent of flowers tickling my nose and birdsong fluttering into my ears. I no longer knelt on hard stone, but lay on my back in a bed of soft grass.

It did not put me at ease. I stiffened, rolled, and was on my feet in three beats of my heart. I stood in a forest glade. Soft ground carpeted in blue grass and vibrant white flowers lay beneath me, and the air held a pleasant coolness.

I could hear water flowing over rock, and a woman's voice humming a quiet tune I felt certain I'd never heard before. Yet, it hit me with a sharp pang of nostalgia.

Seeing that place, *feeling* it, I had a terribly strong urge to lie back down and take my ease. For that reason more than any other, I hardened myself to the quietude and kept upright. I did not trust anything that wanted me to be at peace.

My eyes roamed the glade. It seemed a scene out of an ancient dream. Which, I suppose, it was. Shades of emerald, blue, and silver tinted everything. By the shape of the sky and the high cliffs at my back, I knew I stood on the side of a mountain. The Living Moon, waning and crowned in stars and shining dust, dominated the heavens.

I walked forward, my worn boots drifting with near silence through the blue and white carpet. The sound of water came from a low fall I suspected fed from some cavern in those cliffs, which went into a gleaming silver stream. Grass and moss covered nearly every surface, including the trunks of the ancient trees and the smooth, almost metallic stones stacked around the waterfall.

All shone vibrant, abundant with growth, and untouched by rot. Put simply, a scene beautiful enough to make an artist weep and a poet's tongue fail him.

I closed my eyes and took shallow breaths, trying not to take in the heady scent of the flowers blooming across the grass. My body and mind were telling me I was safe, that this was a clean place, a refuge.

I could not trust myself to know those things.

Instead of drinking in the fey-lit grove, I turned my eyes to the figure kneeling by the stream. She was as beautiful as the setting within which she had enthroned herself. In a way, it *was* her throne. She had not spoken as I'd stumbled to my feet, and I had time to take in details as I cautiously approached her.

She wore a gown fashioned in shades of forest green and moonsilver. Flowers were woven into her midnight black hair, and her skin held a pale shade nothing in the natural world could replicate.

Even kneeling, she was tall. Taller than me. Taller than any human. She possessed an athletic build, though slender, her round shoulders displayed by the sleeveless cut of her dress, her long neck dappled with spray from the waterfall, the dew glinting like beads of crystal on her skin.

She exuded a very faint light.

She was the *source* of the grove's light, brighter even than that titan moon.

As I reached the edge of the stream, I realized that the shining woman bowed her head over the form of a slumbering creature. It looked like a war chimera, though I knew that no mortal alchemist had crafted this beast. It had a wolf's body, all coarse gray fur and lean, muscular limbs, and its head had a distinctly canine aspect as well.

The gleaming antlers growing from its head gave its true nature away, and its back legs ended in cloven hooves. Its tail was long and bushy, like a fox. Its chest rose and fell in long, deliberate breaths, and its jaws hung slightly open to reveal long teeth sharp as any blade.

I approached to stand near the beautiful woman and the creature that was, in its own way, also striking. I studied it for a while longer before I spoke.

"It's dying."

The woman's eyes were closed. One of her hands rested on the creature's chest, the other on its neck. Her head drooped slightly, and I thought I noted a shade of weariness in the movement.

"She is." Her voice was a breathy murmur, so low I shouldn't have been able to hear it, yet every leaf and tree in the grove quivered with the words.

"How long?" I asked.

"She was injured in the year the Gilded Haven fell," the shining woman said. "Most of ten years ago. Not long, I think."

Something wrenched in my chest. This creature then, like me, was a veteran of that war. A kindred spirit.

"Is there anything I can do?" I asked.

A smile touched the edges of the woman's roseberry lips. "No, Alken Hewer, but it does you credit to offer."

A shudder went through me at the sound of my own name. There was power in that utterance, of a kind that made my whole essence respond like a plucked chord on a lute. It wasn't an altogether unpleasant feeling, but it made my guard go up again.

I didn't much care for anything that made me react in a way I didn't want to.

When I spoke again, I did my best to keep anything like anger or disrespect from my tone. "If you and your brethren wanted to speak to me, you could have sent Donnelly, rather than tampering with that poor preacher's dreams. Or mine."

The woman stood, and my initial impression of her height was, if anything, conservative. She stood more than eight feet tall. Her hair hung in a black curtain nearly down to her bare feet, giving it the aspect of a shadowy cloak.

Indeed, it rippled like liquid shadow, as though caught in some unseen current. She turned to me, and her eyes cracked open to reveal a clean, pale light. I was careful not to look directly into them.

The Onsolain regarded me thoughtfully for a moment, then nodded. "Of course. You would resent having your dreams intruded upon, given your past . . ."

She bowed her head, the gesture conveying apology. "Forgive me. If it puts you at ease, know that this is not *your* dream, but mine. I have invited you in as a guest, and I assure you this place holds no danger for you, Ser Alken."

I turned my eyes from her, staring instead down into the clean water of the stream. "I am no ser, Lady Eanor. Not for a long time."

". . . Of course."

The gentle sympathy in her musical voice only made me feel worse. I changed the subject. "I saw your sister recently."

Surprise flickered across Eanor's face, which I caught in the water's reflection. "And you still live?"

I shrugged with one shoulder. "It's not the first time she's tried to poach me, since I started on this path. She gave me the old *we're not so different, join the forces of darkness* speech."

Eanor half turned from me, looking troubled. "Yes, I can imagine." She turned to face me again and spoke more firmly. "Do not heed Nath's words. She dreams of a world baptized in red seas." The immortal closed her burning silver eyes and drew in a long breath, her shoulders drooping a finger's width. "I regret that she has gone so far astray."

They looked so much alike, Eanor and Nath. They *were* twins. Only the eyes were different, and their manners. Nath could give a devil nightmares, and Eanor seemed like some princess's kindly fairy godmother.

They were both equally dangerous.

"Why am I here, Lady?" I asked. "Usually Donnelly passes along word for the Choir."

I hadn't seen the spirit in many weeks, not since he'd passed along the orders to execute Leonis Chancer.

"The Herald is engaged in other duties," Eanor said. "And the old forest you passed through is within my own domain. It was once a meeting place for lovers, blessed with mirth and fertility. The children born from those meetings often had such joyous lives."

The Saint of Love smiled, the expression full of regret. Then, turning to me, she spread her hands out so the strips of transparent cloth woven about her arms rippled like outstretched wings.

"You guard your dreams well, and I would have contacted you another way, but I had need to speak with you in haste, Headsman."

The Onsolain's use of my epithet made me draw in a sharp breath. "Ah. So I'm here for work."

Eanor nodded, her fair face a somber mask. "I am afraid so."

Anger, my old and ill-trusted friend, boiled up. I took a moment to get a grip on my emotions before speaking. "It's been less than a week since I killed that bishop for you and your brethren. You couldn't have given me time to recover from my injuries, at least?"

Eanor laced her fingers together, letting the wings of shimmering cloth form a helix, and bowed her head. This time, it was not a gesture of apology. Her lambent eyes slitted, and her voice once again became that nearly inaudible murmur.

"Time," she said bitterly. "Time is an illusion as delicate as any elven glamour, Alken Hewer, and it is fast slipping from our grasp."

I folded my own arms. "Right. So, who do you want me to kill this time? A warlock? Rogue warlord? Maybe another preost?"

I knew who she wanted me to kill, or strongly suspected. Even so, my bitterness pushed me to play this game.

I snapped my fingers and spoke in a brighter voice. "I know! How about a king this time. I think there are still a few realms I'm not wanted in, may as well get those bounty hunters spread a bit more evenly, don't you think?"

Eanor tilted her head to one side, her shadowy hair shifting like the deep currents of a lightless sea with the motion. "We never claimed this role would be an easy one."

I clenched my jaw. "Why did you need me to kill a high clericon? He was a servant of *your* church."

Not a mote of anger registered on the Onsolain's statue-perfect face. "The Church of Urn is not our instrument, Alken Hewer. It belongs to your people.

It is a channel, an institution of learning and wisdom, a bridge between faith and knowledge. It was fashioned by *your* people, and is thus fallible and prone to corruption."

"So are angels," I said in a voice tight with frustration. "Your own sister fell. She joined the Briar. She is a *force* of corruption."

Eanor fell silent a long while. Once I'd spat the poison, I felt its acid taste on my tongue.

She hadn't deserved that. I am certain she held her own pain. Who was I, a mortal man not yet halfway through his life, to know hers?

"Even so," Eanor said at last, her voice still calm. She unlaced her fingers in my direction, as though releasing cupped water. "In any case, we do not rule the Church, Alken. It is not a court of judgment through which we may extend a punishing fist."

"Then what do you call me, if not a punishing fist?"

I pressed a scarred hand to my chest, feeling the frustration I'd been holding inside for long years surging up and out. "I've been killing men and monsters across Urn for more than five years now at the Choir's will. Most of them I understood the need for it well enough."

I began to pace, caught by a nervous energy. I knew I wasn't truly in that glade, that I still knelt in sleep in the chapel, but the timeless grove *felt* real enough.

"I get that Leonis Chancer was a bastard, but why did *you*," I pointed a finger at the inhumanly tall figure, "and the rest of the Choir need the Headsman of Seydis to send him off? I deserve to know."

"Do you?" Eanor asked, her voice very calm.

I realized then that the birds were no longer singing, and the stream no longer cheerily flowing. The water's song had become a muted, cautious tune.

I suppressed a shudder of fear and folded my arms again. "Maybe not," I admitted. "But I've been misled by those I thought infallible before. I don't care that some might call you and yours gods or angels, lady saint. I want to know the score."

Eanor remained quiet a long while, her impossibly beautiful face set with marble calm. Or maybe not. I couldn't ever really tell with her kind. Too often it seemed like every display of emotion, every gesture, every word was composed like actions on a stage. Rehearsed, so mere mortals could comprehend them.

Some called them lesser gods, some called them angels, others the First Children—there were many names and many aspects to the Onsolain, kinsfolk of the Heir of Heaven and prime spirits of the Choir of Onsolem.

It all meant the same thing. The being in front of me was more ancient than the world, and powerful enough to unmake me with a word. Sheer idiocy of me to try to bully her into answers. But . . .

Damn it, I was so *tired* of being in the dark. I'd played the role of a good little soldier before, and I'd watched a civilization burn. Never again. If I was going to fight, to spill blood, then I would know *why*.

I was the Headsman of Seydis. Before that, I had been a knight. I had fought wars and watched a realm I had sworn to protect burn.

I had been the good, dutiful soldier once. The stakes were higher now.

"Thirty-one," I said in a near whisper, glaring into Eanor's dimly glowing eyes. I didn't care just then that it could harm me to meet her gaze directly. "Thirty-one heads I've claimed in the last five years. Where does it end? I thought the point of this was to kill the bastards who caused the war so they couldn't start a new one. Killing warlocks and leftover Recusants is one thing, but this was a High Clericon, a leader in the Faith. Didn't you think I had enough stacked against me without making an enemy of the goring Church?"

"The Bishop used the conflict to usurp power in the Church," Eanor said, her serene countenance a stark contrast to my bitterness. "Hundreds died at his command, when he began the witch hunt in Idhir. Hundreds more died at the hands of those who followed his example. Do you think that ended with the Llynspring Inquisitions?"

She regarded me somberly. "His influence would have continued to grow, poisoning the faithful until the memory of this last war washed away in the blood of religious revolution."

The Onsolain inclined her head, looking into my eyes as though compelling me to understand. "In his death you have forestalled such a calamity. It was necessary. It was just."

Just. The word rang a discordant note in my thoughts. Despite that, I did consider her words and their ramifications.

They were unpleasant, to put it mildly. Still, having a priest murdered to quell wider change in the realms . . . It seemed so *political*, for the gods to become involved in. I'd thought they had a different objective in mind for me. Something more . . . not noble, but at least something that felt less unclean.

When has death ever been clean? I mocked myself.

"I didn't think I'd be one of the most wanted men in the land," I said, more sour than defiant. "I've heard the stories they weave about me in inns and taverns. The commonfolk call me a devil."

"You *are* a devil, in some ways."

When I started, Eanor's faint smile returned. "You are *our* devil. Yours is a Penance of Blood. You are the Headsman of Seydis, our chosen executioner, the one who delivers the dooms we weave."

The angel's voice hardened. "You accepted this path. Now you must walk to its end. You know the alternative."

I did, but I resented her for reminding me as though I'd forgotten. My head, or I guess my spirit, had begun to throb from looking into Eanor's eyes for too long. I turned away and walked toward the stream, staring into its clear waters. Precious gems glittered at the bottom rather than stones.

Nearby, the dying guardian beast labored to breathe.

After a minute, I sensed the goddess's presence behind me. Light fingers touched my shoulder, making me shiver involuntarily. The strength to break apart mountains lay in those hands.

"You have been deeply wounded by war and betrayal." Eanor's words rang with empathy. "Had it been my choice, I would not have bestowed such a fell office upon an oathsworn member of the Alder Table."

I took a deep, calming breath. "But you're just one voice in the Choir, right? I get it."

I took a deep breath, stepped back, and knelt. I hadn't been holding it before, but in that moment—the moment I decided to accept my role—the axe was in my hand. My fingers tightened around its gnarled grip as I took a knee. Propping the axe against the bank of the stream, I let my head dip so my unkempt hair fell down around my face to hide the bitterness I knew colored it.

"Who is my next target?" I asked, forcing calm into my voice.

"Orson Falconer," Eanor said the name I had known she would, and the grove whispered it along with her. "The Baron of Caelfall."

"His doom?" I asked.

"Death."

A hint of anger crept into the immortal's soothing voice, the first display of it since the audience had begun. "His minions slew the sentinel."

"The troll," I muttered, realizing. "One of yours?"

Eanor nodded. "An old friend and a valiant guardian. My own sworn vassal. A knight, after a fashion. But his death is not why we give you this name, Alken Hewer."

I noted the use of *we*. I felt a twinge of disappointment at that. Part of me had hoped this was a case of personal vengeance on behalf of the being I spoke to. I could understand that. It even held a ring of chivalry.

But no. This was another edict for the Headsman, direct from the Choir itself.

"The Baron has consorted with the Adversary," Eanor said, drawing my attention back to her. "He was once a just ruler, and a scholar of much wisdom, but that was many years ago. His dissolution began even before the burning of Elfhome, and he has grown ever bolder in his heresies of late."

I heard grass and flowers rustle around the Onsolain's white dress as she began to pace around me. I continued to kneel. In this, the ceremony of the thing mattered.

"He gathers forces to him, and may threaten the peace of the Accorded Realms. Already a tenuous thing. He must be stopped before he strengthens his ties to other Recusants and threatens war."

There were many powers in the land who refused to respect the authority of the Accord, the alliance of nations and powerful factions formed to maintain order in a land broken by the Fall. Mostly they were warlords consigned to isolated demesnes where the Accord's influence couldn't easily reach, ruling small domains as they pleased and raiding the larger, battle-weary realms.

But not all were merely petty warlords. Some were powerful warlocks, or militant groups posing as mercenary companies and bandit gangs. Some were wizards.

Some were kings.

In common parlance, these dissidents and warmongers were called Recusants. They were not a united force, but if they ever found common ground it could easily lead to another Fall. They had almost won the war, when they'd all hewn together. Some, myself among them, believed that only disparate goals and ancient rivalries eroding their unity had stopped them from winning, and creating a very different order from what ruled Urn in the present.

Part of my job was to prevent just that outcome. Even if many of the lords of the Accord basically thought of me as *one* of those Recusants.

If Orson Falconer gathered forces to him here, practically in the heartlands of the Accorded Realms, and made nice with other rebel factions . . .

Things could get bad.

"You called him a heretic," I said. "He's a diabolist? A warlock?"

"Yes," Eanor confirmed. "I have felt his darkness pressing on the edges of my own domain, especially here in this forest. I have urged my brethren to act before."

"I'll do what I can," I said. "I'm kind of a mess right now."

Eanor only smiled softly. My eyes felt heavy, and I knew the end of this strange audience approached. My drooping head felt made of iron, weighty enough I couldn't lift it.

"Do not forget," the Onsolain said from directly above me. "You are still of the Alder Table, Ser Knight, bound to that office. It is a calling greater than your penance as our instrument of doom."

"The Table is broken," I mumbled, my eyelids drooping. "And the Church stripped me of my titles when they excommunicated me. I am no knight."

"Mortal nations may not recognize you as such. But your vows are forever binding. Do not forsake them, Alken Hewer, for they have not forsaken you."

Darkness took me.

Damn immortals. They always end up having the last word.

CHAPTER THIRTEEN

DEATH ON QUIET WINGS

I woke still kneeling in the chapel. My legs were sore, my eyes fuzzy, and the moonlight had vanished from the opening above to leave the room in deep darkness.

As I lifted myself out of the communion dream, the aura in my eyes brightened in reaction to the gloom, chasing it away. I saw all the still stone and images of legend in stark, pale clarity.

I knelt there for some time, mulling on my new orders.

Orson Falconer, the enigmatic lord of this dreary, isolated country, had been given the Choir's doom. My left hand drifted across the gnarled oak of the axe, its little imperfections and fire-scarred wood as familiar to me as my own callouses.

I'd carried it for five years now. Five long years of horror and blood.

As I stood, I felt a strange energy. My limbs seemed lighter, less stiff, the pain of more recent wounds barely noticeable. I flexed the fingers of my empty hand. The dream had replenished me. My magic felt different. Less sullen.

Even still, I put my ring back on. Not always an angel who sought me out in my sleep.

I had a mission to prepare for. I needed to know more about this baron, scout out his sanctuary, learn what sort of defenses he might put in my way. The priest had mentioned a castle in the middle of a lake. That seemed an obvious place to start.

As I turned back toward the guest halls, I felt the hairs on the back of my neck stand on end. Instinct, ingrained into us feeble humans from a history of being prey to mightier things, warned me of danger before my magic did.

I dove into a roll just as almost silent wings cut the air, hitting me with the ensuing draft of wind as scything claws missed me by fingers. I came up, teeth bared and axe in hand, searching the darkness.

Something looked back. The light in my eyes did not illuminate the room fully—they cast soft beams of pale gold through the gloom, just shy of reaching the far wall.

Then I began to feel it. A dull drumbeat, like some distant heart quickened in panic. The aureflame roiled in discontent.

Something foul was here with me. Something with wings. My eyes drifted up to the opening in the ceiling—no more moonlight, but I suspected I knew how it had gotten in.

I heard claws scrape against stone, the echo confusing my ability to pinpoint the source.

Some dark predator from the wilds? Seemed a strange coincidence.

I had a different suspicion.

Feathered wings beat once, the flutter producing almost no sound save for the soft shift of air. I tensed, twisted, and swung on pure instinct. If I were even a fraction of a second off my timing . . .

With a bone-jarring impact, the blade of my axe cleaved the thing. I struck it just above one back-bent leg, severing the limb and opening its guts. The steaming, reeking contents splattered me from chin to lowest rib.

Its remaining talons sliced through cloth and flesh, opening my shoulder. I grit my teeth and turned, on guard.

The attacker slammed into the altar, cracking the basin's stone. The water I'd poured into it, darkened by my own blood, began to spill out in a thin trickle. The creature thrashed, dying badly.

I paced around the thing, my shoulder flaring with pain I ignored. The beast looked like an owl the size of a dog, with a cancerous growth of horns around its neck and back. They resembled elfhorn, but lacked the glow of od. Its short, wickedly curved beak was serrated, and it had six beady black eyes.

A chimera. One made to kill, rather than to transport a rider or plow fields.

An assassin.

For me?

No. The lord couldn't know about my mission already.

The preoster died right after he went to confront the Baron. Edgar has been terrified, and we just arrived today . . .

Was it here for the remaining priest, or for Olliard?

Blood soaked through my shirt. Wincing, I clutched at the wound. Bastard thing had gotten me deep.

More fluttering, feathered wings disturbed the chapel's air. The first hadn't been alone. I glared up at the rafters, seeing a scattered constellation of bright, nocturnal eyes watching me, six to each beast.

Shit.

I hefted the axe, ready. With chimera, it's hard to know how intelligent they are. Some are dumb beasts, good for tilling fields or pulling a cart, and some can carry out more complicated tasks. They can even act as spies and messengers, trained to communicate in code.

Probably nothing more complex than *danger, newcomer killed us*, but that would be enough to ruin my element of surprise. I didn't need to be chased out of the demesne like I had at Vinhithe *before* completing my mission.

The monster owls shifted across the ceiling rafters, hunching on wooden beams or stone lips.

Would they all attack at once? Or test me more, as the first had? Its blood had begun to pool around my boots, its death throes gone quiet.

The click of a door latch and a dim haze of lantern light drew my attention from the creatures. The back door to the chapel had opened, and a figure stepped into the room.

"Alken? What are you—"

Edgar. The priest. The young man blinked at me, wounded and blood-stained, then at the corpse at my feet and the broken altar bowl. His face went sheet white.

"Get back!" I barked, making him startle.

All the chimera dove at once. They descended in a fluttering, brown-feathered storm. Their aggression had a terrible spider-like quality—they didn't hoot, or screech, or make any sound besides that of unsettled air.

Edgar dropped the lantern. I lurched toward him, cursing.

Too far. No chance to shape an Art—sorcery takes time, and I had no technique that could be used in an instant, which was all I had.

I am no wizard, but I've fought them. I've fought *with* them too, and learned some tricks.

I lunged forward, skidded on the smooth stone, and hurled the axe. It tumbled end over end, making more noise than the fiendish birds did. It struck one of the beasts just before it would have raked the young priest with its talons.

In the same instant, it erupted with light—a brief, molten nova within the chapel's darkness. The owls scattered, becoming a swirling whirlwind.

Barely in time. I let out a breath of relief.

No time to fashion an Art to kill all the things directly, but the faerie axe was a receptacle for aura. I'd stuck the seed of a sorcery in it before throwing, which bloomed into golden phantasm moments later. Which left me weapon-less, and most of the things still alive.

Had I let them kill the man, I could have destroyed them all at once while they grouped up to maul him.

Still playing the knight, I scorned myself. Even still, my boots beat the stone as I plunged forward. One of the owls, blinded, flapped into me and began to slash with its talons. I caught the blow on my left forearm, taking another injury, then punched it with my right hand.

The creature went into the stone hard, its brittle bones broken, and did not get back up. Blood dripped from the torn flesh on my left arm.

I rolled, sending fiery agony flaring up my injured shoulder, and pulled my axe out of the burnt corpse it had remained stuck in. I rose into a cut, cleaving another of the things. More blood soiled my clothes.

Still more. How many? I counted six, all big, all deadly. They'd remain blind for a time, their sensitive nocturnal eyes scorched by my magic.

Panicked, unable to find their escape high up in the ceiling, they did the only thing frightened, aggressive beasts would do in that situation. They con-verged together where they sensed my heat in the room, and all tried to kill me.

Behind me, Edgar whimpered in terror. I ignored him, pushed the pain down, and started killing.

When the gruesome task was done, it left me out of breath and covered in stinking gore. My right shoulder and left arm burned with pain.

Not even recovered from the last one, I thought as I worked to swallow the pain. *Not the best start, Al.*

Edgar, sitting with his back to the wall near the door, muttered despon-dently to himself as he stared at the carnage. He'd experienced a lot of fear recently, and this must have pushed him over the edge.

I didn't have the patience to be gentle. Once I'd caught my breath I walked forward, making him cower against the wall. I must have looked fell—huge, with burning gold eyes, stained by blood and poorly lit by the fallen lantern.

If it got him to listen, I'd play the part. I grabbed him by the collar of his preost's robe, lifted him, and spoke in a voice that came out like a snarl. The shakes, always there after hard violence, had started to strike me hard.

"Do these belong to the Baron?"

Edgar's mouth popped like a gasping fish. "I . . . what—"

I shook him. "Speak, man. Does the Baron breed chimera?"

Shakily, the priest nodded. "He does. His family is known for it."

I could have kicked myself. It was in the name—*Falconer.*

"He either sent these because he got word you'd taken in strangers from beyond the demesne, or he sent them to silence *you*." I glanced at the corpses, thinking. "Tell me, did your predecessor say or know anything that might be dangerous to Orson Falconer? Anything that might make him want to shut you up?"

"He hates the Church." Edgar swallowed. "It was a point of contention between him and Micah for years."

I met his eyes. He didn't flinch. Telling the truth, then. I released him, letting him slump back against the wall.

The violence hadn't seemed to wake the doctor or the girl, or they'd have made an appearance already. Then again, much of it had been eerily quiet. Just my grunting, muted cursing, the dull cracks of breaking bone, the occasional growl of aureflame and whisper of stealthy wings. No doubt they were exhausted from the long journey.

Well enough. I had a choice to make.

Olliard wasn't just an ordinary doctor. Preoster Micah had called him here for help. I remembered that strange weapon he'd kept hidden in the cart. Lisette's skills were no layman's talent, either.

I could get their help. Only . . .

This wasn't work for some adventurer fellowship. I was the Headsman of Seydis, here to deliver the Choir's doom. Already, the spirits shadowing me had nearly killed the girl. There would be more danger soon.

No. I wouldn't repay them for saving my life, even if they *had* found me only by divine interference, by dragging them into my work.

I turned my attention back to the terrified priest. "I'm going. Tell the doctor and his apprentice that they should leave Caelfall immediately. You should go, too."

"Leave?" Edgar looked like he'd never even considered the notion before. I'd seen it plenty in backcountry folk. They spent their whole lives staring at the same hills, and even when war and famine came knocking, their roots would tie them down—usually by the neck.

I nodded. "The Baron wants you dead, and I don't have the time to play protector. Get out of the fiefdom, far as you can."

"You will stop him?" Edgar asked, his eyes brightening with hope. "Rid us of him?"

I turned my back on him. "I'm not here to save any of you, preost. You got lucky tonight, that's all."

"But . . . I knew you would arrive before you did! And that light . . ."

"That's right," I said darkly, "I'm not here by coincidence either. You want to take this as a sign? Save those two healers. Convince them to leave."

I reached up to wipe at the blood on my face as I started toward the door. Pausing, I took a look at myself. I was a mess, my clothes soaked in blood—some of it my own.

"There were more priests here once." I glanced back at Edgar, who looked at a loss for words. "Were any of them close to my size?"

CHAPTER FOURTEEN

AMID THE MISTS

Not long after my scuffle with the chimera, the greater moon showed its face again. Huge even waning, it cast the bands of languid mist coiling over the marshy fields into sharp luminescence. The skeletal corpses of drowned trees emerging from the flooded land looked flat and eerie, like wounds in the world.

The weather matched Cael Village well. Set just over a mile north of the church, it hugged the region's largest lake in a haphazard tangle of buildings enclosed in a winding barricade. Larger than I would have thought, and possibly once bigger still. I could make out ruins here and there as I approached, the remnants of older satellites to the community lost to flooding and time.

Perhaps it had once been a sizable town. Not so big as Vinhithe, but a definite hub in the region. Now, waterlogged structures of wood and mossy stone dominated, most lifted on high platforms to keep above the water.

Pale, hungry eyes watched me from the distant reeds. The local wildlife, or more of the Baron's creatures?

Was there even a difference?

I'd switched out my ruined traveling garments for new cloth I'd taken from the church. Edgar had managed to find a coarse woolen robe, light brown like most monastic garb and too small to fit me properly. With some modifications, I'd made it into a knee-length tunic of sorts, tying it at the waist. I'd taken new trousers as well, kept my boots, and thrown my worn red cloak over it all.

I approached the village with my pointed cowl raised against the rain. My wounds twinged with every step. I'd sewn up my shoulder and put some of Olliard's medicine—he'd given me some to apply myself after his ministrations had run their course—to my arm.

I was in a rough way, but I wouldn't keel over. I could fight if I needed to.

The barricade, though mostly all wood, was a proper wall save in some spots where the natural terrain provided most of the settlement's defense. It had been raised up from the reeds and drowned trees irregularly, with sharp stakes placed here and there to deter intruders.

The wall had sentries, especially around the main gate. They didn't look like a peasant militia. They wore light armor hammered from good steel, and carried pikes and crossbows.

The mercenaries Edgar had mentioned, I had no doubt. The make of their spears looked very familiar. They'd hung lanterns on tall posts around the village perimeter, and many carried torches.

Even still, this was no fortress. There were many gaps in the wall, some with signs of recent repair but most rotted from the constant damp. This village was old, and the environment had treated it poorly.

Further, the mist was gravid with od.

Not all sorcery is flashy. Battle Art can allow an adept to cleave a foe with a blade of fire or knock him from his steed with a lance of lightning, and these techniques were a mainstay of chivalrous combat in the subcontinent.

But for all the powers cultivated for war, not all are violent. The Sidhe, and some wild creatures who have soaked themselves in the land's enchantments, can use magic the same way they might use stripes for camouflage.

I focused on the flickering warmth of my magic. My aura. Always there, always on the verge of roiling into violent discontent. It took me more than an hour of meditation and effort, but I managed to quell that flame, constricting it into a bare ember.

When done, I breathed out a plume of frosting breath. I shivered, even in my thick robe and woolen cloak. Cold dug its claws into my bones, stark as though a bitter winter had settled into me.

Dangerous, and it left me vulnerable. The light in my eyes dimmed, so only the waning moon gave me something to see by. I wouldn't be shaping an Art as quickly as I had against the chimera now, or healing as fast.

But it also left my presence in the world all but gone, making me a shadow. It wasn't invisibility, not quite, but unless someone were deliberately searching for me, casual eyes would slide away.

The living breath of the world swirled in to fill the empty space I'd left. The mist clung to me more tightly. I let it, drawing it in with murmuring invitation, using that ember of my power I'd left to draw it like moths to a flame.

A basic glamour, all told. I'd known elves to obscure their presence in the world so well they could dance in village festivals without any of the mortals being the wiser. I would have to be cautious, and endure the unnatural chill of letting my own essence dwindle so dramatically.

So obscured, I ghosted into Cael Village. I used the marsh, enduring the cold of the shallow water as I approached the barricade wall like some bog vampire, until I found a section rotted away enough for me to get through even with my bulk.

I entered the village on the verge of hypothermia, but had a plan and only had to keep myself hidden long enough to enact it.

The village had a confusing layout. Larger than it had seemed from the outside, with structures raised wherever they could find solid ground, I could make out signs of regular flooding and methods the locals had used to deal with it. Unsurprisingly, it was a fishing community. Many homes had traps set, nets and other devices, and I could tell they farmed the waters. Wooden bridges and narrower walkways circumnavigated many homes, allowing the residents to visit their neighbors without getting their feet wet.

I kept to the shadows, knowing the moonlight might give me away even with my glamour. Otherwise, I did not walk like a furtive thief—act like you're not supposed to be somewhere, and the place itself will take note. I was there without invitation, and with hostile intent. Even if I didn't cross a home's threshold, the village itself had its own sort of life, like any long-inhabited place. It would not know me and resent my unwelcome presence.

This place *was* a home to these people. While it had seemed almost a slum from the outside, the raised houses were old and had some artistry, with curse traps placed over doors and dream traps over windows, even some metalwork, copper mostly, decorating frames. There were little gardens here and there, hung from roofs or kept in small beds.

This had not always been a place of fear. But I *felt* the fear. I felt it in the silence, in the predatory mist, in the stillness of the water below.

I stopped at the corner of one house as I heard voices. They were making little effort to be quiet, and I recognized the crude jokes of soldiers.

Peeking around the corner, I saw a group of five men—no, four men and one woman—all clad in armor. They wore deep gray uniforms, tunics and tall boots with baggy leggings, and steel breastplates. They were lit by lantern light. Alchemical lanterns, like the kind Olliard had used. It cast them in an eerie paleness somehow sharper than the moonlight.

The most heavily armored one was the woman. She wasn't tall, but wore a longer coat than the others under better armor, and the helm tucked under her arm had a plume of silver hair. She looked old, with sallow skin and bloodshot eyes so wide they seemed lidless.

Her voice, however, seemed almost grotesquely young.

"New orders from his lordship," the lead mercenary said. "He wants third squad pulled back to the island."

One of the men cursed. "We're already stretched thin in this marsh. The damn irks have been out for blood ever since we got rid of the troll."

"It wasn't a suggestion." The leader's tone was more one of weary acceptance than reprimand. "More of the Baron's guests are expected soon, and he wants to make sure there are no"—she seemed to chew on her words a moment—"misunderstandings."

"You mean he wants to let his would-be courtiers know who's in charge," one of the others said, snickering. "Nothing better for it than a wall of steel."

"Just see it done," the leader said. "Have Berregon's men take over patrols in the eastern marshes, keep the damn spiders away from our throats. I'll talk to the captain, see if he can make the Baron see reason. Terrible country to have a guerrilla war."

"Lot of trouble over a bridge brute," one of the soldiers grumbled. "I thought elves and trolls hated one another?"

"Trolls *are* elves," another corrected.

"I hate this land," the grumbler said. "None of it makes any sense. Back home, we kill a monster and someone pays us for it. Here, there are all these fucking *rules*."

"You think he'll send his pet?" one of them asked the leader.

The woman with the bloodshot eyes made a hissing sound. "Keep your mouth shut, Tarkley, or I'll have it sewn. With *wire*. We don't need the local stock more tense than they already are." She glared around at the shuttered windows.

". . . Yes, lieutenant."

The group split then. The lieutenant took one of the sellswords and started making her way down the street, while the rest went to the gate.

I considered for a minute, then followed the lieutenant.

The rot smell of fish and stagnant water grew more noticeable as I shadowed the sellswords. I realized we were drawing closer to the lake. This suspicion was confirmed when I began to hear the creaking of wood in water, from docks and moored boats. I saw them ahead, as the street dipped down into a semi-open area where the fishing boats were moored.

I had a sudden and vibrant memory of Vinhithe. The driving rain, the roar of thunder, metal singing its lethal song as I fought with the Glorysworn. I felt the dagger ram into my leg again, the bolt embed itself in my hip.

I wiped the cold sweat that had beaded across my brow and ducked behind a lantern post. The lieutenant and her crony had stopped near one of the docks, where two more of their fellows waited. They started up a conversation I couldn't hear, and I drifted closer, taking cover again just at the edge of the village proper, lurking behind some drying fishing nets.

The four mercenaries all turned to face the water. Though the air was still, I soon began to hear a distinct sound—the burbling disturbance of water around wood.

A boat approached the shore, emerging as a vague shadow at first in the denser fog that clung to the lake. My eyes drifted upward, and far out across that veiled body I saw an almost phantasmal shape, black within the distant fog and wispy as though half formed—the Baron's castle.

The boat only had two occupants. One wore a cloak similar to my own, though less worn and green rather than red, with a deep hood to obscure their features. They worked an oar through the water, approaching at an unhurried pace. The second was another of the mercenaries, this one huge and clad from head to foot in battered gray armor. He had a chiseled statue's face, pale and stubbly, with a heavy brow and harshly short black hair touched with gray.

The mercenaries shifted, visibly impatient, but kept their silence until the boat reached one of the rickety docks. Almost as soon as the green-cloaked figure stepped onto the dock—they were slim, not very tall, and moved with an eerie grace—the lieutenant stepped forward and spoke with a growl.

"About time. Dawn's only hours away, and we're still waiting on orders. They done in there yet?"

It wasn't the cloaked one who spoke, but the big man. "Ease yourself, Darla. You can't rush the mighty, no point getting out of sorts about it."

The woman spat out a vile curse. "Easy for you to say, Vaughn. You've been kicking your feet up at the castle, while I'm left in command of this mud sty and all its peasants."

Vaughn shrugged. The one in the green cloak turned to Darla.

"Your band's job is very simple, lieutenant." The voice within the green cloak was cold, aloof, and very slightly nasal. I couldn't tell gender—the voice might have been a young man's or a woman's. "You guard my lord's property, and in return he pays and . . . indulges you."

Again, the lieutenant cursed. She did not argue, and Vaughn replied to Green Cloak. "Hard to protect his property when it includes a fucking marsh half as big as most kingdoms. If he wants to properly garrison his keep, we're going to lose more territory to the irks, and that's a fact."

"The Baron's fief would not be threatened by the Sidhe if not for your company's desecration of the forest," Green Hood said coldly. "You should not have killed the sentinel."

I could hear the rattle of Vaughn's armored shoulders as he shrugged. I got the sense he outranked the lieutenant and spoke for the sellswords. "Damn troll was costing us every time we had to use that road. 'Sides, his lordship would have had us off the ugly git sooner or later, just like he got rid of that old preacher."

"Silence, fool!" The hooded figure stepped forward. The four other mercenaries stepped back, hands going for weapons. Only Vaughn remained still, unconcerned, towering over the hooded one.

Despite this, Green Cloak didn't seem intimidated. Their voice came as a raspy, angry hiss through the shadows of the hood, threatening as a serpent. "If the locals overhear you, it could lead to revolt. These people are faithful."

Vaughn snorted in derision. "Let them revolt. Twenty of my boys could secure this entire village and hold it."

Venom crept into Green Cloak's voice. "My lord cannot afford dissent, Mistwalker. Remember that. His subjects are still needed."

"Right, right." Vaughn scratched at the stubble on his cheek. "All right, Darla, what's the word?"

The lieutenant turned her bloodshot eyes on the big man. "The guests at the inn are becoming discontented. They want to know what's going on at the castle, and when they will be invited for the Baron's gathering."

"They'll all get their turn," Green Hood said. "Has anyone else arrived today?"

Darla shook her head. "Just those travelers our scouts spotted on the road. They're still at the old church. Don't think they're more guests for the Baron. Had the look of pilgrims."

"I doubt they will trouble us come morning," Green Hood noted. Vaughn snickered, drawing curious looks from the other soldiers.

My hunch about those chimera had been right. They were from the castle.

"Vaughn will remain here and ensure the guests at the inn don't cause trouble," Green Hood told the mercenaries. "Darla, you will keep him appraised of any activity in the marsh. My lord must not be disturbed while he plays host. These proceedings are . . . delicate."

The cloaked one pulled on Vaughn's arm. He leaned down, letting them whisper into his ear. He seemed to chuckle before straightening. Green Hood left then, taking up the oar and pushing the boat back out into the misty lake.

"Creepy bitch," Vaughn said to the others. They muttered in agreement, and he jerked his head back toward the village. "Ivor, you go with the lieutenant. Petyr, Raki, with me."

The mercenaries parted ways then, splitting into two groups. My eyes tracked the big one, Vaughn. These "guests" at the village inn were curious. I might be able to learn more about this mysterious gathering from them.

Risky. If any adepts were in the inn, glamour might not fool them. An ordinary place, I could ghost in through the front door, pick a shadowed corner, and listen without being noticed by ordinary folk. But I didn't get the sense this village was occupied by "ordinary" folk.

Still, I followed the big sellsword, keeping a distance. The village didn't have many ordinary streets, with most of it raised above the marshland, but central parts of the settlement were on relatively high, dry ground. Here the buildings were older, larger, and I recognized one of them as an inn. Two stories, high-roofed, with inviting light still spilling out of the first floor despite the late hour.

Here the three mercenaries stopped in the middle of the village's main street, two buildings down from the inn. I could see the main gate off in the distance.

Why hadn't the lieutenant gone this way, if she were returning to the gate watch? I paused at the corner of a smithy, frowning at Vaughn and his companions. They hadn't met anyone. They'd just stopped.

A terrible suspicion coiled into my gut, and my heart skipped a beat. At the end, the hooded one had said something to Vaughn.

Directly above me, the tiles of the roof creaked.

I dove into a roll just as something heavy slammed into the ground where I'd been standing. I came up, tossing my cloak back to free my axe.

One of the mercenaries, the Mistwalkers, stared at me from the alley floor, one leg bent beneath him, his head twisted to one side. He'd tried to drop on me and landed badly.

I was confused at first. Then the man grinned wide, revealing blocky yellow teeth. His eyes glinted in the moonlit gloom, eerily pale.

Not human. Not entirely. With a horribly boneless motion, the soldier got to his feet. He resembled a puppet being pulled up on tightening strings. His leg remained broken, and he lurched into the moonlight despite it.

I heard the creaking of armor as Vaughn and the other three soldiers moved to surround me, trapping me between them in the middle of the village street.

"Well well," Vaughn drawled. "When the Baron's pet told me we were being watched, I thought it was one of the villagers out past their bedtime. Instead we caught a jackal."

He drew his sword, and the rest followed his cue.

Damn it all. Not again.

CHAPTER FIFTEEN

THE HUNGRY DEAD

We faced each other in silence, me and those five killers. Mist made nearly lambent by the moon's glow coiled around our legs, anticipatory in its languid motion.

It was one of Vaughn's cronies who broke that silence. "Looks more like a bear than a jackal, vice-captain. Big fucker."

"Lot of meat on him," another said, eyeing me with an uncomfortably hungry attention.

"Not enough fat. These vagabond types never eat right, makes them too tough. Too thin."

Darla, the lieutenant I'd originally followed, clicked her yellow teeth together. "Don't care. He's snooping about like a weasel, we'll skin him like one."

"Now now." Vaughn had a more reserved expression than the others, a more relaxed posture, but his gaze held a similar tension, like a starved hound taut at its master's leash. "Talk, jackal. Name yourself."

"I'm still torn between Jackal and Weasel," I quipped. "Far more charming than most names I've been given."

How had they surrounded me so easily? My more preternatural senses had been dulled when I'd let my aura go dark. Even still, the way the lieutenant and her partner had vanished into the mist, and from my own thoughts, had been uncanny.

They used glamour too. They're not ordinary mercenaries.

Their unnervingly big teeth and unsettlingly bright eyes could have told me as much.

Vaughn snorted. He didn't do anything so cocky as flourish his sword—a heavy, short blade of simple dark steel with a distinctly archaic design. Very well used judging by the nicks and scratches along its weathered surface.

He held it low in one heavy fist, slightly in front of him and ready to come up into a guard with an easy movement. A professional swordsman.

The rest had a distinctly more bestial aspect, hunching and shifting around me, some even twitching as though on the verge of a fit. Darla stared at me with her mouth slightly agape, a trickle of drool running down her chin. She didn't even seem to breathe.

"This doesn't have to be difficult," Vaughn said.

"Right," I said. "Because I'd trust the honor of a ghoul."

Vaughn went very still. Too still, which made sense—he didn't need to breathe.

This was another risk of darkening one's aura. My powers allowed me to feel the presence of many more profane creatures, but it wasn't a perfect awareness. My abilities, though potent and versatile, operated by the same rules and principles as any being with an awakened soul.

Diminishing myself to be hidden came with risks. The stagnant atmosphere of the marshland had dulled my senses too, given me a general air of paranoia, and muffled the true natures of those who inhabited it.

I'd been trained to be wary in places like this. Too often in history had the True Knights, regardless of their order of origin, ventured into environs more suited to their adversaries and found what blessings they had—be they artifacts or innate abilities—weakened or even nullified. The witch hunter who found his quarry seeming no more threatening than a young woman living in the woods, only to end up in her cauldron. The paladin who didn't sense the fiendish thing lurking in his own shadow, because the twisted labyrinth about him was so full of the echoes of horror.

You underestimated this baron, I admonished myself. *He has dangerous friends.*

"You know what we are," Vaughn said. Even as he spoke, his skin seemed to take on a grayish pallor, his eyes becoming less vibrant. He bared his teeth. They were overlarge and the color of ivory, heavy and strong enough to crack bone.

"Your stooges weren't too subtle about it just a moment ago." I nodded to the shivering, drooling soldiers. "Unless they were trying to flirt with me? Sorry, but I'm afraid none of you are my type."

"You're funny, stranger." Vaughn jerked his chin at me. "Kill him."

With uncanny energy, the ghouls shivered into action. Vaughn brought his own heavy blade up in a guard as the others advanced. He seemed to have more control over his hunger, which made him especially dangerous.

I couldn't summon my magic, not quick enough. With my aura cooled down to embers, it would take a minute or more to stoke it back into lethal fury.

Another damned risk of trying to do things the quiet way. I grit my teeth and decided to try a more unpleasant tactic.

I used the axe's magic instead.

I squeezed the uncarved branch that made the weapon's handle with my right hand, pressing my flesh hard against it. I felt one of the little barbs along the length of rough oak bite into my palm, drawing blood.

The oak soaked in the blood, drank it, and came to life.

The air filled with the sound of creaking, cracking bark, and the handle of the axe suddenly writhed in my hand. Roots split out from the bottom, more coiling up from the top to wrap around the metal head, forming a spear point. It grew longer.

I swung even as it grew, taking it in both hands. I might not have been able to summon sorcery then, but I am most of three hundred pounds of muscle and I have been fighting all my life. I twisted, cocking the elongated axe, and whipped it across the air.

One of the ghouls had lunged ahead of the others. The quickest of them, I guessed. Perhaps he'd prided himself on that speed.

I split his head sidelong, cleaving the upper half of his skull from the lower so a lolling tongue remained to lap at the air as he collapsed, teeth flying like bits of shrapnel in every direction.

I'd dodged with the cut, taking advantage of my suddenly longer reach, so the corpse went past me and rolled across the street. It stopped in a sprawl between two of its comrades.

Even still, horribly, the body continued to twitch with more than just death spasms. Its fingers searched for its sword dumbly, rancid blood pumping out of the cavity of its open throat.

A lightning bolt of pain shot through my shoulder. Immediately after, I felt damp warmth begin to spread. *Pulled my damn stitches.*

The rest paused, resizing me. Their leader spat out a curse.

"He's a fucking adept!" one of them hissed. That one's eye sockets seemed too large for the rest of his face, his eyes deeply recessed so they seemed lost within shadowy pits. He bared teeth too big for the mouth in which they were set.

I wasn't about to hold back with ghouls. I didn't know how these had been made, exactly, but I could guess—usually, ghouls are the product of starving or nearly dead men, who in their desperation for life devoured the freshly dead. The lingering traces of aura left in those bodies kept the cannibal alive, strengthened them, and left them hungry for more power to stave off their encroaching end.

They kept starving and kept eating. The more they ate, the more they hungered for that energy, until they even went so far as to break into crypts and dig up graveyards, seeking any trace of soul-essence they could from rotting flesh and bone marrow.

They became trapped, forever, in a state very near death. They were *always* dying, always at its very edge, and always kept from that end by the aura they consumed.

That stubborn grip on their ruined bodies, and the power they ate, made them very hard to kill. Even with his upper skull missing, the one I'd struck might still be dangerous.

"Ain't this a surprise," Vaughn said with an eager laugh. "That's a queer magic, friend. Yours, or that fancy axe's?"

"You should take it, vice-captain!" One of them laughed. "A handsome trophy!"

"It'll be for the captain," Vaughn growled.

"We have to share him with the others?" One of the other ghouls said, a thin line of drool beginning to emerge from his lips as he stared at me.

"Company rules," Vaughn said. "Don't worry, boys—we still get first taste."

They began to advance again, heads bent forward and backs hunched, moving with a twitching, graceless celerity. When they sprang, it would be with preternatural speed.

I tensed, crouching as I prepared to throw myself at the vice-captain. The axe grew another several inches in a single crackling burst as it sipped more of my blood.

Would their discipline crack without their big commander? It might be my only way out of this, *if* I could overpower him.

My shoulder throbbed with pain, and I felt dizzy. *Lost too much blood recently.*

Before anyone could move farther, a shrill voice cut the night air and froze all of us.

"Vaughn! What are you doing?"

All four remaining ghouls flinched as the voice cracked across the buildings, sharp as a well-oiled whip. All of us turned to see a figure standing on the raised porch of a house, one lifted above the street by a set of stairs.

She looked to be in her mid-twenties, perhaps a bit older, average height and thin, clad only in a white night dress. She was pale, perhaps made more so by the eerie light glimmering in the mist, her face partly shrouded by an unkempt mop of chestnut brown hair. Her dress slipped from one shoulder, making me think she'd just woken.

"Catrin." Vaughn eyed the newcomer warily. "Leave it. This isn't your business."

The woman tossed her mane of frazzled hair as she lifted her chin. Her position at the top of the stairs allowed her to tower over us, like a queen looking down over a disappointing court, for all she looked like a skinny peasant woman in truth.

"To the Pit with that," she said. "Baron's expecting guests, and here *he* is tossing sorcery and looking fit to rip an ogre's head off."

She nodded in my direction without actually looking at me. "Call went out, boyo. I heard it. You heard it. So why don't you lay off the evil minion act for a night before something nastier than you sends you off to the Caves, eh? Looks like poor Jonas already got it. Someone help him get his skull back on, already?"

The half-beheaded corpse continued to crawl about, twitching and spasming as it pumped rotten blood onto the street. Two of its companions glanced at it uncertainly.

Vaughn's expression darkened. Something ugly rippled under his skin, an anger unbound by anything like restraint or dignity. It passed quickly, but while it was there it transformed his face, made him look as hideous as any demon I'd ever seen.

Then it passed, and he bared his teeth in a savage grin. "You shouldn't toy with us, whore. Captain's already warned you once."

He pointed his gladius at me. "He was snooping about, and isn't expected. He tells us who he is, then he dies."

"Looks like you were skipping right to the dying part," Catrin shot back, apparently unintimidated by the rage that'd overtaken the corpse eater. "If he's here to answer Falconer's call and you off him, others who've come will start to think they're not so safe here. They'll leave. Don't know about you, but I imagine his lordship won't be too pleased about that."

"He was eavesdropping on me and the Baron's herald," Vaughn growled. "He's a fucking spy."

Catrin blinked and turned to me. "That so, big man? You a spy?" She folded her arms, her posture challenging.

I stared at her, nonplussed. This hadn't been a conversation I'd been anticipating.

Eanor had told me the Baron gathered forces to him. I hadn't considered playing at being one of those who'd heard his summons—there were too many details I wasn't privy to, too many variables I couldn't anticipate.

It wasn't the plan, but I wasn't above improvising.

"I heard the call," I said, and shrugged. "That Lord Orson was challenging the Church, maybe even taking the fight to the Accord. I was curious."

Edgar had said the Baron was at odds with the clergy. I decided to make some educated guesses and play along with this strange theater.

I turned my gaze back to the ghouls. "Wanted to know more before I threw in on a rumor."

Vaughn narrowed his eyes, unconvinced. Catrin, however, was nodding.

"This is nonsense," the vice-captain snarled. "Catrin, we've all grown tired of your games. The Keeper's reputation can't protect you forever, and your mischief will end up getting you in over your head if you aren't smart."

"Bet she'd like that," Darla sneered, very ugly in that moment even ignoring her sallow face. "Filthy little strumpet."

Catrin sniffed, but only that and her narrowing eyes gave away any reaction. She kept her eyes on Vaughn.

The vice-captain turned his glare on me, his fingers wrapped tightly around the hilt of his ancient sword. The muscles of his face shifted dramatically, almost as though they were trying to break free of the skin. I could see anger, suspicion, and sheer ghoulish hunger all urging him to kill me.

I tensed, waiting for him and his comrades to attack.

Catrin rolled her eyes and let out an annoyed huff. "Bleeding Stars, Vaughn, are you that hungry? You going to act like I didn't see you and your Mistwalkers raiding the graveyard the other night?"

To my surprise, Vaughn and his cronies suddenly looked chagrined. He glanced at Catrin sidelong. "It's not the same as eating an adept." He looked at me again and his voice lowered into a bestial growl. "*Fresh.*"

I bared my own teeth at him. "Try it. Might burn, though." I lifted my axe to show him the bright, brassy gleam playing along its edge. I'd had time to work up my aura again, and was on the verge of being able to shape an Art.

"If everyone's done comparing their cocks," Catrin said in a dry tone, "this little spectacle is going to draw a lot of attention. The mist won't keep the villagers asleep through anything."

I paused at that. Tentatively, I felt at the coiling eddies of pale, ever-so-slightly lambent mist in the street with my magical senses.

It was subtle. I hadn't detected it until I had looked, but there *was* a power in the mist. That explained why none of the locals had come out to investigate the commotion me and the mercenary ghouls had caused. Some sort of subtle enchantment to keep the villagers asleep, I guessed.

Almost as though responding to this, a shirtless man came out of the door at Catrin's back. He had the same mussed hair and sleepy eyes as the pale woman.

"What's all this noise?" he asked groggily, shivering at the cold and hugging himself.

Catrin arched an eyebrow at us. Vaughn cursed and sheathed his sword. He made a sharp gesture, and the other ghouls did the same. One was *trembling*, I noted, physically forcing himself not to lunge for my throat.

I'd never met ghouls this disciplined, or even this sane. Though my guard stayed up, part of me was in awe that the half-dead soldiers had actually listened to reason and stopped the fight.

Vaughn growled an order to his men, threw one last glare at me, then they collected their maimed companion. One handed over the upper half of his skull, which he put back into place with a grotesque noise, bone clicking together and meat squelching.

He hadn't put it back on straightaway. His eyes and mouth faced different directions as he spat a curse at me. With his missing teeth, it came out slurred and unintelligible.

Vaughn turned to the woman on the balcony before they left.

"He's your problem then, Catrin. Next time he crosses the company, he's ours. So are you."

With that disturbing remark, they vanished into the mist.

Catrin said something to the man who'd emerged from the house. He glanced at me and the retreating mercenaries, his confusion evolving into alert concern. The woman murmured into his ear, and his eyes became glazed. She laughed quietly, turned him toward the door, and gently pushed him back inside. Then she turned to me and the amusement in her eyes faded.

"You," she said, "should get to the keep before the Mistwalkers decide to make a meal of you."

"Not the inn?" I asked.

Catrin lifted an eyebrow. "You really want nothing but thin wooden walls and a bunch of drunk travelers around you when Vaughn's cronies come knocking?"

"Will they even let me in?" I asked. "It was my understanding the Baron's guests had to wait in the village until called."

She studied me a moment, her thoughts unreadable behind a neutral mask. I waited, tense and prepared to quit this place and try another tactic. I clearly didn't understand enough about the strange situation unraveling itself in this gloomy land.

"I've got a pass into the castle," Catrin finally said. "Just don't like it there much, so I've been staying here." She shrugged. "I'll show you the way."

Couldn't be that easy. "Why?" I asked.

"Because I'm bored," she said. "And because the marrow lickers might try to get back at *me* now, too. Best to have a big lug like you at my shoulder when they try to get even, eh?"

She grinned, revealing crooked teeth. "Besides, I'm technically supposed to be *at* the council for the Baron's little club. I skipped class. Better late than a no-show, right?"

Before I could say anything, she pushed off the railing and vanished back into the house, reemerging a minute later with a yellow dress over her night shift and a satchel around her waist. She had a pair of shoes slung over one elbow by the strings as she pattered down a flight of stairs. She flashed a crooked grin as she looked up into my face.

"You aren't scared of water, are you, big man? Lake is awful deep."

"I can swim," I said, still nonplussed.

"Good, good. That'll make one of us. Let's go."

Before I could protest, Catrin had started off toward the lake.

Is this another bit of divine interference, I thought, *or some darker providence?*

Hard to say. But I needed to get into that castle.

I followed her.

CHAPTER SIXTEEN

CASTLE ON THE LAKE

The mist lingered. I imagined it would so long as whatever will was behind it wanted it to. It writhed and curled around the edges of the boat as the vessel cut the murky water of the lake, wispy tendrils parting reluctantly around the wooden hull.

Lanterns attached to the boat helped light our path, but I moved us forward slow and cautious all the same. I propelled us through the mist with a long oar while Catrin sat at the front, occasionally giving me direction.

She seemed to know her way well through the fog-laden expanse of the those waters. Which was, I felt certain, a problem. She'd known the ghoul mercenaries by name. She was a guest of the Baron, with an invitation to his council.

Perhaps, like the mercenaries, she wasn't what she seemed. But what, exactly? Another ghoul? A witch? Something worse? She seemed very human, almost mundane in her peasant dress, her ruddy brown hair, that occasional flash of slightly crooked teeth.

But that meant little for some beings. There were glamours even my golden eyes could struggle to break, if woven cleverly enough. And even if I tried, she might sense me doing it. If I revealed her fully, it would mean violence.

Better to pick my moment.

"You listening?"

The question ripped me from my thoughts. The slow, steady rhythm of my rowing faltered, and it took me a moment to realize I'd missed the last thing Catrin had said.

I glanced at her where she sat at the front of the small fishing vessel. Even in a dress, shift, and badly laced brown bodice, she looked underdressed for the cold air over the lake, the skin of her neck and shoulders exposed. I felt chilled even under the weight of my heavy cloak.

When I still failed to reply, Catrin arched an eyebrow at me. "I asked you what your name was, big man."

I hesitated a beat before replying. "Alken."

"Ooo . . ." Catrin lifted both eyebrows then, leaning forward with interest. "Haven't heard that before. Sounds fancy. You some kind of lord?"

I struggled to place her accent. It sounded like a marchlander a bit, from the subcontinent's eastern regions, but she spoke with an impatient, breathy haste that made her words blend together. It seemed more the product of a verbal tic than a dialect.

"Not a lord," I said in response to her question. *Not anymore,* I added silently.

Catrin folded her arms, studying me as though I represented some interesting puzzle. "So what are you? I don't think *mysterious wanderer* is an official profession. Tends to be more of a cover for something, right?"

I didn't reply. I doubted she'd take too kindly to learning I was an assassin, or that she was guiding me right to my target. I could have made up a story, but the more fiction I wove the more suspicion I might draw. I'd never been a good liar.

Silence was easier.

Catrin narrowed her eyes at me. She had large eyes, expressive and a shade of brown only a touch lighter than her hair, set beneath thick eyebrows. "Not much of a talker, are you, big man?"

I turned my eyes back to the lake and sent the boat forward with another rotation of the oar. "No."

Catrin snorted. "Suit yourself, then, but I'll tell you this—you're about to go into a nest of vipers. You've got a mighty fine cutter there . . ."

She nodded to my axe, which remained elongated from the blood I'd fed it. I'd had to lay down on the boat's floor to use the oar.

"But where you're going, this castle? Lot of nasty in those walls. Falconer's been putting out the word nearly a year now, and those corpse eaters aren't the only ones who've answered."

She leaned forward and propped her elbows on her knees. I avoided her eyes, looking out over the lake instead, but her eyes were intense, losing some of that drowsy nonchalance she'd kept up so far.

"Just want to make sure *you're* sure about this, big man. Don't know if you're some hard killer or what, but you can always turn this boat another way. I'll lead you safely from the marsh and have you gone before sunup, my word on it."

I did look at her then. "Why? You don't know me." I paused and added, "For that matter, why did you intervene with those ghouls?"

Catrin spread her hands out in a helpless gesture. "Because they were going to eat you? Even if *they* didn't, the rest of their band of killers would have."

"So it was altruism?" I asked, spurring the boat forward with another push. The water rippled beneath us, our boat the lone disturbance in its black stillness.

Catrin leaned back against the edge of the boat and made a shooing gesture. "Sure. Why not? You think I've got some ulterior motive?"

"You knew that one by name," I said. "That vice-captain. Maybe you're one of them. Maybe you're taking me somewhere private to make a meal of me yourself."

Catrin was silent awhile. My comment hadn't been a joke—I had every reason to suspect she *was* dangerous. If so, I'd rather know before she brought me into the midst of a den of darkness. Out here on the lake, with just the two of us, I might have a chance.

Quietly, I started to burn my magic again, feeling the first crackle of power flow through my limbs, anticipatory and ready to surge forth in a burst of amber flame. Even the wooden oar in my hands could prove a deadly enough weapon if I imbued it with aureflame.

Catrin parted her lips and bit lightly on the tip of her tongue, studying me with a detached sort of focus, like a painter planning a future stroke of his brush. "That's rather forward of you, big man, seeing as how we just met and all. Not even going to offer a girl a drink first? Bring me flowers?"

My rowing faltered for a moment. Catrin laughed, a low and throaty sound of genuine mirth. "Ah, you stoic types are always fun. We're almost there, so we'll put a rain check on that. Careful here, there are rocks."

I didn't have time to reply, or even process her words, as the waters of the lake began to grow treacherous. I had to put all of my focus on the dark, fog-shrouded abyss beneath the boat, looking for the telltale shadows of sharp rocks jutting up from the depths. Catrin murmured the occasional direction, and soon a larger shadow formed in the thinning mist ahead of us. It clarified itself into tall pillars and spikes of rock emerging like broken teeth from the depths, which soon began to coalesce into cliffs.

A barren island lay ahead, and on that island rose a castle. I couldn't make out its true dimensions, but the cliffs, the darkness, and the fog made its walls seem a monolithic shape. I could make out the hazy outlines of towers and rampart walls crawling with writhing fog, as though the fortress were some congealing phantasm.

Perhaps it was. It wouldn't be the only one in the world.

More, there were other, smaller structures rising from the water, which I had at first taken to be more rocks. They weren't. They were pieces of wall or the shattered remnants of drowned towers. Evidence of a larger structure, I thought, or even a town lost to the lake.

I swung the oar, and a lance of pain went through my injured shoulder. I tried not to show it, but its intensity caught me off guard. I flinched, gritting my teeth. I felt more warmth against my already damp preost robe, and another wave of dizziness.

"You're wounded," Catrin said.

I glared forward. "I'm fine."

She shook her head, causing her unkempt mop of hair to swing, no sign of mirth on her face. "You're not. You're bleeding."

She nodded to my shoulder, where the light brown material of the clothing I'd borrowed from Edgar had begun to darken.

"Let me take the oar," Catrin offered. "You should get that seen to. I've got some string in my bag here . . ."

She began to root around in her satchel. I let the boat drift, hesitant to let her take charge of our course.

Well, she already *was* in charge of it. Besides, it would free me to grab my axe if I needed to.

We switched off, the strange woman rowing the boat while I redid my stitches and worked to quell the bleeding.

"So, Alken." Catrin kept her eyes on the water as she spoke. "What brings you to Caelfall? Didn't get much back there with Vaughn and his cronies."

I snipped off a bit of string with my teeth before answering, using the motion to give me time to think. I decided for fragments of truth, which were easier than lies. "I'm a soldier, and I haven't had a lord to fight for in a long time."

"You a Recusant?" she asked. "Fought in the war?"

Angry, I opened my mouth to deny it. I was *no* Recusant. But I suspected Orson Falconer and his guests probably were. I clicked my teeth shut, then forced calm into my next words.

"Yes, I fought in the war." Not a full answer, but she seemed to accept it.

Catrin hummed as we passed beneath the sunken tunnel of an ancient arch. "I remember the war. Didn't see the worst of it—I'm no fighter. Far as House wars go though, it was an epic show."

"It wasn't just a House war," I snapped. "The Fall wasn't just another brawl between nobles. The Golden Country *burned*. It changed . . . everything."

Catrin glanced back at me, one brown eye peeking out of brown hair. "Right. Sorry, I forget how touchy that sort of thing is for some people, soldiers especially. I'm sure it mattered a whole lot to a lot of people. Especially the fey folk, seeing as how their city got turned to rubble."

She turned her attention forward again. "But to a lot of other people? Didn't matter if you were Recusant, Ardent Bough, or any of the big factions. Just your village getting burned down again. More starving, more fear. War tends to look like war."

"This war had demons," I said. "It involved the Magi, and started with the Archon's murder. You can't tell me it was *just another war.*"

"Lot of wars tend to start when someone with a golden hat gets chopped." Catrin waved a hand.

I clenched my jaw. "The Archon was the *voice* of the Choir of Heaven, king of all the Sidhe, an immortal who dwelt in this land before humans ever stepped foot in it. He was chosen by *God* to act as arbiter for Urn's monarchs."

Again, the infuriating woman shrugged. "So he had a *very* shiny hat. Most every big war starts with fancy titles like that thrown around. King so-and-so gets poisoned by lord such-and-such, then everyone's got some cause to die for."

I remained silent, frustrated with her dismissive attitude and with myself for letting it get to me.

"Besides," she added philosophically. "*Every* war has demons."

"And what would you know of war?" I growled. "You said yourself you're no fighter."

"Maybe not." She glanced back at me again, her face aloof. "But you warrior types don't always fight on some empty field. Whenever you march out, villages burn and innocent people die. *That*, I've seen."

She shrugged and turned her attention forward again. "Not that I'm any innocent. I don't mean to toss around mud, big man. Don't mind me. I'm always running my mouth, and getting into trouble for it."

Those ghouls certainly hadn't seemed to like her. They'd also been wary of her, which I hadn't forgotten.

Before either of us could continue the conversation, my attention redirected to the snap of leathery wings above. I tensed, reaching for my axe. Again, I heard the sound of huge wings beating, disturbing the pale white haze. The echoing sounds of claws scrabbling across rock filled my ears as something unseen crawled over the lake-drowned stones.

My instincts screamed that this was the trap. I bared my teeth and grabbed my weapon, starting to rise from the floor of the boat.

Catrin had her eyes up, but turned when she heard me move. Her eyes widened when she saw me.

"They're not going to hurt you as long as you're with me!" she said. "They're the Baron's sentries. Just . . ." She swallowed. "Just calm down, all right?"

She clutched the oar tightly to her chest, letting the boat drift. She looked ready to defend herself. Not from the things above, but from *me*.

I realized that flickers of amber fire were playing along the edge of my axe, accompanied by the scent of burning wood. I studied the woman for a long moment, waiting, but neither she nor the creatures lurking in the surrounding rocks made any move to attack me.

I let the power fade but kept my weapon in hand. "Are we near?"

Catrin nodded. "Yes. Just a bit further now." She turned her attention ahead, the motion stiff.

Once the tension of the moment passed, I felt a stab of guilt. *She's helping you. That wasn't courteous.*

I buried the foolish notion and focused on the task ahead. This woman was dangerous, and possibly not human. I hadn't missed how the cold night air didn't trouble her.

Up above, the hazy shape of curtain walls and steepled towers solidified. We'd arrived at the castle of House Falconer. My fingers tightened on my weapon as I inwardly steeled myself for what came next.

I had no specific plan. Couldn't have one, until I knew what I was dealing with. But I went into the dragon's den, no mistake.

Catrin guided the boat into a narrow ravine sinking into the depths of a cave. There were torches ensconced on the sheer rock of the cave's entrance, and the water extended through a tunnel within. This eventually brought us to a dock, little more than a wooden platform built along the cave's wall. A passage had been cut into the wall, torches illuminating it, and a set of stairs leading up. We pulled the boat up alongside the dock and clambered up onto the platform.

Catrin looked far less relaxed after we'd spotted the castle. I think my hostile reaction to the things flying above the lake had much to do with that. But that wasn't all of it.

She looked up at the cavern ceiling above and shivered. "I hate this place. Let's get this done quick, all right?"

"You're taking me to the Baron?" I asked.

Catrin shrugged. "To where his special guests are gathering, at least. Man's a recluse. I've seen him all of three times since I got here a couple months back."

I still didn't understand why she had helped me, and I didn't trust her. Still, I was within the fortress where my quarry made his abode. I followed her out of the cave, keeping my senses alert both to her and to my surroundings.

We ascended a steep set of stairs carved into the solid stone of the cliffs. This soon transitioned into something more artificial, smooth walls giving way to layered brick. Catrin lit our path with a lantern taken from the fishing boat, but even still the darkness seemed to press in behind us the farther we went, as though agitated by the presence of the light.

Farther, I could make out a very faint scuttling sound. I focused on it, certain it wasn't my imagination. Like insects crawling across the walls by the hundreds. The ground seemed to pulse beneath my feet, as though reverberating with the beating of a great underground heart. My magic stirred in discontent, troubled by the feel of the place.

This castle was unhallowed.

Catrin turned to look down at me, lifting the lantern. I had stopped, letting her get a ways ahead.

"You all right?" she asked.

I suppressed a shudder and nodded. "Fine."

I wasn't. I felt lightheaded from blood loss, my shoulder throbbed with agony, and I had broken out into a sweat from the ugly feeling in the walls around us. The shadows seemed a beating summer heat pressing down with eager energy.

Catrin nodded slowly. "You feel it, don't you?"

She licked her lips and glanced nervously around the walls. Though, I thought perhaps there was a glimmer of something besides fear in her eyes. A nervous excitement.

"Lot of bad's happened here," she said. "A man I knew used to say the walls of Castle Cael are made as much from bone as stone."

"You're a local?" I asked. I'd thought she was like the Mistwalkers, here for the Baron's gathering.

Catrin shook her head. "Not a local, but I've got connections here. I've never called any place home for long, really."

She considered a moment before adding, "I guess that's part of why I'm here. If the Baron's not full of shit—and I'm not saying he isn't—might be that could change."

"What do you think about what he's doing?" I asked. "The Baron, I mean. This gathering."

Catrin shrugged one pale shoulder. "Do I think a Houseborn recluse who's dabbled in the forbidden arts can bloody the Church's nose? I don't know. Wouldn't mind seeing it done, though."

"You're not fond of the Church." I didn't make it a question, or put any special emphasis on the statement.

Catrin's voice turned bitter. "It's more like they're not fond of *me*. Still, I'm not here for any vindictive reasons. Orson's talked about making this place a sanctuary for . . . well, folk who don't have an easy time most other places."

She flashed a sad little smile. "Wouldn't mind it, you know? Planting roots. But I'm not holding my breath, and I'm here for work in any case."

"The Keeper," I said, remembering Vaughn's warning. The name sounded familiar, but I couldn't place it.

Catrin nodded. "I'm sort of his representative?"

And not taking it very seriously, I silently noted.

There wasn't any conversation after that. I followed in the wake of Catrin's swishing yellow skirts until we finally reached the end of the long stairway. It brought us to a short tunnel with a heavy oak door at the end. Catrin rapped on it three times with her knuckles, and it opened to reveal a large chamber with the look of a foyer. Halls branched off in various directions, and a chandelier of intricate design hung from the ceiling.

The door had been opened by a gray uniformed Mistwalker. I tensed, knowing instinctively that he was also likely a ghoul, but the mercenary—a younger-looking man whose half-dead state was hinted at only by an unnaturally gray pallor—ignored me and dipped his head at Catrin.

"Cat! Thought you were staying in the village tonight."

"I was," Catrin said, jerking a thumb over her shoulder at me. "But one of the Baron's guests got lost. Thought I'd bring him over before the rest of you tin-heads got the wrong idea."

"Guest, huh?"

The guard turned his attention to me, and his welcoming attitude vanished. He studied me with a casual disinterest, as all the best sentries do. He was average height, leanly built, and somehow made his drab uniform and battered cuirass look fashionable. He had pale blond hair, and a thin face dominated by a crooked nose.

He fixed ice-chip blue eyes on me and pursed his lips. "Fashionably late, is it? His lordship is hosting some others who just arrived."

Catrin scrunched her nose. "More?"

The Mistwalker, Quinn, just shrugged. He laid a hand on the sword at his hip in a casual, easy gesture. "Scared, Cat? Don't worry, you're safe enough." He patted his weapon and flashed an easy smile, though it was perhaps too wide and manic to look quite human. His teeth were the color of old ivory.

Catrin snorted in contempt. "I'd rather roost with cairnhawks than trust a corpse eater to keep me safe." Her expression tightened with concern. "Quinn, there's not many people in Caelfall, if all of these predators Falconer is bringing in start getting hungry . . ."

Quinn scratched at his neck. "They're not *all* maneaters. I think one of them is just a necromancer, or something."

Catrin's lips pressed into a thin line. "Don't be dense. If the Baron loses control of his guests, people will start dying. He promised he would keep his subjects safe."

Quinn's lazy smile returned and he leaned forward, his voice turning conspiratorial. "Don't worry, Cat, I'm sure there will be plenty enough for you. Speaking of, you free tomorrow night? I've got a shift in the village."

Catrin's voice emerged encrusted with a layer of frost. "I'll be occupied."

"I'll bet." Quinn flashed his too-wide grin again, then turned to me and lost the smile. "He wasn't invited to the council. All the guests who weren't asked to come to the castle are supposed to be waiting in the village until called."

"*I'm* supposed to be here," Catrin said, jabbing a thumb into her shoulder. "I'll vouch for him."

Quinn shook his head, sucking at his cheek. "It's not gonna fly, Cat. You can't keep doing whatever you want and expect your master's goodwill to stave off the consequences."

Catrin's lips thinned, and she enunciated each word she said next. "The Keeper is *not* my master. He's my *employer*."

Quinn shrugged. "Sure. Doesn't change it. I'm just saying you're playing with fire."

"Let's just call him an attaché," Catrin said, her voice taking on a wheedling quality. "Come on, Quinn, I'll take the heat!"

Instead of answering her, he turned to me and shifted into a solid stance. I was taller, and heavier, but he didn't seem intimidated. Like Vaughn, he had a professional control. Size and weight weren't everything in swordplay, especially when I wasn't wearing armor.

"What's your story?" he asked.

Catrin glanced between us, clearly worried.

I set my axe—long enough to function as a walking stick just then—against the ground, resting my hand on its head to keep any threat out of the motion. Even still, the soldier's eyes flicked to it.

"My profession is war," I told him. "It's obvious to me that this lord is preparing for one. He will want to meet me."

I worked to put absolute confidence into my voice, even though my forehead beaded with sweat from pain and nervousness. If my voice was perhaps too low and too tight, I just had to hope it came across as stoic bravado.

Quinn lifted a blond eyebrow. "That so? Confident, aren't you?"

I said nothing, holding his gaze. His eyes narrowed, and he broke the contact first.

"Sellsword, then?" Quinn scoffed, though it seemed more an expression of appreciation than skepticism. "I can appreciate that. Well, if you're no joke, then perhaps Cat might earn herself some goodwill being the one who found you."

Catrin folded her arms and straightened, adopting a serious expression. "Exactly! See, I knew you'd catch on."

The Mistwalker sighed. "Well, it won't be on me. Fine, fine. This way."

He turned and started to walk deeper into the shadowed castle. Catrin traded a nervous glance with me, her earlier confidence almost completely gone. I kept my own demeanor neutral.

"Your injuries . . ." Catrin swallowed. "How bad are they? You *really* don't want to show weakness where we're going, big man."

"I've had worse," I said honestly.

Inwardly, I cursed myself as a fool for going through with this. I'd taken the opportunity presented, but I was in no shape to fight. Even having tended to my shoulder, I'd lost a lot of blood in the past week, much of it just that night, and had used my body and magic hard.

Just then, I had to put effort into standing upright and keeping a straight face. How long could I hold the act?

As long as you need to in order to survive, I told myself.

Catrin didn't look fooled. Even still, she nodded. "All right. Well, once we're in there I can't do much for you other than an introduction."

I nodded. Then on impulse added, "I should thank you. And . . . apologize. Before, on the boat, I was discourteous."

Catrin shrugged and started to say something, but Quinn interrupted us from the stairs.

"Hey, I don't have all night! Get moving."

We did. Injured and uncertain what I faced, with a dubious ally at my side, I strode deeper into that lair of darkness and dark things.

CHAPTER SEVENTEEN

ENEMIES ABOUND

Quinn brought us through the winding halls of Castle Cael. Seeing it from the outside, I'd expected something more decrepit, but the interior of the ancient redoubt turned out to be clean and well furnished. We passed by empty suits of armor, polished and festooned with the Falconer sigil, rich tapestries, and various forms of art spread across the castle's many corridors.

Lord Orson, it seemed, was something of a collector.

I lingered by one work. The painting, tall as a man and dominating one wall between two pulled curtains, showed a knight brandishing a broken spear as a dread wyrm threatened her, curved teeth flickering with sickly flame.

The image didn't seem fashioned to glorify. The knight looked old, tired, and afraid. The dragon was an enormous thing, its jaws large enough to swallow the warrior—no larger than my thumb in the image—whole. The beast was a thing all of cancerous scale and bursting horn, wreathed in fire and the souls of its victims, stylized by the artist as disintegrating skeletal shapes.

I inhaled deeply, and for a moment found I could smell the sulfurous reek of it, hear the painful grinding of its ill-formed mass.

I had never laid eyes on a dragon. It was a memory of older knights, echoing through the power sewn into me.

Quinn made a noise of impatience. "No time to dally. You'll have plenty of time to enjoy the art, I'm sure."

Catrin had noticed my pause as well. "You all right?" she muttered.

"Fine," I said. I breathed in deep, working to refocus myself on the present reality.

As we went farther on, I noticed a distinct lack of guards. Besides the empty armors, there were no true knights or sentries wearing the Falconer sigil. The castle lay eerily empty, for all it seemed regularly maintained by servants. I didn't see any of those, either.

The sense of dread I'd felt below had faded as well. Even still, I remained tense with nerves.

Quinn eventually brought us to a large set of doors. Here he stopped, nodding to the ostentatious portal.

"Dining hall. Baron's other guests are in there, waiting on his pleasure. And here, I must leave you."

He gave a mock little bow, to which Catrin rolled her eyes. She went to the doors, though Quinn gestured for my attention before I followed.

"Not going to ask your story, stranger. All the Baron's guests got one, and they're all fit to give me bad sleep."

I grunted a noncommittal reply. I knew what this man was and didn't like lingering so close to him. With my not quite natural senses, I could detect the faint odor of rotting bones and grave soil on him, for all he looked like a well-groomed fop.

Quinn glanced at my guide, lifting an eyebrow. "Odd to see her taking a risk for a stranger. You one of her regulars or something?"

I frowned. "What do you mean?"

Quinn's eyebrows lifted further. "What, you mean you don't know?"

"Hey," Catrin said from the doors. She'd cracked one open and waved for me to follow. "This thing's heavy, come on."

I left the Mistwalker behind to follow her, putting his words out of my mind. Catrin ushered me into the dining hall.

It was a theatrical space, meant to express the power and lavish taste of the castle's lord. A tall flight of stairs led up to an upper balcony set just below a row of narrow windows paned in foggy glass, reflecting light from the chandeliers hung from the high ceiling. A long table dominated the room.

The Baron's guests waited for us inside. Not all of them were human.

As Catrin and I entered, a silence fell over the hall of the sort that occurs in the midst of an interrupted discussion. More than half a dozen figures sat at seats around the long table, their arrangement seeming random and casual, many of the chairs left unoccupied. A score or more could have been comfortably seated there, and the hall itself was large enough for a more formal gathering, making the room feel cavernous and empty. Shadows clung deep to every corner.

Eyes turned to me as the door shut at my back. Catrin paused next to me, eyeing the gathering with a cool indifference, though I didn't miss how she went tense at my side and didn't approach the table. I stood there, draped in my red cloak, waiting for this strange drama to play out.

"Catrin!" A shrill, hissing voice cut the brooding silence. It came from an old woman clad in an archaic gown of deep maroons and velvety blacks. A high collar supported by metal spikes enclosed her long neck, making her seem like some regal vulture. An elaborate headdress crafted from ivory secured her thin silver hair.

"Lillian," Catrin replied neutrally, sniffing.

The old woman sat near the head of the table, just by an empty seat very much like a throne. She leaned forward, revealing almost black teeth. "Why, my dear, I thought you'd decided these meetings bored you. What brought . . . ah, and who is this?"

Her eyes, which had sclera yellow as a ghoul's teeth and irises so faded I couldn't tell their original color, flickered to me. Her nostrils flared beneath a hooked nose, as though she were inhaling my scent or preparing to charge.

"This is Alken," Catrin said, waving a hand at me. "He's here to see the Baron." She glanced around, frowning. "Where is his lordship, anyway?"

"Fashionably late." Lillian enunciated the words with a distracted air, her eyes having never left me. I felt a distinct discomfort from those bloodshot orbs. They were corpse eyes, even more than Vaughn's or Darla's had been. "Why don't you take a seat, dear? You and your . . . friend."

Before we could, a snort came from a man sitting across the table from the old woman in the red gown. He was clad in simpler garb, all greens and browns like a hunter. He even wore a tricorn low over his shaggy blond hair, shadowing his eyes. He had pushed his chair back and kicked his feet up on the table.

"Hold on a breath." The hunter glared at me with one piercing hazel eye through the shadow of his pointed hat. "I wasn't told there would be any other voices at this council. I know who everyone in this room represents, except this one."

He nodded to me. The rest of the guests stirred, including the woman at my side.

Two figures made into twins by their matching black robes and cowls whispered to one another, the hems of their hoods nearly pressing together. A dark-haired, heavily bearded man in sooty armor at the far end of the table from Lillian ignored everyone, focusing intently on the plate of meat in front of him. He ate loudly and messily, heedless of the hush that'd fallen over the room.

He'd been eating since I walked in, and hadn't even seemed to take a moment to catch his air.

There were others. A thing out of nightmare sat in the deeper shadows opposite the table from the door. He had gray-green skin and a malformed aspect, with a lumpy head that merged with a neck that vanished into a formal aristocratic outfit very much too small for him. The ensemble was held together by crude stitchwork and ill-matched pieces of salvaged cloth, for all he looked like some eccentric aristocrat. His hands ended in four long, gnarled fingers tipped in green nails, and green were the glassy orbs of his eyes as they peered at me from the gloom.

Instead of buttons or lace, his bright doublet was sewn with pieces of bone.

An elf? Some lord of Briar, or perhaps Bane? Or a changeling?

Either way, he flashed sharp teeth at me in a threatening snarl.

Monsters. In that room I stood surrounded by monsters. Even, I suspected, of the human variety.

A rumbling, basso growl rippled through the room. The hairs on the back of my neck stood on end, and my muscles went tight with instinctive fear. A heavy foot came down on the floor, large enough to make the stones of the ancient castle shudder, as something enormous emerged from the shadows between two columns.

This one had not been sitting at the table, but lurking beyond the chandelier light. I turned to face it as its bulk strode forward.

Calling it big would be like calling a redwood tall. A hulking mass of muscle more than nine feet in height approached me with steady, thunderous steps. Its skin was the color of old rust, and it was clad all in heavy furs and hides, a few pieces of metal sewn here or there. They seemed more decorative than functional. Skulls, some human, hung from a heavy belt.

The hulk's brutish face wasn't quite human. It had a simian aspect, with a slightly elongated muzzle and a sloping forehead. Its features emerged from a neck set lower on its torso than a human's. Deep-set yellow eyes—piss yellow, ringed in deeper orange—burned with a manic, violent intelligence.

Catrin shifted away from me, having gone utterly silent when the beast had emerged. I took a step back as well. I couldn't help it. The fear I felt was primal, instinctive, woven into the fabric of my blood and bones.

Prey animal fear. There were few things in all the Alderes more deadly than a war ogre.

A city garrison's worth of muscle and pent-up rage loomed over me, wrought in dark laboratories to dominate ancient wars. Yellow eyes burned like the cores of candle flames, scorching me with malice.

The ogre leaned forward and sniffed. Then it growled again.

"He smells of sun-stained groves and gilded trees." His voice rumbled in my chest, more something I felt than heard. Again, that rippling growl filled the room. "He reeks of *elf*."

The room became very still. My attention remained fixed firmly on the monster in front of me.

I didn't mean monster in the poetic sense. Ogres are, to put it mildly, nightmares. Bred in dark lands in dark days in distant edges of the world beyond the shores of Urn, they had been made for a singular purpose—to kill, and to do so without restraint or mercy. They lived for a very long time, every year of that centuries-long life dedicated to the arts of violence.

Worse, some of the skulls the ogre wore belonged to its own kind. Its craggy exterior, marred by countless scars, hinted at a long and terrible succession of battles it had *won*.

I sensed this particular ogre was old. No runt of the litter.

"Elf friend," the ogre accused. It bared wolf's teeth the color of iron. "Spy."

I've been in danger many times in my life. I have escaped death by the narrowest of margins, danced with it, befriended it, even gone beyond its threshold.

Few times have I been as near to it as in that room.

All eyes fixed on me, bright and predatory within the deep shadows of the dining hall. Sweat beaded on the back of my neck, even as I remained very aware of how injured I was, how little strength I had left.

Foolish. Coming here had been foolish. I hadn't expected to meet an entire gathering of rebel leaders, for that *had* to be what this was. Remnants of the enemy who hadn't been slain or cowed during the war. Those who continued to defy the rule of the Accorded Realms, the Aureate Church, and the remaining Seydii elves who'd survived the Fall.

Recusants. My enemies, one and all.

CHAPTER EIGHTEEN

SHADOW COUNCIL

In my mind, I moved through the series of actions I would take next.

Draw my dagger, move under the ogre's legs, and hamstring it. If Catrin comes at me, I use the ogre as a shield and wield my axe. Make for the window on the far side of the room, cut down anyone who gets in my way. Use Art if I have to, even if it burns my aura out.

The ogre bared his gray fangs and flexed fingers near thick as my wrists. I tensed.

"Hold, Karog." Lillian's rasping voice filled the room. "He is the Baron's guest, and it is Orson who should decide his fate. Stay your hand."

Another growl ripped out of the ogre's throat, impossibly loud. "I do not answer to you, witch."

The old woman's face darkened with anger. She wore many rings and bracelets, and toyed with one of those accoutrements now as she contemplated the hulking warrior. Some of those sitting nearest to her shifted nervously.

The hunter remained relaxed, his feet propped up, and the two in the hooded cloaks kept whispering to one another. The man in the battered armor kept eating, ignoring everyone.

Catrin muttered a curse behind me.

I noticed something else then. The shadows around me and the ogre had deepened, the already wan flames of the chandelier seeming to retreat from us. A heaviness hung in the air, and the very faint sound of many tiny, scuttling legs.

The same thing I had felt in the lower levels of the castle.

Karog didn't seem to have noticed it. One of his hands went to his belt, where a weighty blade, like a cleaver, hung in a crude sheath.

I didn't think I could match him, not in my condition. But when dealing with predators, you never show weakness. Couldn't fight, probably couldn't flee, so . . .

Time to play a part. All those around me were high-class villains of one sort or another. I'd been called one myself, more than once.

Time to wrap myself in the aspect.

I propped my axe down on the floor, resting my hand on its head as I cast a disdainful look on the hulking creature. "I can tell you're a stranger to these lands, *kin fomori,* so I'll do my best to explain something I assume obvious to everyone else here."

Karog paused at the old name I'd used, his heavy brow furrowing. The silence took on a sharper aspect, broken only by the feasting man.

"What are you doing, big man?" Catrin lingered behind me, as though using me as a shield against the behemoth. Perhaps she was doing exactly that.

Ignoring her, I kept my focus on the ogre. "You're from the continent, aren't you?"

Most war ogres were, crafted by western alchemists in bad old days to act as shock troops and suicide soldiers.

"I know things are different there," I continued, "but here in Urn, *everything* has some faerie meddling in it. This land is gravid with old enchantment. It has a way of sticking to things."

Lillian leaned forward, an amused glint flickering in her corpse eyes. The hunter lifted his fingers to his tricorn, propping up its brim as his attention focused on me.

Out of the corner of my eye, I noticed the hobgoblin in the aristocratic garments stroke at his thorned chin. He was nodding.

"We mere mortals don't always ask for their *gifts,*" I said, letting a bitter note enter my voice. I desperately hoped none of the sweat beading on my brow would be noticeable through my unkempt bangs, or that it would trickle down to my chin.

Karog grunted, one corner of his lip curling to show his teeth again. "You mean to say this stench on you is the result of some curse?"

I let a grim smile cross my lips. "No, I consented to it. Just didn't understand the cost at the time. That's how the Sidhe work—give you what you think you want, then leave you to spend your days in regret."

"Hear hear!" the monstrous noble called, banging a fist down on the table. It made several plates jump, startling one of the hooded twins. The armored man growled, but didn't stop eating.

Not an elf, I thought as I glanced at the hobgoblin. *Not entirely. A man changed into that, or a changeling cursed with a mixed nature. Guess I found one sympathetic ear in this audience.*

The hunter also looked attentive, his head tilted to one side as he studied me.

Karog didn't look convinced. His hand lingered on the cleaver.

"Why did you bring him, Catrin?" Lillian spoke to the woman shrinking behind me.

"Well, uh . . ." Catrin coughed, stepping out so everyone could see her. "He seemed scary enough, and I figured the Baron would want to meet him. More the merrier, right?"

She shrugged, looking as unconvinced as everyone else by the excuse. I hid a wince.

"We don't have time to indulge your tastes," Lillian hissed. "If he suits your fancy, you could have kept him in the village."

Catrin's eyes flashed with anger. "Oh, shut your wrinkled trap, Lilly."

"Regardless . . ." The ghoulish woman turned her attention back to me. "The scent of elves, and an axe wrought from the branch of a Malison Oak . . ." She leaned forward and sniffed again. "Yes, that is a fell thing. Where did you get such an accursed treasure, Alken?"

I did not answer, taken aback that she'd recognized my weapon for what it was.

"He is probably a ranger or some questing knight discarded once his purpose was done," the monster nobleman growled. He had a burbling, lisping voice tinged with something more bestial. "I have seen it often enough before. Is this not so, man?"

I glanced at him. "It is near enough. My tale is for the Baron, if he chooses to ask it, and if I decide to pledge to him."

The hobgoblin chortled. "True enough! I say we let him stay."

"And if he is a spy?" Karog snapped.

The changeling shrugged. "Such magic suffuses the lands far and wide, Karog, just as he said. It is not that uncommon, nor does it mean he is a danger to us."

"So you are here to pledge to Orson?" one of the shadowed twins asked. They had an androgynous voice, some enchantment woven into their garment masking it. It came out buzzing and artificial from the fuzzy blackness beneath their cowl.

I'm not suited for this, I thought. I could not tell a direct lie—my powers would punish me for it, and I couldn't afford to be any weaker just then. I'd already skirted around the truth, and eventually one of these blackguards would sniff out the deception.

"I heard of this council through rumor and hearsay," I said. "From those wiser than myself. I can say no more. All you need know is that I can fight, and well."

I turned my stare on Karog, working to keep my expression and voice dispassionate. "If you need me to demonstrate now, I am willing."

The ogre lowered his head. A threat, not a surrender. He bared his prominent lower fangs and tensed, as ready for violence as myself.

Lillian scowled. "If you were not given invitation to this council, then our discussion is not for your ears. Catrin, this was ill done. You have already stretched our patience!"

Catrin folded her arms, looking nervous, and said nothing.

"I agree," the one cloaked twin who'd already spoken said. They poised their hands, wrapped in dark cloth, on the table. "Our enemy has eyes and ears across all of Urn. Their puppet priests, yes, but others too. Spirits disguised as trees, birds, dreams . . . even men."

The hooded gaze fixed on me, the voice within falling silent. I felt that hostile attention from all sides once more. Catrin was of no help—I could tell she regretted bringing me here by her silence and nervous expression.

He is no spirit.

I went dead still. The voice had not come from anyone sitting at the table, or standing in the shadowy alcoves as Karog had. It came from all around, a shivering, manifold thing as though many quiet, ghostly voices spoke at once, their collective presence becoming something more substantial.

It slithered from every shadow. With every syllable it changed, sometimes deep and masculine and sometimes airy and effeminate, a profane chorus forming one voice.

He smells of fire and blood.
And pain.
Regret.
He is mortal.
Touched by an immortal flame.
He is marked.
Claimed.

The sound of many insectile feet scuttling across the walls intensified, as though excited. Karog's eyes were going everywhere, his fangs bared, his cleaver half drawn.

Claimed by mine own kin.

Everyone in the room was scared. I could see it in their panicked faces. Even the armored man had stopped eating.

The scars over my left eye itched. I made an effort of will not to lift my hand and feel the old wounds, though the discomfort grew worse by the second.

The hobgoblin swallowed, his entire neck bulging like a frightened toad's. Lillian seemed to sink into her chair. All around us, unseen things skittered in the shadowed corners. The source of the voice.

A new shadow appeared on the balcony at the back of the room. My eyes went up to it, and Karog saw my attention and turned himself.

A man had appeared there, atop the stairs overlooking the dining room. He was tall, in his mid-fifties, clad in a princely white robe of ancient design woven with patterns of red and blue, winged in flaring sleeves lined in black netting studded with small gems. He looked like some dark emperor out of an old fable, not a country lord at all.

The gems woven into his outfit glittered in the candelight like eerie green eyes as he lifted one hand to the balcony railing, letting ringed fingers trail across it. Though heavily shadowed above the hall, I could see his eyes as the firelight caught them. They were a bright shade of violet.

"My lord," Lillian breathed. Her face, already pale, had turned ashen. "You assured us that creature would not be present during these discussions."

The Baron did not answer her. He had begun to descend the stairs without hurry, his fingers lingering on the railing. Without looking at him, he spoke to the ogre.

"Will you not take your hand off your weapon, Karog?"

The Baron had a melodic voice, soft and deep as dark waters, yet it seemed to fill the room.

The scuttling noise grew louder. I couldn't tell where it came from—everywhere? It seemed to fill the shadows.

Karog's eyes, orange-rimmed, showed little fear. Indignation, and calculation, but no panic like the hobgoblin or Lillian. I saw him consider killing the man.

He chose reason instead, slamming his blade back into its sheath as he stepped back into the columns, hunching there like some enormous guard dog. He said nothing else.

"I bid you welcome," Orson Falconer said. I realized he spoke to me, as his violet eyes drifted toward my face. "I regret that the hospitality of my hall is not what it might have once been, but I offer it all the same."

A second figure followed the Baron. The one in the green cloak, his herald. They—*she*, I recalled Vaughn's crude insult—drifting behind the lord like a silent shadow.

I inclined my head, deciding to show respect. "I apologize for arriving unannounced, my lord. I did not fully understand all of this before arriving. I only knew it might interest me."

"The Keeper's representative told you of this meeting, I understand?"

Orson had reached the bottom of the stair. Now I saw him level, I got a better look. He had short hair receding into a sharp widow's peak, black striped with gray, and a dusky skinned face that remained handsome in age. He had a scholar's build despite his height, not a warrior's, thin and long-limbed, with shadowed eyes and gaunt cheeks.

"That's right," Catrin offered nervously. "Seemed like someone you would want to meet, your uh . . . your lordship."

"We were just discussing this one," Lillian noted as she tracked the Baron's movements with her maniacal eyes.

"He was not invited!" the talkative twin said. "I do not wish to speak of delicate matters with an unknown element listening, Orson."

Before the lord had a chance to speak, an armored fist slammed down on the table with thunderous force. All eyes, including my own, turned to the figure sitting at the far end of the table. The feasting man.

He'd finally raised his head, revealing a heavily bearded, wild-haired visage. He wore battered armor that had seen at least one hard campaign, and probably many. There were deep shadows around his pale eyes, and beneath the mane of gray-streaked hair he was painfully gaunt.

He'd eaten the entire leg of meat he'd been working on. Even the bone.

"I've had enough of this," the armored man growled. His voice was dry and rasping, as though he badly needed water and had for a very long time. "I came here to discuss war. I don't care about the rest."

He took a scrap of his ruined gray cloak and wiped it across his mouth, doing little to clean his matted beard and further soiling the garment. "If we're not here for business, then I'll take my Mistwalkers and go."

The Baron inclined his head to the ghoul. "I do not want that, my friend. And I concur. Let us return to business." He gestured toward me again. "Will you sit, Master Alken? You as well, Catrin."

I was still shaken by the thing in the shadows—or *was* it the shadows? But I nodded and moved to a chair. I found one as far from any of the others as I could, which wasn't an easy feat as unevenly spaced as they all were. Catrin chose a seat right next to me, though I sensed it was more a bet for safety than any camaraderie.

She shot me a furtive glance and shrugged, then went about inspecting the array of food and drink set on the table. A whole feast, though only the mercenary captain had partaken so far.

"Excellent." The Baron ran his eyes across the gathering one more time, then took his own seat. He adjusted his sleeves, then relaxed into the high-backed chair.

"Then let us begin."

"Why don't we start with why you've called us," the black-robed figure suggested, the only one of the duo who'd spoken. Their companion remained silent and still, a vaguely humanoid shadow slumped in their fine chair. "I have my suspicions, but I am curious as to the true purpose of this . . . council."

There were murmurs of agreement from the others. I folded my arms, idly running my eyes over the feast to avoid meeting anyone's eyes.

The captain of the Mistwalker Company had already eaten much of it. He started in on another leg with noisy, vaguely sickening sounds.

The Baron nodded and steepled his fingers. "I have called you all here to discuss, as Captain Issachar so succinctly put it, *war.*"

The hush in the room deepened, an air of eager anticipation falling over the guests. I fixed my attention on the Baron more firmly as well. The mercenary leader even stopped his ravenous eating to hear the lord better.

"Ten years." The Baron paused, letting those words sink in. "Ten years since the forests of Seydis burned, since the towers of Elfhome fell and the Archon, voice of the Choir of God, was slain. Many in this new alliance which professes to govern the land, this *Accord* . . ."

His voice turned bitter. "Believe *that* was the beginning of the land's woes. But that is not true, is it?"

An anticipatory silence followed that statement. I did not rush to break it.

The Baron continued. "For long centuries have the ancient powers who profess to guide us let their idle whims and favoritism chart our fates. For long centuries have they professed to rule on behalf of their Golden Queen, while Her voice remains *silent.*"

Blasphemy, an angry voice in my soul warned. I quelled it. Now was not the time.

The sanguine calm in the Baron's violet eyes cracked like glass as he spoke. His voice never changed, never rose, but an edge of cutting anger *was* there—in the way his left hand clenched and relaxed in tandem with his jaw, in the deadly quiet of his every word. A quiet that filled the hall. Drowned it.

"We all know the elves are their puppets," the Baron said, and the hobgoblin let out a low, throaty growl of agreement. "We all know the Church is their tool, for all its infighting and factionalism. Even the Accord and its representatives bend to the whims of our so-called *gods.*"

The blond man in the tricorn shifted. A subtle motion, his slouching posture remaining relaxed, but I sensed him to be more alert than he let on.

"I have had enough." The Baron drew in a deep, shuddering breath. "Enough of my people worrying over whether their crops will die because they did not direct their prayers to the east with enough fervor. Enough of bending to the fey whims of lesser immortals whose petty, childish antics are enabled by the world's insistence on wallowing in nostalgia. Enough of fearing for the souls of mine own blood, whose very peace in death isn't even a guarantee."

Layers of cloth rustled as the two black-robed figures stirred in their seats.

Lillian leaned forward, her feverish eyes intense with interest. "Is this why you had the bridge troll butchered? Are you declaring war against the Sidhe, Orson?"

"They are vulnerable enough," the goblin lord said with a laugh. "Scattered, their eldest driven mad by old Tuvon's death, those blessed champions of theirs all gone. It's a ripe time for it, I say."

"You gave that order?" the talkative twin asked the Baron.

Issachar let out a hollow, rasping laugh. "Fucking thing kept trying to get my men to pay his toll. Never heard that old saying, *you and what army*, I suppose."

The huntsman at my side tensed and adjusted his cap.

"That was a stupid thing to do."

It wasn't until all eyes present turned to me that I realized I had been the one to say the words. Catrin winced at my side, shifting as though to put more distance between us.

The commander of the ghoul mercenaries fixed his hungry eyes on me. "Come again?"

Inwardly, I winced. I'd meant to draw as little attention to myself as possible, but the troll's death kept flashing through my mind. The brutal way it had been dismembered, the callous cruelty of the display made from that violence. I recalled its terror and confusion as it had been killed, that echo passed into my aura now, part of it—possibly forever.

The anger boiling up in me couldn't all be blamed on the golden ghosts sewn to my soul.

"It was a stupid thing to do," I said again, letting my own voice drop into an angry growl to match the ghoul's. "Settled trolls are arbiters for their domains, centers of balance. Magically, and socially. I crossed that bridge on my way here. Saw what your men did."

I met the ghoul's eyes and held them. "You didn't just kill it. You *desecrated* it. That bridge will become a locus of hostile od, probably for centuries, and that's not even mentioning the attention it drew. I heard your Mistwalkers talking before I arrived at the castle. Something about irks raiding from the forests? Why do you *think* that's started up all the sudden, corpse eater?"

The ghoul's chair screeched as he stood and slammed his palms down on either side of his mostly empty plate. He glared at me, too-big teeth bared, his face a rictus mask of anger.

"Maybe you are an elf friend," he hissed. "I don't remember you being given a voice at this council. I was willing to overlook it while the Baron did, but keep your trap *shut*."

Bits of food and spit flew from his lips as he spoke, his foggy blue eyes wide with threat. I held his gaze, my jaw clenched. I felt very aware of Karog still lurking between the columns, and of the subtle ambience of skittering insects in the shadows. That *thing* which had arrived at the same time as the Baron was still here.

A chuckle coiled mockingly through the room. It had come from Lillian. "Ah, so our vagabond friend here is not just a thug who caught the Backroad wench's eye. I misjudged you, Master Alken."

She dipped her head in my direction, the elaborate coils of her silver hair remaining fixed in place as firmly as if they were made of ceramic. Then she turned to the Baron. "The newcomer is right. Killing the troll was preemptive and poorly done. It exposed us before we were ready."

"I agree," said the young hunter at my side.

"It was the most dangerous threat in this region," Issachar said, sullen now that he'd been ganged up on. "And it had wendgates all over the damn wilderness. I need my troops to be able to move freely, and not have to worry about paying every time. No matter where we went, we'd find that damn bridge."

"What was its toll?" I asked.

Issachar glared at me, his lips forming a thin line. I met his stare and asked again. "*What* was its toll? No troll's passage price is ever the same. What did it ask for the use of its bridges?"

I could nearly hear the ghoul's teeth grinding.

"Don't know, do you?" I asked, flashing my own teeth at him. "Didn't even bother finding out. He might have just wanted a riddle, or a cup of spring water. They don't always ask for *coin*."

"Fingernails."

It was Catrin who'd spoken, though she seemed reluctant to do it. She'd made an effort to avoid notice through the meeting, but sighed as all the attention went to her.

"Fingernails," she repeated. "That was his price. He preferred those from the left forefinger."

She held up her left hand to demonstrate. It might have been my imagination, but the nail on the first finger of that hand seemed shorter than the rest.

Lillian laughed. It was a severely unpleasant sound, a screeching cackle that echoed off the ancient castle walls, a show of mirth to put even the most fell witch to shame.

"What, you death eaters prize your pretty nails that much? Oh, that's rich!"

Issachar's face turned red. "He was an Onsolain bondsman. He would have challenged us in time."

"Fingernails!" Lillian chortled, still caught up in her amusement. Issachar growled and reached for the sword at his hip.

Another, much deeper growl filled the chamber from the ogre still lurking in the shadows. The ghoul froze.

"Peace!" Orson held up his hand. He sighed. "I think, perhaps, we should retire this discussion for now. The matter of the bridge troll is not an insignificant one. I must consider. I *will* speak to you of it later, captain."

Issachar looked to the Baron and nodded sharply. He looked half caught between rabbit terror and canine rage, and unable to decide which beast to be.

"I will speak to you now, Alken"—the Baron looked to me—"in private."

Chapter Nineteen

THE RECUSANT

I followed the Baron, accompanied by his green-cloaked servant, deeper into Castle Cael once the council had dissolved. The rest went their separate ways, vanishing into the labyrinth of the keep. Catrin had thrown me an apologetic look before slipping out, as though to say *sorry, hope you don't die!*

A strange woman. Who exactly *was* she? Who was this Keeper? Lillian had called her the *Backroad wench*. What exactly was the Backroad?

I had more pressing questions just then. I followed in the wake of the lord's regal white gown, his shrouded servant taking up position behind me. A not-so-subtle threat. Braziers clutched in iron hands along the walls burst alive as the lord passed them, the castle responding to his presence.

Not a bad trick. His own sorcery? Some device? Or did this ancient house simply respond to him, like an eager hound raising its head for its master?

Some places are like that. A good commoner family might be blessed by a fey sprite in their hearth, who will light and warm the place of its own volition. Villages might be protected from threats such as savage beasts or disease by similar powers.

The great castles of Urn often enjoy even more dramatic blessings. Long generations of pride, war, loyalty, and secret rites bind the nobility to the land itself, much of that power sewn up in the bones of their great manors and fortress palaces. The very stone soaks up the aura of the inhabitants, drinking in the will of rulers and those who love or hate them alike through long centuries.

In the end, the legends we tell about the land's greatest names can become real as spring rain. I had never heard of House Falconer, but I sensed this place was very old and storied.

Which would make its lord mighty within its walls. I suspected him to be an adept, and possibly more.

Orson brought me to a small, comfortably furnished room with the air of a study. The door shut behind us, the hooded servant took up position in the corner. The castle lord turned to face me.

"You upstaged me," he said. The words held no heat, no petulance. The lord seemed, if anything, curious.

I turned my head to one side. "When I interrupted your speech to talk about the troll, you mean."

The Baron shrugged. "That, and your entrance. I daresay you were the focal point of that entire discussion. I do not criticize you . . ."

He trailed off and pursed his lips. "Are you a knight? Shall I call you *Ser* Alken?"

I hesitated, then shook my head. "No, lord. Just Alken will do."

The Baron's expression hardened. "You will tell me why you are here, and whether it is on another's behalf. You will speak truth."

Not a magical command. Just the certain authority bred into all members of the peerage. For all he seemed the aging scholar, this man was the son of warlords. He held the proper mien.

The fingers of my right hand flexed. The motion was hidden by my cloak, and I clenched that hand into a fist before I gave away my tension. He had not demanded I surrender my axe, which I still rested like a walking stick on the floor.

Perhaps he just didn't fear it, or me. Did he know how weak I was just then? Or was Orson Falconer a very dangerous man in his own right?

I swallowed through my dry throat, wishing I'd taken some of the drink on offer in the dining hall.

The Baron wasn't aware that outright lies weren't something I could easily conjure, not without cost. It wasn't like I could tell him that, however, so I had to try to convince him. I took a moment to gather my thoughts before speaking.

"I spent much of my life fighting for the realms of Urn," I said. "For lords, for the priests. I was loyal." I tightened one fist, as though it could quell my steadily rising heartbeat. It galled me to deceive him with scraps of my truth.

"I fought and fought, and it didn't earn me gratitude, or peace." The bitterness in my voice wasn't entirely feigned. "I risked my life countless times, until one day I was called to account for my failings, as they were."

I showed the lord my teeth. It wasn't a smile. "Eventually, I decided that if I couldn't live without sin, couldn't make the world better without it, why bother avoiding it? The realms wanted me to be a fighter. A killer. Let them reap what they've sown."

"Revenge, is it?" The Baron nodded, taking this in stride. "Yes, I can understand that. I can ally myself with that. You do understand, should you decide to join this affair, it will be under my leadership? I have enough conflicting motives out there."

He waved in the direction of the dinner hall. "If you are truly independent, truly in this for your own ends, I will have your agreement to obey me. I don't expect loyalty—that, I know, I must earn. But I will have obedience so long as you are a guest in my hall."

I inclined my head. "So long as I am a guest in your hall."

Inwardly, I felt amazed at how easily he'd accepted my shallow justifications for rebellion. Were all Recusants so vapid in their motives, in their petty vengeances? I'd thought my improvised speech flimsy at best, had expected him to challenge it.

Perhaps he sympathizes with it, I considered.

"This gathering is a delicate affair," the Baron said, smoothly moving on from the topic of my own motives. He paced to the far side of the room to stand in front of the hearth, which had also lit of its own volition upon our entry. My back tingled thanks to the presence of the servant. She remained by the door. Silent. Watchful.

"Not much of an army," I said. "I admit, I expected more when I heard of this gathering."

The Baron let out a snort. "Some war council of Recusants, you mean, like back during the Fall? No. Those armies are scattered, their captains dead, gone into hiding, or made little better than brigands. *This* is something more . . ."

He paused, thinking, then waved a hand. Green Hood glided forward to place a wine cup in it. He nodded his thanks to her. I noted a ring set on the thumb of his right hand. A signet, stamped with the image of a diving falcon. The servant offered me wine. I refused, and was offered water instead. That I took. If he wanted me dead, I imagined poison wouldn't be his method with all the deaths available to him in this place.

He didn't finish his thought. He sipped from the goblet, thought a moment longer, and then turned to me.

"I have no allusions that I may sweep aside the Accord and the Church in some glorious crusade. No. I am the backwater ruler of a small fiefdom."

His eyes narrowed with some subtle emotion. Again, I noticed their violet color. Many Houseborn have vibrant eye and hair colors, the product of old alchemy in their blood. The nearly red shade of the Baron's eyes stood out from his darker skin.

"I am ill prepared for open war," he said. "And it is hardly something I want in any case. I am rebelling against *them*, not my fellow man. Though, I will fight him too if necessary."

He waved a hand vaguely skyward and eastward and sipped wine before continuing. "I am connected. With elements of the highborn, yes, but also with factions within the occult world. I believe, with enough time and coordination, a sort of . . . resistance, I suppose you could call it, can be formed."

"A resistance against the gods?" I asked, not bothering to hide my skepticism.

Again, the Baron scoffed. "The Onsolain are not *gods*. Demigods, perhaps. They are powerful and ageless, yes, but not immortal. Not truly. That was proven during the Fall."

I hid my clenched fist under my cloak. What he said was blasphemous, heretical . . .

And true.

The Baron continued in a musing tone, unaware of my inner turmoil. "Even the Church only acknowledges one true God, and where is She? More than half a millennium gone, with no telling when or if She might return."

"It's prophesied that the Heir of Heaven will return," I said, trying to make my voice bland and not argumentative, as though I were just speaking from rote. "When She has reclaimed Her true kingdom."

A pale smile traced Orson's lips before he returned his focus to me. "I will make my plans without the assumption that God will appear in the flesh to cast me down. If that happens, then I suppose we were always fated to lose."

He pondered that for a moment, then shrugged. "But I digress. The Onsolain are the true threat, and while I question their inherent divinity, I do not doubt their power. Still, they tend to act through proxies and intermediaries, rarely displaying their power in truth. I imagine it will take much to draw them out as happened during the last war. I intend something more . . ."

He held up the fingers of his left hand and pinched them together. "Subtle. A network of allies, working in tandem to discredit the Church, diminish the magics and pacts with which the gods . . ." He let irony slip into that last word. "Have riddled the land. Believe me, this is just a seed from which something much larger might sprout."

I nodded slowly, while inside I roiled with indignation, and let him do all the talking. May as well get it all out before we got to the point. It just made my next decision easier.

"I intended to explain all of this to the rest of my guests," the Baron said. "I will, in time. They will have concerns. Questions. Demands." He chuckled darkly. "I'm not so deluded as to think they're doing this for the same reasons as I, or want what I want."

"What *do* you want?" I asked.

The Baron glanced at me, and then toward the fire. I almost didn't hear his reply, so quiet was it.

"A choice."

I didn't understand. In truth, I wasn't sure I wanted to. Orson Falconer was, in every way I could think of, the kind of madman my position had been created for. He consorted with fiends and Recusants. He allowed his allies to butcher and desecrate, and planned far worse. I suspected him to be responsible for the untimely death of Caelfall's former preoster, Olliard's departed friend and Edgar's mentor. He had openly admitted to planning rebellion against the divinity and all their works, a crusade that would likely drag our already-wounded land back into war.

I wasn't there to understand him. Just to kill him. I could do it right there in that room. He was unarmed and alone, besides the cloaked servant. It might be the best chance I got.

I would die. Already near my last legs, it took all my focus just to not show how fatigued and short on reserves I was. After I cut him down, I doubted I would escape the castle and all its horrors.

Even still . . . this was my duty.

I exhaled, long and slow, easing tension from my limbs. In my thoughts I concentrated on the words of an Oath, and felt the first thrum of power course through me. Orson, who'd been lingering by the room's window, shifted as though he'd been disturbed by something.

I would have to move quick. Quicker than whatever hid under that green shroud lurking by the door.

I almost did it. I almost lifted my axe and had this entire farce done right there. Even if I *did* survive, it would hurt me to do it, perhaps permanently— false pretenses or no, I was a guest in the lord's house, protected by the rights attached to that status and bound by his authority as the master of that hall. My powers had deep ties to those same rites.

If I killed him this way, it would be murder.

I had been given great power by the Alder Table. It came with costs and restrictions. Among those were this—the ancient laws that tied the powers of the land together, its traditions not least among them, were bound into my bones and blood.

Shirking those laws came with great risk. Even with the Bishop in Vinhithe, I had approached him openly and declared his doom. I had done it in a temple. It had been as official as I could make it.

And it had gone to shit. I could have killed the old man in his sleep, and been miles from the city with no one the wiser until dawn.

My role was to protect the sanctity of the land and its peoples, not my own. I wasn't convinced what was left of mine was even worth protecting.

In the moment before I convinced myself to go through with it, as my senses sharpened in anticipation of battle, I heard something that gave me pause. The sound of many tiny, scuttling insects in the deeper shadows along the room's edges.

I wasn't alone with just the Baron and his retainer. That thing from the dinner hall was there with us. Watching. Ready.

I knew what it was. I knew by the way my magic warned me, and even more so by the burning scars over my left eye. Hate and fear more intense than anything I could possibly feel toward Orson Falconer shot through me.

No wonder he'd let me keep my weapon and only brought one retainer. Orson had no fear of me. With that thing in the room, he may as well be at the top of a curtain wall.

Orson saw none of all that agonizing I went through in those moments. He finished his quiet contemplation by the window and turned, forcing me to refocus on him. The moment had passed.

"You have proved yourself wise in the ways of the Sidhe," the Baron said. The lord paced as he talked, violet eyes unfocused. "Further, you have shown restraint. With Karog, and in your council regarding the troll. I need that kind of thought in all of this. I already have muscle. The Mistwalkers are capable in the ways of violence, and that war ogre . . ."

He shook his head. "Well, suffice to say I have all the potential for bloodshed I need, at least on the scale I'm currently operating."

He whirled on me. "Are you a ranger?"

I was taken aback a moment. "I've learned from them, but no."

The Baron nodded. "That explains some of your knowledge, and the fae magic Karog sensed on you. I won't pry into your personal affairs, Alken, but I won't deny that I'm suspicious of you. You arrived out of nowhere, without announcing yourself, and have skills and motives that are of great value to me."

His lips curled up at the corners. "But I am not in much of a position to look a gift chimera in the mouth."

Realization struck me. "You don't trust the others." *Of course he doesn't. None of them trust one another. Why would they?*

The Baron's smile became more genuine and he inclined his head in a brief nod. "They are either working toward their own ends or representing other factions with goals only tangentially aligned with my own. Many of them see me as a safe bet. A petty mortal lord with some knowledge of the occult, who can act as a neutral intermediary. They have nothing to lose by indulging me, and much to gain by using me. My connections among the Houses are of special interest to many of them. My family is very old, very tied to the land."

"So where does that place me?" I asked. Idly, I observed that Orson had barely for a moment stopped pacing, while I'd remained planted and still throughout this interview.

"You have not proclaimed yourself representative of any other interest," the Baron said. "You claim to seek retribution against the Faith. And the powers behind it?"

I didn't reply. The Baron seemed to take that for confirmation and smiled. "That is what is arrayed against us, Alken. This is not just a petty rebellion against a mortal theocracy. The clericons and preosters of the Church are but one arm of the denizens of Heavensreach. They are deeply embedded into this land. The elder folk, the elves and all their cousin kindreds, are their vassals and students. They have blessed knights, rangers, armies of the zealous, and have wrapped this land so deep in enchantment it can be hard to tell dream from reality in some places."

He sounded so bitter, as though it were all some sort of hell. Our land had been beautiful before Recusants like him had set fire to it.

The Baron's smile fled, and his nearly red gaze became intent. "So I must ask—are you and I kindred spirits?"

A coldness crept into me. *Don't deny it*, I thought. *This is what you need.*

I wanted to deny it. Very badly. To growl that he was *nothing* like me.

"I'd like to call you mad," I said. I very much wanted to. "But I don't imagine I'd have taken an interest in anything less. You have my attention, Lord Baron."

Orson Falconer looked pleased. "The first step is securing my own land from Eld influence, be it Onsolain or the Sidhe. I've committed to this, now that the Mistwalkers have forced it."

He sighed and rubbed at his temple. "I intended something slower, more subtle, but I have waited long enough. You want to strike against our mutual enemy? I intend to send you at them, and sooner rather than later."

I schooled my features, not wanting to let him or his servant see the frustration I felt then. I wasn't there to fight against the Baron's enemies. The farther I was from him, the fewer chances I would gain to complete my true objective.

On the other hand, gaining his trust could get me more information, more opportunity. This was bigger than just one traitor hiding in a back country. Powerful forces, possibly greater than Orson Falconer himself, gathered in Caelfall.

Politics. I suppressed the scowl the thought nearly brought to my lips. I'd believed I was done with all of that. Even still, if the seeds of a new war were being planted here . . .

Stopping that was also my duty. Wasn't it?

I felt the sharp barbs of the axe's branch against my skin, almost like an admonishment. I ignored it. I could bide my time in this improvised cover, potentially do more damage to this league of traitors. Besides, I needed time to recover and complete my real mission.

Aloud I said, "What would you have of me, lord?"

The Baron studied me a moment, thinking. "I will consider. For now, however, I believe you've had a long journey and could use rest. Priska will see you to a room where you will be able to refresh yourself."

He didn't quite wrinkle his nose, but I got the message. I inclined my head. "I wouldn't mind a bath," I said. I also had the mysterious servant's name now.

"A bath, fresh clothes, and a clean bed." Orson Falconer quirked a smile. "The hospitality of my house is not what it once was, but I will not be called a poor host. You are my guest. You will be taken care of."

I tried not to read too deeply into that statement as I was led from the study.

Chapter Twenty

NIGHT VISITOR

Priska led me from the Baron's study. She kept her green shroud on, giving me no indication of what lay underneath.

Was she human? Something else? I couldn't tell, got no read on her like I had with the ghouls. She neglected to provide me any clues, other than the uncanny grace with which the hem of her cloak seemed to glide across the castle floors.

"You will be provided your own room," she told me after some time. "There will be materials to wash and clothe yourself. The garments you've brought will be cleaned."

"I haven't seen any other servants," I noted. "Who maintains this place?"

Fishing for information, but I *was* curious. The halls of the castle, while dimly lit and largely austere, were also clean and well maintained.

"There are servants," Priska said mysteriously. "They simply avoid being underfoot."

We passed by some Mistwalkers, all in worn gray uniforms and battered steel armor. Mostly they ignored me, probably because of Priska. I saw Quinn chatting with two of his comrades as we navigated the upper balcony of a grand foyer, who gave me a nod and a friendly smile.

Strange. The mercenaries didn't seem to be keeping guard or acting as the castle's standing garrison, just milling about. I still hadn't spotted any men-at-arms bearing the Falconer sigil.

It almost seemed like the castle had been empty before all these "guests" had arrived.

Priska led me to an upper hall, stopping in front of an innocuous door. She handed me a key, one long-fingered, almost impossibly pale hand emerging from the folds of her cloak. Ignoring its color, it was human, and feminine. I accepted the key.

"It will only work on this door," she told me. "I would suggest you lock it. The Baron holds the comfort and safety of his guests in high regard, but precautions must be taken nonetheless."

I nodded, remembering the hostile eyes in that dining room. Issachar in particular hadn't seemed stable, and all the soldiers in the castle were his men.

"Leave your clothes in the hall and they will be tended to before you wake," Priska added. "Most of the other guests keep odd hours, so there is no rush to rise with the sun. You may take your meals in the dining hall, or in your chamber."

Priska left then, leaving me to my own devices. I watched her until the whispering hem of her long green cloak had turned down a further hall and vanished. That left me accompanied only by the silence.

Living on the road for months at a time, it is easy to forget how divine simple pleasures can be.

Even as I was given new clothes, allowed to bathe and shave, I did not forget that I intended to kill the man who offered these indulgences. I took no satisfaction in the thought, no irony. It only made me feel dirty, ill at ease.

The Baron's a madman and a murderer, I reminded myself as I studied my reflection in the bedchamber's vanity. *He's trying to fashion himself into a nascent Dark Lord. This isn't the time for misplaced honor.*

As a distraction, I studied the mirror in my comfortable chambers. Like much in the castle, it was old, over-designed, and beautiful—a piece near tall as myself, worth a small fortune all on its own, its bronze border worked into the shapes of dozens of entwining serpents.

It had been a long time since I'd taken a good look at myself. I ran a hand along the freshly smoothed edges of my jaw, trying to remember the last time I'd made use of a razor. My own skin felt cool and unfamiliar.

I looked . . . not old, precisely. My skin was still smooth, my red-blond hair still untouched by any traces of frost. I looked ten years or more younger than I was, and would for decades yet—another of the Table's blessings.

No, it was something else that made me see age in that tired reflection. Myriad faint scars, a permanent furrowing in the center of my brow, a weary distance in my bright golden eyes.

I ran a hand along the scars crossing my left eye. They began just above the eyebrow, running down from my temple at a sharp angle in four thin, long grooves. The marks ended below my cheekbone, a single line of scar nearly touching the corner of my lip. They were not so faded as my other scars, still dimly touched by red as though on the verge of infection.

They hadn't stopped itching since I'd entered the castle. I knew why, and what Orson's pet truly was. I needed to deal with that, before it figured out what *I* was.

I tore my eyes from my own tired image as a knock rapped against the door. I finished lacing the shirt I'd been provided along with the room—a dark green tunic with roomy sleeves—and cautiously approached the door.

I listened, waiting for the telltale signs of heavy breathing, the creak of a great weight, or even a betraying stench. Anything to let me know if the ogre or something similarly dangerous lurked on the other side.

Nothing of the sort. I spoke through the door. "What is it?"

The answer came without pause. "It's me. Just wanted to check in on you."

I hesitated. Then, against my better judgment, opened the door.

Catrin stood on the other side. Like me, she'd changed into a finer set of clothes. The yellow commoner's dress and bodice had been replaced by a thin gown more than a century out of fashion, pale blue in color, with winglike sleeves and silver-green trim. Her unkempt mop of chestnut hair had been combed, proving it to be longer than I'd thought. It fell around her shoulders in a mane of red-brown curls.

She studied me a moment and made an appreciative sound. "Heh. You clean up well, big man."

I didn't quite hide the glance I threw to the hall, checking to see if she'd brought anyone else. Armed guards, or the like.

She didn't miss the suspicion. "Not here to put you under arrest." She quirked a misshapen smile very at odds with the courtier's dress. "Though, I think I could make the look work. Me in a breastplate, little cape maybe? Long boots."

"What do you want?" I asked.

I didn't truly mean to be rude, but my nerves were frayed. I was exhausted, my freshly wounded shoulder burned beneath my new shirt, and I didn't have much more conversation in me.

Catrin arched an eyebrow. Without another word, she ducked under my arm to move into the room. I tensed, but the movement was so fast and smooth I barely registered it before she went past me.

"They gave you a nicer room," Catrin noted studiously. She glanced at the mirror and let out a small laugh. "Classic."

I suppressed an annoyed growl as I turned.

Catrin spoke as she began turning the mirror around to face it toward the wall. Its weight made her next words strained. "Wanted to check in on you, big man, make sure you were still . . . alive."

She finished turning the mirror with a grunt of effort.

"What are you doing?" I asked.

"Making sure we're not being spied on," Catrin said, adjusting the sleeves of her dress. "Mirrors, you know? Baron's an occultist. So's that creepy old crone, Lillian."

A spike of cold shot through me. *Idiot. You should have thought of that.*

"Why are you here?" I asked.

Catrin's eyes flicked to the door. "You gonna leave that open? Walls have ears."

I glared at her. After a deliberate pause, I shut the door, then folded my arms and waited.

Catrin propped a fist on her hip, exactly as she had when she'd intervened with the Mistwalkers in Cael Village. "You're not actually here to throw in with the Baron's little gambling club, are you?"

I noted the position of my axe where I'd propped it against the bed. "I don't know what you mean."

Catrin rolled her eyes. "You're a bad liar, you know? I knew you were improvising back in the village when I gave the corpse eaters that spiel about you being a guest, and you've looked ready to take that cutter to every shadow since we got on the boat."

She nodded to the axe. "I'm not blind." Her eyes narrowed. "You're no Recusant."

I went very still. "You figured that out from how tense I am, did you?"

She shook her head, disturbing her lazily combed hair so it fell over one eye. "Nah. You practically told me, remember? When I suggested you were one back on the lake, you got *real* angry. You were put out when I suggested the old elf king wasn't all that, either. A Recusant would have agreed with me, with *fervor.*"

My heart sank. Had I really been that transparent?

I considered killing her. I felt disgusted with the part of me that considered it so readily. I waited and kept silent. If she wanted me to admit anything, I'd keep her in suspense.

Catrin saw my stonewalling and rolled her eyes. "I'm not tricking you. Not this time, and I didn't help you get here for Orson Falconer's sake."

"Then why?" I asked. "Is this where you blackmail me?"

"Something like that," she said, surprising me with her honesty. "But it doesn't *have* to be that way."

I grunted, considered a moment, then decided there wasn't any reason not to hear this out. "What do you suggest?"

She studied me a moment, as though trying to reach a decision. Then in a more quiet voice she said, "I work for the Keeper of the Backroad Inn. You know who that is?"

I did not, though again the names sounded familiar. Catrin took my silence in stride and moved to the room's small window, pressing her ear against the foggy glass as she continued.

"Not everyone who lives outside the grace of the God-Queen wants to wage war on the Church. It's not like we're *fond* of them—they can be right cunts more than half the time. But the land's still recovering from the Fall. Who knows how many people will die if Orson plays this out? Even in a best-case scenario, he brings more attention down on all of us. *No one* wants another inquisition."

I quietly shuddered at that name, and couldn't disagree.

Catrin turned from the window to face me, her expression losing some of its wry mask. "You work for the Church? Or, any of its factions? I know the clergy aren't really centralized, but I could figure you as some agent for the Abbey, or maybe even the Priory."

I canted my head to one side, considering. "Would you believe me if I said no?"

"Depends," Catrin said, serious. "Answer the question."

I unfolded my arms, hesitated a moment longer, and decided to play along. "No, I don't."

Catrin let out a sigh of relief. "Good. I believe you. Second question."

And here she met my eyes again, and there was something harsher in that look, something with teeth. "Did you kill the Bishop in Vinhithe?"

I froze, even my breath stopping for a moment.

Catrin moved away from the window, back toward the turned mirror. She never took her eyes off me, and there was something catlike in her movements. Cautious. Taut. Ready to spring into action.

"Part of my job's to gather information," she said. "I'm good at it. Heard a rumor that a man with an axe killed the priest who instigated the Llynspring Inquisitions. A man in a red cloak."

Her eyes drifted to the faerie-forged axe propped against the bedpost, and then to the red cloak hung by the door. That, I hadn't tossed out for the servants to clean.

"So it *is* blackmail, then," I said. "I do what you want, or you go to the Baron."

Catrin snorted. "You *are* paranoid, aren't you? Listen, big man, I'm not here to start trouble with you." She held up a placating hand. "I'm here to help. I brought you to the castle to keep the Mistwalkers from throwing your pieces into the marsh, and I'm telling you this now so you know how deep the shit you're in is."

She said all of this without her previous air of flirty nonchalance, her demeanor very businesslike.

"I'm good at collecting secrets," she repeated. "But this news about the Bishop's death?" She shrugged. "It's going to spread here before long. The Baron could learn it from his own sources, or the villagers will hear it next time the clericons come to collect their tithes. Either way, you're working on dying time, you understand?"

With a sinking feeling, I realized she was right. I'd made a spectacle of myself in Vinhithe, and—while it was no great city—it was an important enough hub in the region that word would spread of the red-cloaked man who'd murdered a high clericon and cut his way out of the streets.

I'd hoped they would assume me dead after I'd fallen in the river, but I wouldn't trust to convenience there.

"Why'd you do it?" Catrin asked, more curious than accusing. "Kill the Bishop, I mean. Who are you?"

It was a moment before I drew myself back to the situation at hand. "You wouldn't believe me if I told you."

"Oh, I can believe a lot." The woman—the spy, or whatever she was— flashed her crooked teeth in a sharp smile. It faded near as quick as it had appeared and she added, "Your secrets are yours, but my point is this—we can help each other."

I leaned against the wall by the door, using the motion to bring myself another foot closer to my weapon in case I needed to lunge for it. I folded my arms as I spoke. "I still don't really know *who* you are, or what you want. How do you know I didn't kill the priest on Lord Orson's behalf?"

Again, Catrin shrugged. "Could be you did. Would be a smart play for him, drawing attention away from his own lands to create a crisis in a larger city. But I don't think that's the case, otherwise he'd have been expecting you and I wouldn't have had to pull you out of a pit."

"Point," I said. Who exactly *was* this woman, who knew so much and saw to the truth of things so easily? "But that only answers one question. Who are you? Who is this . . . Keeper?"

I'd never heard of a place called the Backroad Inn.

"A man whose business it is to know things," Catrin said.

"An information broker," I said, realizing.

Catrin nodded. "Hit it on the head. He specializes in dangerous clientele, and dangerous secrets." She placed her left hand against one breast, a note of pride entering her voice. "I help him get those, and got more than a few of my own too."

"And you're not here to sell them to Orson Falconer?" I asked, scratching at my freshly shaved chin with a thumb.

"There are old powers in the land, boyo." Catrin's smirk had a dark edge. "Older than the Accord, older than the Church even, and certainly older than the likes of Orson Falconer. Not all of them are happy about the attention this petty aristo could bring down on them. Killing that bridge troll was a poor move. That's another thing that caught my attention."

She took a step forward, lowering her voice. "It made you angry, what they did." Her eyes lit with a flash of fierce approval. "Trolls are old magic. Sacred, and I don't mean that like a priest would, trying to sell the word *holy* like it's an old piece of hacksilver."

She took another step closer. Dangerously close, almost blocking me from my weapon. I tensed, but she caught my eyes in hers and suddenly I felt . . .

At ease.

It's difficult to explain what happened. All my tension, my fear, my uncertainty, it all faded away like morning fog. I felt relaxed. Safe.

And more than a bit enraptured. Catrin had large, expressive eyes, and I noted for the first time they were mismatched—it was subtle, but one eye was just a slightly darker brown than the other. It was distracting. Even interesting.

She had thick eyebrows for a woman, but it didn't make her look masculine. Just expressive, intense. Her furtive motions and quick, almost breathless voice kept my interest, though I hadn't wanted to admit it.

"I'm your friend," she said, lowering her voice. It wasn't quite seductive—her voice wasn't smooth or liquid enough for that, but there *was* a comforting quality to it. She sounded kind, quick of wit, confident.

"Leonis Chancer killed people I knew back in the west. I'm *glad* someone finally called him to account. Anyone who's willing to anger the preosts to make the world right again is someone I'd like to know better."

She reached out a hand. The motion was slow, hesitant. It made me want to take her hand and let her know it was all right, that I didn't mind. She brushed long fingers over the material of my shirt, so lightly I only felt it as a rustle of cloth against my skin.

It had been a long time since anyone had touched me. Wanted me. My reaction was . . . not controlled. I inhaled sharply, closing my eyes. Catrin noted this and let out a breathy little laugh.

Not a pretty sound, but an honest one, endearing. I found myself wanting to hear more of it.

"Why are you here?" Catrin murmured. "It's all right. You can tell me."

I opened my eyes, and once again they were caught in her gaze. Catrin had stepped closer. She was much shorter than me, and had to look up to meet my eyes.

"I'm here for the Baron," I said, my voice near as quiet as hers. "Because he killed the troll, and because . . ."

Here I hesitated, some remnant of caution tying my tongue. "He's dangerous. He needs to be stopped."

"You're some kind of vigilante, are you?" Catrin's asymmetrical smile returned. She still barely touched me. Teasing. "It fits. I like it."

I shook my head slowly. My thoughts were coming slower than usual, like thick molasses filled my skull. "It's a curse. I don't want to be here, don't want to . . ."

"Don't want to what?" she asked, eyes narrowing. Her words were so quiet I found myself leaning down to hear them better, bringing our faces closer.

"I'm not here by choice," I finished lamely. I wanted to tell her, to tell *someone* about my burden, my penance of blood.

And why not tell someone? There was no vow against it, no oath I'd sworn to keep the truth of my duty a secret. I'd only done so out of necessity.

Out of shame.

"Pretty eyes," Catrin almost whispered, her cool breath tickling my nose. Her subtly mismatched eyes seemed to swirl like liquid, dark and inviting, warm pools to sink into. "Such an unusual color. Almost shiny, like gold coins."

They hadn't always been that color. I wanted to tell her that, too.

"It's all right," Catrin said. "It won't leave this room, I promise. You can tell me. You can *trust* me, Alken."

Our lips were nearly brushing now. Again she flashed that thin smile, and my eyes were drawn to her teeth. Strangely pale, with very sharp canines.

Her words cut through the fog in my thoughts. She was not the first to say them to me.

The scars on my face were burning.

With an effort of will, I shut my eyes tightly to block out the sight of hers and focused inward. It was only then I realized how loudly my senses were warning me of danger. The core of golden power in me practically blazed in alarm.

I inhaled through my nose, breathing in Catrin's clean scent—a subtle perfume, clean linen, woodsmoke . . . and something else beneath it all. Something sharp, alarming, copper scented.

Blood.

I opened my eyes, and pale golden aura shone through them. The shadows in the room crumbled away, every line of furniture and wall sharpening. Catrin winced, her eyes caught by the sudden gleam that shone from my irises.

And I *saw* her. Not as she'd been, this attractive young woman with her crooked smile and mussed hair, but as she truly was.

She was a pallid thing, like a corpse, her skin hugging her bones. Her mismatched eyes clarified into bloody spheres. Her teeth were all pointed and dipped in red, and pointed were her ears where they protruded from hair that had gone dun, losing its warm luster. Dark veins crawled across her flesh, poisonous, webbed. Her neck was too long and her mouth too wide.

Without thought, without hesitation, words snapped from my lips. Not a prayer, but similar—an invocation of repulsion against the Adversary. The creature in front of me was not a demon—not truly—but it wasn't many steps removed.

A flash of nearly white light burst in the room, and Catrin let out a shout of surprise. She recoiled faster than I could follow, retreating to the window on the far side of the room in the time it took me to blink. Her masque was gone now in truth, not just in my auratic sight, revealing the thin, macabre thing only superficially like a woman, the folds of her blue-green dress hanging from sharp bones and thin skin.

I lunged for my axe and had it between us by the time she recovered. The creature's pointed features shot up, recovering from the backhand of power I'd hit it with. It let out a loud, serpentine hiss through wolf-sharp teeth.

"Stay out of my head," I growled, lifting my axe and letting amber flame play along its edges as I channeled aura through it. "Vampire."

CHAPTER TWENTY-ONE

THE DHAMPIR

Catrin stared at me, bloody eyes wide with shock. She lifted the fingers of her left hand, the ones she'd touched me with, and studied them. They were blackened and blistered, trailing smoke.

Her true form was very different from the "girl next door" look she'd had before. Her hair looked closer to ash than chestnut, her skin corpse pale, her eyes deep vermillion in the room's dim light. Even the sclera had darkened to red, giving her a manic, starved look. The pointed ears and narrow features made her look like a gothic artist's paranoid depiction of an elf.

Her fangs had been so close to my neck. I breathed to calm my racing heart, aware of how close I'd just been to disaster.

Fool, I berated myself. *You let your guard down in the enemy's own house. Fatigue is no excuse.*

I expected her to attack, tensed for it. I knew she could move faster than the human eye could track, perhaps even do nastier things like assume a bestial form or become a devouring mist. There was no room for mistakes or hesitation.

She didn't do any of those things. Instead, Catrin clutched her burnt hand to her chest, wincing as a look of pure indignation crossed her transformed face.

"The fuck was that?" she asked, distress coloring her voice. "Are you some kind of fucking priest? That *hurt.*"

The pain and disbelief in her ghoulish features were genuine enough to give me pause, despite my better sense. I frowned, watching her. *Another trick? Trying to get me to let down my guard?*

"Bastard!" Catrin scowled at me. "And I'm not a vampire, fucker. Rip your arms off if I was. *Ow.*"

She shook the injured hand, wincing.

What is this? I stepped to one side, giving myself space from the bed so I could move more freely. "I've faced your kind before," I growled. "You were about to go for my neck."

Catrin's pallid features shifted into something almost petulant. "I mean, sure. I might have gone in for a sip, but I wouldn't have hurt you. Not much, anyway. I already fed tonight."

"You were in my head," I snarled. I could still hear her voice in my thoughts, drifting there like a stain of oil through water.

The rage, and the fear, struck fast and venomous as a viper. I took a step forward as amber fire boiled along the axe, smoldering within the already-scarred wood of the handle. The vampire flinched away.

"It was just a trance," Catrin corrected hastily. "Not so different from being drunk, really. I wasn't reading your thoughts or anything. And you were being so *vague,* dodging all my questions or giving me half answers."

She patted down her dress and sat against the window, folding her arms as she took a calming breath. "I got impatient, you know? I shouldn't have gone in for the whole *dark seductress* act so hard. I'm sorry, all right? So can you put the axe down?"

The axe remained between us, dimly burning as I glowered at her. She caught my gaze and winced again, unable to hold it while I used my powers. Now it saw the truth of her, the light in my eyes was not gentle.

"I should kill you," I said. "You'll go right to the Baron."

"I won't," Catrin insisted. She stood then. When I tensed, she lifted both of her hands in a gesture of surrender. Her vampiric form was starting to fade away, I noted, her hair darkening to its normal chestnut hue, her skin taking on a healthier pallor.

"Listen, big man, everything I said to you was true. Besides, from where I'm standing you're pretty short on friends. You want to make it out of this alive?"

She studied me a long moment, one eyebrow lifted. She finished when I kept my silence. "It's only a matter of days before his lordship hears about what happened in Vinhithe and takes the half step of logic he needs to figure out you're the same man who killed Red Leonis. If you're really here to bring him down, then I *can* help you . . . but you're going to need to put the cutter down and *talk* to me."

"I can't trust a word out of your mouth." I took another step toward the door. I wouldn't let her retreat to rouse the castle. She was near the window. I didn't think using a cant to stop her would be very effective.

The magic she used to lower my guard was stronger than any command I could muster, and far more subtle. Aura has many uses, even when not shaped into a distinct phantasm by Art, and using it to influence another's will is among the most common.

I could do it, to compel truth, stop aggression, and pull others from more hostile trances. My method wasn't subtle—more like taking a hammer to brittle stone. I suspected this creature had a far more insidious method.

Vampires are proto-fiends—not quite demons, but most of halfway there. Damned souls fashioned in the world rather than in the boiling darkness of the Abyss, hungering for blood, undead, vicious. They came in many varieties, and I'd faced my share of the creatures. I had learned to hate them.

They were repelled by sanctified aura same as demons too, which was a fine thing to me. My magic had been cultivated through long, dark centuries by knights of old to fight such creatures. I showed the intruder that power.

"You chose the wrong man to try to make your thrall," I growled. "I'll send you back into the Dark."

Catrin rolled her red eyes. "All right, I'm certain of it now. You're some kind of knight, aren't you? Warrior priest, maybe? Had my suspicions about it. Should I call you *milord*?"

She dipped into a mocking curtsy, and in the same motion stepped back into the shadows. And *vanished*, sinking into the wall itself.

I waited, expecting her to emerge from another shadow and go for my throat.

"If I wanted you dead," Catrin said from right behind me, "I could make it happen."

I spun, swinging my axe with a single hand. It trailed a golden blur as it went. I cut nothing but air.

My vision went dizzy. Still too injured, too low on blood. The aureflame helped heal injuries faster than natural, but not instantly. It would be days before I fully recovered.

"*You're hurt,*" the hemophage's disembodied voice said from everywhere and nowhere, drifting out of the shadows in a strange echo. "*I'm not some dread badass, big man, but I think I could take you right now. The fact I'm not should tell you something.*"

"It only tells me you want something other than my death," I shot back, searching the darkness. The aura in my eyes illuminated patches of it as they drifted across the room's corners, but I found no sign of her. How did this trick work?

"*Of course I don't want your death!*" the voice snapped back, annoyed. "*I want an ally. I'm just as isolated in all this as you, and in just as much danger.*"

A long pause. Then, "*You ready to talk?*"

Frustrated, my hand clenched tightly around the oaken branch of my weapon. "If you mean to get into my head again, it won't be so easy. I know you can probably do it through conversation, but not now that I'm wise to it."

I wasn't so sure. With my energies diminished and my mind foggy with blood loss, I might not be able to push her out if she made a real effort again.

Catrin's voice drifted from the shadows. *"I won't try that again, trust me. Didn't realize you were hallowed."*

There was a thoughtful pause before she continued. *"My employer wants to see Orson Falconer's faction undone before it's properly formed. And I . . ."*

Here she hesitated, her disembodied voice fading into a weighty hush.

"I want revenge."

"Revenge?" I asked.

"Preoster Micah was a good man," Catrin said. *"A kind man. One of the few priests I've ever met who wasn't a right cunt. It was the Baron who gave the order to have him killed."*

"How do you know this?" I asked, turning a slow circle to try to pinpoint the source of the fell presence she exuded.

"He told me," she said.

I paused, taken back. I almost sensed a sad smile from the unseen vampire. I could feel her presence filling the shadows, one with them. Was that why I couldn't find her even with aura? Had she gone somewhere *beyond* this room?

If so, her power was far more potent than a mere glamour.

"I spoke to his ghost a few weeks back," she continued. *"That witch, Lillian, kept his soul from departing. I guess the Baron was worried his plans might get out that way."*

Very possible. Orson meant to challenge the ancient spirits who governed the land's natural order. Even in death, it could be difficult to keep secrets from such powers.

Catrin waited for me to absorb all of that before speaking again. *"And that's all I know. Really. I was sent to observe and report, nothing more, but I can't leave things as they are. I owe Falconer a bit of payback, and you're the only one here who I think might be willing and able to help me. So will you put the damn axe down already?"*

I bared my teeth, jaw clenching, fighting to keep hold of the anger in me. Anger at having my thoughts and will tampered with, mostly. I couldn't trust her, not if she could affect my mind.

And yet, I sensed no deceit in her words. I didn't use powers for it, just my own intuition. And *if* she told the truth . . .

The Baron himself had said it. There was no room to look a gift chimera in the mouth. But working with a Thing of Darkness . . . the idea made my stomach churn.

"You tried to make me your thrall," I said to the shadows. "Whatever your reasons, that's a damned sour way to start an alliance."

Another pause. *"You're right. It's just . . ."*

I heard the rustling of cloth at my back and turned. Catrin stood there, fully human again. She took a long, shuddering breath. "I'm not going to pretend like I don't make impulsive decisions sometimes."

"You're a blood drinker," I said darkly. "You're driven by impulse."

Anger hardened the malleable edges of Catrin's face. "I'm a dhampir, you cockwart. I was born this way. Now do you want my help or not?"

That gave me pause. *Dhampir.* A type of changeling. That *was* a difference from what I'd assumed.

Changeling is a catch-all term for any variety of creature with nonspecific origin. They might be a Sidhe switched out with a human child in the cradle, or a half-breed born of mixed ancestry. Sometimes a darker entity could corrupt a seed in the womb, giving birth to something terrible, a parasite with unknowing human parents who became little more than haunted victims to the demon babe.

That last tended to have a different name. If Catrin was that, it might explain the itch in my scars. Or it might just be this accursed place. I hated this, not being able to trust anything around me, or anyone.

Regardless of the kind, changelings are often preternaturally strong, driven by unnatural hungers, and difficult to destroy. Their most dangerous ability, however, is their predilection for creating a masque—a nearly perfect human disguise. They tend to learn the trick in infancy in order to survive and get better at it as they age.

And they are not all wholly evil. Not always, anyway. Unlike true vampires, who are little more than hateful souls bound inside a corpse, changelings are misbegotten children tossed into the world.

There'd been one in the woods near the village I'd grown up in. Old, mad, and harmless as a leaf.

Catrin was *not* harmless. Even if everything she said was true, she'd still tried to subdue my will with her own. She'd tried to taste my blood.

When I still hesitated, she let out a contemptuous scoff and turned back toward the shadows.

I gritted my teeth. "Wait."

She stopped and half-turned to glare at me.

"Do you have some kind of plan?"

The smile that touched the corners of Catrin's lips was sharp as razors, revealing teeth sharper still. "Maybe. If you're still alive by sundown tomorrow, we'll talk again. Keep your head until then, big man."

Then, before I could stop her, she walked into the wall and vanished into a patch of darkness. I took a step forward, lifting a hand as though to grab her shoulder, but it was too late.

"Shit," I said aloud. My eyes went to my axe, which still dimly burned with amber flames. I quenched the flow of power and let them fade, then set it down against the wall by the bed. I sat myself. I took a few minutes to calm myself and think, twisting the ring on my right forefinger in idle habit.

Had I just made a devil's bargain? Because Catrin was certainly a *kind* of devil, and very dangerous.

I would have to keep my guard up, and hope I hadn't just been duped.

You're in a house of devils, I told myself. *Maybe this is the least of all available evils.*

I was far from certain. Sometimes the most insidious evils can seem fair to the eyes.

I waited for a long while, suspicious she might be lurking in the room's shadows still, waiting for me to let down my guard. As I stood there, my breath came shorter and shorter. My shoulder burned with agony, and I felt hot.

A fever. Had those chimera had venomed talons?

I had some resistance to poisons, and little fear of disease, but I'd been injured many times recently in quick succession. Enough for a lethal toxin to do me in?

The room swam around me. I took a step toward the bed, stumbled, and caught myself on the post. My skin ran with sweat. It dripped onto the floor beneath me. I focused on those tiny droplets, trying to use them to center myself.

I lost time. Lost thought. All I could think was that I shouldn't rest, couldn't afford to, that I was in danger . . .

I had a dim memory of throwing a blanket over the mirror, and curtaining the windows. I latched the door, managed to drag a chair over to use as an extra barrier. It all went in a blur, one action swimming into the other, the time between each scene gone.

I think I vomited. I had little in my stomach, so it mostly came as spittle and dry heaves.

I fought against the encroaching darkness.

There are some wars that can't be won, no matter how hard you struggle.

The dark took me.

CHAPTER TWENTY-TWO

DARK COMPANY

I woke on the bed. Consciousness came slow, my thoughts foggy and disconnected. When awareness did come crashing fully in, it wasn't unlike a splash of ice water.

I shot awake, rolled off the bed, and had my axe in hand in the same motion. No memory of where it had been before, either propped against the bed frame or perhaps even already under my hand, like some macabre lover.

Silence. The castle loomed around me, huge and cavernous, its presence felt even in that enclosed space. Cold sweat clung to my skin, and my throat was very dry. I'd been down awhile.

Not dead. Not yet. I stood slowly, winced, and felt at the wounds on my shoulder. If those assassin chimera had carried some venom, the aureflame had burned it off in my sleep. I got my bearings, throwing the curtains wide on the window. A crisp glow touched the opaque glass. I opened it, letting fresh air in.

An overcast day again. I guessed it to be late morning. Still too cool for the season, but the clean gust I let in invigorated me, helped clear my head.

Once I'd gotten my heartbeat down, I spent an hour whittling my axe's handle down to a more manageable size. That helped settle my nerves, as it often did. Damn thing was always growing, even when I didn't feed it blood for more dramatic transformations. Just as much of a hemophage as the woman who'd barged into my room in the middle of the night.

Catrin's offer floated through my thoughts as I ran a dagger over the oaken branch. I considered my situation too, and what I should do next.

Orson Falconer needed to die. Little doubt about that. But this situation was far more complicated than Eanor had led me to believe. There were secret powers at work here, factions that could threaten the Accord with or without this marsh baron bringing them together.

I was in a position to do something about it. More than that, I needed time to recover from my injuries and wait for a chance at Orson's life. That meant understanding the nature of the creature he'd bound, the dark spirit that scuttled through the castle's shadows like insects. I suspected I knew what it was, but I needed more information.

I checked my ring. Almost fully red now. Either the spirit, or some other inhabitant of the castle, had tried to get into my dreams. I clicked my tongue and ran a thumb over the ivory band.

Biding my time, then. Not something I enjoyed, but I could be patient.

I heard a knock at the door. Thinking it might be Catrin again, I moved the chair I'd propped against the latch and opened it.

No one waited outside, but the clothes I'd pilfered from the chapel were lying in a neat bundle on the floor. I took them, shut the door, and changed. The clothes left in the chamber were finer, but I preferred the rougher, more inconspicuous garments Brother Edgar had lent me.

So clad, I threw on my red cloak and left my room. Navigating the castle halls—I'd memorized the route Priska had taken so I could find my way around without help—I made my way back to the dining hall.

I saw no guards. No Mistwalkers, or otherwise. The castle, touched by muted daylight filtering in here and there through slim windows cut into the stone, seemed very different from the night before. Less dark, less threatening. I felt no profane presence, which had seemed so omnipresent before.

Still, I didn't let my guard down.

I found my way back to the dining hall, entered, and found food set out. No one else occupied the room. I sat, ate, then continued to sit for about an hour.

It's getting late, I thought. Most of the morning had passed already. *They can't all be nocturnal, can they?*

Considering how late the meeting had been held the previous night, they very well all may.

I was just about to leave when the doors opened. I turned, and saw the young man with the shaggy blond hair and the hunter's greens enter. I'd never gotten his name.

He didn't look like he'd slept any better than me. He gave me a cursory nod, sat, sniffed at the lavish meal set out, then tucked in without a word. He ate with gusto, not coming up for air until his plate had been cleaned. After the man had wiped his mouth and realized I hadn't left, he raised an eyebrow.

"Creepy place, eh?" He leaned back in his seat, his brown eyes drifting across the hall.

I couldn't disagree.

"William," the man introduced himself. He wasn't wearing his tricorn, and had less of an air of performance about him now.

Dropping the act now we're not surrounded by the others, I thought. "Alken," I returned his greeting.

"Tense stuff last night," he noted, tossing an apple from hand to hand. "I thought that sellsword was going to try and open you."

I grunted, leaning back in my chair. "I figured it would be the ogre."

William nodded slowly, pursing his lips. "Karog's a scary one, and no doubt. I hear he and Issachar fought together in the west. They're both veterans."

Experts on war. More evidence that Orson's plans weren't exactly of the gentle kind.

"And you?" I asked, keeping my tone conversational. "What do you bring to this table?"

William's lip twitched into a smirk, and he bit into the apple without answering. Fair enough.

The doors opened again, cutting our conversation short. The shadowy form of Priska glided in, eerie and silent, with the ghoul soldier Quinn trailing her.

"I trust everything is to your liking?" the servant asked in her oddly buzzing voice.

I murmured an affirmative while William just shrugged. Priska went straight to business.

"My lord has judged it prudent to grant you both opportunities to serve this council."

William frowned. "Doesn't waste time, does he? Fair enough, this castle air was getting stale. What's the task?"

"You are both needed in the village. Quinn will take you across the lake, after which you will meet his vice-captain at the inn. You will be provided details there, and follow his lead."

William accepted this easily, while I quietly felt trepidation nestle into my gut. *Vaughn again.*

Trouble, but it was too early to start butting heads with the Baron. If he wanted me to prove myself, then that just meant an earlier opportunity to earn his confidence. The more he let down his guard, the more chances I had to understand all the elements at play here.

And take his head, I reminded myself as I stood with my meal half eaten. I couldn't forget my true mission.

Perhaps I could take a few of these others as well. Besides, Catrin was supposed to meet me that evening. I was curious what she intended, and could use a firmer plan of action than what I'd come up with.

We passed a man I didn't recognize as we left the dining hall. An old man, dressed in a fur-lined robe that might have been fine in his grandfather's day.

He walked with a cane, and his face was pale with nerves. Priska greeted him with a bow, ushering him to a seat at the now-empty table.

"The village headman," Quinn told us after we'd entered the hall. "He's been here a handful of times since the preacher died."

He glanced back at me with a knowing smile. "Doesn't like my lot being about. Been trying to get the Baron to clear us off."

Putting no heat in my words I suggested, "Perhaps he'll succeed?"

Quinn only laughed.

The trip across the lake proved both tense and boring. Quinn rowed the small craft while William and I sat with our own private thoughts. The young hunter had dressed in his woodsman's outfit and tricorn again, while Quinn had donned a short cape of gray wool to protect his armor from the damp air. I had whittled my axe down enough to wear it on my belt again, hiding it under my cloak. I kept my pointed cowl up as our boat floated through the mist perpetually clinging to the surface of the lake even in daytime.

When we'd gone about halfway across, I felt a . . . shudder. That's all I could describe it as. Perhaps some instinctive dread any human would feel, or perhaps some warning from the aureflame. Even still, I stiffened and stared down into the dark waters.

Something was below us. It moved through the lake, circling, following our little craft.

Quinn noticed my sudden attention and grinned. "Ah, noticed it, did you?"

"What is it?" I asked, my eyes fixed on the water.

"Orson's family are chimera breeders," William said quietly. He also cast a nervous eye out over the lake. "They've been doing it for centuries. He's started incorporating western alchemy. I think that's part of what Lillian is helping him with."

"Breeding monsters," I said, trying to settle despite knowing something dangerous swam within the murky depths just below me.

"Think about it this way," Quinn suggested, looking undisturbed. "At least it's on *our* side."

If only he knew the irony of that statement.

The village was much transformed in the day. People lingered outside, tending to their small gardens, fishing the foggy waters, repairing rotten boards on roofs or the walkways they'd built over the marsh. They spoke little, even to one another, and avoided looking at us.

I felt their fear. I felt it in myself as well, even knowing some of their tension was directed *at* me.

If they knew I was here to help them, would they be grateful? I remembered the old man in that window in Vinhithe who'd called the guards on me.

Better not to fantasize. I wasn't here as the knight-errant.

Those villagers who lingered in the streets cleared off as Quinn, William, and I made our way to the inn. Conversation stopped as we passed. The smell of rot and fish hung heavy in the air. Gorcrows lingered on rooftops and ivy-choked fountains, or circled overhead, as though waiting for the town to finally breathe its last breath.

Quinn, for his part, seemed to enjoy the atmosphere. He nodded and called out greetings to the locals in a jovial tone like he were some well-liked constable. The villagers did little more than murmur back without meeting his pale blue eyes. I caught him chuckling at their nervousness.

William kept professional, refraining from toying with those scared people, which I appreciated.

The inn, like much of the village, showed signs that this hadn't always been such a poor and decrepit place. Two stories, sturdy, with decorative copper around the doorframe and a handsome sign, though faded, which read *The Cymrian Sword*.

We entered a large common room made cavernous by its near total lack of customers. Small, circular tables dominated much of the space, and an unlit hearth formed the centerpiece to a brickstone chimney on one wall. A distant-eyed girl in her mid-teens listlessly swept with a broom near one wall. When she saw us, her devotion to the task became more determined.

I gave her the same courtesy and ignored her, instead fixing my attention on a man in his middle years behind the bar, heavyset and almost fully bald, a heavy beard grown to compensate. He ignored us as well, occupying himself by cleaning glasses. I could almost feel his tension from across the room.

There were a few patrons, most of them gathered around one table near the bar. None looked like locals, and all were dressed innocuously, like traveling peddlers or vagabond sellswords, with dun cloth draped in layers to hide any more vicious gear they might carry.

I saw Vaughn, huge and still clad in his battered armor, sitting with the larger group. Quinn led me and William to that table. I could feel eyes on me as I moved, every click of my boots echoing within the common room with uncomfortable volume.

I didn't want to make an impression, but that can be hard when you're a finger over six-and-a-half feet tall and scarred as heavily as I am. I'd grown my hair long and left it unkempt to hide the glint of aura in my eyes, but it only went so far. I avoided meeting anyone's gaze.

Quinn indicated some empty chairs at the corner table where Vaughn and some of the travelers sat. William and I took our seats. Quinn slipped into one not far from his vice-captain.

They were playing cards, and betting. A pile of coins lay in the center of the table, mostly hacksilver and bronze. No gold. Gold is sacred, and rarely used as currency outside of the clergy.

Vaughn gave me a neutral look, shrugged, and nodded to the table. "Deal them in."

"I was told you had work for us," I said, having no desire to play.

Vaughn's jaw clenched. "You'll play. Deal him in."

I glowered at him, frustrated, but didn't push back. Instead I turned my attention to the game. They were playing *Phalanx*, a common enough pastime for gamblers across the subcontinent.

I had once enjoyed such games well enough back during my days as a soldier. After I'd sworn my oaths to the Table, I had enjoyed them less. Lying is difficult for me, sometimes even painful, and such games require deception.

We played awhile with little conversation. I took the time to study the others. A tall, handsome man with the look of a merchant sat by Vaughn, wearing a rich outfit woven all in shades of charcoal gray, even the lumpy hat. Gray, too, were his eyes, and there were streaks of it in his brown hair and trimmed beard, though he didn't look older than thirty-five otherwise.

The other three men at the table were a rougher sort, vagabonds like myself in rough cloth, with unkempt hair and scraggly beards, their gear stained by hard roads. I took them to be sellswords, perhaps even hired killers of a more dubious sort.

We played several rounds. I spoke little, and mostly ended up folding. This pleased Quinn, because he had luck and enjoyed attention, and annoyed Vaughn. The vice-captain kept throwing angry looks at the table and muttering darkly.

The gray merchant ended up winning the pile. He was patient, personable, and in the end very ruthless. He chuckled on the last hand, earning scowls and bitter curses from most of the others.

"I'm going to stop playing with you, Carlisle." Vaughn drummed his heavy fingers against the table, still trying to figure out why he'd fallen for the merchant's bluff.

Carlisle leaned back, stroking his gray-streaked goatee in quiet satisfaction. "You always say that, old friend, and then you always invite me for another round. But you still haven't introduced me to this pair?"

His flinty eyes went to me and William, lingering on me.

"They're part of the Baron's little club," Vaughn grunted. "Apparently, I'm to break them in."

"They're not joining the Company!" Quinn laughed. "His lordship just wants to see how they handle themselves."

The innkeeper's daughter brought us drinks, quiet as a mouse and trying not to be noticed. She failed, and Quinn wrapped an arm around her when she tried to leave. She went very still, her face blanching, but the mercenary seemed not to notice as he grinned at the vice-captain.

"I see," Carlisle muttered, still running his hands through his long beard. "And when shall I be invited to one of these council meetings?"

"We've been here nine days," one of the vagabonds snarled. "You'll get your turn after us, peddler."

The merchant rolled his eyes to the man who'd spoken, the motion lazy as a well-fed cat's.

"And when did this one arrive?" Another of the thugs put in, gesturing to me with a thumb. "I don't recall him waiting in this dump with the rest of us."

The girl mumbled. I don't think anyone caught it besides me and Quinn, whose yellow eyebrows went up.

"The Baron decides when he takes his guests," Vaughn said, gathering his cards. "Though, it was Catrin who took this one into the keep last night. He got to skip the line."

All three of the vagabonds turned their angry eyes on me. One of them sneered.

"Must be the slut's type. Can't believe we got someone from the Backroad here, and she ain't even available. Just our luck . . ."

"I hear she's letting one of the villagers bounce her. No accounting for taste. Just look at these peasants, living in the mud . . ."

"Tired of this pit," the third agreed, glaring into his tankard. "Piss beer and piss air."

Vaughn snorted, somehow expressing agreement with the sound. The girl trapped in Quinn's arm closed her eyes, her mouth pressed tight.

"I think our young friend here disagrees!"

I drew in a sharp breath. *Damn it.*

All eyes went to Quinn, who'd been the one to speak. He was grinning, his eyes malicious as some fox spirit's as he jostled the girl.

"What was that you said, dear?" He leaned in to the terrified girl, adopting a conspiratorial look. "Go on, tell them! I'm sure they value criticism, and we're all friends here."

She just shook her head, all the color drained from her face as she shook her black curls. "I didn't . . ."

"But you did!" Quinn caught the vice-captain's unamused look and winked. "Here, I'll say it, I don't think they heard you. She said, '*My pa's inn isn't a dump.*' Isn't that precious? Defending her family's business, now that's a loyal daughter for you!"

One of the vagrants ignored the jovial ghoul, lifting his tankard to take a drink. Another of the trio stared at the innkeeper's daughter, rubbing at his chin with one thumb. He was the one who spoke next.

"Well, if she's so worried about her da's business, maybe she'd like to earn him some extra coin?"

Horror entered the girl's face. Behind her, I noticed her father staring at us from behind the bar. His fists were clenched over the countertop, and he opened his mouth to speak. He was caught between anger and terror, and it choked him.

A hand slammed down on the table, making the whole thing jump. Many of the coins Carlisle had been studiously counting as he ignored the scene went flying, making him curse savagely.

William stood, causing all voices to fall silent and all eyes to go to him. The young hunter had a dark look on his face, almost bestial with rage beneath the brim of his tricorn.

I sighed in relief, letting my hand slide off my axe.

"If this is the sort his lordship treats with," William spat, "then I want nothing to do with the lot of you."

His glare went to Quinn. "Release her, corpse eater."

Quinn's eyes widened in surprise, though the expression had a theatrical quality. He raised his arms with deliberate slowness. The girl darted to her father, who ushered her into a back room and out of sight. Smart man.

William scorched everyone at that table with his angry brown eyes, including me, then turned to the door. He'd gone three steps before Vaughn spoke.

"You are in Caelfall under its lord's protection, William Garou. You walk out that door, that goodwill is revoked. You sure you want to make that choice?"

The hunter froze. Then, in a tight voice he said, "I won't work with men like them."

Vaughn snorted. "You're not an aristo anymore, boy. This is the world you've stepped into. Men like them *thrive* in it. Time to grow up."

William glanced back, locking eyes with the vice-captain. "Orson was supposed to be better than this."

Vaughn nodded. "He can afford to be, in that fancy castle on the lake. Out here, dirty hands get dirty work done. Don't be naive. The girl's trotted off, you've made your point. Now sit down."

Quinn studied his nails, pretending like he hadn't been the one to instigate this little show. The three thugs tended to their drinks, looking bored.

William hesitated, uncertainty warring with indignation in his expression. For some reason, he looked at me.

I shrugged. "If you weren't here, worse might have happened."

William's face twisted with anger. "So you're saying you would have let them do what they wanted?"

I hadn't meant to say that, but I felt the rest of those hard eyes on me as well. The role of blackguard suited here, much as it stung me.

"He's right," I said, tilting my head to the vice-captain. "Can't afford to be naive here. Even still . . ."

I turned toward the three vagabonds. They all had similar features, so I guessed them to be brothers.

"These are your employer's people," I said, letting my voice turn steely. "His subjects. Orson Falconer is no back-alley thief lord. He is a *lord*. Blood of the Houses. You touch these people, and he'll have you flayed."

I stood then, rising to my full height to tower over them. To my immense satisfaction, they all shrank under my shadow.

"I am entertaining a decision to join the Baron's household," I said calmly. "I would take immense pleasure in carrying out his justice."

One of the three, whom I judged to be the eldest, adopted a bored expression and shrugged. "As the Mistwalker said, we was just playin'. No need to make such a fuss over it."

The merchant, Carlisle, chuckled. "Well, this has been entertaining, but I think everyone has made their point. Shall we play another hand, gentlemen?"

Vaughn studied me, his foggy half-dead eyes lidded in thought. "Nah," he grunted. "We've got work to do. You with us, Garou?"

William stared at me as well, but looked to the mercenary as he was addressed. His face calmed and he nodded. "Fine."

"Good. Quinn, you're with us."

"But—" the blond man started to protest.

"What's that?" Vaughn growled.

Quinn swallowed and shook his head. "Nothing. Right you are, vice-captain. Glad to be part of the team."

Vaughn stood, navigating around the table to draw up next to me. He lowered his voice so only I could hear.

"You talk a good game. Let's see if it's all talk."

He lifted his voice. "Time to move."

"Where are we going?" I asked.

"You'll see," Vaughn said, a cruel smile twisting his mouth. The rest followed him out of the inn, only the merchant staying behind.

Carlisle drew the string over a small satchel, the bag fat with his winnings over the card game. He smirked at me. "Would you have really killed all three of them?"

He hadn't missed me reaching for my weapon. Even during cards, he hadn't missed anything.

"Not sure," I said honestly. "But I wouldn't have let them hurt the girl."

"Dangerous friends to show scruples around," he warned me mildly, sipping at his cup. "Don't want to show weakness to predators."

"They're not my friends," I said as I turned. "And it's not weak to have scruples."

Lot of things would be easier without them, I added to myself.

His quiet laugh followed me out of the inn.

CHAPTER TWENTY-THREE

DARK DEEDS

Our band traveled out of the village as the morning aged into afternoon. Sullen gray clouds hovered low over the marshlands, threatening more rain.

Still plenty enough light for me to tell where we were heading without trouble. The chapel soon clarified itself on its high hill. I could guess well enough why we went there. I kept myself marching, while inside my mind went into panic over what to do.

Those chimera the night I'd arrived in Caelfall had to have been assassins sent by the Baron to murder the demesne's last priest. They had failed thanks to my presence, and now I suspected he'd opted for a more simple tactic.

Still, sending killers in broad daylight? If he wanted to keep the villagers from discovering his hand in the deed, why would Orson do it this way?

My silent turmoil was interrupted when Quinn sidled up next to me, falling back to match my pace. Our group had formed a loose line across the trail leading out from the village, giving us room to talk with relative privacy.

"Wanted to apologize for back there," he said with a quick smile. "Wouldn't have let them touch that barmaid. Just having a bit of fun."

I glanced at him out of the corner of my eye and kept my silence.

Quinn coughed. "Well, anyway, I suppose you haven't been told what we're about?"

"No."

"Just like the vice-captain. Surly brute . . ." Quinn shrugged. "Well, there's a priest in that church up there."

"There are priests in most churches," I said philosophically.

"Right . . ." Quinn struggled to match my longer strides as he talked. "Well, this one's a problem. Been skittish ever since the last one bumped off. The Baron's worried he might get a message out in a prayer or something."

He paused before asking, "Can they really do that? Our band's from the continent. Things are different in the west. We have monsters aplenty, but these seraphs, these . . . gods?"

He frowned.

"Onsolain," I said. "They're servants and kinsfolk to God, but not quite gods themselves."

Quinn shrugged, as though to say *what's the difference?* "Sure."

"They can hear prayers," I admitted. "And they *do* watch the land. They can travel about in disguise, and they use lesser spirits as messengers and watchers. It's possible for a preost to communicate with them."

Quinn shivered. "Creepy."

"A ghoul thinks *that's* creepy?" I asked.

The mercenary tossed me a yellow-toothed grin, apparently taking no offense. "Nothing more natural than a man wanting to live, *and* to eat. We're not the first mob of killers to catch the grave hunger on campaign. The Mistwalkers have been in a lot of wars. There's always war in the continent."

His manner turned thoughtful. "Well, admittedly, it can be dark sometimes. But most times? I still live, still enjoy myself. Being undead isn't so bad."

I had nothing to say to that, though it did remind me of something else. "How do you know Catrin?"

Quinn glanced at me and raised a blond eyebrow. "Cat? Why do you ask?"

"I just wanted to understand why she helped me," I said. "She didn't know me, but stuck her neck out when your comrades thought I was an intruder. I asked her, but she didn't really give me an answer."

No, I thought. *She did, you just didn't believe her.*

Quinn ran a gloved hand through his blond goatee, considering. "Cat is . . ." He laughed. "Well, she's an enigma. One of the Keeper's girls, so it's no surprise."

"Who is this Keeper?" I asked. I'd heard his name a lot lately.

"No one really knows," Quinn said. "Not really. He runs the Backroad Inn. It's a sort of gathering place for the outcast and the misbegotten. Sorcerers, changelings, witches, hired killers, lost wanderers . . . they come and go, but their secrets tend to stay. The Keeper collects secrets and bargains with them."

"He sounds like a devil," I observed.

Again, Quinn let loose that easy laugh. "Maybe he is! As I said, no one knows. But he's been around a long time, and he's got a whole coterie of helpers. Cat's one of them. She serves drinks at the Backroad, entertains guests, and learns things for the Keeper to add to his collection."

His expression sobered and in a less easy tone he added, "I'd like to say she's harmless, but be careful what you tell her. They say the Keeper's used his secrets to bring *kingdoms* to ruin."

I frowned, considering this. How had I never heard of this man in all my years with the Table? Surely the knights, or at least the legion of scholars who dwelt in the Gilded City, would have known about some sort of dark spymaster lurking like a shadow in the land?

Then again, I'd never known all of their secrets, had I? Maybe they *had* known. The idea formed a bitter kernel in my thoughts.

"What's a barmaid doing here?" I asked. "Involved in all of this, I mean." I waved back in the vague direction of the castle.

"Haven't you been listening?" Quinn asked, grinning to take the edge off the words. "She's a spy, man. The Keeper's a spider, and she's one line of his web. The Baron could hardly deny him a part in all of this—the old crow's too well connected. But that doesn't mean his lordship or any of the others are happy to have the Keeper's fingers stuck in their business, so they go out of their way to disclude her."

I recalled the council's attitude toward her. It tracked.

"More than that," Quinn added as his voice took on a conspiratorial edge, "I hear it was the *Keeper himself* who got the invite to Orson's little party. So, him sending one of his wenches in his place . . ."

Quinn tossed a hand dismissively. "Well, she's not ordinary, but she serves drinks in a pub. Something of an insult, isn't it?"

I answered with a slow nod, chewing on these new details. Perhaps Catrin's opposition to the lord of House Falconer wasn't feigned, after all. Still, it set me ill at ease to think what kind of man this Keeper might be, to employ changelings as his eyes and ears.

"So how do you know her?" I asked. "You two seemed well acquainted."

Quinn coughed. I think there might have even been a blush touching his pallid cheeks. "Well, the regiment's made use of the Backroad more than once. Soldiers and ale, you know?"

More like soldiers and wenches. I kept my silence.

"And them?" I asked, nodding to the three brothers ahead of us. They lingered close to Vaughn, silent and grim as they trudged along the muddy road.

"The Mourner Brothers," Quinn said in a theatrically ominous tone.

That name, I certainly had heard. "Assassins."

"Indeed. Good at it, too."

"I thought they were all hanged not long after the war." I frowned. The Accord had made a big show of it, executing the infamous trio at Kingsmeet as a show of solidarity among several monarchs.

"That was the rumor," Quinn agreed. "Yet there they are."

Vaughn stopped then and turned, cutting our conversation short. The big soldier waited for our little band to gather up before speaking.

"All right, here's the job."

He shifted, resting a hand on the heavy pommel of his broadsword. The chapel hill rose above us, the first short wall marking sacred ground rising just thirty paces behind the soldier.

"The priest up in that pile o' bricks is a problem, and the Baron wants it taken care of. Should be simple. Far as we know, the bastard's no true cleric, but sacred ground is sacred ground, and his predecessor apparently said his prayers every night. That's where you lot come in."

He nodded to me and William. "You two shouldn't have any trouble getting in there. Go say hello. We're not in a hurry, but don't dally."

William shuffled, checking his bowstring with a practiced hand. "What about them?" He tilted his chin toward the three brothers. One of them spat, glaring at the young hunter.

"The rest of us are going to surround the hill," Vaughn explained. "The new preoster has some guests, ones his lordship didn't invite. If any of them try to make a run for the woods, we'll have them."

"So we're playing the bloodhounds," William said, realizing the same thing I had. "Scaring them out of their refuge."

"Should be easy," Quinn piped in with a wide grin. "The church's gargoyles flapped off ages ago. Neither one of you are secretly undead or fiendish, right? Be awful embarrassing if we brought you for nothing."

William shook his head, his expression distant as he focused on the church.

Deciding honesty wouldn't hurt me with this lot I said, "I'm an apostate, but it doesn't prevent me from entering holy ground. I'm just not supposed to." I shrugged.

One of the Cullers laughed. "Well, if you catch fire, there are plenty of ponds to leap into."

I looked to Vaughn. "We approached with plenty of light left. They'll have seen us already."

Inside, I was toying with the decision to kill all of them right here. I wouldn't kill the young priest, the doctor, or the girl. I wouldn't let any of these villains do it, either. How did I deal with this without blowing my cover?

Vaughn dashed all my hopes when he grinned, the expression near macabre as Quinn's manic smile. "Oh, I hope they have. I've had more of the Company spread across those fields since before dawn this morning. This isn't our first show."

I looked out over the misty, flooded fields. If the dead were hiding in those stagnant waters, and Olliard and his companions tried to make a run for it . . .

Damn. This was bad.

I glanced at the Cullers. If Vaughn had brought plenty of backup, and had me and William to invade the church, then what was their purpose?

I didn't like this, but the three in that chapel were lucky I'd been given a part. If the ghouls and other creatures the Baron had gathered couldn't invade sacred ground, then I could hold there. Not forever, but for a time.

"Fine," I said. "Let's get to it, then."

"Not so fast." Vaughn stopped me, stepping into my path. We were of the same height, and he seemed an iron wall in his heavy armor. "Take this."

He handed me a curved horn, fashioned from some beast I couldn't readily name. Perhaps some western monster. It was an ugly thing, brown with strips of sickly white, banded in iron.

"They make a run, you sound this. Don't try and steal all the glory for yourself. You fuck us, I'll kill you."

I took the horn, then began to ascend the hill without any riposte. I suspected Vaughn would have his chance at my throat soon enough.

William and I walked up the trail to the chapel's front door side by side. I tucked the horn under my cloak, securing it at my belt. It made my hand itch, though I couldn't tell if the item was profane or if it just felt so having been held by the undead so long.

As we went, I focused on the ember of sacred fire in me. I'd kept my aura subdued since the previous night, wary of the dark things around me sensing too much about my nature. Karog had smelled the magic on me, which was disconcerting, and I hadn't wanted to risk any of the others getting more than a suspicion.

It had been easy enough to keep my powers low key, especially weak as I'd been. I stoked it now, anticipating battle. Not against the three in that church. Against the ones behind me.

I felt something from William as well. The young man seemed to shiver every few moments, as though from cold, and I felt a trembling pressure emanating from him. I got the distinct feeling of walking beside a dangerous predator all of a sudden, something more instinctive and physical than any impression through my aura. The hairs on the back of my neck stood on end.

Vaughn had called him William Garou. A House name? Or a moniker?

"Let me do the talking," I told him as we walked.

"Suit yourself." His voice had become a gravelly snarl, far different from the soft, almost boyish voice he'd had before.

He'd gotten angry at the inn when that Culler brother made a crude pass at the innkeeper's daughter. Could he be a potential ally? Should I risk outing myself to recruit him?

Wait until we're in the church, I decided. *Out of sight of the others. Then I give him a choice.*

We passed through the rows of grave stones climbing the hill, soon enough reaching the yard below the bell tower. My eyes scanned the building. Silent. Still.

I noticed something else too. Or, more precisely, the absence of something.

William shuddered as we approached the steps leading up to the knave's front door. "You ready for this?" he asked. "Killing priests . . . even hard men can balk at that."

He said this with an eager hunger, as though he *wanted* me to back off and let him loose. His brown eyes had taken on a more amber gleam, not unlike the color of my own, though less clean.

Garou. I realized what he must be. "You're a lycanthrope." I frowned. "Are you going to need an invitation to get in?"

The laws protecting sacred ground and other thresholds were mostly for the dead, but changelings and other misbegotten creatures can be repelled by them as well.

William shook his head. His hair, which looked thicker and darker than it had, shook with the motion. "This is just my Art. It's a bit more unpleasant than most, but I'm human."

His aura was *boiling.* It took an effort of will not to step away from him and draw my weapon.

I stepped up to the door, reaching out for the auremark worked in faded gold into the oaken barrier. I paused, glancing at William to meet his bestial eyes.

"Don't do anything until I say," I ordered him.

He bared his teeth. "I don't take orders from you."

A shape had begun to congeal around him. Something with claws, horn-like protrusions or perhaps tufted ears, all hackles and spasming muscle. His soul, given shape.

I studied it a moment. This wasn't some undirected tool. His power was unrefined, rough, but very potent. He was practically salivating to hurl it at the innocent man inside this building.

This young man knew hate.

I nodded, turned, and pushed at the door. Locked.

"Let me," William Garou hissed.

"Don't waste your Art," I said. "This might not be the last barrier."

I closed my eyes, focused, and murmured a word of command. Not a spell. Apostate or no, I had once been of the Table, a holy knight.

Would it still matter? Even after I'd spilled that bishop's blood on his own altar?

Sacred gold and blessed oak answered my command, and the door unlatched at my touch. I wasn't certain whether to take that as reassurance or admonishment.

At the very least, it meant this was still hallowed ground.

We stepped inside. The darkened knave where I'd fought the chimeric owls greeted us. I could still make out the crack in the sacrificial bowl. The corpses, however, had been taken out, the bloodstains scrubbed clean. Otherwise, silence greeted us.

"Think they ran already?" William asked, his gleaming eyes searching the dark. "Out the back, maybe?"

"The Mistwalkers would have warned us," I said. I doubted the horn at my belt would be the only such device the ghouls carried.

I stepped closer to the altar, considered the silent church, then turned back to my companion.

"Stay here. I'll look around."

He started to protest, but I gave him a hard look and he fell quiet.

"If they make a run for it," I said, "I'd rather have you here where you can do something about it."

A weak excuse, but he accepted it. I took my time searching the church and its attached buildings, making certain of my hunch. I used the time to consider my options.

William had seemed a potential ally, but he was clearly unstable and eager for violence. He was also young, and might listen to reason. Did I risk it? Catrin had proven herself at odds with the Baron. Perhaps there were other personal motives that might be turned against the renegade lord.

I was still chewing on it when I returned to the nave. William waited for me, impatient and angry, his magic flexing away from his body like a hound straining at its leash.

"Well?" he asked.

I licked my lips and glanced toward the doors. "They *are* gone. Probably before this trap was ever set."

William glared at me, confused. "How do you figure?"

I paused a moment, then made a choice.

"Because the two who were enjoying the church's protection came with a wagon and a chimera. The wagon is still out there, but the beast is gone. They've cleared off. Probably, they expected this."

Olliard had been invited here by the last preoster, who'd been feuding with the Baron. My suspicion about him being more than an ordinary physician solidified into certainty.

Had he taken my warning to heart? Taken his apprentice and the monk and left Caelfall?

I doubted it.

William blinked, nonplussed for a moment. "How . . ."

He went very still a moment, then took a step back. The eerie sense of presence around him suddenly flexed and seemed to grow larger, like a wolf raising its hackles. "Wait . . . you arrived yesterday. Same time as those two . . . you *know* them."

I focused my attention on the younger man. "William, this situation is complicated. Earlier, you didn't like how those brigands acted. I think maybe you've got a sense of right and wrong in you, so I'll give you a choice."

I turned to face him fully. His back was to the still-open door, but he held his ground. His confusion shifted more into anger by the second. I kept my own voice calm, my posture nonthreatening.

"The one the Baron wants us to kill is an innocent monk," I said. "The other two are an old man and a young woman barely out of girlhood. They're decent people. I won't let them die for Orson Falconer's mad ambitions."

William's bright eyes flashed with fury. "Traitor."

"Traitor?" I tilted my head at him. "Boy, this whole mad gathering are Recusant leftovers, the same powers who waged war against the faithful Houses of the Ardent Bough. *They* are the traitors."

It was the wrong thing to say. William's eyes widened further. "Karog was right. You *are* a spy."

"I don't serve the Accord," I said, taking a step closer to him. He tensed. I went still. If he bolted, and I didn't catch him before he made it outside . . .

"You want to save that fucking preacher," William snarled. Again, the power unfolding from him roiled. It was a disconcerting image, like he'd split double, only the double didn't resemble anything human and my eyes struggled to fix on it.

"I have no reason to kill him," I hardened my voice. "Neither do you."

"I have every reason!"

William's voice came out as an inhuman bellow, blaring through the chapel as two voices.

He's not in sync with his own aura, I realized as I watched him. *It's influencing him as much as he's directing it.*

I had some experience with that.

I kept calm as I took another step forward. "I am willing to hear them." I began to draw my axe from its belt loop, hiding the motion with my cloak.

"Who are you?" he demanded. Then, shaking his head he said, "No, doesn't matter. Where are they?"

"I don't know," I said honestly.

"Liar!"

He lashed out with one hand, his fingers forming claws. The boiling phantom around him made the same motion, only it had far more reach, and its claws were sharp as iron.

Rather than recoiling, I shot forward, freeing my axe from the folds of my cloak in the same motion. I ducked, letting that wild swing go over my head. Its heat prickled at my neck, set my hair to fluttering, but missed me. I imagine there wouldn't have been much left but a bloody smear had it connected.

I flew forward in relative silence compared to his echoing snarls and whirling, wind-shearing claws. Only the quiet ripple of my cloak marked my forward momentum. I took my axe in both hands, went low as he tried to reform his broken phantasm for another attack—it had come undone with his miss, his concentration breaking.

Strong as his power was, William's magic wasn't *truly* an Art—not yet, anyway. It was on the cusp of forming one, but for now it remained an unstable phantasm, rippling in and out of reality.

More, he had warned me of its every movement through his display of rage. He had a rare power, but little refinement. Perhaps, in time, he might have cultivated that into something truly dreadful, a weapon for the likes of Orson Falconer to unleash on the realms.

I never gave him the chance to fulfill that dark destiny. I stamped a boot on the chapel floor, pushed off, and swung in the same motion. My axe parted the air with a sound almost like a cough.

I slid a ways past him before I came to a stop. He started to say something, his voice young and confused. I straightened, letting out a slow breath.

He hit the floor with a muted thump behind me.

I hadn't killed him instantly. He groaned, writhing on the floor as he tried to stand. I turned, unhurried, and approached the lad. His struggles were leaving red stains all over the stone.

I'd carved a gash across his stomach. A lethal wound, and a bad way to die. He glared at me, his eyes normal now and full of confusion. When he spoke, blood burbled up from his throat. He couldn't form the words.

"I would have heard your story," I told him. "It didn't have to be like this."

He had a dagger at his belt. He was trying to reach for it, but his struggles were weakening.

A long succession of kings, knights, and angels stared at the scene from the chapel's decorated walls. I accepted their judgment, and watched William Garou's life leave him.

"—Elp . . ." All the anger left William's face in a rush, replaced by terror. He hacked up more blood, freeing whatever clot had choked him. "No . . . but I haven't . . ."

What am I doing? I gritted my teeth, lifted my axe, and swung. The young man's struggles stopped. I knelt, heedless of the blood soaking into my clothes, and closed his eyes. All the while, I fought against the surge of self-loathing and disgust threatening to choke me. I failed, and vomited.

After I'd wiped my mouth, I made myself look at the empty, frightened eyes of the boy I'd just killed. Eighteen at most, now I saw him without that mask of mature confidence he'd kept.

"Who were you, William Garou?" I asked him the question, but he couldn't answer anymore.

It is much easier to slay the minions of darkness when you have not seen their humanity.

CHAPTER TWENTY-FOUR

THE PREOSTER

'd pulled my damn stitches again.

I took the time to fix them as I considered what to do next. I leaned against one of the knave's columns, staring at the corpse lying in the middle of the floor as brooding clouds moved overhead and my time ran short.

I'd learned this a long time ago. Everyone's got a story. There are no faceless minions, no bit players whose only purpose is to be a foe to slay. There are those who deserve death, but no one's life is simple. For every villain like Vaughn or those Culler brothers, there is someone like William.

That empty shell on the floor had possessed a story, ambitions, hopes, hatreds, just as I did. Now he cooled in a pool of his own blood, killed by a man he'd known less than a day.

Perhaps I would end up the same.

When I'd killed William, his awakened aura—his soul—had detached from the corpse. I could still barely make it out, shivering and writhing, resembling nothing human. The boy had been using it hard in the moment I'd killed him. The shade he'd left would be dangerous, likely feral.

I considered banishing it. I could, with my powers. I am no cleric, and I couldn't do it gently.

I didn't need more problems. I stepped forward, focused on the congealing presence in the air as I spoke the ritual words of a banishing rite. I lifted my axe slowly—the ritual motions mattered in this, gave direction and purpose to what would otherwise just be raw power. I wanted to hurl this fresh ghost away from this place, not maim it further.

I swung, amber fire flickering along the path of the cut. The shade writhed, twisted in on itself as it was illuminated for an instant by the golden embers, then vanished as some fissure in the fabric of the world took it.

Would William's remnants end up in the Realm of the Dead? Or lost in the Wend? I couldn't say. I only knew he wouldn't trouble this place anymore.

The gnawing pain in my shoulder reminded me *I* was still alive, and still wasn't out of danger yet. My playacting as a minion of darkness had run its course. I wouldn't be able to explain William Garou's death to the Mistwalkers, not in any way that'd satisfy them. Vaughn would see the way he'd died, and recognize it as my axe's work.

Had my free trip to the castle been for nothing? Should I have tried for the Baron's head there, my own life be damned?

A more pressing mystery drew my attention. How had Olliard gotten himself and the other two out without Vaughn's killers knowing about it? Especially with that big beast of his. He would have had to leave just after I'd departed the previous night, before Orson became aware of the first failed attempt.

Get yourself out alive before worrying about how they did it. I took a deep breath, snipped the last bit of string off with my knife, and readjusted my clothes as I sheathed the blade. All my recent wounds pained me, but the discomfort helped me focus. No more time to get lost in thought.

Sound drew my attention. I had my axe in hand in an instant, grabbing it from where I'd leaned it against the column.

It had come from deeper in the church, not the front door. Soft footsteps. I narrowed my eyes and went to the back door.

"Olliard?" I called out. "Edgar? It's me, Alken. If you're there, come out. You're all in danger, and . . ."

I stepped into the back hall. It split two ways, one going to the living quarters and the other descending into the catacombs.

My eyes went down those stairs to the left. Was it just my imagination, or did I feel a cold draft coming from below?

I started down the stairs. Every click of my leather boots on the stone echoed down into the dark. It grew colder, making me shiver even in the embrace of my woolen cloak.

Every church in all of Urn has a catacomb. The dead dwell beneath the land, and the surface is full of predators. Ghouls like the Mistwalkers, who feed on the dead, and necromancers who use them for even darker purposes. The remains of the deceased are guarded in sanctums of earth and stone, warded by the blessings of clerics and kept at rest with prayer and offerings.

I felt the cold sharpen into something more than cold. The stair formed a long, wide spiral that I suspected conformed to the shape of the circular prayer hall above.

As I'd suspected before, this house of God had been here a long time. The stairs went a long ways, and split into many dark passages. The rotations became shorter as I descended, as though I sank into a whirlpool of dug earth and chiseled rock.

It leveled after a time into a long, narrow hallway. The floor here was rough dirt, hard-packed and dry despite the surrounding climate. Probably why this place had been raised on one of the few patches of high ground to be found. The corridor split into side passages.

Every wall had been perforated with rectangular hollows, where caskets of sanctified wood had been nested. Some of the smaller chambers had sarcophagi of stone, probably holding the remains of other preosts or even Orson Falconer's noble ancestors.

All of them held bones. The smell of death hung heavy in the air.

Such places were very dangerous to those who weren't meant to be in them. Dangerous especially to me, because what I carried called to the dead.

I lit no torch. No need to disturb those who dwelt down here more than I needed to. I let the aura in my eyes light my way, making it to the end of the hall before I felt a prickling cold run up my spine. Something had taken note of me.

"Who are you?" I asked the darkness.

A voice, faint but very real, answered me. It was male, aged, and full of a sad weariness.

"A stubborn old fool. And a friend, if you would hear me out."

I took a deep breath of the crisp, stale air. "Preoster Micah. I'd heard you hadn't been allowed to depart."

I turned and saw him there. An old man, thin and below average height, with iron gray hair and a thin face. I could make out his bones through transparent skin, though even the skeleton wasn't truly real. Just phantasm, the echo the man's soul had burned into reality.

"You killed that angry young man," he said, frowning.

I nodded. "He would have killed me. And your junior."

When the priest moved, he left afterimages of himself behind for brief moments. He shuffled to one side, his frown deepening. "Yes. Yes, he would have."

"Where did they go?" I asked. "Brother Edgar, and the doctor?"

The preoster let out a sigh. "Ah, yes. Olliard, my dear old friend. He got my message after all. I had thought us lost."

His form was fading. Even here, in a sanctum of the dead, this soul had been abused. I could see it, where his misting form had sharp protrusions like thorns and fragments of bone twisted into abstract shapes.

Catrin had said Orson and Lillian hadn't allowed him to depart. She hadn't mentioned they'd also tortured the spirit. My fist clenched at the sight.

"Where are they?" I repeated. I didn't want to use my magic to compel him, and risk hurting him more. I would if I had to.

"You will save them?" The preoster's face came apart as he spoke, becoming a smoky skull. It reformed in time for me to make out his next words. "You will stop *him?*"

I nodded. "That's why I'm here."

"Golden eyes . . ." Micah's own eyes became hollow pits. "A red cloak. I saw you in my dreams."

"The Choir sent me."

"*The Headsman,*" the ghost whispered.

I inclined my head. The spirit's eyes went to the axe.

"*The dead whisper about you.*" I could barely make out the cleric's form in the darkness then. "*They are so angry.*"

"I have failed them terribly," I admitted. No point lying to the dead. Then, as firmly as I could, I asked, "Where did Olliard go?"

"*These catacombs lead out near the woods,*" the ghost whispered, almost too faint to hear. "*Olliard sent his beast away to mislead the Baron's hunters, and used the old tunnel. You will find it behind the sarcophagus at the end of this hall.*"

I turned, seeing an open section near the end of the passage.

"*They've gone into the Irkwood,*" Micah continued. "*The Sidhe are angry. They are not safe.*"

My jaw clenched. "I cannot protect them and wage war on our enemy at the same time."

"*You are one of the True Knights.*" The ghost drifted forward, a skeletal hand reaching out as though toward a campfire. "*That light . . . ah, I understand now, why they say the dead are drawn to the east! You are like a torch flame in the dark.*"

I stepped out of his reach. His fingers became wispy claws of shadow, which quickly faded.

"I'm not a knight anymore," I said, my voice bitter even though I'd meant to speak without heat. "What you feel are just embers."

The walls were shifting. More shadowy forms congealing like a miasma. The dead were being drawn out by my presence. No more time.

The ghost wasn't done. "*With no one tending this place, its protections will fail. You should go.*"

I understood. Once the Mistwalkers realized the church was empty, they would gain the courage to approach. Once the sun set and the mists came in, gravid with Orson and Lillian's power, they would be able to enter. An abandoned house has no threshold, and the same is true of most sanctuaries.

As for the dead . . . that was a bigger problem. Left undisturbed down here, they were harmless. If Orson decided to make use of them . . .

I wouldn't let him get that far.

"Thank you," I said to the dead priest. Then, studying his desiccated form I asked, "Is there anything I can do for you?"

"*Save them. Stop him.*"

The phantom's strength failed. He faded out of reality, sinking into the surrounding earth. Stronger, older spirits bubbled up to replace him.

"I will stop him," I said. Then I turned and made my way for the hidden passage.

CHAPTER TWENTY-FIVE

THE HUNTERS

The hem of my worn red cloak glided over twisting roots and undergrowth. I'd left the catacomb passage some time ago. It had gone very far, more than a quarter of a mile, and brought me out at the edge of the marshland just like the dead preoster had said. Beyond those flooded fields rose the shadowed forests that ringed Caelfall.

The air hung heavy and thick in the shadowed depths of the Irkwood, damp and smelling of rotting plants. My eyes kept wanting to track movement at the edges of my vision, flitting phantom shapes that might have been mist, or my nerves, or the wraiths I knew would haunt the trees.

Human shades had followed me out of the catacombs. I didn't fear them as much. They would weaken out here, and eventually retreat back to their crypts.

The forest spirits were made of sterner stuff. Those, I was well wary of.

I could hear whispering. There was no wind, no singing birds or insect sounds, so the murmuring voices in the near distance provided the only ambience besides my own crunching boots in the undergrowth.

I knew better than to try to listen to those voices. Elves don't die—immortal is immortal—but their flesh can still expire just as a human's can. Their souls are made of hardier stuff than a man's, though. Anywhere I'd find the Old Children, I'd find their shades lingering. Whispering.

Bitter.

So many of them had died during the Fall. The land was infested with fey ghosts, undying, refusing to forget. Or forgive.

"*He's here,*" a voice muttered, louder than the rest.

"*He's come!*" another answered, outrage and excitement melting together in the words.

"*Which one is he?*" a third asked.

"Doesn't matter, they're all oathbreakers. They let the towers burn, let the Archon die."

"Didn't just let him. They did it!"

"Betrayers!"

"Liars."

"Murderers."

I ignored the vague shapes in the deeper shadows and moved on, farther into the wood. Emaciated claws and eerie faces with huge, lidless eyes watched me from the gaps between branches and roots.

"He bears the Axe. The Doomsman's Arm."

"The Headsman."

"Headsman!"

"The Headsman has come."

I stopped in a small clearing. Mist wrapped around the forest floor, curling around the trees and clinging to the hem of my cloak. I wore my hood up to shadow my features—not to disguise, but so the mild enchantments woven into the garment would help keep the wraiths and wild od from interfering with my senses. I'd had an ally, one of few left to me, weave it some years before.

I spotted something half-lost amid the undergrowth and knelt. A saddlebag. It was old, worn, and—when I inspected it—empty. So innocuous. But I knew it must belong to Olliard. One of the packs he'd kept in the cart, or a saddlebag for Brume, his chimera.

They *had* come this way. And left this behind. Were they chased?

Something changed in the forest. The wraiths had stopped their constant murmuring, and its absence hit me like a scream. The hairs on the back of my neck stood on end.

I tightened my grip on my axe, resting its butt on the ground so I could use it to push to my feet.

A rustling in the surrounding trees. I narrowed my eyes to slits, focusing on the subtle impressions from the world around me. Every living thing has aura, even if not everything is aware of it. I am aware of mine, feel it always, and it lets me feel the world around me. The alien sensations were near constant, and I'd long learned to shut them out.

Only when something unnatural drew near, something that didn't *belong*, did my powers truly shout warning. The rest of the time, I was better off using my more natural senses.

I did now, sharpening my ears. Every muscle in my body clenched, an instinctive anticipation.

I heard the creaking of a taut string, quiet as a whisper.

I whirled and swung my axe in the very moment the crossbow fired. Something hurtled from the undergrowth, and the edge of my weapon caught it. The impact jarred my arms, set my teeth on edge—no mere bolt. Something heavier—

Hollow. Whatever I'd struck shattered, splattering me with a viscous warm liquid.

Glass?

A shape moved in the bushes. Not whoever had fired at me, but something bigger. I lunged, not to attack, but to get out of the way.

Too slow. An enormous thing, all gray and brown hair and snorting rage, with chomping teeth and goring tusks, exploded from the forest. It hit me at speed, barreling me straight out of the air. It bucked. I went flying, hit a tree hard enough to ring my bones like a struck bell. I fell.

The world split into fragments. My shoulder let out a screeching protest as I wrenched it. Damned stitches *again*.

Maybe a cracked bone too. Whatever had hit me had been huge and strong as a war chimera.

Not far off the mark, I realized as my brain caught up.

Brume.

I rolled, coming up to my feet, and flinched as another of those glass balls zipped by my ear. A near miss. It erupted against the tree at my back, splattering me with more of that odd liquid. This time, it scalded where it touched me.

Brume, the huge hog beast—more a warthog now—stamped one hoof and snorted. The sound was so deep it seemed to rumble in my chest. The mass of gray fur started another charge, not so placid now.

I heard iron mechanisms clack into place. Tracking the sound, I lunged out of Brume's path. The chimera hit the tree, cracking the trunk nearly in half.

I dashed into the woods in a flurry of red wool, taking my axe in a backhand grip. Didn't want to use it for this. A startled gasp met my ears, cut short as I struck the source without seeing it. We both went tumbling down a shallow slope. A whirl of confusion as we rolled, branches and thorny bushes catching and scratching, grunts, a half-formed curse.

The roll ended with me on top at the bottom of the slope. Snarling, I brought up my axe and planted a boot on the crook of an arm as I caught the flash of a blade, pinning it.

And looked straight into the aged face of Olliard of Kell.

"Doctor," I greeted him, once I'd managed to catch my breath.

The old physik had lost his glasses in the tumble. Half blind eyes blinked up at me, then widened. Olliard's thinning hair was in disarray, and his brown robes were covered in leaves and mud. He had pulled a knife, a thin, curved blade with the aspect of a scalpel, which I'd trapped under a boot.

He'd lost his grip on the weapon he'd tried to shoot me with. It lay several feet away. That fancy crossbow of his, fitted with some new mechanism it hadn't had before—a long tube, like a very thin cannon.

"Alken?" Olliard asked, breathless and confused. "What are you—"

"Master!"

I turned just in time to see Lisette burst from the woods. Her hands moved in a complex series of patterns. She had a mesh of string held between her hands cat's-cradle style, string wrapped around each finger. She pulled the strings taught between her outstretched fingers, revealing a pattern between.

A pattern, I realized, which formed a rune.

There was a flash of white-gold light, and suddenly I no longer crouched atop the old doctor. I was ripped into the air like a doll with barely a chance to shout. My back slammed against the trunk of a large tree, *again*, and all the wind went out of my lungs in a rush.

When I was next aware of anything, I lay on the ground. I blinked, getting my bearings, and found I couldn't move my arms or legs. They were held by something solid as good rope or iron links.

Looking down, I saw thin lines of pale golden light tying my legs together. I suspected the same bonded my arms behind my back.

A dramatic rustling disturbed the woods as Brume reappeared. I tensed, expecting the huge beast to stomp over and crush my skull, but she just moved to loom over me. She snuffled at my hair, and I almost gagged at the animal reek.

Lisette scurried to her master's side and helped the old man stand, all without letting the pattern of strings between her hands go slack. Her attention remained fixed on me, a bead of sweat forming on her brow. She murmured what sounded like a litany of prayer under her breath.

Olliard winced as he stood, favoring one leg. He didn't glance at me as he limped to his fallen weapon and picked it up, sheathing the blade he'd pulled in some pocket hidden beneath a fold of his robes. He took a moment to check the crossbow, then turned his attention to me with a weary sense of inevitability.

"So," the doctor said with a sigh. "We meet again, Alken."

I didn't reply at once, instead taking in a few details. I tested the magical bonds and found they had some slack. Lisette narrowed her eyes in concentration and they tightened, hard enough to make me wince in pain.

"Doctor," I greeted the old man through clenched teeth. "Nun."

Lisette scowled, but didn't stop her murmuring incantation.

I glanced down at myself, and found I was covered in some metallic, pale gray substance. The contents of whatever the doctor had shot at me, I realized. "What is this stuff?"

"Liquid mercury," Olliard said. "Quicksilver." He pursed his lips. "I suppose you're not one of the Baron's creatures, or it would have set you afire. The substance is quite ungentle to the undead."

"Azsilver?" I asked.

Olliard let a tight smile flicker across his face. "Of course. I am no amateur."

"So that story about you just passing through Caelfall on your rounds as an itinerant healer was troll shit," I said. "You're hunters."

I could think of no other reason why the doctor would be packing weaponized moonsilver.

"Vampire hunters," Olliard confirmed. He loaded another missile into the strange crossbow. The weapon had four arms instead of the customary two, several strings, and what looked like an iron tube in the gap where a bolt would normally go. Instead of a bolt, he placed a small gray ball inside before pulling a latch, producing a solid *ka-clank.*

"The Baron isn't a vampire," I said. I felt certain of that, at least. I'd sensed no corruption in him even when we'd been face-to-face.

Then again, he'd been shielded by that skittering, whispering thing. Had it hid his true nature? *Wouldn't be the first time you'd missed it,* I reminded myself. My golden eyes were far from infallible.

"No," Olliard agreed, surprising me. "He isn't. But he does ally himself with such creatures, and he is responsible for Micah's death. I believe he plans much worse."

"Where is Edgar?" I asked. No sign of the young priest.

"I will be asking the questions," Olliard said, aiming the crossbow at me. I gritted my teeth.

"Doctor—"

"After you left last night," he cut me off, "telling Brother Edgar nothing, I started to look at the facts. Orson is gathering allies to him. Sorcerers, undead things, killers of every stripe. He's even recruited the Culler Brothers, and they are truly depraved. It struck me as strange that we found you where we did, *when* we did."

I met his eyes. "I protected Edgar from the the Baron's beasts."

"Indeed." Olliard nodded. "Which is why you are not dead right now. So I will have answers. Who are you? Why are you here?"

Lisette's murmuring had halted. Even still, the auratic bonds remained strong. She watched me with sad, thoughtful eyes, but made no move to jump to my defense. Brume snuffled, ready to leap into violent action at her master's command.

"Your apprentice knows what I am," I said tiredly.

"Some kind of holy knight?" Olliard lifted a bushy eyebrow. "Yes, that was quite the show with those forest spirits. But it gives me no facts, and I am a man who much prefers facts to poeticism."

"I'm not a knight," I said, almost reflexively. "Not anymore, anyway. I *was*, once. It left its mark."

I tried to straighten, so I could talk to them from my knees rather than face down in the wet grass, but Lisette's litany suddenly rose into a harsh onslaught of words and the golden bonds around my arms tightened. I gasped, fearing for a moment my arms would break, then slammed against the tree again as the auratic tethers dragged me to it like a magnet.

"I wouldn't move," Olliard suggested. "I've seen her use those to break bones. The same technique she used to stitch your wounds, you know. People never consider how easily the healing arts can be turned to the purpose of *unmaking* the body. The alchemists in the west know this fact well. They've made all sorts of tools just as potent as any elf magic in this land . . ."

He lifted his crossbow and aimed it at my skull. "What I shot at you before was just glass. This one is iron."

"I'm not your enemy!" I hissed.

"I am not so sure," Olliard disagreed. "I have been watching the village. I saw you with those undead soldiers. *Those* creatures, I have faced before. The Mistwalker Company. They are . . . evil."

His expression darkened. I didn't see any of the kindly, worried old man who'd tended to my wounds and told me stories on the long road to Caelfall. His eyes had a steely, merciless quality to them.

"I do know what you are," Lisette said.

She kept the binds taut, though it seemed she didn't need to pray to keep the magic up. I imagined the prayers were just a focus, like the string between her fingers. I turned my attention to her.

"Oathbreaker," she accused. I flinched, but the girl's face remained calm. "Those spirits in the woods, they said it themselves. I've heard the stories, that the Knights of the Alder Table turned against the elf king and slew him, betraying their vows. They are the worst of the Recusants, born of the land's most fabled order."

She stepped forward. Olliard started to protest, but she ignored him and focused on me. Her blue eyes were full of anger, which I had gotten used to facing, and pity, which was much worse.

"It has happened before," she told me. "When I was with the monastery, we studied this. When a True Knight, a paladin, breaks their vows, they don't lose their powers. They steal that fire, wielding it as a weapon even as it burns them. Just like what I saw happen to you, though I didn't understand it at the time."

She glanced at her master. "He is just as much a servant of darkness as those soldiers, or any of the Baron's other guests."

Olliard nodded. "I am no student of myth and legend, but it tracks. I have fought death knights, and other such horrors."

"He can become that," Lisette said darkly, turning her angry blue eyes back to me.

I opened my mouth to say more, to tell them they had me wrong and that I was Orson Falconer's enemy as much as they—but I stopped. They wouldn't trust anything I said while held prisoner with a weapon aimed at my skull, and the truth wasn't something they'd easily believe in any circumstance.

Better to show them. I gathered will for a Command, shaping my aura to freeze the doctor in place before he could shoot me. After, I'd break Lisette's auratic bonds and we would continue the conversation on more equitable ground. Her magic was good, clever, strong as steel cable, but no Art is stronger than its wielder's will.

Just as I started to gather strength, Lisette's eyes widened. In a flash her fingers danced through a series of complicated motions. The thin strings in her hands altered their pattern, and the quality of her murmured prayers changed.

Before I could speak a word, golden light shot through my lips. Down, then, up, and then repeating the process a dozen times in the blink of an eye. My lips slammed together and stayed there, neatly stitched.

Olliard frowned and glanced at his apprentice.

"He was about to use magic on us," she explained. "Not sure what kind."

"Ah. Good thinking then, my dear."

"What are we going to do with him, doctor?" Lisette asked, as I struggled futilely against the bonds. I tried to speak, but my words just came out as an incoherent mumble.

"We don't have time to interrogate him. We need to get back and check in on Brother Edgar, see if he managed to find those old maps for us. Our time is short, and our enemy watchful."

He pondered a moment before asking, "How long will your magic hold him, once we've departed?"

Lisette grimaced. "Not long."

Olliard nodded and lowered his weapon, then approached me. He pulled something from within the layered folds of his monkish robes—a metal syringe.

I struggled, but the small man was quick, decisive, and stronger than he seemed. He plunged the metal needle into my neck. Within the space of three breaths my eyes were growing heavy. My quickened heart pumped whatever he'd spiked me with through my veins at speed.

"Not a deadly concoction," Olliard muttered. "I just need to make certain you don't interfere. I don't know how you're involved in all of this, and I've no time or patience to sift your lies from truth. I should kill you, but you *did* save the girl's life, and Edgar's. I can't decide if you are an enemy or not, so this is my compromise. You will sleep for a while, and when you awake . . . well."

He shrugged. "I don't imagine we're likely to meet again. Get in my way, and I will not show mercy."

No, I thought through the spreading thickness in my blood. *You don't know what's in the castle, how bad things are. You can't handle him alone, can't—*

I couldn't say any of it aloud, not with my aura-stitched lips.

Lisette said something, but I didn't hear it through the spreading haze in my thoughts. I closed my eyes, and everything became dark.

CHAPTER TWENTY-SIX

BANE

When I woke again, the light in the woods had changed.

Must be near dusk, I thought. *Fell asleep again. Rupert's gonna give me a lecture.*

As the fog in my skull cleared, I realized in a flash where I was. The following realization—that the old soldier had been dead more than twenty years—was an almost physical pain.

I lay in damp undergrowth in the woods beyond Caelfall, not on the borderlands of Karledale. I was in my middle years, world worn and tired, no longer an eager young man set to challenge all the tyrants and monsters of Urn with nothing but a sword in hand.

Everything ached. I guessed I had whatever the doctor had injected me with to thank for that. *Bastard old man,* I thought. If he'd only let me explain . . .

But I hadn't really tried to explain, had I? I'd tried intimidating them instead, and the old physik's clever apprentice had shut me down hard. I'd underestimated them both. Even still, they'd get themselves killed if I didn't get back to the village and stop them from trying the castle's defenses.

If I wasn't too late already.

I started to get up, but some subtle noise in the surrounding forest stopped me. I went still. Instinctively, the fingers of my right hand searched for my axe. Cold logic told me the doctor had probably taken my weapons, so I was surprised when I found it lying at my side.

Must not have wanted to leave me defenseless, I thought. Softheartedness seemed a foolish trait for a pair of fiend hunters. They should have killed me.

Like you should have killed that novice back in Vinhithe? I asked myself.

That had been different. He'd been an innocent.

Carefully, without a sound, I shifted my muscles to readiness and tightened my grip on the axe. There was another rustle. I felt a subtle coldness, an itch along my skin. Small voices whispered through my blood.

Something of the Dark was approaching. Some beast of the woods, perhaps, or one of the Baron's creatures sent to deal with a loose end.

It wouldn't find an easy meal. I waited, and when my instincts shouted I twisted, spinning into a low and savage kick. My boot connected with something. It fell, letting out a high yelp. I was on my feet and had my axe up in a flash.

For the second time that day I froze before delivering the killing blow. Instead I lowered the axe and stepped clear, biting off a curse.

"Vampire."

The young woman stood, wincing and lifting one foot clear of her skirts to rub at the ankle I'd bruised before hurling a glare my way. "It's Catrin, you ass. Have trouble keeping names in that hard skull of yours? All the knocks you've taken to it, maybe?"

She still wore the old blue courtier's dress she'd been given, or pilfered, from Orson's castle. She'd opted to go without shoes, which made the ensemble somewhat less elegant.

"Bleeding Gates," she complained. "You're a jumpy one. Is every conversation with you going to involve violence?"

"How did you find me?" I asked, wincing as I worked some kink out of my neck. I'd been lying still for hours. It had left me stiff and groggy.

The dhampir sniffed. "I turned into a ghulbat and flew around until I saw you lying in the mud."

I glowered at her, unamused.

Catrin sighed and held up her hands in surrender. "I heard you got sent out on some job with Vaughn and Quinn. It gave me an uneasy feeling, so I went out. Then . . ."

She trailed off as a troubled, distant look entered her eyes.

"What is it?" I asked.

"Micah," she said quietly. "He found me on the lake shore. Told me you needed help."

So, I thought. *When the preoster's ghost vanished in the catacombs, it hadn't just been too weak to keep talking. It had gone to find an ally.*

Didn't lead me to trust her. Undead things can command lesser spirits.

"So you came all the way out here?" I asked. We were several miles from the lake.

"I can move around quicklike if I want," Catrin said with an evil little smile. "Maybe I can't grow wings like some of my kind, but I've got my ways."

I remembered how she'd moved through shadows during our conversation in the castle the previous night and didn't comment. I turned and started walking, guessing at the direction of the forest edge.

"Hey!" Catrin scurried to catch up, her skirts rustling through the brush. "Where are you going?"

"Back to the village," I said. *Before that old fool gets himself and his apprentice killed.*

"All right, fine enough, but could you at least tell me what happened out here? Why I found you lying on your face in the bloody wilderness?"

She sniffed, then scrunched up her face in disgust. "Did you shit yourself?"

I paused, then sighed. I had. "I was drugged," I told her.

Maybe I'd just let Olliard die.

"Drugged?" Catrin asked, confused. Her eyes fell like well-trained arrows on the puncture wound in my neck.

I didn't miss where her eyes lingered and turned, half-raising the axe. She stepped back out of my reach, both of us going on guard at once.

"Not here to fight," Catrin said slowly, watching me with wary eyes that shone just a touch too bright in the deepening forest gloom. "Came to make sure you were alive, not finish the job. You have my word, big man."

I considered her a long while, torn by distrust, doubt, and need. I had no allies in this, and the situation kept getting more complicated. Perhaps I couldn't trust her. Shattered Hells, maybe she'd been about to drain me in my sleep.

But she hadn't told the Baron about my duplicity, and she'd tried to find me after I'd gone missing. She'd stuck her neck out for me with the ghouls and even offered to help me escape the province, knowing nothing about me at the time.

She'd taken risks on my account. Whoever she was, *whatever* she was, everything she'd done told me she wasn't an enemy. Yet my instincts, and the sacred magic in my blood, screamed at me not to trust her.

Well, my instincts tended to compel me to swing steel first and ask questions never, and I had reason to suspect my magic to be a touch biased in this regard.

"What do you know of a man named Olliard of Kell?" I asked.

Catrin frowned, recognition passing across her features. "Yeah, I know him." She didn't seem too pleased by the fact. "Why? He the one who made you shit yourself?"

I scowled. "Matter of fact, he is. He's also a vampire hunter packing Edaean weaponry. He's planning to raid the castle and kill all the heretics and monsters inside with a fancy crossbow. Him and his nun apprentice, anyway."

Catrin's eyes widened. "Oh." Her frown turned thoughtful as she propped a fist on one hip. "Seems like he might be an ally, if he's also after the Baron's head. Not that I'm eager to work alongside a man who's made it a profession to hunt down my like, but you know what they say about beggars and choosers."

"He has no clue what's in that castle." I rested my axe on a shoulder and started walking again. "Some moonsilver and a few prayers aren't going to make a difference against that ogre."

Or that whispering thing, I thought grimly. "I need to get back there and warn him."

"What makes you think he won't just drug you again?" Catrin asked, keeping pace with me. Despite the dying light, she glided easily over the tripping roots and tangled vines.

"He'll listen to me after I've knocked his skull a couple times," I growled.

I wasn't in the mood to be patient or gentle with either of the hunters. They'd get out of my way and let me do my work. Orson Falconer and his coterie of darkness were a problem for the Headsman to deal with, not some vigilante.

"Well, it's a damn shame you and he ended up having this misunderstanding," Catrin stated cheerfully as she danced along at my side. "I'm sure it's awful embarrassing he made you go and soil your trousers, but you should really see this as a good thing, big man."

I lifted an eyebrow as I walked. "That so?"

The woods were too still. I frowned, slowing my pace. Something felt off. I stepped forward, ducking under a tree, then saw what lay ahead and drew in a sharp breath.

"Of course!" Catrin said brightly, not noticing what I had. "This time yesterday, you were one man against a small army of frightful things. Now you've got a pair of professional cutters roaming about on the same job, and a cute dhampir to—"

"Quiet."

Catrin's teeth clicked shut. She glared at me, but when her gaze followed mine the annoyance vanished.

"Bleeding Stars . . ."

He had been impaled on the branches of two trees. They speared into his neck just within the circle of his collarbone, up under his ribs, between his legs. A single long point of wood erupted like a tortured tongue from his open mouth. More came out of his eyes.

I stepped forward cautiously, studying the corpse. Even so destroyed, I recognized him.

"One of the Culler Brothers," I said. "Vaughn must have sent him into the woods to hunt for me when he realized I wasn't in the chapel anymore."

Catrin ran a hand across her mouth, lines forming between her eyebrows. "I think that's Jace, the oldest. Can't say I feel too sorry for him. I know the Cullers. They are . . . well, they've done worse to others." She shook her head. "What *happened*?"

"The forest didn't like him." I paced around the body. It looked like he'd been grabbed by the trees mid-sprint. There were roots bursting from the ground as well, stabbing into his legs, holding up his ragged brown cloak.

"How did I not smell him?" Catrin murmured, rubbing at her chin as she studied the corpse. "I should have gotten a whiff of blood half a mile away . . ."

"There isn't any," I said. "See how sunken he looks? The woods drank it all."

Catrin shivered, taking a nervous step away from the grisly scene. "How do you know the *forest* did it?"

"These trees are Malison Oaks." I lifted my axe to show her the gnarled branch it had been fashioned from. "Same thing this is made of, though these are younger than the tree mine was carved from."

She gave the weapon a dubious look. "That's why I smelled blood on you last night. You're carrying that thing around, and you call *me* a vampire?"

I ignored the comment. "Do you know if he was with the group that killed the bridge troll?"

Catrin shrugged. "No clue. Those three showed up around that time, so maybe."

I nodded. "We're probably in danger. I doubt Vaughn would have sent him in alone. Keep close to me."

Catrin lifted a brown eyebrow. I caught her expression out of the corner of my eye, but focused on the surrounding woods. She didn't seem terribly disturbed by the dead man.

"There were two others," I said. "They might still be about."

The dhampir nodded, then indicated the speared corpse. "You should burn him."

I frowned. "Why?"

"The Culler Brothers are necromancers," she explained. "If even one of them is still alive, he'll bring the others back. It's how they operate."

I recalled the rumors of the assassin trio's execution. It made sense.

"No time," I decided. "If they manage to get him out of this wood, we'll deal with it then."

Catrin shrugged. "Fair. So who offed him?"

The woods were still too silent. I focused on the subtle emanations of the world around me. As I'd thought, too still. Like all the world held its breath. Even the shades had gone quiet, though the encroaching night would usually bring them out in number.

"Alken." Catrin's voice took on a nervous edge. "You're freaking me out. Who killed that—"

She never got to finish that sentence. Something flashed from the shadowed woods. It punched into her left shoulder, making her jerk back into a stumble.

I blinked, catching the image of feathers winging the top of a thin, black shaft. An arrow.

I moved without thought, on pure impulse. All my suspicion, uncertainty, and revulsion toward the changeling forgotten, at least in the moment. I caught her in one arm and lifted my axe with the other, snarling with rage at the woods as amber flame burst to life across my weapon.

It came fitfully, with a sullen reluctance. The aureflame was burning off the poison in my system, but whatever Olliard had used had been strong. Or was it just my tired, abused body catching up to me?

I'd fight through it. I had before.

And they were there, all around us. I knew it before I truly saw them. The sun had finished its descent, and my eyes saw through the darkness—but not so far as they should have. Another power was there, working against mine. An older magic.

Fey lights blinked to life through the trees. Bobbing blue will-o'-the-wisps. They giggled like ghostly children, flitting in and out of sight. One light passed in front of a tall shape, wild haired and clutching a warbow near as tall as they.

An elf. Not just one.

The denizens of the old woods had come.

"I don't want trouble," I said, calming my rage. More of the ghost lights appeared in the corner of my vision. I tracked them, but saw no more of our ambushers. They lurked in the darkness. How many?

Too many. Even one would be dangerous enough in this place.

"*Es tiirien valre, es'curunai.*" The serpent voice coiled through the darkness, spoken in nearly a murmur yet filling every gnarled edge of the wood. "*Yet you bring trouble with you, mortal. That thing in your arm is an abomination.*"

I thought at first the elf meant my axe. The elves had made it, long ago, but they did not love it. Then I realized he probably meant Catrin.

"We are no threat to you," I said. "If you seek revenge for the sentinel, neither I nor this changeling were responsible."

"*We know this,*" the hidden elf said. The slithering words were punctuated by more surreal laughter from the wisps. "*But there are grievances besides those held against the Falcon Lord to be answered.*"

A pause. Then, in a darker voice, "*You have much to answer for, Alder Knight.*"

A cold shiver ran through my blood. They knew what I was.

"Are you all right?" I muttered to Catrin.

The dhampir shivered in my arm, pressed tight against my side. She felt very cold, though I wasn't sure if that was her injury or her natural state. The arrow in her shoulder was black and fletched with pale green feathers. A subtle silver-hued light radiated from the wound, as though the dart had been a burning comet fallen from the stars.

"I feel sick," she said. She looked very pale, almost as much as when she'd briefly taken her true form in my room the night before.

I clenched my jaw. The elves had hit her with azsilver. Banemetal, as humans called it, or Moonsilver. An alloy that harmed the soul along with the flesh, and was especially effective against the undead.

"Hold on," I told her. "I'll get us out of this." I wanted to rip the arrow out, but didn't dare take my other hand off my weapon. Had she been human, I'd have left it in to avoid blood loss, but the magic dart did harm for every second it remained embedded in her.

"Knew you were some kind o' lord," Catrin said with a weak smile. There was blood on her teeth, and the whites of her eyes had darkened to red. She shivered violently, as though from deadly fever. Her accent had thickened— definitely a Marchlander. "Just my luck."

I tore my attention from the dhampir and fixed it on the darkening woods. "I was sent by Saint Eanor of the Choir Concilium to execute Orson Falconer. We are on the same side, my word of honor on it."

Like with William, I chose the wrong words.

"*. . . Honor?*"

The wisps ceased their laughter. The forest went deadly silent. The chill in my blood became a winter wind, ice crackling through my veins.

The immortal voice in the darkness spoke, and each word was a brand, each sentence a pronouncement of doom.

"*You think to claim honor now? You, who wields Faen Orgis?*"

"*You, who let the greatest of our havens burn?*"

"*You, whose order betrayed our archon?*"

"*You, who allowed the Adversary into the very heart of our most sacred places?*"

"*Even now you bear that creature's mark upon your flesh.*"

The scars on my face burned. I opened my mouth to speak, but couldn't muster a word. What could I say?

It was all true.

"I was deceived," I croaked. "I didn't know—"

"*You should not have come here,*" the elf said. "*You will not leave alive.*"

Movement in the surrounding trees. More wisps congealed, little motes of faerie fire burning themselves into reality. Only then did the true Sidhe make their appearance.

They were all tall as lords, all graceful, and an unearthly light clung to them. They were so beautiful it hurt the eyes, their weapons and armor shining with witchlight. Their faces were stern, wolfish, and utterly without mercy. Some looked as they are often depicted in art and story, as beautiful humans with pointed ears and vibrant youth, but others took stranger forms.

They had the strength of ages, and a hatred born of the death of their civilization.

A death I'd helped bring about.

They gathered close, aiming shining spears at my neck.

"We will bring you to our lord for judgment."

CHAPTER TWENTY-SEVEN

ELVES

I have an old memory that's never left me. It's from when I was a boy, back home in the Dales.

I wasn't born a lord. I earned my knighthood, before I'd gone and lost it, through deed, a touch of luck, and the whim of a certain iron-willed highborn. Half my relatives were woodcutters. I'd even taken my House name from those roots—Hewer.

I'd thought it a fine jest at the time, though Rose had rolled her royal eyes.

When I had still just been the son of a clerk and a laundress, I'd gotten lost in an elfwood near my home. It had been my first experience of just how strange the world could truly be, how frightening. I'd gone from the tedium of life in the country castle my family had worked in, into a world of whispering shadows and dreaming trees.

A world without death. One that didn't forget.

There'd been wisdom in the roots of that ancient wood. And horror. The priests say the elves mentored humankind when we first came to these shores, took us under their wing and taught us how to wield our souls, the best weapon we have against the Adversary.

I'd once thought of elves as my mother talked about them. Kind, whimsical, beautiful, and bearing the wisdom of immortals.

She'd never mentioned how immortality can make you go goring mad.

The elves brought us deep into the Irkwood. So deep, in fact, that I suspected we drew very close to the border of one world and the precipice of another.

I knew the signs. The trees grew taller, and less quiet. More will-o'-the-wisps and wraiths began to gather, their ethereal voices intermixing to form a ghostly ambience. The shadows sank into depthless pools of liquid shadow, and light clung to the woods from no apparent source, as though it grew as moss or mushrooms might, or gathered in lambent springs.

It might have been beautiful. It *was* beautiful, yet it held a dreadful alien quality. My eyes were tormented by confusing shapes, overwhelmed by half-heard sounds or phantom scents.

I focused on the elves who'd taken us captive instead. They were unearthly in their own way, but in a manner I felt at least somewhat familiar with.

"My companion needs that arrow taken out," I said. "It's hurting her."

Two elven warriors guided Catrin along, both clad in light armor of a pale metal inscribed with intricate patterns like overlaid leaves. What I could see of the bodies beneath were tightly bound in strips of cloth, as though they were mimicking the mummies of ancient human kings.

Each held one of the dhampir's arms in an ungentle grip. She shivered violently, her flesh pallid and coated with a thin sheen of sweat. Her form seemed nearly liquid, shifting from the lean, attractive woman she usually resembled to the gaunt, undead thing I'd glimpsed the night before, then back again. The banemetal arrow remained embedded in her left shoulder.

The one leading the band was a tall elf clad in armor fashioned of a pale blue star metal, beautifully made, with a horned helm revealing nothing of the face beneath. A faerie knight in truth, wrapped in odlight. They had been the one to shoot the dhampir, and the towering warbow in the elf's hand quietly hummed with sorcery.

The elf knight turned an eye that shone like distant starlight from the depths of their helm on the changeling. Though I couldn't see it beneath the helm, I could almost imagine immortal lips curling into a sneer.

"The half-dead will live. The azsilver tortures the dark spirit in her, but it is bound in her tightly as any living mortal's essence. Her fate is for the Oradyn to decide."

That word took me aback. An Oradyn is an elven military commander, like a knight-captain, but the word holds more meaning than that. A champion. A war chief. A hero of their people.

My trepidation grew teeth.

They hadn't taken my axe. None of the elves seemed willing to touch it, but neither had they allowed me to put it away beneath my cloak.

"You are the bearer of Faen Orgis, mortal, and our lord will see as much when we bring you before him."

"If he isn't too distracted by the smell of you," another added. They'd all laughed, and that preternatural sound was pain on my mortal ears.

I ignored their jibes, instead considering the weapon I held. Faen Orgis. The Doomsman's Arm. It was the first time I'd heard the weapon's true name since it had been given to me along with my penance.

Wraiths, very much like those that had attacked Lisette during the journey to Caelfall, swam through the shadows like silverfish with faces like hateful glass, murmuring invectives at me.

We were brought deeper into the heart of the Irkwood until we reached a great manorhall. It was built atop a low cliff where a waterfall fed a forest stream, rising among the trees like a fragment of the moon. Light seeped from the very stone of the hall, obscuring the spaces within as much as any amount of gloom might have. It was nearly too bright to look at, but my eyes began to adjust as we drew closer—or some trick of distance made the light fade into something more subtle—until I could make out more details of the building.

It reminded me of Elfhome, the capital of Seydis before it had burned. I could see similarities in the painstaking detail of the craftsmanship, in the way each pillar or overhang blended seamlessly with the whole. Every coiling arm of ivy, each fragment of glowing moss that clung to the lower walls, even the branches of trees tall as castle towers seemed a deliberate part of the structure, as though the forest had grown itself in accordance with the maker's vision rather than the other way around. Platforms mingled with curling boughs to form a complex series of walkways encircling a central structure capped by a crystalline dome.

We were guided up a switchback formed of smooth jutting stone along the cliff until we reached the entrance to the manor. Living wood entwined around supporting pillars on either side of an arch more than ten feet in height, funneling us into the building's interior. Wisps chased us like carefree children as we were pressed inside the manor, whispering nonsense syllables in voices like little bells.

And there were wraiths here too. Many of them. Though the great hall that formed the central core of the structure's interior was nearly empty, shadows filled every wall and corner as though reflecting a great congregation. They murmured, sullen, their voices just barely on the edge of hearing and beyond the edge of understanding. A sullen chorus.

"Alken?"

I glanced aside and saw that Catrin had managed to open her eyes somewhat. Her guards held her up, and I suspected without them she wouldn't be able to stand on her own.

I glanced at the elven guards, seeing if they'd stop us from talking. They didn't meet my eyes, but didn't make any motion to stop the changeling from speaking either.

"I'll get us out of this." I knew I'd said it already, but hoped the repetition convinced her. "You should save your strength."

"Course you will." Catrin's smile came strained, but she held an edge of iron in her as she fixed me in her gaze. She winced, and a mercurial ripple paced over her features. For a moment she was a vampire in truth, pallid and fanged, eyes red as freshly spilled blood. Then the fit passed and she was just a brunette village lass again.

I tried not to show my discomfort with the change, but some of the same disgust in the faces of the guards must have been on mine as well. Catrin's smile turned brittle.

"Not very pretty, is it? Listen, Alken." The sound of my name caught me off guard, made me pay closer attention to her words. "I know we barely know one another, and your kind and mine don't tend to get along . . . I heard what they called you. You're some holy knight, right? Slayer of monsters and all that. I get it, I really do, but listen . . ."

We reached the entrance to the manor. There wasn't much time left for talk, and Catrin's words came out in a rush of haste, tinged with pain.

"Reason I helped you back in the village wasn't because I needed an ally. Not just that, anyway. Hadn't even sorted out what was going on before I opened my big mouth, and that's always been the way . . . and I'm babbling. I just need you to remember this wasn't all some plot. I wasn't trying to use you, not at first. Shouldn't have tried what I did last night."

She fell quite a moment, taking several labored breaths before continuing. "I don't think these Fair Folk will let me go, not knowing what I am, and I need to tell you something because I've got a suspicion you're not as royally fucked as I am."

"We're *both* going to—"

"Damn it!" Catrin hissed, cutting me off. She struggled a moment, and her guards tightened their grip with dispassionate strength, causing her to bow lower. She looked at me through a gap in her disheveled hair, revealing sharp teeth.

"That *thing* in the castle . . . all the other guests think it's a demon. I don't know what it is, not for sure, but the Baron's got it bound to him. I couldn't figure out how, but it's the reason they're all here, the reason they're all taking him seriously. You want to take him down, you find a way to get rid of his pet."

She shuddered, and the motion caused her to go vampire again. "It's evil, Alken. Truly evil. I can *feel* it. It calls to the worst parts of me. It scares me. That thing is why I was avoiding the castle."

Those words coming from her transformed face made them seem truly dire, somehow.

There was no time for me to respond. We were brought into the belly of the manor, a great hall as fine as any mortal lord's I'd ever seen. There were many elves. Some looked as they are often believed to—fair humans with pointed ears, light clinging to them.

But not all Sidhe are fair, and they choose their forms over their ageless lives, or have them chosen. I saw creatures that looked like giant spiders scuttling about along the walls or branches that wove through the ceiling like rafters.

Cant Spiders. There were irks and trolls, and stranger things. I saw wisps and wraiths were everywhere, and there might have been a mortal or two. Captives or guests, I couldn't say.

At the end of a hall rose a throne woven of living roots, and sitting upon it was an elven lord. Male, with a lean and muscular frame and skin a very faint color of pale silver-green. He nearly seemed to glow in the relative gloom of the hall's interior, very much as the Lady Eanor had, though to a lesser degree. A pale and distant star to her luminescent moon, as all elves are to the Onsolain.

His hair was such a deep blue it was nearly black, grown into a wild mane that hid his pointed ears. He wore a white toga fastened at one shoulder, a sleeveless tunic of midnight blue beneath.

He'd been handsome once, even by Sidhe standards. That fair countenance had been marred by brutal scars. Deep gouges were carved on the right side of his face from temple to neck, narrowing the eye into a permanent squint, turning his mouth down into a macabre scowl. The wounds were angry, badly healed, still faintly red as though suffering infection. The marred eye seemed wet and bloodshot, the flesh around it swollen.

The scars on my own face, not so severe but unnervingly similar, itched.

The disfigured elf leaned forward on his root throne. "So it is true. A paladin of the Golden Aldertree is among us, come out of the shadows once more to tread these tired lands."

He all but whispered the words, but they rang from every corner of the hall. The onlookers fell silent, though the shades and wraiths continued to murmur, almost seeming to echo the Sidhe lord's words.

"My lord," I began, deciding it worth indulging the wood elf a touch if it got me and Catrin out of this. "I'm here to—"

"I know why you are here," the elf interrupted. His voice had a mild rasp to it, as though his throat were damaged, but its tenor filled the space with supernatural volume. His left eye was slitted lazily, like a cat's, but his scarred eye fixed on me with lidless intensity.

That's a cheap trick, I thought. *Makes it easier for him to talk over you.*

I hardened my own voice. "Then you know I am also carrying out the order of the Choir Concilium. Saint Eanor—"

"—Does not speak for us," the elf drawled. "The Onsolain are our elders and teachers, not our gods. It is only you humans who insist on treating them as such."

He paused and regarded me a moment. His eyes were very dark, little of the fey light shining through them. It hung *around* him instead, a tangible aura that made the Sidhe lord seem much larger than his mere physical body.

Elven spirits grow larger as they age, until their shells of flesh and bone can no longer contain their own aura. I guessed this elf was very old. Not the oldest I'd met, but no youth either.

He'd be powerful, and maybe a touch mad. Most of the older Sidhe were.

"I am Oradyn Irn Bale," the elf said. "Lord of this haven, one of few left from your order's failure. It is my judgment which will pass here, not that of the Lady Eanor."

I wanted to show him my empty hands, but I was still holding the damned axe. I settled for keeping it at my side, my grip loose, as nonthreatening as I could be. "I am bound to the service of the Choir, not just to Eanor alone."

Irn Bale snorted, his marred lips twisting with contempt. "I know who you are, Alken Hewer, *Headsman of Seydis*, and why you are here. Do you even know the lineage you pretend to? The thought of a mortal man holding that title twists my gut, and you dare to enter these woods uninvited, trample grass which has grown undisturbed since before your brutish kin first benighted these lands, claiming such ancient names?"

I swallowed my frustration and took a step forward. Guards moved to stop me, but their lord made a cutting gesture with one hand and they remained at bay.

"I am honorbound to this duty," I said. "It wasn't one I chose, wasn't one I sought—it's a penance. I'm *trying* to atone for my failures. Lord Irn Bale, the man known as Orson Falconer is—"

"Your treacherous order lost any claim it had to honor ten years ago, when they let *Tiir Ilyasven* burn." Irn Bale's voice was cold as glaciers. He used the Sidhe word for the city humans called Elfhome—*The Haven of the Falls*. "There are even rumors that some among the Table assisted in the murder of the archon. It is difficult to pick apart the truths from the babblings of those scorched wraiths who managed to escape the city's destruction . . ."

"I would be willing to give you my own account," I said, cautious of my tone but wanting to say the words through gritted teeth. "But I am here for a purpose, and every moment I am away puts more people at risk, and raises the chances our enemy might learn my purpose and take precautions."

Irn Bale shrugged. "That is no moment to me. You mortals spread like flies, and you're always in a rush. Another can take up this burden."

"And if Orson Falconer strikes at you?" I challenged him. "His allies already murdered the Troll of Caelfall."

Irn Bale's marred face hardened. His scars exaggerated the small show of anger, making it seem a devil's snarl.

Another figure at the elf lord's side stirred before he could say more. In a moment of surprise, I realized I'd missed their presence entirely—they'd been sitting within the tangle of roots that made up one section of the throne, so still and unassuming they'd blended with it.

She was a slender elf dressed in a blue toga, with blue-black hair like the Oradyn's, hers done in a long rope of braid that hung almost to the floor.

A relative, perhaps, though it can be hard to tell with elves. She rested a lute of intricate craftsmanship on her lap.

The female elf leaned toward the Oradyn and murmured something, then caught my gaze. She had mismatched eyes. One was shadow blue, the other molten gold like a coin before the metal has cooled. Not so different from the color of *my* eyes.

Irn Bale calmed, though with obvious reluctance. "I am aware of this misdeed. The old sentinel was my friend, and the Baron will answer for his death. His crimes, however, are not why you stand before me now."

He pointed a finger at the weapon in my hand. "That arm does not belong to you. You will surrender it."

I closed my eyes, swallowing the sigh that wanted to escape my lips. This was what all this theater had been leading to—the old captain wanted the weapon of power I carried. Everything else was minor in his eyes, a fleeting problem for a passing season.

I watched him in silence a moment before lifting the axe. The weapon softly hummed with magic as potent as any that clung to the elder wood and ensorcelled stone all around me. It had been forged long ago, wrought of strange alloys for a grim purpose before being refashioned for my use.

I held the axe out, letting it rest on my upraised palms. The elf's eyes narrowed, the fey light in them subtly changing hue with the motion. Sea blue to venom green.

"I never wanted this," I told him, meaning it. "It's been nothing but a burden."

Irn Bale nodded sharply. "Then I shall free you from it."

CHAPTER TWENTY-EIGHT

CLASH IN THE ELF LORD'S HALL

are to catch me up?" Catrin asked.

Her voice was strained, but still had some strength. Enough for sarcasm, which I took to be a good sign. I knelt at the dhampir woman's side near one pillar of Irn Bale's hall while a goblin tutted over her wound.

"The scarred elf wants my weapon," I said, indicating the axe I held. "It's a relic of their people."

"Uh-huh." Catrin nodded, then winced as the faerie physik pulled a fragment of azsilver from her shoulder with long, scalpel-sharp claws. He didn't use any tools—didn't seem to need them. "That doesn't tell me why my wound's being treated. Why doesn't he just take it from you?"

I lifted one shoulder in a shrug. "Custom. The elves—all the Sidhe really—bind themselves to old traditions. If he takes the axe from me by force, he loses face, tells his whole court that he's a tyrant who does as he pleases . . . gives them implicit permission to do the same. You can't afford that sort of recklessness in a society with memories as long as theirs."

"So, what, he's trying to butter you up? Get you to give it to him?" Catrin eyed the monstrous gathering. "Funny way of going about it."

I shook my head. "Not quite. He's going to fight me for it, but I have to agree to do it of my own will. He can't just attack me."

Catrin winced again. The goblin said something in its own language, its voice a bubbling hiss. I spoke back to it in the same tongue, and it grumbled incoherently back. Catrin eyed me and I coughed.

"You're full of surprises, aren't you? First you show up as a vagabond looking to join Falconer's little fraternity, then you're a spy and assassin, then some sort of noble warrior . . . now I find out you speak goblin."

"Sidhecant," I corrected. "All the Sidhe know it."

"Sure, sure. So why don't you just refuse to give it to him?" Catrin asked, eyeing the axe.

I grimaced. "If I refuse, he can just keep me here long as he wants. I'll die of old age eventually, and he isn't going to mind waiting. I'm the only one on a time table, and he knows it. So if I want to leave, I accept his bargain."

I sighed. "We fight."

"Any chance you just give him the axe?" Catrin asked. "I mean, it's a fine cutter, big man, but I'm not sure it's worth our lives."

I contemplated the weapon a moment. The brassy alloy reflected my tired features back at me. "If I did, they'd tear me apart. They hate the axe, but it's also precious to them. Part of their history. I treat it with disrespect, they won't take it well."

Catrin sighed. "Fucking elves." Then, startling, she looked at the physiker. "Uh, no offense. I'm sure you're lovely."

The goblin said something and let out a bubbling chuckle. Catrin glanced at me and arched an eyebrow.

"He agrees with the sentiment."

"Thanks," Catrin said to me. "For catching me back in the woods when I got shot, and asking them to take the banemetal out. Thought I was done for." She frowned. "Thought I repulsed you, though."

I shrugged. "I didn't trust you. Still don't. I'm willing to believe you're not just after my blood, though."

Catrin nodded graciously, though the mockery was somewhat subdued by the way she stiffened with pain. "Mighty understanding of you, milord."

I winced.

The dhampir flashed her sharp, crooked teeth. "I knew you were a noble. You had the look, even with all those scars, those dire eyes."

I stood, adjusting my red cloak. "I'm barely a noble. I'm the only member of my House, and I've been living as a vagabond for most of a decade. There's no point standing on ceremony."

"As you say, big man." The humor fled from Catrin's face. "So what now?"

I turned to the elf lord's throne. "Now I try to survive."

I moved to stand again in front of the root throne. Irn Bale still sat, consulting with his council. The elf with the golden eye reclined at his side, toying with the strings of a lute and seeming to ignore everything. An enormous faerie spider lurked in the shadows above, an eerie whisper emerging from within its mandibles. Wraiths murmured into the Oradyn's ears. His ancestors, maybe. Parents, cousins, aunts and uncles, grandsires, all eternal advisors.

His eyes were closed, but they opened as I moved to stand before him. "Your companion has been seen to. Are you prepared?"

I just nodded.

"I'm ready."

"So be it."

Oradyn Irn Bale stood. As he did he drew something from within the depths of the roots. A short sword forged of volcanic glass, yellow-green, a dim light smoldering within. The hilt was brass and iron, the grip wrapped in white leather.

The elf brandished the sword. It emitted an audible hum, and my auratic senses quivered at the sensation that passed over me. *That is a potent arm,* I thought.

"You were one of the Archon's warriors," I said. "A Knight of the Falls."

The elf followed my gaze to his sword. A pale smile touched his lips. "No. My sister was. I took this from her hand and used it to slay the same demon who ate her spirit."

He held up the blade, which flashed as though touched by a beam of sunlight that wasn't there. Liquid shapes curled beneath the transparent surface of the faerie sword.

I unclasped my red cloak and let it fall to the ground. Neither I nor the elf wore armor, though his garb was much finer than my borrowed clothes. He also didn't smell like half-day-old shit, but I'd fought in discomfort before.

I put all from my mind except the next few minutes. All my weariness, my uncertainty, my worry for the future and my regrets. I pushed them all down and locked them away, at least for the moment. Energy sung through my limbs as my instincts, honed through many wars and countless fights, took hold of my more cautious mind.

It was a thrill. A familiar, welcome one at that. Fighting had always been simpler than all the complexities of the world, all its vagueness and disappointments. I didn't have to concern myself with uncertain motives or self-doubt. There was no room for doubt and no purpose in empathy when life and death lay no further apart than the width of a blade's edge.

Live or die. Kill or be killed. Simple. Clean.

Pure.

The elf and I had both agreed to this. Both of us knew the consequences and had accepted them. We didn't have to pity one another or worry about whether the other deserved death. There was no deceit in us, no ulterior motives or mistrust. Irn Bale had made plain what he wanted, and I had done the same.

I twirled the axe in my hands—a needless bit of theater, but that was part of these sorts of confrontations. There is a poetry in war, no matter what any cynic might tell you. It fills a dark need in the human soul. To fight. To struggle and triumph.

Hate can be a balm to the spirit.

I felt hatred in the elf. It was in me too, though I felt none toward him. Mine was all a mirror.

I ended my brandish in a two-handed grip, bringing the crescent-moon blade of the axe above my head. I stood my ground, waiting. Irn Bale was the instigator of this fight, and the lord of this hidden realm. It was his right to make the first move.

The court watched from the sidelines, their inhuman visages cast in shadow as all the light in the hall seemed to gather around me and the fae warrior. Their eyes shone out of that darkness and their forms seemed distorted. Monstrous. Goblins and elves, cant spiders and wraiths, giggling wisps and stranger things.

Catrin sat among them. She seemed more one of the fey than human herself, cast in shadow as she was. Worry and anticipation warred in her face. Her red eyes seemed huge in the gloom. Hungry.

I tore my eyes from her and fixed them on my opponent.

Irn Bale adjusted his grip by the smallest fraction—my only warning. His form *shimmered*, like a sea-born mirage beneath bright daylight. He lunged forward, aiming his blade in a piercing thrust.

He aimed for my gut. My body moved without thought, muscle memory guiding my limbs into a parry. My axe didn't bat the stabbing shard of elf glass aside. Instead, the bronze bit of my weapon passed *through* the blade, which rippled before vanishing.

An illusion. The real Irn Bale lurked just behind the mirage, aiming his blade a hand's width lower. It scored across my hip, carving through cloth and flesh. Pain flared and I gritted my teeth.

Ignoring the pain, I took a single step forward and punched the elf lord—or tried to. Again his form rippled like a reflection in a disturbed pond and faded from reality.

I stumbled, caught myself, and brought my weapon up in a guard. Looking around the center of the hall, I saw how deep in trouble I'd gotten myself.

Six Irn Bales stood around me, a pack of dire wolves all with gleaming green swords and cruel, laughing eyes.

More illusions? The glass sword that'd cut me just a moment ago hadn't been one. I could feel the pain throbbing in my side, the warm blood dampening my trousers. The same hip I'd taken that crossbow bolt in back in Vinhithe.

Bastard.

"Clever Art," I said, taking a step back and falling into a stance better suited for multiple opponents.

"It has been the death of many a foe," Irn Bale said from six mouths, his voice forming a fell chorus.

Despite my flippancy, a bead of sweat formed on my brow. I was in trouble. Soul Arts are the mainstay of combat between two sorcerously trained opponents, and there are few better at this particular magic than the Sidhe. They had immortal centuries to refine their craft, not to mention the potency of their spirit.

There are plenty of mortal adepts who can awaken a powerful Art, only to have it fail them in the fury of battle through lack of combat experience. Irn Bale would have had lifetimes to refine his own tricks and incorporate them into his swordplay.

Didn't mean I had no tricks of my own.

Six elven warriors flourished their blades, and three pressed in for the attack. The others began to rush about in converging circles, forming a confusing dance my eyes struggled to follow. Worse, the dopplegangers shimmered and rippled like liquid light, creating a disorienting effect that made the whole pack seem a kaleidoscope of color and motion.

They laughed too. Sound, vision, scent, a throbbing pressure in the air—the elf attacked all my senses.

I didn't bother trying to match the display of sorcery with muscle. If all six blades were capable of cutting me, then it was a fool's game. Instead I narrowed my eyes to thin slits, concentrating on the words of a vow etched into the fabric of my soul.

My aura reshaped itself in response to my will, from a shadow of my physical body to something more complex, sharper, brighter.

My aura is more potent than an ordinary human's. I heal faster, can see in darkness, feel magical forces in the world. My commands and suggestions can leave powerful impressions on a weak mind, forcing a fearful enemy to freeze or a panicked mind to calm. I can imbue my weapons with aureflame, a potent weapon against Things of Darkness.

If this seems powerful, then you haven't ever encountered adepts of true potency. I once witnessed one of the Magi conjure a hurricane of epic strength, and a mage-knight sever that same storm in half with a sword stroke. I can't wield blades of lightning or conjure elemental beasts, though I know these things can be done, have seen them done.

That is not what the Table was made for. It was made to illuminate darkness, banish the creatures of the Adversary, to protect, to ward, and to dispel illusion.

I am the sword in the darkness.

I am the torch on the roads of night.

The hall darkened briefly, then filled with pale golden light as I thrust out a palm in a shoving motion. An expanding ring of light burst into existence around me, rippling out like a glimmering golden-white wave. Wyldefae flinched back from the burst as one body, some crying out in alarm, others hissing in anger. Wraiths scattered like insects when a rock is lifted.

All but one of the elven warriors converging on me were drowned in the blast of light and unmade. The last winced at the flash and fumbled his cut.

I took my axe in both hands, judging my range on instinct, and swung. I turned the bit at the last moment, and struck Irn Bale's wrist with the back end of the weapon. His wrist broke with an audible *pop*. His glass sword clattered to the ground.

Irn Bale did not fall to his knees or cry out in pain. His brow furrowed, but that was his only reaction. He leapt back, quick as a fly dodging a swatting hand, out of my reach. He lifted his broken wrist and studied it with mild concern.

I stamped a boot down on his sword, wary of his grabbing it again.

"How did you know they were illusions?" he asked, curious. "I cut you with one."

"Hunch," I said. "That sword was reflecting light. I guessed the bodies were just mirages, but the sword was real no matter who held it."

Irn Bale nodded. "Because of the one you destroyed after it cut you." His scarred lips widened into a bright grin. "Well done. Well done indeed!"

Then that form rippled and vanished. So did the sword I'd trapped beneath my boot.

The hairs on the back of my neck stood on end an instant before I spun. I caught Irn Bale's sword on my axe's blade. Sparks danced as both our enchanted weapons slid against one another, filling the air with an almost musical sound. Our weapons slid from one another, and the shower of sparks their passing made writhed and flitted in the air like living fireflies, at war with one another.

I parried another blow, Irn Bale's sword quick as a viper, then stamped a boot into his guard and brought the axe up in a savage rising swing. He dodged it, and I brought it down again in a chop.

The Oradyn shimmered an instant before I struck him. My axe cleaved him from head to pelvis, but he only dissipated like mist, my swing meeting no resistance. The real Irn Bale stood a few steps behind.

I'd been ready. I kept the swing going, the savage shout escaping my lips thrumming with aura. Faen Orgis flickered with golden fire as it struck the moonstone floor of the elven hall.

A small but very bright detonation of light bloomed to life from the ground at my feet. It grew into a shock wave of golden flames that traveled nearly twenty feet forward in an expanding teardrop shape.

Irn Bale's scarred face loosened into an expression of surprise as the wave enveloped him. The auratic fire kept moving, causing wyldefae to recoil as it drew near the sidelines.

The wave of aureflame nearly touched the root throne, but broke barely feet before it into wisps of amber-tinted flame. The elf with the golden eye reclined, unfazed, as the magical fire drifted harmlessly past her. She even strummed her lute once, punctuating the Art's end.

Sweat dripped from my face as I knelt there, axe in one hand, and sunk several inches into the floor. The aureflame had singed me, mostly along my forearms. My flesh prickled as though from a bad sunburn, already turning red and peeling in some places.

I fought to catch my breath.

"That exhausted you," Irn Bale noted from behind me.

I sucked in a breath and stood, turning. The elf stood about ten feet away, shimmering slightly with that telltale distortion of mirage. "Have I hit you even once?" I asked.

He held up his broken right wrist. I realized he held his sword in his left hand now. "Was that your own Art?" he asked in curiosity. "Or the axe's?"

"One of the Table's," I said. "So was the one I used to dispel your illusions earlier."

"You can still use them, even with the Table broken." Irn Bale lifted his chin, seeming impressed. "I wasn't certain."

I could, but they cost me a lot more than they once had. I managed to steady my breathing and took my axe in both hands, bringing it up so the blade hung level with my head. It flickered with aureflame.

Irn Bale dipped into a fighting crouch, smooth as a reed, his blade parallel with one outstretched leg. His weapon glowed with faerie light.

Round two.

Irn Bale flickered forward. He was preternaturally fast. His speed combined with his illusory bodies made him seem to teleport with each small movement. One scarred elven warrior blurred toward me, and another went low to swipe at my legs. There was no telling which one's blade had the cutting edge—both, perhaps.

I swung the axe without the graceful finesse the elf displayed, sweeping the mirages away in a flare of auratic flame. Less dramatic than my earlier blast wave, more concentrated, but it did the trick.

The illusions vanished, and the real Irn Bale spun through the fire like a top, swiping at my eyes with a savage cut. I batted the attack away, the impact jarring my bones and making my teeth clack together.

Again, our weapons made a sonorous wail as they clashed. It hung in the air, like some ethereal lute string had been plucked.

His blade had *grown*. Not literally, but the light in it was brighter, encompassing the glass casing and effectively extending the weapon. When had that happened?

Heat flared across my right arm. The blade had cut me. No time to see how badly.

Weapons can have Art wrought into them, to give a fighter more tricks in their arsenal. It is very rare for anyone, even an ageless elf, to develop more than one Art from the fabric of their own aura. I guessed the trick with the mirage bodies was Irn Bale's own magic, and the blade of light he wielded to be a property of the glass sword.

Combat between two adepts is often a mix of skill and the potency of their Art—sheer power can make a difference, but the more refined magic, wielded more competently, will tend to have the advantage.

No matter how mighty, sorcery is a tool. It needs a fine hand to wield it properly.

I had a whole arsenal of Soul Arts I could wield, but none of them were my own. They were all phantasms carved into the Alder Table, hammered into me when I swore my oaths. Some were more difficult to access than others, and some were beyond me. I didn't have much subtlety or skill with more than a handful of them, because I lacked the intimate understanding you'd normally gain manifesting your own inborn magic.

I'd never be able to wield anything so refined as Lisette's trick with her golden threads, or so complex as Irn Bale's illusions. My powers were more about brute force. Blasts of light, bursts of golden flame, repelling auras, and smiting blows.

I had one I thought might work well against this elusive elf.

While Irn Bale danced away from my aura of flame—more a deterrent than a real shield—I narrowed my eyes to near slits and concentrated. I murmured more words under my breath, and once again my aura reshaped itself. Unseen forces rearranged themselves, becoming denser, blunter.

For a moment, reality tilted on my axis.

I brought my axe down, using the dense rectangular back end of the head, and that ethereal hammer came down with it. My axe struck, and the shadow struck, and the floor *cracked*. Lightning bolt fractures raced across the center of the elven hall, intermingling or scattering, each filled with a fast-fading glow.

All of the Irn Bales around me continued their eerie dance, save one. One stumbled and lost his balance along with the rest of the watching fae as the entire structure trembled.

I locked eyes on that one, dashed forward, and slammed an elbow into his jaw. He went down hard, but the elf lord was tough. He twisted into an acrobatic spin, lashing out at me with a kick. I caught the blow in the shin, growled, but kept my feet. I sunk my axe into the ground by Irn Bale's head, making him flinch, then pressed a knee to his chest.

I slammed a fist into his face. Once. Twice.

Again.

On the fifth blow he let his sword drop and went still.

I paused, my bloodied knuckles still poised. "Do you yield?" My words came out as a bestial snarl. I breathed like a beast too, nostrils flaring.

The Oradyn looked more amused than anything. His nose was broken from my fist, and I'd cracked one of his immortal teeth. He held up one hand in limp surrender. "I yield, Sir Knight, I yield."

I stood, walked several feet, then staggered drunkenly. My entire body shook with fatigue, as though I'd been fighting for hours without stop. Using so much Art so quickly had been a foolish idea, but I'd wanted this over.

Wanted to win.

The crowd murmured from the shadows along the hall's sides. By their reactions, I might have just made a scandalous remark rather than won a life or death bout with their leader. No fanfare in the victory, no drama.

More like I'd completed a tiring chore. When had I lost the thrill in this?

Catrin appeared at my side as I ripped my axe from the ground. "Are you all right?" she asked.

"I'll be fine," I grunted. Small tongues of amber fire still flickered around my arms. I clenched my left fist, the other wrapped tightly around the oaken branch of the axe.

Not here. Keep control, damn it.

Irn Bale picked up his own sword and limped back to his throne. Wraiths congregated around him the whole while, their muted whisperings forming their own sort of weather around him. He sat, wiped at the mask of blood on his face, and regarded me with wolfish intensity.

So did the rest of the faerie court.

"Alken?" Catrin reached out to touch my shoulder.

"Don't," I snapped. She pulled back, startled.

The aureflame surged, embers burning to life around my left arm. They raced upward to my shoulder, the same conflagration beginning on my right.

The pain was tremendous. My skin blistered and peeled even as the same magic worked to heal me, a cruel cycle, the power at odds with itself. I gritted my teeth, squeezed my eyes shut, and focused on that inner flame.

"I am the sword in the darkness," I breathed. *"I am the torch on the roads of night."*

More words, more vows sewn into the fabric of my soul. I chanted them in a mantra I'd repeated thousands of times.

The fire roiled hotter, and did not calm. I fell to one knee. Distantly, I heard Catrin call my name. I could barely hear her, was barely aware of the hall around me.

I hissed the words of my Oath, golden fire crackling from my throat.

"The flame is mine aegis. I kindle it so the faithful may know its warmth."

"I hold the door against the shadow. I guard the ways and walk the paths."

Again, the fire surged with bitter fury. It had caught in my hair now, forming an ember halo around my neck. Or perhaps a noose. The elves looked on, pitiless, and did not intervene.

"Alken . . ." Catrin's voice found my ears as barely a whisper, full of pity and concern. But she couldn't help me with this.

It was the result of my sins. My failures.

"I am gold and iron. I am the . . . sentinel flame."

I choked, coughing blood. The vows stuck in my throat, burning it. I struggled to breathe.

"I am the . . . bough from which . . . the Alder's shoots become a phalanx."

Irn Bale regarded me coldly from his throne of roots, waiting.

Waiting for the fire to consume me.

I squeezed the branch in my hand so tightly it bit through my palm, sending trickles of blood down the scorched wood. The gnarled grip had begun to burn too, lit from within like a log in a campfire. I refused to let it go.

I met the elf lord's eyes and growled the final words in a voice that echoed with the Alder's magic.

"I tend the flame so it may never die."

With a sudden, fierce eruption, the fire engulfed me and—

Vanished. The silence came sharp as a thunderclap. I staggered, stumbled, and would have fallen if Catrin hadn't caught me. She was surprisingly strong, for such a skinny lass. I let her support my weight as the last embers of aureflame burned out in the air around me.

I had more scars, and my throat felt like I'd swallowed a furnace, but I was alive.

"I did not believe you could still wield the power granted to you by the Archon," Irn Bale said as I lifted my face. "Much less control it. The axe is in worthy hands, Knight Alder. Keep it, with my blessing."

I nodded, too tired to speak. His sudden change in attitude didn't confuse me, or satisfy—he was fey, and it was his nature. I couldn't muster any indignation just then.

Irn Bale sheathed his glass sword in the roots, lifted his broken wrist, and with an audible *pop*, corrected it. He tested the fingers. The skin beneath the hand had started to purple.

"It heartens me that the rumors surrounding the First Sword of Karles were not exaggerated," Irn Bale continued, rubbing at his swollen wrist. "You fight like a warrior of the Fall. You will need that ferocity to face the evil Orson Falconer has unleashed on this land."

"Quick to praise you now, isn't he?" Catrin muttered sullenly. "Now you've whipped him in front of his court."

I hushed her. In truth, Irn Bale looked hardly winded, and I struggled not to sway on my feet.

"So you'll let us leave?" I asked. My voice came out hoarse.

The elf lord nodded slowly. "Yes. First, though, I will have your wounds tended and your hunger eased." The ghost of a smile flickered along the half of his lips not ruined by scars. "Perhaps a bath, as well."

The whole court erupted with inhuman titters.

I'd have laughed with them, if the sound of it hadn't been so damn unsettling.

CHAPTER TWENTY-NINE

TALE OF A FALLEN HOUSE

An hour later, I was clean and in a fresh set of clothes. They weren't too different from what I'd been wearing, consisting of a tunic and sturdy warrior's robe. The elves even cleaned my red cloak, restitching some of its worst injuries.

They stitched my wounds with strings of moonlight.

Catrin and I were brought to a smaller hall. A round table of deep blue marble waited for us, set with dishes of food and drink. Elfin servants with silver leaves in their hair guided us, whispering conspiratorially to one another. Their laughter resembled that of the will-o'-the-wisps—fey, carefree, and a touch unsettling.

We were left alone for a long time. Music drifted from somewhere, bitterly sweet. There was wine on the table, but I didn't drink it, though I knew it would help ease my aches. I drank the water, and ate some of the food.

Catrin eyed the ensemble dubiously. "Aren't we not supposed to touch this stuff?" she asked, poking at a plate of fruits.

"It's not going to ensorcel us, if that's what you mean." I took another sip of water, wincing as the movement disturbed an injury. "Not unless we have too much, leastways. A lot of the stories are true, but we've been given hospitality. They won't try to trick us unless we prove ourselves ungracious guests."

In that case, the tricks would become malicious.

Catrin lifted a cup of rich blue wine, hesitated, then shrugged. She downed it fast enough that I lifted an eyebrow.

"They're not at all how I imagined," Catrin said after lowering the cup and wiping her mouth with the back of her hand. "And . . . everything like I imagined."

I nodded. I'd had the same realization, once.

"When I was a girl . . ." Catrin fell quiet, though the hall had been emptied. Only a few wisps bobbed in and out of the open windows. "When I was young, I daydreamed about who my real parents might be. I liked to imagine my real father might be a great elf lord, like in the stories. Wise, just, good. I liked to think he'd come and find me someday, take me away to be some sort of great lady. Or maybe my mother was the faerie, and she'd teach me all her magics and songs . . ."

Catrin laughed. The sound held a subtle note of grief. "Or maybe both my parents were false, and when I found my true family, it would be a full set. Happily ever after."

She fell silent. I studied the food in front of me. Kingly fare. I had no appetite, but I methodically dismantled the food, old habit compelling me to eat when I had the chance.

"You ever find out who they were?" I asked, after I'd eaten awhile. "Your eld parent?"

This time, Catrin made no effort to hide her bitterness. "Yes. I'm no faerie princess, that's for certain."

When I didn't respond, she threw a withering look my way that I caught in the corner of my vision. "Disappointed?"

I shrugged. "I wasn't born noble."

Catrin's eyebrows lifted in surprise. "You're serious?"

I nodded. When I refused to elaborate, she leaned back and folded her arms, studying me. I carefully refused to meet her gaze, instead focusing on getting enough water and food in me to take my mind off my wounds.

But she wasn't going to let me off the hook.

"I thought I'd imagined some of what the elves were saying earlier," Catrin began. "That the banesilver made me delirious. But it's true. You're not just a knight. You're a bloody *Knight*. A paladin of the Alder Table. You're . . ." She seemed to struggle for words. "I mean, they're—"

"Gone," I said. "Most of us, anyway. Lot of the order died when Elfhome burned, and the rest . . ."

I shook my head, a grimace forming. "Order was founded to safeguard the city and serve the Archon, the elf king, act as a bridge between the eld and human realms. Their broken oaths turned on them, turned them mad. Most of the rest died that way, after the fighting. There's no Table anymore, no order. It all just . . ."

I stared into my cup. "Faded away."

"Not you, though."

Catrin and I looked up as Irn Bale entered the hall. He'd also changed into garments free of blood and sweat, and entered the dining chamber trailed by a gaggle of whispering wraiths, all lurking in his shadow like ghostly courtiers.

I followed his entry with my eyes. "I swore a new oath after the war. Helped keep me sane."

The Oradyn nodded thoughtfully as he sat along one edge of the round table. "Your penance. Yes, I heard aught of it."

Catrin glanced between me and the elf, curious, but I refused to meet her eye. This was something I wouldn't speak of. Not to her.

Irn Bale didn't miss the dhampir's confusion. "Your paramour knows nothing of this?"

Catrin and I both spoke at once.

"She's not my—"

"He damn well wishes!"

We both fell silent and glared at one another. The elf smiled at our irritation. Goring fae.

When an awkward silence had fallen, Irn Bale laced his fingers together and studied us a long while. "I should apologize for that theater before. You understand, it was necessary to keep you safe from the others."

Catrin half stood from her seat, her palms striking the bluestone table. "Necessary!? You dragged us here against our will and tried to kill him. Your cronies *shot* me!"

I winced at the changeling's outburst. The mutterings of the wraiths grew more agitated.

"I understand, lord." I inclined my head to the Oradyn. "I hold no grievance toward you or yours."

Catrin's outrage gave way to disbelief as she turned her glare on me.

I explained before Irn Bale could. "You wanted them all to see I still had the Blessed Country's magic in me."

Irn Bale smiled and nodded, the expression pulling at his scars. "In part. You understand, the *Eldarine* are angry, Alken Hewer. Many hold your order responsible for these dark times, and they will take that anger out on you. And those near you."

His ageless eyes flickered toward Catrin, who hadn't sat back down. "I am not just the ruler of those who've taken refuge here, but their voice. If needed, I am their rage. Their hate. Their *grief.*"

He placed a hand to his chest. "I cannot be seen to disregard their feelings. My role is to *express* them. For that reason, today at least, I was the wrathful war chief. Now they have seen your oaths have not abandoned you, that you still wield the *aures*—the Golden Flame—they will be less likely to challenge my decision to host you."

I waved a hand, as though brushing away so much mist. "I get it. I don't take any offense for myself . . ." I let my voice harden. "Your people did hurt my companion."

Catrin's anger turned to surprise. Irn Bale unclasped his fingers, letting them spread like slow unfolding wings. "My warriors were overzealous in this. What weregild would you and the *malcathe* ask for this injury?"

"What did you just call me?" Catrin almost spat the question. I placed a hand on her elbow and she fell silent, sitting down with a sullen huff.

"You've already healed our injuries," I asked. "All I want now is for both of us to be allowed to leave in peace. That, and information about the lord of Castle Cael." I smiled, not bothering to try to make it look friendly. "I know that's half the reason you had me brought here in the first place."

Irn Bale didn't reply at once. Instead he stood and moved to one of the balconies separating the dining terrace from the otherworldly woods beyond. I stood and moved to stand beside him. Catrin followed too, though hesitantly, and she kept some distance back, looking uncomfortable and out of place.

The Oradyn placed his hands against the railing and contemplated the eternal trees. The wisps were trying to braid his hair, or tangle it, their laughter like tiny bells.

"I am among the last," he said. "This refuge here . . . there are very few of us. Save for the little ones and the Faded, there are perhaps a hundred Sidhe in these woods. All of them follow me. Perhaps a few thousand might still reside in living body across all the land men call Urn. Perhaps some more if you include the Briar, but even then our numbers are small."

He lifted one shoulder in a shrug. "And yet, our bodiless spirits riddle the land. Who knows how long it will be before our stray shades reincarnate, or the lesser spirits choose to manifest in the flesh?"

He held out a hand and one of the wisps alighted in it. Its light grew dim, as though saddened by the elf lord's mood.

He turned to me then, still holding the tiny mote of flame in his palm. The symbolism wasn't lost on me.

"We have no where else to depart. No ancient land to sail to. The west is lost to the Adversary's champion, the east wrapped in wrathful seas. The Wending Roads have been closed to us, along with the realms beyond them. This is all we have."

He indicated the twilit forest. "This, and a few other enclaves. We have little left to us, Ser Alken, and must defend it."

"Don't call me that," I said, too hasty. When Irn Bale raised a blue-black eyebrow, I turned away from him. "Don't call me Ser. I'm not a knight anymore."

"Ah." A sad smile played across the elf's lips. "The Church?"

I sighed. "I'm an excommunicate. I can't claim knighthood anymore."

"Among mortals, maybe. Your priests do not decide such things among my kind. You are a paladin of the *aur enhar*—the Golden Bough."

"Maybe once. Nowadays I feel more like a shadow. I've . . . done things. Things I'm not proud of."

I didn't want to speak more on that, not with Catrin listening.

Irn Bale nodded. "It is a fell role, that of Headsman. It was not meant to be bestowed on the True Knights. But this was not my choice, and I cannot gainsay it. Nor can I stop what must come to pass."

More elven prophecy, I thought, annoyed. Irn Bale smiled.

"I don't like having my thoughts read," I snapped.

"I do not need to be in your mind to see them," the elf said. "You wear them on your face."

The knowing smile faded as he placed both hands on the railing. "Orson Falconer must die. I do not wish it. His family has suffered enough harm they did not earn. But we cannot have his poison spreading, and he threatens my people. You know what he intends for these soldiers from the continent?"

"Not exactly," I said. "He implied it was for prestige."

"In part, I imagine." Irn Bale nodded to the forest. "They are for *me*, or so I believe. He wants the magic in this place—it is an old fountain of Light, preserved since the Dawn Days. He is a petty threat now, but he could make himself Magi with the right tools."

"Why?" I asked. "What drove him Recusant?"

Irn Bale turned his eyes upward and closed them, as though drinking in old memories from the primeval light. "He is the scion of a once-great house. Caelfall was not always the sick land it is now. Once it was bountiful, the Falconers mighty among men. But the city now called Vinhithe, and other enclaves of your kindred at the time, were suffering great famine. The priests cried out for aid, and the Onsolain answered. They diverted rivers, changed the wind, raised hills to save larger lands from ruin."

He opened his eyes and turned them to me. "It was ill considered. The Onsolain are not infallible. My people know this truth better than yours, I think, for we have seen such things through the ages of this world. It is why we venerate them, but do not worship them as your people do."

I took in that fact. Sacrilegious, if you asked most modern priests, yet this man's people were supposed to be blessed. How should I take that?

The elf continued. "Tens of thousands were saved, but Caelfall . . . it suffered. The changing of climate, the restructuring of the land, it turned it into the marsh it is today. Its greatest township sank, only that old castle remaining above the stagnant waters."

I considered this, a bit disturbed at the idea that the Onsolain might be responsible for such woes. "When did all this happen?"

"Long ago," Irn Bale said. "Many lifetimes of your kind. But House Falconer never recovered, and darker forces began to take advantage of their fall. Orson's mother was an exile with reason to hate the present order. She seduced his father and taught her son the truth of his blood's history. She poisoned his mind against the world that took his birthright, made him believe his destiny had been snatched."

Irn Bale shook his head sadly. "He might have been a king. Instead he is a backwater noble of little worth in the eyes of the wider world."

"So this is revenge for his ancestors," I said. "And his ploy to regain what he thinks he deserves."

"He has the potential to become a new dark lord," Irn Bale agreed. "We've had enough of those, I think. He must be stopped."

"I've already sworn to do it," I said. "Or been sworn. Whatever."

I leaned my hands against the railing, sighing. "I'm not sure how I'll do it. That castle is full of monsters. I've gone up against long odds before, but . . ." I shook my head. "He's protected. Some kind of dark spirit."

"You know what it is," Irn Bale said. "The sacred fire in you could not fail to recognize it."

I did know. I hadn't even needed the aureflame to tell me. The scars on my face had warned me well enough.

"Abgrüdai," I breathed.

"A demon," Catrin said. She leaned against the railing a short distance away, her arms folded. The elf's dark eyes flickered to her.

She caught his look and shrugged. "I had my suspicions. I'm more fiend than fey myself."

"I don't think I'll catch him by surprise with that thing shadowing him," I said. "I'm still trying to figure out why it didn't recognize me for what *I* am when it got close."

"Then don't try to surprise him."

When I turned to him, surprised, the elf lifted his chin. "You are no assassin, Alken Hewer. You are an Alder Knight and the Headsman of Seydis—the chosen executioner of this land's most ancient powers. You are no thief in the night, and it diminishes you to act like one. Face the evil."

He laid a hand on my shoulder. "Punish it."

He stepped back and turned his gaze once more to the woods. "I sense a darkness in the forest. The Baron is searching for you, I think. You and her." He nodded to Catrin.

"He sent me out to see if I'd murder a man for him and I ended up vanishing among the wyldefae," I said, folding my arms. "I don't think I'm going to have a warm welcome back."

"Do you intend to continue your ploy of alliance?" Irn Bale asked, curious.

"I don't know." I glanced at Catrin. "You never told me what your plan was."

The dhampir shuffled, glancing nervously at the elf lord. "Might still work, but we need to get back to the castle."

"I have slowed time in the forest," Irn Bale said. He said it casually, as though he were saying he'd put out more guards or felt confident about the weather. "I cannot do so for long, but it should give you the time to recover. From there, you will be on your own. I have something for you as well, Sir Knight."

I turned to the old elf, surprised.

"Your enemies are many, and strong." The Oradyn moved to stand in a column of moonlight. "I am forbidden from leading my people to war against a human lord, though I would gladly take vengeance for the death of my friend. All I can do is prepare to defend myself."

His expression became stern, and for a moment I saw a glimpse of what old humanity must have seen when they first encountered the elves—a grim, deathless hunter, terrible and ageless. No less than a god to those ancient men.

"It is your task to deliver Orson Falconer his doom," Irn Bale told me. "I will arm you for the task. But that will come in time. For now, you must rest."

His eyes went to my ring, which I'd been fidgeting with.

"I know." I understood his meaning, though I didn't much like it.

"Your dreams will be safe here," he assured me. "You must dream to heal the wounds in your soul."

"One night won't heal my soul, Irn Bale." I turned my back on him, tucking my right hand beneath my cloak.

"But it will give you the strength for the battle ahead," he said as I began to walk away.

"I'll rest," I promised him, still fidgeting with my ring. "On my terms."

CHAPTER THIRTY

RESTLESS

When Catrin and I were alone in a room within the elven manor, she whirled on me.

"What the fuck was all that?"

I met her glare, bemused. "What was what?"

The dhampir lifted a hand, gesturing in the direction of the dining terrace and the Sidhe lord. "*That.* These bastards took us prisoner, *shot* me, forced you into a fight for your life in front of an audience, then sent you on your merry way to fight their enemy. And you just . . . just . . ."

She made a clawing motion with her hands, baring her teeth in frustration. "You just bowed and thanked the scarred bastard like he was the blessed emperor of Urn!"

I turned and walked toward the single window in the room. It was more spacious than the one I'd used at the Falconer castle, all blue stone walls and faerie lights, a narrow window without glass cut into the far wall. It contained a bed, a small basin for washing, and an armoire. Outside the window, I caught sight of a garden bounded within the estate, with little streams and bridges. Music, serene and subtly sad, curled like smoke through the scene.

Like a painting. Or a dream. I scoffed. It *was* a dream.

"Well?" Catrin asked at my back, when I pulled the curtains on the little window and didn't reply.

I sighed. "They're immortals. There's no point getting mad about anything they do. It won't sway them, and won't get us what we need."

Also, I thought tiredly, *they had good reason to treat me like they did.*

"It just doesn't seem right," Catrin groused.

"Yeah, well . . ." I turned to the armoire and checked it. No wisps or wraiths. I knocked on the inside in several places. No illusions. "If you want quick justice from the elves, you're going to be disappointed. You want to call in a debt with them, do it, but I'm not going to sit around waiting for the Oradyn to balance the scales. We're lucky I won that duel."

"Lucky?" Catrin propped a fist on her hip, watching me search the room. "Looked like you thumped him good from where I was sitting, big man."

"He wanted me to win," I said. "I think. Not real clear on that point. Anyway, if he meant to kill me I don't think I'd have made it out of that intact."

I turned a hard look on the dhampir. "And you need to be careful how you talk to the Sidhe. They're quick to forget trivial things, but not slights. The Oradyn gave you slack because his people shot you with banemetal, but his indulgence will only go so far."

Catrin scoffed. "To the Pits with that. I don't let human nobles treat me like I'm mud to be stepped on, and I won't let him do it just because he's ancient and glowy."

She folded her arms and studied me thoughtfully. "Though, I suppose you're used to dealing with the like, being some sort of righteous crusader."

"*Don't* call me that," I snapped.

Catrin reeled back, surprised at the venom in my voice.

I fought to control my temper a moment before speaking again. "I'm not some dogmatic zealot, persecuting heretics in the God-Queen's name. That is *not* what the Table was for."

Catrin watched me in neutral silence.

You were quick to persecute her, I reminded myself in a flash of guilt.

She's a predator. She tried to ensorcel you and take your will.

I didn't know what to think. Hadn't for a long time. Catrin was dangerous. Even if she didn't work for the Baron, this Keeper she served might be just as much a villain. Perhaps a worse one.

"What was that he called me before?" Catrin asked, changing the subject. Her brow furrowed as she searched for the word. "Malcathe?"

"It means misbegotten," I said. "They use it for most things that aren't men or fae." *Mostly things of fiendish origin,* I added silently. One more reason not to entirely trust the changeling.

"I'll bet," Catrin said. A bitter smile curled her lips.

"We need to get ready to leave after we rest," I said, changing the subject. "What's this plan of yours? You left before I could ask last night."

"Yeah . . ." I could tell Catrin hadn't forgotten the subject, but she let it pass for the moment. She moved to the bed, sat, then let out a small sound of surprise as she nearly sank into it. She patted it a few times, marveling at the softness.

When she caught me glowering in impatience, she coughed self-consciously and crossed her legs beneath her long skirts. "Remember when I thought we were both going to die and I told you about the Baron's pet?"

I nodded. "You already knew it was a demon."

Catrin's face drained of some of its color. "Yeah. I can . . . I don't know. *Feel* it. Like it's making my blood shiver."

She did shiver, as though to demonstrate. "But it's not just my hunch. All these factions sending representatives to treat with Falconer are taking him seriously because he bound some dark spirit leftover from the wars in the east. And . . . you don't look shocked."

I shook my head. "I sensed it too, with my powers. Remember when you brought me to the castle?"

Catrin's eyes widened. "I thought you were some kind of mage. That was because of this paladin thing?"

"It's a gift of the Alder Table," I confirmed. "I can sense Things of Darkness."

Catrin's smile turned a touch shy. "Didn't sense me."

"No," I said quietly. "I didn't."

Seeing my expression, the changeling's humor faded. "Well, in any case, everyone's wondering how the bastard bound the thing to him. It's a powerful weapon, and he's the one keeping it in his armory. I didn't see the fighting during the Fall, but most everyone knows the stories—whole countries afire, thousands dead, armies getting lost every month. If Orson Falconer has one of the monsters involved in all that at his beck and call, he could unleash a little bit of that hell anywhere he pleases. It's his main bargaining chip."

I leaned against the wall by the window, considering. "You want to break Orson's hold over the spirit."

"That was my plan," Catrin said. Her tone turned sly. "But you're some kind of hallowed warrior, aren't you? Can't you just take that cutter, and . . ."

She indicated my axe, which hung on my belt, and made a chopping gesture.

"You can't kill demons," I said. "Not really. They're like elves and Onsolain—eternal. You can wound them, destroy their physical bodies, seal them away or banish them into the Wend, but you can't truly get rid of them."

My voice turned grim. "Believe me, we've tried. They're . . . difficult to fight. And the one at the castle isn't manifested in a body, I don't think. It felt more like it was in the walls, or a shadow. If it's not flesh, there's less direct harm it can do, but it makes it harder for me to hurt it in any meaningful way."

That was another disturbing thought I didn't voice. If the demon wasn't manifest yet, but Orson Falconer intended to use it as a weapon, then it stood to reason he planned to give it form. There were no gentle ways he could accomplish that.

"So . . ." Catrin lifted both hands in a helpless shrug. "Back to Plan A—we cut off the Baron's control of the thing. Without it, he's got no allies and no leverage. He's just some petty provincial ruler, and all this blows over."

"I'm not going to release a demon on the world," I said.

"Then what should we do?"

"Kill him," I said. I met her eyes. "That's what I was here for in the first place. If he's not a fool, then his death shouldn't free the thing. It's probably bound to the castle itself, or some edifice inside it."

Catrin swallowed. "Well, I don't think you're going to get close to him with that nightmare guarding his back, not to mention Karog and the Mistwalkers. So unless you've got a better idea . . ."

She had a point.

"Do you know how he's got the thing bound?" I asked the dhampir.

"I think I might." Catrin leaned forward, one pale foot bobbing in thought. "You remember that creepy cloaked attendant? The one called Priska?"

At my nod she continued. "I think she's got something to do with it. The Baron vanishes into the castle's dungeons every night, and she's always with him. I've tried spying on them down there, but every time I get close I can sense the spirit . . ." She shook herself. "It's like they're all down there in some secret council. I bet Priska knows, and she's not nearly so well guarded as Orson is. We grab her, get her to talk."

I considered in silence a moment. Catrin arched an eyebrow. "Not working for you?"

"It makes sense," I said. "But it's a bit short on details."

"Details," Catrin scoffed. "What's all that muscle for?" She appraised me for a moment, then amended. "Well, I can think of a few things."

I ignored the comment. "So your secret plan is to . . . use me as a thug."

"Yep," Catrin confirmed brightly.

I scoffed, but inwardly admitted I didn't have a better idea. It might have taken me days or weeks to learn what Catrin had already provided, and her knowledge of the castle and its inhabitants would prove invaluable on our return.

"There's also the trouble of those two hunters," I said. "I've got no clue what they're planning to try, but they'll get themselves killed."

Olliard had mentioned maps. Were they trying to sneak into the castle through some hidden way? It wouldn't save them from what waited inside.

"My coin's on the Baron," Catrin said dryly, as though reading my thoughts. "Still, I see what you mean. Those two could be trouble . . . or a nice distraction."

I didn't much like the thought, but she was right.

"What of the others?" I asked, beginning to pace. I hadn't gotten the chance to investigate the other members of Orson's council while at the castle.

That must be why he gave me a mission, I thought. *He had to be suspicious of me, and sending me out prevented me from gathering intel while he learned more about how I operate.*

Play and counterplay, and the Baron had outplayed me.

"Well, there's Lillian." Catrin's face twisted in distaste. "She's a sorceress. Not a true Magi, but a dangerous sort all the same. Don't know much about her, being honest. You've met the Culler Brothers, and they're right bastards, but not real *badasses* like Karog or Issachar."

"What about those two hooded ones?" I asked.

"Don't know their identities," Catrin admitted sheepishly. "They never take those hoods off, and they only really talk to one another outside of those dinner parties. The others seem intimidated by them, so I think they're important. Just don't know how."

"They probably represent some other faction," I muttered, scratching at my chin with a thumb. "How about that hobgoblin?"

Catrin blinked. "Hobgoblin? Heh, wish I'd thought of that. You mean the guy who likes using bones to sew up his doublet? Yeah, I know him. That's Count Ildeban."

I whirled on her. "You're joking."

She shook her head, causing her chestnut hair to swing and fall over her left eye. "I'm not. He's a regular at the Backroad, just like the Cullers, but he likes to take different guises."

I knew of Count Ildeban. He'd been mortal once, but he'd run afoul of the Briar. The wicked elves hadn't made a Briar Brother of him, but they had made him a monster in his own right. There were grim stories about the mad nobleman dating back nearly three centuries.

"There were rumors he joined the war," I said. "But no one could track down his castle. He likes to hunt knights for sport, and he didn't take a side, so we never managed to verify if the stories were true . . ."

"Guess he picked a side," Catrin observed.

Our conversation lapsed into silence as I chewed on what I planned to face the next day. A whole coterie of deadly villains stood between me and my target.

I only needed to deliver my doom to one of them, but I wouldn't weep for the others.

"Go get some rest," I told her. "The Oradyn has time slowed in these woods, so we can recover. Use it."

She nodded, hopped off the bed, and started to leave.

Another thought struck me, and I spoke even as it came. "How did you know Micah? Seems strange a preoster would be friends with—"

"A bloodsucker?" she asked. Then, her voice turning mocking she added, "A *malcathe?*"

I'd spoken thoughtlessly. Still, I waited for an answer as Catrin paused by the door.

After a minute, she answered in a sudden rush. "I was letting him fuck me. Is that what you need to know?"

I think she meant to say the words with spiteful challenge, but they came out like a nervous blurt.

I turned to look at her. "You were feeding on him, weren't you?"

The changeling folded her arms, shifting uncomfortably. "A bit. He . . . look, he knew what I was, all right? Caelfall's attracted my sort for a long time."

"He was an old man," I said in a hard voice. "Have you considered *you* might have killed him? That his ghost keeps seeking you out because it's *tethered* to you?"

Catrin's cheeks turned an angry red. "You're a real bastard, you know that? Micah was a good man! I wouldn't . . . I didn't . . ."

She jabbed a finger at me. "Fuck you!"

She slammed the door on the way out. That left me alone, wondering if I'd been right. And whether it changed anything.

CHAPTER THIRTY-ONE

IN IRON BOUND

I didn't sleep quickly. I paced awhile, fretting. I dwelled on the conversation with Catrin, which left me irritated and little closer to rest.

I took half an hour to shave my axe down, though it hardly needed it. I fretted some more. The soft bed called to me, but I couldn't get myself to sit despite my weariness. I realized I still wore my red cloak, and hung it on the bedpost. I stared at it awhile.

An elf maid entered the room some time later, carrying water and a tray of food. I nodded my thanks to her after she'd set it down, but she didn't depart. She waited by the door, hands folded. I went to the tray, took a morsel off it, then glanced at the elf.

She wore a very thin dress of pale blue, toga style, just transparent enough for me to see the shadow of a slim figure beneath. Long limbed, smooth skinned, slender arms bare up to the shoulder. Impossible to tell her true age, but were she human I'd place her at twenty at the oldest. She had mismatched eyes, one green and one gold, foggy blue hair, and a pair of dragonfly wings longer than she was tall, folded like a patterned cape.

I realized I recognized her. The one with the lute who'd sat among the roots of Irn Bale's throne.

She caught my look and smiled invitingly. I had to bite back my frustration.

"Please tell the Oradyn I appreciate it," I told her, "but I must decline."

The elf maid's smile faded. "Do I not please you, lord?"

I shook my head, choosing my words with caution. I didn't want to give offense to a faerie—I had enough problems. "I'm just not in the right mind to enjoy your company," I told her. "I promise, it has nothing to do with you."

It had been a lifetime since I'd needed courtly words. I was out of practice.

Who was I kidding? I hadn't been good at this even when I'd lived at court.

"I am not unwilling," the elf said, taking a light, graceful step forward on one dainty foot. Almost like a step in a dance, done with a controlled poise a mortal would need years to master. Her thin dress whispered around her ankles as it settled, teasing the shape of the legs within.

Again she smiled. "I like your scars, and . . . ah! Your eyes. I have heard the eyes of the Table's champions shine gold, but I have not seen it. Do you like mine?"

She batted her eyelashes, tilting her head so I got a better look at her golden eye.

"It is striking," I said honestly, still trying to decide how best to disentangle from this situation without causing offense.

She took another step, her dragonfly wings shivering. Perhaps a tell of excitement. I felt more certain of that when I noticed that the tips of her breasts had hardened against the almost transparent material clinging to them.

"I can help you rest," she told me. "You *need* rest, Ser."

She reached out toward the claw marks on my left cheek. Reflexively, I brushed her hand aside. Her face fell. It was like seeing a beautiful sculpture of ice crack.

I clenched my jaw and turned toward the bed. "I'm tired. Please, just go."

She fled from the room with tears in her eyes. I sighed after she'd gone, feeling miserable and satisfied at once. It can be cathartic to be cruel.

I did need rest.

I did sleep. I did not remove my ring.

Even still, my mind swam with surreal thoughts in the spaces between waking and deep sleep, and those I did not lose. Images curled through the darkness behind my eyes, one blending into the next with little thought or order.

My tired thoughts lingered on the events that'd led me to this place. I replayed the death of the Bishop in Vinhithe, my bloody, desperate flight from the city. I recalled nearly drowning in the river, could practically still feel the relentless rushing water, the crash of the storm.

I dwelled on my conversation with Nath. Had that been a dream, like with her twin sister some nights later? It can often feel like dreaming, when one meets the Onsolain.

I did not think so.

In my thoughts, I killed William Garou many times. Each time, I felt worse about it. I could have reasoned with him, if I'd chosen my words better. Couldn't I have?

Trying to push that ugly death out of my mind proved to be of little help. The pretty elf who'd tried to seduce me had half-succeeded, and I sank into sleep still mostly aroused. I imagined her with me in the soft bed, her dark hair under my lips, those thin dragonfly wings fluttering weakly against my stomach as she clutched the pillow, gasping into it while I moved atop her.

I felt ugly about that too, even as I indulged in the fantasy.

Damn it. I don't need distractions.

The thought was lost in the mad jumble of my exhausted mind. A blacker sleep claimed me just when the wings in my imagination began to take a different shape.

I don't know how long I slept. A long time. When I woke, I felt much less stiff. My restless discontent from before had relaxed, replaced by a sense of calm purpose.

Some quality of that surreal place, or just my will focusing, I couldn't say.

I met Catrin. She nodded a greeting to me, but remained coolly aloof. Fair enough.

We were led by a guard back to the Oradyn, who waited for us in a room more austere than most of the rest of the faerie manse. A space for meditation or some other quiet purpose, perhaps.

"I hear you rejected my daughter's advances," Irn Bale said without preamble. He'd been staring at an object near the far window, covered by a dark cloth so I couldn't see what lay beneath.

I grimaced. "That was your *daughter*? My lord, you have my apologies, I did not intend offense. I just—"

Irn Bale held up a hand, stopping me. "*I* do not take offense, Ser Alken. I told her you suffer from deep wounds, and would likely refuse. Still, you suited her fancy and she tried anyway."

He shrugged and added, "Personally, I think it is good for her to endure rejection. She is still young, and it will color her youth before conceit has a chance to plant roots."

I had seen the work of scorned, vengeful immortals often enough not to disagree. Even still, I had also daydreamed about fucking this elf lord's daughter. Best to keep my lips tight.

I caught Catrin studying me out of the corner of my eye, her expression thoughtful. I folded my arms and ignored her.

The Oradyn moved to the thing by the window. He ushered me forward, then nodded to it. "I will not send you against Orson Falconer ill prepared. He is our shared enemy, even if I cannot move against him openly."

"And why the hell not?" Catrin asked, ignoring the glare I shot her. She hadn't taken my words about courtesy with the Sidhe to heart, after all.

"The Heir's Laws," I explained as Irn Bale quirked an immortal eyebrow. "Back when men first started settling these shores, we warred with the elves.

The God-Queen worked out an accord with their leaders, the Archon in particular. One part of that agreement is that the nations of the Sidhe cannot wage open war against us."

I glanced at her. "It's part of the same rules that govern the Dead, and restrict the actions of the Onsolain. Without them, the land's more supernatural elements would rule us as tyrants."

"Or compel your kind to hunt us," Irn Bale countered.

"Oh." Catrin blinked. "So, you can't just send your fancy faerie knights to knock down Orson's door?"

"Even so," Irn Bale confirmed. "However, the God-Queen's laws do not prevent me from arming him for this task." He nodded to me. "It is the very reason why the Choir employs him as they do. *He* can be our instrument."

With that, he swept the cover off his gift.

I stared at it for several minutes, struggling to find words. Finally, unable to name the emotion in my gut, I shook my head.

"I can't accept this," I told the elf lord.

"You must," Irn Bale said, his voice melancholy. "You cannot afford to refuse it."

I raised a hand—one that trembled slightly—to feel the mesh of metal links that formed the armor. The coat of chainmail, a hauberk made to fall from neck to calf, was of elven make. Each ring had been riveted with an immortal master's hand, wrought of an iron alloy so dark as to be nearly black. The strange, living light of the Oradyn's home made shades of green and blue undulate along its length, so the armor almost seemed to be fashioned of liquid shadow or the water at the bottom of a deep lake.

Considering I had threads of literal moonlight fastening my wounds together just then, I considered the possibility that was *exactly* what it was made of. Shadow, water, and aura. The elves rarely used only ordinary materials for their craft.

"My wife wore this sixteen hundred years ago," Irn Bale said. "In our war against the Cambion."

He brushed his hand along the metal, and its substance seemed to ripple at his touch. "Its magic has faded, but it will guard you well all the same. It will not weigh you down, even in water, nor will it make sound to give you away in stealth. Should you wish it to, it will sing of your approach to an enemy you wish to terrify."

Elven chainmail. *Dark* elf chainmail, made to wage war in old nightmare wars. A raiment of fear.

It was an invaluable gift, if a fell one. A treasure of the Sidhe.

"If it wasn't for us," I said in a bitter voice, "your wife would still be alive."

"Perhaps," Irn Bale said thoughtfully. "Perhaps not. Do not bear all the failures of the world on your back, Alken Hewer, lest it break. You are but one man, and your battles are not done."

He nodded to the armor. "Hers are."

"I am not a knight anymore," I insisted.

"But you *are* a warrior. We will prepare you for war."

My fingers curled into a fist. I bowed my head in assent.

Several elves fitted the armor. The sides of the hauberk's long lower half were slitted on the sides, allowing more freedom of movement for the legs—my thighs and waist were instead protected by a heavy belt strung with solid iron faulds. On its original wearer, the chainmail would have fallen to mid-calf, like a robe or gown. On me, it barely passed my knees. The sleeves were short and topped by a pair of spaulders studded with round spikes, and a harness of heavy elf-iron disks was hung over my chest. The set came with greaves and vambraces of the same shadowy metal, which were adjusted for my size.

I was much bigger than Irn Bale's wife would have been, but somehow the elven armorers made the whole thing fit, and fit well. When I stood, it rattled ominously, the sound seeming to echo in the room.

The armor had seen many, many battles. I could see scars along the closely riveted links of each and every ring, and deeper grooves on the finely detailed segments made of more solid plate. Links were missing along the sleeves and skirt, giving the whole thing a somewhat frayed appearance.

"I will not give you her helm," Irn Bale said. "That, I keep for my house."

I nodded, accepting this without question. "It is a kingly gift. What was your wife's name? So I can remember."

"Irn Raya."

Finally I donned my red cloak, wrapping it around my neck twice before letting the rest fall about my new armaments. Catrin watched by the door of the fitting room. As I took my axe and approached her, I saw her eyes widen slightly.

"The Baron's going to piss himself," she muttered. "You look like Death's own executioner."

"That's the idea," I agreed.

Catrin turned to one of the elves. "Where's my fancy armor? I'm going in there with the big man too."

In answer, Irn Bale handed her a dagger. The blade was banemetal, the grip trollbone.

"The arrow we struck you with was worked into that blade," the Oradyn told her. "And the handle is from the bridge troll Orson Falconer's minions slew. You will deliver its justice to him, I trust."

Catrin swallowed, all the humor fled from her. "Yeah. Sure thing."

"Let's go," I told her. "If you still want to be part of this."

"Hey, I was part of this before you showed up." The dhampir sheathed the dagger at her belt, careful not to touch the cursed metal. "Believe me, I've got no qualms about sticking this thing into that bastard's heart."

More serious she said, "Alken . . . all this new gear is going to make it pretty obvious to the Baron that you're tight with the elves. Once you make it back to the village, they're not going to just let you through the front door."

I nodded. "I know."

So armed, we went to war.

CHAPTER THIRTY-TWO

DEATH BY DAWN

In the depths of the irkwood bordering Caelfall, a lonely campfire crackled in the last hours of night. Two men warmed their hands at it.

Two *living* men.

"Hate this fucking forest," the first complained, casting a dark look at the surrounding trees. He was the younger of the two, though his sunken features and graying hair so closely matched his brother's it wasn't easy to tell.

The older brother coughed, hacked up something foul, and spat it into the fire. The log within split, scattering sparks as though trying to cough the thing back out.

"You don't like any forest," the older grunted. He produced a blade, the motion so quick it blurred, and began cleaning his nails. "Suck it up. We'll head back to the village come sunrise and report."

"*Report.*" The younger Culler scowled at the word. "Like we're fuckin' soldiers. I didn't sign up for no militia. Since when do we take orders from the likes of Vaughn?"

"We're not taking orders," the older Culler admonished, picking a chunk of dead skin from his thumb, most of it callous. "This is a commission. You've done this before."

"Haven't died like this before," the younger man said, his eyes wandering to the third of their trio. They'd managed to fish their eldest brother down off the trees. The evil things had grown their branches and roots *into* him, and they'd had to leave most of that still riddled through the carcass's bones, opting to hack him down.

The one cleaning his nails shrugged. "Death is death. He'll come back, same as always. We should get it done before sunrise. A whole day in this climate will make him rank, and I don't need to hear his grousing again."

The youngest Culler couldn't take his eyes off the corpse's face, where two spear points of wood emerged from its empty eye sockets.

"Shouldn't we . . . get all that shit out of him? Before, I mean."

"And how the fuck we supposed to do that? We'll just mess him up more. Best leave it."

"He's not going to be happy," the younger warned.

The older shrugged again. "He's never happy. Besides, it'll make him look right terrifying. Might even earn him a name, like . . . the Willow Man."

The younger made a face. "The Willow Man? That's stupid."

"I don't know. I kind of like it."

Both men were on their feet in a flash, pulling blades as they spun on the source of that new, third voice. Their eyes alighted on the low arm of a skeletal tree. A woman sat there, cast in moonlight, slippers dirtied by a day in the woods swinging beneath the frilled hem of her blue dress. She flashed the two men a mischievous smile, revealing slightly crooked teeth.

"Catrin!" The younger Culler's shoulders slumped. "You scared the shit out of us. There are devils in these woods."

Catrin gave him a somber nod. "There are, yes."

The older Culler didn't sheath his knife. "Why are you out here? Vaughn send you?"

She scoffed. "Vaughn doesn't tell me to do shit, and you know it. Why are *you* two out here?"

"None of your business," the older said.

At the same time the younger said, "Looking for a man. One of the Baron's guests ran off after killin' that Will kid. You seen him? The one with the red cloak, pointy cowl. Big bastard, ginger hair, scars over his left eye like so."

He ran a thumb down the left side of his face at an angle, from temple to cheek.

"William's dead?" Catrin frowned, leaning forward.

The Culler nodded, ignoring his brother's scowl. "Killed him in the chapel! Fucking sacrilegious, that. He'll earn a century in the Pits for it, don't you doubt."

"I don't doubt," Catrin agreed, quirking an eyebrow. If either of the assassins detected the irony in her voice, they didn't comment on it.

A sound disturbed the quiet woods. It sounded very much like a light, muffled laugh. Both of the men glanced into the darkness warily, though the woman seemed undisturbed.

"Oh! Right." The younger brother flashed a gap-toothed grin. "Why don't you come warm yourself up by the fire, Cat. It's nice and toasty."

The older wheeled on his brother. "The fuck are you doing?"

The younger frowned, confused. "What? Just being friendly."

The older man thrust his knife in Catrin's direction. "She's fucking *undead*, you git. You're not supposed to invite them into the light of your campfire. The Law of Draubard, *remember*? It lets them at your neck."

He shook his head, exasperated. "What kind of necromancer are you?"

The younger brother scratched at his stubbly neck. "I mean . . . we're undead, ain't we?"

"Not like her!"

"Right," Catrin said with a laugh. "Not nearly as pretty."

She spoke from little more than a foot away from him. The Culler startled, spinning to raise his blade as he backed away.

"Get away from me, bitch!" He bared his teeth. "I don't want what you're offering, and I'm not willing to pay your price."

"Speak for yourself," his brother mumbled, flashing another smile at Catrin. She returned it, though hers was a bit more sheepish.

"So what's going on back at the castle, boys?" She knelt, holding her palms out toward the campfire. If she noticed the dead Culler lying half hollow and branch-riddled within arm's reach of her, she didn't comment.

"No clue," the younger Culler said. "Kimber and I have been hoofing it in this mess. Vaughn wants the red hood, that priest, and the other two found before the ritual."

Catrin's eyes shot up to the man, suddenly intent. "He's doing it today?"

The Culler nodded, feverish eyes flashing with eagerness. "So we've guessed. Why do you think he was so intent on choking the priest? He needs that hallowed ground *un*hallowed, you read?"

Catrin nodded slowly, pursing her lips as her eyes wandered back to the fire. "I read, Riley."

Kimber, the older brother, narrowed his eyes at the dhampir. "Aren't you part of his inner circle? Why didn't you know? For that matter, didn't you just come from the castle?"

Her eyes slowly raised to meet the man's. Riley blinked, confused by the sudden air of tension that passed over the camp. He noticed something about the changeling woman then, and he spoke in a hesitant voice.

"Hey, Cat, why are you . . . glowing?"

Catrin blinked, nonplussed, then lifted her hand. It hadn't been obvious before in the moonlight, but a soft silver glow clung to her frame.

"Huh." She flexed her fingers, watching the light blur. "I guess a bit of that mansion stuck to me. Neat."

"Mansion?" One of the brothers asked her.

"Yeah. The elf mansion."

Kimber took a lurching step forward. "You know where the irks are hiding? You've seen their sanctuary?"

"Sure." Catrin looked up at the assassin and shrugged her bare shoulders. The cold night air didn't seem to bother her, and the courtly dress showed plenty of skin around her neck and arms. "I just came from there."

Kimber turned his bloodshot eyes to his sibling. "Baron will want to hear this."

Riley grinned wide as a ghoul. "He'll reward us for sure."

"Yeah," Kimber agreed, turning his eyes back on Catrin. "Where'd you say this place was?"

"I didn't," Catrin said, her eyes still on the fire.

Kimber took a step forward, his blade glinting red in the firelight. "Don't toy with us, whore. You might be one of the Keeper's favorite pets, but out here you're *nothing*."

Catrin studied the sharp nails on her right hand, adopting a bored expression. "Kimber, Kimber, old friend, think about what you just said, and where you are. These are the deep woods. This is my *kingdom*."

Riley swallowed, his throat bobbing. His older brother was less impressed.

"Fine," Kimber spat, clutching the knife tighter. "You'll tell us where those irks are hiding, one way or another. How much of your guts I pull out first is up to you."

Once again, ghostly laughter stuttered out of the dark.

"The hell is that?" Riley asked, a bead of sweat forming on his brow as he lifted his own weapon, aiming it at the ghastly trees rather than the dhampir. Little lights had begun to form in the distant woods.

"Will-o'-the-wisps," Catrin told him. She still hadn't risen from where she knelt by the fire.

Kimber began to mutter with a susurrous, manic energy, his bloodshot eyes wide, almost inhuman in their hateful intensity. A flickering, whispering static began to form around him as he shaped his Art.

The corpse on the ground started to twitch, flickering in the same way as its living brother.

I never got to see how his magic actually worked. I took that moment to step out of the shadows around the little camp and swing. My axe cut the air with an almost musical hum.

The man's severed head hit the forest floor a moment before the body.

Riley cursed savagely, spinning to hurl his blade. I batted it out of the air in a burst of sparks as metal struck metal. The necromancer's eyes widened as he saw me standing there at the edge of the campfire's circle of light.

I must have cut an intimidating figure, with my blood-red cloak draped over my shoulders, the pointed cowl over my face, my coat of black iron rings making the interior of the shroud an almost solid darkness. Will-o'-the-wisps formed around me, burning themselves into reality like little violet stars as I lifted my axe.

A good distraction. Catrin's knife touched Riley's throat while he still gaped at me.

"Bye, Riley," she said into his ear, baring her fangs in a humorless smile. "This is for what you and your brothers did to Beth."

She cut his throat, then pushed him into the fire. The blade hadn't killed him—he'd been raised too many times, and was more like a ghoul than a man. But the fire caught on him like dry tinder. He writhed and wailed as he burned.

Catrin watched the entire time, her brown eyes reflecting the scene so they turned hellish. I didn't interrupt her, and didn't much care to hear the story behind that vengeance.

We burned the other two bodies, and the Culler Brothers were no more. I felt no melancholy at the death of that grim little legend.

"Dawn's not far off," I told her. "What's this ritual they were talking about?"

Catrin shrugged, checking the knife Irn Bale had given her idly as she answered. "Don't really know the details. Something Lillian has been helping the Baron set up for weeks. It's supposed to give that demon of theirs physical form, let them use it for real."

I rested my axe on my shoulder, considering. "That would require a profane vessel."

"Like?" Catrin asked, curious.

"Could be any number of things. None of them good. Ritual sacrifice is the most common, of a beast or a person. Could even be a place."

Catrin's eyes widened. "The church."

I nodded. "That's my thought. He clearly wants the priests there dead, so the sanctuary isn't protected. Once that's done, he can sully the place. It's sort of like . . ." I searched for words. "It's like making a wound in the world. The demon is an infection, or maybe a parasite. It can burrow through the wound to enter our world."

"You seem to know a lot about them," Catrin noted.

"It's not my first time dealing with demons," I admitted.

"I guess it wouldn't be," the dhampir agreed. "Just don't go turning that golden fire on me, all right? I'm no demon."

I wasn't so sure about that. She was no typical changeling, born of a union between fae and mortal in the traditional sense. Like the ghouls, she had a presence my powers didn't like.

I kept my peace on the matter. "We should go." Then, considering the situation I asked, "Did Micah know about this?"

I felt hesitant to mention the priest, after our last conversation about him. But Catrin kept her calm, shaking her head at my question.

"I don't know. He seemed to suspect Orson was planning something bad, but he never told me all the details. He . . . well, he had plenty of his own secrets."

Which meant he hadn't trusted her fully, either.

"Then he might have passed something on to Olliard," I said. "If the doctor knows Orson is leaving his castle for this ritual, then he might be planning to take that opportunity to kill him. I'll need to get to the Baron first."

I thought about it a moment longer, then let out a frustrated scoff. "No, Olliard was talking about Edgar finding maps for him. Whatever he plans, it involves the castle."

"And then what, if you do reach the Baron and axe him?" Catrin asked. "Die while all his allies rush in to rip you apart?"

I hadn't really thought that far ahead. Taking the Recusant lord's head was my first priority. My duty.

You are no thief in the night, Irn Bale had said. *Face the evil.*

"Let me worry about that," I said. "Besides, it would make a good distraction for you, wouldn't it?"

Catrin shrugged and sheathed her knife. "Yeah. I guess it would."

Our strange alliance had been born of a mutual enemy. We both wanted the same man dead. I didn't trust her, and she didn't trust me. Well enough.

"In any case, we need to get back there. Whatever Orson plans might have already started. There's not much dark left, and he won't want to perform this kind of sorcery in broad daylight."

I needed to have this done by dawn. Otherwise, it might all be for nothing.

CHAPTER THIRTY-THREE

UNHALLOWED

Something's wrong," Catrin said, as we approached the village.

I had noticed the same. There were no guards at the gate, and no sentry torches as there'd been the night I'd arrived. The streets of the lakeside community seemed quiet. Empty.

Out over the lake, the black towers of the Falconer castle jutted from a shifting haze of fog, cast in its own eerie glow against the black horizon. A ghost castle, brooding and watchful.

I wondered if the Baron watched us even then.

"Maybe something's happening at the keep," I said.

"Or maybe your hunter friends killed everyone," Catrin suggested, half joking.

I grunted. I didn't think the doctor was that dangerous, but it paid to be ready for anything.

We approached the village cautiously, but openly. Tiny blue lights flitted around us, illuminating the overcast gloom. They giggled like little bells and chased one another, toying with the frayed hem of my cloak or flitting in and out of my raised hood. They played with Catrin's hair too, though she swatted at them, half annoyed and half charmed. They'd followed us from Irn Bale's manor.

"*You remind them of the Gilded City,*" Irn Bale had said. "*They are fickle creatures, but perhaps they will give you some comfort. Remember, Ser Knight, there is beauty in this world still worth fighting for.*"

I wish I could believe it.

I glanced at the old church atop its lonely hill. It, too, lay quiet and dark. Had Olliard and Edgar returned there, tried to take sanctuary on hallowed ground? With two clerics, it could act as a veritable fortress against the Mistwalkers.

But not that ogre. And not Orson. He was human, and noble born.

I considered what to do next, my mind lingering on the chapel. Was William Garou's body still lying in the nave, cold, his blood dried on the stone?

"Let's see what's going on in the village first," I said. "I've got a bad feeling."

Catrin nodded. "All right."

We passed through the gates, and no one challenged us. I didn't even need to use glamour this time. It wasn't until we were in the village square that we found anyone.

"Bleeding Heaven," Catrin cursed.

A corpse had been strung up on a post above the square's fountain. The fountain was old, some remnant of more bountiful days, a piece of clever masonry bearing the image of an Onsolain herald, which had likely once filled itself from some underground spring. Nothing emerged from the stale waters below anymore.

Now the stone basin was filled with blood. The body had been beheaded and disemboweled, though his old, threadbare robes with their fur lining remained to make it clear who it had been. The head adorned the fountain itself, eyeless and tongueless. Night insects swarmed it.

"The village headman," I said. "He was at the castle yesterday morning, to see the Baron."

"Meeting must have not gone well," Catrin noted, grimacing at the sight.

"I'm guessing this was the Mistwalkers," I said. It reminded me of the dead bridge troll.

"Fucking butchers," Catrin hissed. Her voice held a strained note, almost desperate. She inhaled sharply through her nose, taking in the fountain's gory scent, then shuddered. A blush formed on her cheeks.

"We . . ." She licked her lips. "We should get moving. Get away from this." She cast her gaze around, trying to look anywhere but at the fountain. "Where do you think everyone else is?"

I swallowed my disgust at her reaction and thought it over. My senses didn't warn me of anything inhuman nearby, save for the subtle pressure of threat from the dhampir at my side.

"Let's check all the buildings," I suggested. "Inn, too. If anyone's here, they can tell us what's going on."

We split up, Catrin melding into the shadows. How that trick worked, whether it was Art or some kind of inherent power of her nature, I couldn't guess. If it helped us search the village quicker, I wouldn't complain.

I went door-to-door. Every house lay empty. I found meals left half eaten, laundry left out in the damp, doors unlocked or even ajar. But no signs of violence. No bodies. Even the inn had been abandoned.

Just empty rooms and eerie quiet. My sense of unease blossomed into a heart-pounding anticipation.

The Baron will need a sacrifice.

He wouldn't. These are his people. He is sworn to protect them even as they are bound to him as his subjects. That is the law of Urn, the sacred duty of the lord.

Orson Falconer consorted with monsters. He was Recusant, and professed to defy the god-saints and their priests. Why would he consider any law sacrosanct?

I had believed he did all of this for his people, his house. For honor and respect.

Catrin found me some time later. Dawn was little more than an hour away, the time limit I'd imposed on myself closing fast.

Perhaps it no longer mattered.

"Nothing," she said, confirming my own suspicions. "Place is a ghost town."

I looked to the hill. One more place to check.

The muddy trail leading up to the chapel had seen hard use, and recently. No rain had fallen that night, so I could still make out the tracks marring the path as we ascended. There had been many feet trudging up this hill that night. Scores, at least.

Less than a hundred people had occupied the village. There had been less than half a hundred ghoul soldiers. I did the math, and didn't like where it settled.

The chapel, like the fountain, was older than much of the rest of the settlement. Its bell tower rose high above the surrounding land, made even higher by the low hill it sat on, almost a castle in its own right, competing with the steepled towers of the Falconer palace rising through the mist in the distance.

Catrin eyed the church dubiously. "Need a quick pray before we head back to the keep? I'm not judging, but I think I'll wait out here."

I moved to the entry and, as I had with William, inspected the auremark worked in solid gold to the double doors. I sensed very little power in it. The metal seemed faded. Tarnished, more like dull brass now. Several wisps flitted toward the door, drawn perhaps by its faded energy or my own attention. Their light dimmed as they touched it and discovered, to their disappointment, its lack of magic.

Every preoster's ritual, and every supplicant's prayer, puts a bit of aura into Urn's temples. Over long generations, they become like fortresses against the fearful things that would prey on the faithful. When I'd been here last, that blessing still held strong.

Not anymore.

I glanced back at the dhampir. "This place is barely hallowed. You should be fine."

Catrin shook her head, her mop of hair swinging with the motion, and remained planted on the trampled grass. "I'd rather not take any chances with holy ground. Sorry, big man. I'll be out here when you're done. Keep watch, yeah? Make sure no ghouls sneak up on you."

I didn't trust her. This reluctance felt suspicious.

Well, better to have her out here than at my back if she planned anything. I shrugged, as though it were of no consequence, and tested the door. Unlocked.

I stepped inside, and nearly gagged on the smell. The wisps retreated into the shadows of my cloak, hiding from what I found.

I'd found the villagers.

I'd been too late.

They had been piled around the dais basin. All of them, so far as I could tell. Blood dried within the floor's many grooves and cracks, like a hundred miniature charnel rivers. I could barely see the holy basin for all the corpses piled around it.

My eyes, with their cursed blessing, saw the entire thing clearly. No detail was hidden, no shadow so deep I couldn't capture every facet of the nightmare in my memory. My gaze fell on the innkeeper from the *Cymrian Sword*. His eyes stared unblinking from the mound, rimmed with red. His teenage daughter lay against him, as though clutching him for safety.

The soldier's spear had stuck both of them to the pile together. They'd all been killed with weapons, so far as I could tell, and many of those tools had been left behind, as though the killers had thought it more aesthetic.

I'd known. I'd known there was no way the diabolist nobleman could properly use his minion without something profane. *This is what he needed the mercenaries for. As butchers.*

Too late. I was too damn late to make any sort of difference. Was I at fault for this? Had Orson Falconer moved quicker than he'd anticipated because I'd killed William, made him feel threatened?

I stumbled toward the altar. The smell of rotting meat, feces, and blood made me want to flee from that place, empty my guts out under the clean sky. I moved toward the slaughter instead, some unseen gravity tugging me onward on unwilling legs. I kicked something and nearly fell. When I looked down to see what I'd struck, the corpse of a child stared up at me. It had rolled off the mound.

I did vomit then.

When done, I wiped my mouth and half turned to leave. Something gave me pause. Movement in the edges of the room? I tightened my grip on Faen Orgis and turned slowly, glaring at my surroundings.

The domed ceiling and pillars of the chapel were carved with complex scenes, all meant to depict the history of the Faith. Ranks of archaic knights battled the slave armies of Recusant kings, the original ones who'd pushed the faithful out of the west. Alongside them congregated images of ancient lords offering their crowns to the God-Queen. Great storms and floods swept across the plains and mountains of the continent as the converted Edaean kings led their armies into Urn, to fashion new bastions against the chaos in the west.

The long march of history and legend, inscribed into ivy-wrapped stone.

Blood had been splattered across all of it.

My eyes took in more scenes, more wars, more fables I'd known since childhood stretching across those walls. My gaze lingered on the pillar that showed a group of knights surrounding an elven youth. The elf held an axe, very much like the one I carried, his image superimposed over a towering tree encompassing most of the stone pillar's length. Lines of gold had been worked into the stone to add definition and color to the scene.

I knew the elf. I knew the tale.

And the greatest lord of the Sidhe, wisest among all who walk the world in flesh, took an axe to the great Golden Alder which had stood in that place since the silence of the world was broken. And he, the elf king, hewed down that tree, and from its ruin shaped a power then bequeathed upon Men, so they may hold a candle against the hungering dark. And the Autumn King knelt before the Golden Queen, She who is Heir to the throne of God. And the God-Queen gave unto him the services of chosen knights among Her followers, who bound themselves to the Alder, and made of this act a covenant.

Legend. Myth. I had thought that once, before it had become my world.

My heart began to beat faster. I blinked, and the image changed.

The stone-etched image of the elf had fallen. The knights had driven their swords into his back, pinning him to the ground. The tree became a blackened, charred husk less than a third its original length. The scenes of war carved along the other pillars took on a more visceral aspect, until very real blood trickled down like miniature waterfalls, pooling into the open space in the room's center, even dripping from the ceiling to form a macabre rain. Fiendish things danced within the chaos, crouched on the shoulders of kings, spurring them on to slaughter and worse.

I could hear them laughing.

I blinked again. The images were as they had been. The knights bowed before the elf, who stood tall again, their swords held in supplicant hands. The rest of it remained cold stone, unmoving. Dead.

Profaned.

I moved closer to the basin, using some of my cloak to cover my mouth and nose, though my gorge gibbered threats with every step. I could still make out the crack in the altar from when I'd fought Orson's chimera.

There was something in the bowl where I'd given blood to speak to Saint Eanor. Something moving.

I leaned over the piled bodies and looked into the receptacle. It was full of crawling insects. Centipedes, spiders, maggots, beetles . . . they swarmed over one another, devouring, breeding, dying. Many had spilled into the piled corpses of the villagers and the same horror repeated itself there.

Somehow I knew—though I couldn't say whether it was some insight from my oaths or a more primal instinct—that a hollow lurked within the basin, an emptiness just under that crawling, writhing mass. A hole in the world.

Something had been born here. Something terrible, just as I'd feared.

Too late.

"They said this was justice."

I whirled, a snarl half-formed on my lips, only to see a figure slumped against one of the pillars encompassing the room's center. He was young, overweight, dressed in the plain brown robes of a chapel brother. His black hair had been matted to his head. Blood and worse soiled his robes.

Edgar.

The young priest's eyes slid up to me. They were bloodshot. "They said this was justice for our sycophancy, that the Onsolain would not save us for all our prayers."

"They?" I asked. "You mean Orson and his guests? Where is the Baron, Edgar?"

He didn't seem to hear me. He lifted cracked fingernails to his temple and clawed at the raw flesh there. His words took on a hysterical edge. "She made me pray as they killed them. She said they could not hear me."

"Who?" I asked.

His eyes remained unfocused. "God. Oh, Golden God, Queen of all the world, why did you let this . . . why did you have to leave? Why haven't you come back?"

I approached the monk and knelt at his side. He shied away from me.

"Was Orson here?" I asked him softly.

He shook his head. "No. It was . . . it was that old woman, Lillian. The witch in red."

Orson hadn't been here? That struck me as strange. "Who else?" I asked.

"There were two in hooded robes," he told me in a shaking voice. "And this . . . monster. A man who dressed like a nobleman, but his face was . . ."

I recalled the goblin lord from the council. Count Ildeban, Catrin had called him. Another dark legend, just like the Culler Brothers. Lillian had been here, and those shrouded twins. The Mistwalkers were here too, doing all the murdering, which likely meant their captain Issachar had been present.

But not Orson? The instigator of all this?

"They said no one could hear my prayers!" Edgar sobbed. "Not God, not Her saints. They wouldn't stop!"

I showed him Faen Orgis. The Doomsman's Arm. Will-o'-the-wisps emerged from the shadows of my cloak to flit about the weapon, illuminating the elven patterns engraved into the axe blade. The monk's eyes widened as he saw the gleam of aura clinging to it, the same light held in my eyes.

"They heard you," I told him.

SMITE

When I stepped outside, I no longer stood alone on the hill. The restless dead gathered in the bell tower's shadow. Mistwalkers all, clad in the raiments of a dead kingdom, pallid faces framing hungry eyes.

They had emerged from the marshes at the hill's base, or crawled out of upturned graves beyond the road, mud still clinging to them. Waiting for me.

Well enough.

Dawn had come and gone. Thunder rumbled above. A light rain began to fall.

"You were a fool to come back." Vaughn faced me from the center of the scattered pack of undead. Encased in a set of old, battered armor, he was as tall as me, his wide shoulders made into metal hills by studded pauldrons. He held his heavy broadsword in his fist, the nicks of many campaigns marking its blade.

Unlike the rest, he had a mount. A brutish chimera of a kind I hadn't seen before, perhaps brought over from the continent or bred in the Baron's labs. A massive hyena, long tailed, its purple tongue lolling. It snickered at me as the ghouls spread out to cover the churchyard.

More than a dozen ghouls surrounded their vice-captain, forming a half-ring around the front of the church. In the rain and mist, their armor seemed formed of pale shadows and their eyes gleamed with odlight.

No sign of Catrin. No warning from her about this ambush, either. She'd betrayed me after all, then. Perhaps this had always been her plan. Had she known what waited inside the church?

It didn't matter. All that mattered was the task I'd been given. The doom in my hand. I tightened my grip on the axe.

"We should thank you for offing that William boy," Vaughn continued, his tone conversational. His mount lurched forward, letting out a hungry cackle.

He forced it back with a savage jerk on the reins. "He would have been a problem."

I started to understand this strange situation better then. It didn't change my next steps, or my goal, but a clearer picture formed in my mind of the previous night's events.

I regarded them without words, and saw a few take nervous steps back. The will-o'-the-wisps lurking within my pointed cowl made the inside of the hood glow with eerie blue light, masking my face. More of that light spilled from the narrow gap down the front of my cloak. I couldn't see the effect myself, but I imagined it would be uncanny.

The wisps giggled playfully, the sound just on the edge of hearing. More of the ghouls began to lose hold of their bravado. They weren't mindless creatures. Their undead state stemmed from a gluttonous desire to remain alive, after all, and what is more human than that?

"I'm here for Orson Falconer," I said, my voice emerging from the elf light with a faint echo. "Step aside."

"Sure." Vaughn lifted his scarred blade. Unlike the others, he wasn't impressed. "We'll do that."

Fine, then.

I lifted my axe as amber fire played along its edge. I ran the fingers of my right hand along the brassy alloy, leaving tiny trails of golden light where I touched.

"This is pure aura," I said to the Mistwalkers. "It cuts you, and your spirits will lose their grip on those borrowed bones. Won't take much more than a nick."

Vaughn bared his yellow teeth in a snarl. "I've had enough of this. Take him."

The Mistwalkers were veteran soldiers to a man. They didn't hesitate, didn't falter. I hadn't expected my attempt at intimidation to work. Hadn't wanted it to, really.

They'd earned this for the old troll, for the villagers, and for five centuries of murder.

I waited until the nearest ghouls were perhaps five paces away, then flashed into motion. I went forward in a rippling flurry of blood-red cloak and dancing faerie light, lashing out with the axe.

The bell atop the chapel tolled. I couldn't say who was responsible. Maybe Brother Edgar, the one survivor of that nightmare I'd failed to stop. Maybe it was the wind, or the tortured spirits bound forever within that desecrated hall.

Maybe it was the ghost of Preoster Micah, whose spirit remained bound to this place.

The gladius of the nearest ghoul shattered along with the hand holding it. The mercenary stumbled back, maimed hand burning with a molten light. I stopped my forward motion, brought the axe up, then down to cleave into the undead soldier's shoulder.

There was a bright flash, a smell like nothing so much as one might find in a sunlit glade, and the ghoul fell to one knee. I'd severed his right shoulder down to one lung. The edges of the wound burned with golden flame. He opened his mouth as though to scream, and more of that light spilled from it. No sound came other than something like the rumbling of a furnace.

He fell, a smoking husk, and the spirit tethered to the corpse came free in a ghastly wail before it too was consumed by aureflame.

I lifted the axe as the rest of the Mistwalkers froze in their tracks, lifting arms and shields to cover their eyes from the flare of light. I let out a breath, and it emerged as a dawn-lit plume.

I began to kill.

Distracted by the dramatic death of their comrade, two more Mistwalkers fell as my sanctified weapon lashed out. I wielded it more like a greatsword than a proper axe, cleaving and slicing, blessed bronze sheering through chainmail and severing paper-thin ghoul flesh. Each undead soldier who fell erupted in a briefly lived plume-molten gold, their undead spirits losing hold on ancient bones as sacred fire consumed them.

It was a painful, nasty way to go, an unmaking that tormented the spirit as much as the body. There would be no peaceful rest for these. The flame would hurl them into the Dark, where they would burn for centuries.

Outnumbered as I was, the mercenaries should have been able to easily overwhelm me. Instead, terrified of the doom I brought, they backed away and lost their coordination, allowing me to dance through them, swinging my burning axe as I went.

I went through them like a killing wind, and within moments three more ghouls had fallen before they'd barely had the chance to muster a defense.

Then Vice-Captain Vaughn spurred his ghastly mount forward. Huge, a nightmare of stinking fur and grinning teeth, the chimera lunged at me. A heavy head alchemically engineered to snap bones surged forward, maw wide. Its carrion reek filled my senses.

It died on the first swing. Faen Orgis clove the beast's skull, but its forward momentum didn't halt. Hundreds of pounds of war chimera struck me hard in a shower of burning fur and gore, and I went down into the mud. Only my new armor saved my life, dampening the impact.

Vaughn rolled from his saddle expertly, landing on his feet. He planted a boot on his dead mount's shoulder and brought his sword up to take my head.

The ghoul's scarred sword met the edge of my axe as I rose, battered but intact. I batted the swing aside, but the Edaean legionnaire was wicked strong. My bones quivered from the shock of impact, my abused muscles groaning.

The ghoul warrior let out a shout, surging forward with a terrible fury before I could get my proper balance. I barely caught another killing strike on my weapon, ducked the second, then fell back as his onslaught went unabated.

We dueled beneath the bell tower, moving around the mound of the dead chimera. He didn't stop, didn't need to breathe or rest, didn't need to care if his muscles tore and his bones fractured. He had the strength of the dead, and the hate of lifetimes dedicated to war.

Vaughn was an old ghoul as well as a veteran of many wars. He'd probably fed on many potent bones across a hundred battlefields, and I'd have had difficulty finding anyone with that kind of implacable killing potence outside of the oldest elves. He was stronger than Irn Bale had been. Less graceful, true, but he had a wicked cleverness and a cruel edge to his swordplay.

Vaughn jabbed his sword at my eye, intending to puncture my skull. I flinched, bringing up the vambrace encasing my left forearm. The blade skidded off the elf metal, leaving a shallow groove to join a hundred others. I had an opening and tried it, but another Mistwalker swung at my legs with a pole-axe. I bared my teeth in effort, dancing back before the hooked blade could hamstring me.

Vaughn had distance again and used it well, shouting as he chopped one-handed. His blade skidded off my hauberk.

"Your irk friends give you some new toys?" Vaughn hissed through teeth nearly too large for his mouth.

I had no interest just then in banter. I took my axe in both hands, bringing it back behind my head—not for a swing, but to block the sword of a ghoul who'd gotten behind me. I used her own momentum to carry the swing around, letting it go harmlessly into the trampled grass, then punched her in the jaw hard enough to shatter marrow and crunch teeth. She went down, letting out an almost jackal-like yip.

I flicked the blood from my knuckles as I caught my breath. The Mistwalkers, still numbering more than half a dozen, paced around me like a pack of starving dire wolves.

I was out of breath. They didn't see it through the wisp light filling my hood, but heard it. My injuries accumulated from more than a week of near-constant fighting, most only half healed, screamed protests at my senses.

Vaughn barked out a laugh. "Orson told us you were some kind of holy killer. I admit, you put on a good show, but we've killed your like before. You tire like any man. Still . . ."

He clacked his yellow teeth together. "I bet that's some ripe aura in those bones."

"I want one of his ribs," another ghoul said. He drooled like a hound.

"We'll all get our share," Vaughn growled, the same hunger making his voice rough. "Company rules."

Discipline broke, and several of the undead mercenaries lunged forward ahead of their leader. Ready, I swung my axe up. A sunburst of auratic light blazed to life from the runic blade. The ghouls stumbled back, screeching and blind.

I sprinted at Vaughn. He was the most dangerous enemy present. If I killed him, the others would fall like chaff.

Eyes scorched, the Mistwalker commander spat something in a language I didn't recognize. Grating, harsh syllables, a blemish on the fabric of the world. His iron sword began to boil with a green-black smog, the same power writhing up one steel-clad arm.

His aura. He was a fucking adept, too.

Of course he would be.

He swung, and the smog boiled across the ground in front of him, erupting in a curtain of poisonous fumes. I barely stopped before barreling straight into the curtain, my cloak carried forward by wind and momentum. The edges of the red cloak sizzled where they touched.

Art. I should have expected a fighter as experienced as the vice-captain to have one. It reminded me of the choking smoke of battlefields, of alchemical craft erupting in toxic clouds that scalded the lungs and blistered the skin. A manifestation of a soul steeped in gore and iron hate.

I threw an arm over my face to shield myself from the fumes and leapt away, silently cursing. Too late. Some of the fumes had gotten into my hood. My mouth became suddenly, horribly dry. My eyes started to itch, then burn. Several of the wisps hiding in my cowl withered and died, dimming the light inside my cloak.

"Stings, doesn't it!?"

Vaughn came through the black fumes, a titan of iron with yellow teeth bared in a macabre grin. The fumes clung to his armor and shaved scalp, writhing around his huge frame in a protective cloud. Blood vessels burst in his eyes, turning them red and terrifying.

The wisps in the cloak with me whispered fearfully. I couldn't understand them, but got the message well enough—I was in trouble.

Vaughn brought up his sword, and once again it boiled with hateful fumes. His grin widened until it seemed to split his face in half. His skin was pallid as the corpse he should have been centuries before.

Before he could bring that finishing blow down, he staggered to one side. A look of confusion crossed his twisted features, then pain. He reached up with his free left hand, and found the elf-forged dagger embedded into his neck just below the right ear.

His neck twisted to one side, his features contorted into something truly nightmarish as he fell to one knee. A strange keening sound came from his lips as the banesilver tormented the ghost trapped inside his body.

"Thanks for giving me a bunch of darkness to hide in, you marrow-licking bitch."

Catrin emerged from the billowing well of fumes, apparently unaffected by their bite. I could barely see her through the red haze my vision had become, but her expression was nearly as frightening as those of the ghoul's—her skin had turned paler, her brown hair taking on an ashy hue.

When she peeled back her lips, her canines had elongated into sharp fangs.

Vaughn groaned, still shivering from the cursed metal's touch, but he wasn't out of the fight yet. He twisted and swung, moving with a jarring speed. Catrin let out a yelp, hurling up her arms to defend herself. She took a deep cut above the elbow that sent her stumbling back. She tripped over her long dress and fell into the mud.

Vaughn rose, ripped the elven blade out of his neck, and hurled it. It missed Catrin's face by inches, making her flinch. He advanced on her, insane with rage.

I squeezed the branch of Faen Orgis, letting it bite into my flesh. As it took my blood, the branch crackled and grew several inches. I lunged.

Vaughn lifted his sword.

I swung, mostly still blind from the stinging in my eyes. If I misjudged the cut—

I didn't. Vaughn's head went tumbling through the air several times before landing in the mud, plopping in the muck like some grotesque pumpkin.

The huge body, clad in iron and somehow still intimidating, stumbled. I recalled how that one ghoul had survived even with half its skull lopped off. I tensed, prepared to parry.

I hadn't used aureflame on that ghoul in the village. This time the headless body fell, erupting with amber fire, and did not get back up.

It took another moment for my own magic to counteract Vaughn's. My mouth and eyes still burned. I could see well enough, though the edges of my vision hazed. Catrin stared up at me, muddy and shocked but alive.

I turned to the rest of the ghouls. My hand tightened around the axe's grip, making the oak creak. Aureflame rippled along my arms, blazed in my eyes.

The Mistwalkers stared at me and the dhampir, blank-eyed and bestial.

I took a step toward them.

They fled.

CHAPTER THIRTY-FIVE

THE HEADSMAN'S MIEN

Once the ghouls had retreated into the mist encircling the chapel hill, I closed my eyes and made myself breathe. I meditated on my vows. Not just the ones I'd made to that elf tree, but those I'd sworn to my queen as well. The ones that'd made me a knight before I'd been wrapped up in all this horror and myth.

I knew Catrin was watching me, but she'd seen this before. She didn't interfere, or get too close and risk getting hurt. After several minutes, I had the fire under control.

When I opened my eyes, I turned to the dhampir and spoke in a soft voice. "I thought you'd betrayed me."

She lifted one shoulder in a shrug. "No way I was going to stall all those marrow eaters on my own, big man. I knew you could handle yourself. Just needed to pick my moment."

She glanced at me, then at the corpses, then back to her blade. In a hesitant tone she said, "I *did* consider abandoning you. If the Mistwalkers thought you dealt with, it might have given me my shot at the Baron." She blew a stray lock of brown hair out of her eyes. "But I figured my chances were better with you alive, so I stuck around."

Catrin reclined against the edge of the old fence lining one part of the churchyard. Edgar, or perhaps Micah, had kept a little garden there. It would go untended now, and already ivy crept from its bounds. She had one ankle crossed beneath her long skirts, an elbow propped on the fence.

The image of casual indifference. Her eyes were on her elven blade, distant and aloof.

Her mask cracked when I went down on one knee at her side, that neutrality scattering into shock.

"Hey, big man, what are you . . ." A nervous laugh escaped Catrin's lips. "I'm flattered, really, but it's just so sudden!"

"I owe you an apology," I said, ignoring her jest. I bowed my head, just as I might have done before a great lady in the court of a High House. "I've treated you with suspicion and distrust this entire time. Twice I nearly attacked you, and my words and thoughts have been . . . unkind."

I lifted my face to meet her gaze. "You've saved my life twice. Even if you hadn't, my behavior was not worthy. Please, forgive me."

Catrin's cheeks were bright pink. "You don't have to be so dramatic about it, big man, I forgive you. Bleeding Gates, you really are some shining knight, aren't you? I'm not one of your high ladies, so there's no need to—"

I shook my head, voice firm. "*Yes.* There is a need. I owe you, and you're the only ally I have in all of this."

"Well . . ." Catrin's expression turned sly. "Tell you what, you do something for me and I'll call us even."

I hesitated, my contrition evaporating as trepidation took its place. "What?"

Catrin hopped off the fence and patted at her castle gown, like a village woman brushing off her apron. "Call me Cat. Not vampire, or bloodsucker, or malcathe. None of that." She met my eyes. "Just Cat. It's what I prefer friends call me."

Friends. When was the last time I had one of those?

I stood and looked down at her. "I'm not sure you want me as a friend. This . . ."

I gestured at all the carnage. Ghoul bodies, smoldering and butchered, lay scattered in front of the chapel. "This is the world I live in."

"Al . . ." Catrin—Cat—sighed and patted my elbow. "Can I call you Al?"

My lips pressed into a thin line. *I'm going to regret this,* I thought. "I'd rather you—"

"Listen, Al, because this is important." Catrin pressed her forefinger and thumb together and held them to her lips, which widened into an exaggerated smile. That grin revealed long, needle-sharp canines.

"I'm a dhampir, boyo. I drink blood, and more than half the time I *like* it. You really think all this is going to scare me off?" She waved at the bodies. When she saw my expression she laughed. "Don't look so glum. I'm sure you were trying for the whole noble sacrifice thing, but save it. You're stuck with me, least until this mess is done with."

I turned my back to her, mainly so she couldn't see the smile threatening the corners of my lips. How long had it been since I'd smiled at anything, without it being bitter or mocking?

"So . . ." Catrin coughed and glided to my side. "You looked like a devil coming out of that church, big man. What did you see in there?"

Any thought of smiling was forgotten then. "They killed the villagers," I said. "All of them, I think."

Catrin's face bled what little color it had. "No . . ."

She looked to the chapel, and hate twisted her face. "That *bastard*," she spat. "He said he was doing this for them."

She blinked several times, but a tear still fell.

I recalled, on my first night in the village, she'd been with a local. "You were close with one of them?" I asked softly.

Catrin wiped at her eye with the back of a hand. "Not really. I haven't been here longer than a few months. Not much time to get close, you know? I spent most of my time those first weeks with Micah."

"I remember there was a man," I said. "That night we first met."

"Oh." Catrin let out a shaky laugh. "Just a bit of blood and warmth. I can't even remember his name." Her gaze went distant. "That's awful, isn't it?"

I shook my head. "It does you credit to weep for those you didn't know well." The admission she'd been feeding off the man unsettled me, but I let it go. This wasn't the time.

"I can't believe he would do this," Catrin said as she stared at the silent church. "I knew he was ambitious, but not insane."

"I don't think this was Orson," I said. When Catrin startled, I indicated the church. "There's still a survivor. Micah's disciple, Brother Edgar. He told me the Baron wasn't here last night. It was his guests instead. Lillian, the hobgoblin count, and those two in the robes."

I studied the bodies. "I think these Mistwalkers were left behind for Olliard and Lisette, if they tried returning to the church. Maybe for us, even. Loose ends."

Catrin got what I implied quickly. "You think they betrayed him? Did a nastier version of the same ritual he intended, and stole his pet demon?"

"It's possible." I fixed my eyes on the distant fortress. "I'll need to get to the castle to be sure. I still have a task to complete. You—"

"If you tell me to stay behind, I'm going to bite you." Catrin glowered at me and bared her sharp teeth. "I'm going. That aristo prick is going to get Shivers right in his gut."

I raised an eyebrow. "Shivers?"

The dhampir woman patted her elven blade and flashed a wicked smile. "Your cutter has a fancy name, so mine gets one too. Shivers. Cuz the bane-silver makes the dead shiver, ya' know?"

I snorted. "Let's go, then. I'm sure they're already shivering."

"Hey! I saved your ass back there, big man, so don't go making fun."

Before I could reply, I heard the doors of the church opening. I turned to see Brother Edgar standing there, eyes wide as he surveyed the carnage.

"You . . ." the young monk's voice trembled as he pointed a finger at me. "Just like last time, you . . ."

I sighed, having had a stomach full of piety. However, rather than proclaiming some devout supplication, the monk's features twisted with rage.

"Where were you?" he spat. "Where were you when we needed you? When they were butchering them?"

He began to descend the steps, flinging one wide sleeve toward the dead ghouls. "What does all this do now? What's the point? You should have just let those beasts kill me the night you arrived if it was all going to come to *this*."

I didn't know what to tell the young man. I had no words that could assuage his grief. Had I been even half the man I'd wanted to be—a true paladin, a proper knight—I'd have told him something to calm his fears, give purpose to his anger. I would have sworn some noble oath and breathed a bit of light back into that darkness.

But I didn't have the words, and he was right. I hadn't done anything for them. I'd spent the night trying to be clever, dining in an elven hall, making plots and plans to defeat my enemy.

Instead, hardening my heart against the monk's despair, I turned to face him fully. "Where are the other two? Olliard and Lisette?"

Edgar's face darkened further. "He did nothing for us either," he hissed.

"Where are they, Edgar?"

Hugging himself beneath the cold rain, a blank, dull nothingness filled the monk's eyes. "I gave him some of the preoster's maps of the castle. Micah had been at odds with the Baron for years, making preparations to stop him . . ." He barked out a hollow laugh. "I thought him a paranoid old fool chasing after imagined sins!"

"They're trying to infiltrate the castle?" I asked, trying to keep the man on topic.

Edgar nodded miserably. "Castle Cael used to lie at the center of a large township. You can still see its ruins across the lake. They make the waters treacherous, but there are a few routes you can use to get through and enter the castle. The maps were of the old town, showing places where the sunken buildings might not stop a boat."

"Not much use to us," Catrin noted. "I already have a route in."

Edgar's eyes went to Catrin, and lit with fresh fury. "You!"

Catrin sighed. "Here we go."

"Deceiving slattern! You're one of his creatures!" Edgar pointed a trembling finger at the dhampir. "Seductress! Succubus! Micah was healthy and strong before you crawled into his bed!"

Catrin winced, turning her face away from the monk's anger. I grabbed him by the wrist, hard enough he let out a hiss of pain. I kept my voice very low, speaking slow and calm to break through his mania.

"She isn't a succubus," I told him firmly. "The Baron wanted the preoster dead. He tried to kill *you* as well, so he could use the chapel to raise his beast. *He* killed Micah."

"He kept to his vows for decades before she arrived," Edgar hissed. "She weakened him."

"Maybe," I admitted. "But she's on our side now, and we can't afford to refuse help. This isn't done."

I let him go. He stumbled back, almost tripping over his robes into the mud.

"What of the monster?" I asked. "Orson was keeping something in the lake. A chimera, I think, and a big one. Did you warn them of that?"

Edgar nodded. "Of course. But Olliard insisted he could deal with it. He is . . . very capable. I think he's some sort of monster hunter."

I'd guessed the same. Still, a few fancy tools and his apprentice's clever magic wouldn't save them from the lake monster. Much less Karog, if he remained in the castle.

"Was there an ogre with the ones who did this?" I asked, nodding to the church.

Edgar shook his head.

Was Karog not one of the betrayers? I wondered.

"What're you thinking, big man?" Catrin asked, folding her arms and glancing nervously at the church. Brother Edgar had slumped down on the stairs and buried his head in his hands. I think he was praying. Or weeping.

I closed my eyes, thinking. Orson Falconer might already be dead, his castle full of enemies. If not, then I was still duty bound to deliver his sentence.

Even if he *were* dead . . .

Olliard and Lisette had saved my life. I still owed them, even if they had pissed me off.

"I'm going to the castle." I turned to Catrin. "I probably won't come back out alive, if there's a manifest demon and an army of other horrors inside."

Catrin nodded, grinning without humor. "Sounds like a party. After you?"

CHAPTER THIRTY-SIX

THE TUNNEL

The boat glided across the murky waters of the lake. The overcast sky, and the ever-present mist of Caelfall, cast the world in a dreamlike veil. Quiet, still, and depthless.

Catrin's eyes locked on the shadow of the castle looming from the depths of the lake ahead, enthroned within its drowned field of ruined, shattered buildings. She rowed this time, while I watched the depths of the mist, wary of ambush.

"I don't hear those sentries from before," I noted. I recalled huge, winged things clinging to the sunken buildings.

"They're night beasts," Catrin said. "Might not run into them." I didn't miss the hopeful note in her voice. "They're not all the Baron's got in his kennels," she added. "The Falconers are chimera breeders."

I glanced in the general direction of the sun—I couldn't see it through the overcast sky or the thin veil of mist. The castle was a black monolith dominating the lake, the capstone to the shattered sprawl.

Did the Onsolain really cause all this? I ran my eyes across the ruins. Hard to believe this had once been the site of a small kingdom in its own right, this stagnant swamp and its marshy surrounds.

It didn't matter. Orson Falconer had made his own choices, and he'd chosen to be a monster. Even if he hadn't been present in the chapel, he would have made plenty of similar tragedies with the war he sought. His actions had brought this about.

Once we reached the castle, there wouldn't be time for idle talk. Something else had been lingering in my thoughts as well.

"What Edgar said," I began. "What *I* said back at Irn Bale's house, about you and the preoster . . ."

"Doesn't matter anymore," Catrin interrupted without ceasing her rowing.

"It *does*. It was cruel."

She kept rowing. I couldn't see her face, or tell her thoughts.

"Did you love him?" I asked.

I heard her scoff. Then, after some time she said, "No. Micah was a lonely man. He took his vows seriously, and didn't get into relationships with the locals. They looked up to him, you know? But he wanted company, and didn't mind feeling my fangs to get it. That's all it was."

She pushed us forward with another long sweep of the oar. "As for *love* . . . well, I've never gotten on with churches and priests."

"You didn't choose to be born this way," I said, repeating her own words from the castle bedroom. Hypocritical of me, maybe.

Catrin snorted. "You know that doesn't matter. And as for what you said back in the forest . . . preosts get their magic from faith, yeah? Even ignoring the blood I took, I think I might have weakened his will. And *that* let the Baron beat him."

She glanced back at me with cold, remote eyes. "So yeah, maybe it *was* my fault. You were right."

Our conversation lapsed into silence. We passed by something as the boat drifted through the ruins. A dark mound resting on the surface of the water.

Not resting. *Floating.* It was shiny black and oily, big as a house. Nearly a score of spears protruded from its leathery, puckered flesh. I'd seen something similar before, when fishermen had used javelins to hunt a leviathan off the coast. I couldn't see much of it, but a shiny black eye stared unseeing up into the sky near one end.

"The lake monster," Catrin said as we passed it. "Looks like your hunch was right. The Mistwalkers turned on Orson."

"Question is whether he's still fighting them," I added as we passed the carcass. The castle seemed ominously quiet, just as the village had. No song of battle echoed over the sunken ruins.

Catrin guided the boat into the long tunnel where we'd entered the keep before. As the open sky vanished beneath solid rock, I tightened my grip on my weapon, growing tense.

"You feel that?" Catrin whispered.

"Yes," I said. We weren't alone in the tunnel. My aura shivered with apprehension, but it wasn't just a supernatural sense telling me danger lay ahead. A very real stench filled the cave, overpoweringly foul. It reeked of carrion.

It hadn't been there the last time.

"Alken . . ." Catrin was tense as a bowstring. "Maybe we should find—"

Something hurled itself at me through the darkness. The depths of the waterlogged tunnel were nearly pitch black, but not to me. I saw the shape of the thing, bat-winged and leech-mouthed, and swung on pure reflex.

My axe came down in a vertical chop even as I ducked. The axe's sickle moon blade clove the fanged nightmare from skull to chest cavity. Its bulk splashed into the water some distance behind us.

"Shit!" Catrin swore.

I rested the axe on my shoulder. Its edge glowed slightly, like hot metal. "Keep moving forward," I ordered, scanning the tunnel ahead.

Catrin did, though her hands shook slightly on the oar.

I sensed more of the enormous bat things ahead. Some kind of chimera, I guessed, as Catrin had warned me. My magic alerted me of danger, but not of anything truly profane. Not fiends, but rather ill-formed beasts bound by the Baron's magic or bred like the war chimera used by armies across the world.

Still, something foul had gone into the make of these.

They had enormous wing spans, and the tunnel was only wide enough for one to take flight at a time. I had that advantage, but the edges of the cavern walls were well beyond my reach. If they simply waited for me to pass, then swarmed me all at once, they wouldn't need to take to the air . . .

Black shapes moved along the walls as Catrin spurred us forward with the oar. I ground my teeth, and decided there was no choice.

"This might be uncomfortable for you," I told Catrin. I felt her worried eyes on my back. I narrowed my eyes and murmured the words of one of my Oaths.

An Oath is the core of a paladin's power. It is a pact made with the self, sometimes with a supernatural intermediary that can back the vow to make it more potent, as in my case with the Alder Table. It is not always necessary, and there are True Knights in the world whose vows are entirely personal, born of their own convictions, but those are very rare.

The rituals involved in this brand of magic are old, and much of the might granted to us comes from that long refining.

"The flame is mine aegis," I whispered, my words causing the very air to shudder. "The flame is my sword. I kindle the flame so the world may know its warmth. Its light is our shelter against the Dark. I bear the torch on the roads of night. I *am* the torch."

Saying the words aloud was not necessary to draw on my powers, not always. But saying a thing can do much to make it real.

You do not believe me? I am certain you have experienced this yourself. Have you not apologized to someone you've hurt, and known even as the words passed your lips you felt genuine contrition? Have you not told someone that you love them, and felt the utter certainty that it is true in that moment?

To keep a thing locked inside is to never let it be born into the world.

I felt my aura reshape itself in response, the process fast and smooth. My soul had been restructured by the Table for this very purpose.

The pain came too, starting from deep within and rising as a feverish heat to my skin. It burned me, body and soul, but I'd grown callouses. I endured it.

I lifted my axe up with one hand as though to measure the width of the tunnel. Almost metallic olden flames flickered across the rough length of uncarved wood that formed its handle, illuminating the complex patterns etched along the crescent moon blade. Those flames raced up my arm, my shoulder, enwrapping me until I became a living torch of amber-hued fire.

"Holy shit," Catrin said.

Indeed.

Light spilled through the tunnel, illuminating the flock of monsters lurking within. They were hideous things, gray skinned and emaciated, with most of their muscle powering long, avian legs and huge leathery wings. Their heads were like sinuous worms, or lampreys, ending in tiny, sucking mouths lined in needle teeth.

They recoiled from the light and screeched, filling the tunnel with tremendous sound.

None attacked. When the boat drew close, they practically fought each other to pull away from the crackling bonfire of aureflame I had become. Sweat beaded on my face as I maintained the aura, knowing I couldn't do it for long. I burned my own spirit away with every second I kept this up.

Catrin whimpered behind me. That I had also been worried about. She was only part fiend, but the holy fire was near as repulsive to her as to the Baron's chimera, born of dark alchemy as they were.

The tunnel began to widen into a larger cave. I caught sight of the dock ahead, which would lead us up into narrow hallways where these creatures, with their huge wings, wouldn't be able to follow. I hoped.

"We're almost there," I said to my companion. I had begun to feel cold, and breathing had gotten more difficult.

Once, I could have let that power burn for several minutes without effort, but that had been back when the Table had been intact and the elves still ruled their own city. It was like a cracked fountain basin that drained as fast as it filled now.

Just like that altar bowl I'd damaged back at the chapel. I could fill myself with duty and resolve, but it would always leak back out.

"It's too bright," Catrin hissed. "It burns. I can't—"

"I know," I said. "Just hold on. We're almost there."

The dhampir steeled herself and rowed forward. The monsters watched us from the shadows, their eyeless heads chewing at the air.

We passed into the cave. Another minute, maybe, and we'd reach the dock. I gritted my teeth, fighting to keep the aureflame burning. It had died down somewhat, letting the shadows fill in to half-conceal the hellish swarm around us. In this wide space the chimera could take flight more easily. Several of them cracked their leathery wings in anticipation, as though sensing my strength failing.

We reached the dock. Barely a flicker of the flame remained now, wisps of it running across my body so I was more a gently shining figure in the darkness rather than a blazing one.

"Run!" I snapped at Catrin. She shot toward the doorway in the cave wall, faster than any human could have, feet slapping against the dock.

The hairs on the back of my neck stood on end and I spun, swung, and carved the wing from a chimera that hadn't deigned to wait for the fire to fully fade. It crashed into the dock in flailing, snarling chaos, cracking the wood and nearly upturning the boat. The edges of its wing-arm's severed stump exuded a molten glow.

I rolled onto the dock. Red heat flared across my left arm—the thing had managed to graze me with its claws. No time to tell how bad the wound was. More screeches and more wingbeats filled the cave.

I ran to the door. As Irn Bale had promised, my new armor didn't slow me down, the shadowy links of elf-metal like a second skin beneath my red cloak.

Something heavy landed on the dock at my side. I turned, ducked the thing's head as it snapped at me. Their wrinkled necks could extend incredibly far, I noted. Charming.

I took the chimera's head off with an upward swing, shouting, my weapon leaving a white-gold blur in the air. The creature fell, its headless body writhing in its death throes. More of its kin beat their wings, and I knew they'd pile on me and bring me down, their leech mouths finding the gaps in my armor as they devoured me alive.

"Alken!" Catrin was at the door, waiting for me. She had her dagger in hand, but the small weapon would be of little use against that hell swarm.

I wouldn't make it. With a surge of will I made the aureflame aegis burn again, hoping to repel the swarm even for a moment. Most of them balked. One didn't, its momentum carrying it forward.

The chimera hit me in the back. It was smaller than me, but dense with muscle and heavy enough. I was thrown forward through the door. I felt its claws scrabble at my back, tearing my cloak but fouling on the armor. It hissed in rage, and even as its flesh sizzled and burned at the touch of my aura, it bit at my neck with its sucking mouth.

I reached back with my wounded left hand. A flash of pain erupted as the gouges near my elbow were pulled. The creature's teeth clamped down on my vambrace. It snarled and shook its head viciously, nearly wrenching my arm from its socket. I couldn't turn, couldn't get its weight off my back or bring my weapon to bear.

Catrin saved me, again. Screaming in fury, she hit the thing from the side and stabbed at it with her dagger. It wasn't undead, and the banesilver did little to hurt it more than regular steel would have, but neither was it preternatural enough for that to matter. She ripped the blade out, stabbed again, then again. Eventually she found its small brain.

The chimera went still. Catrin helped me get its weight off. As I stood, I saw she'd been covered in brackish gore. The creatures had purple, almost mossy blood. My eyes flickered to the still-open doorway. More of the monsters were advancing on it.

I took a single step forward, swung, and hewed through the membranous flesh of one lamprey head as it darted through the doorway. My weapon hummed musically as it parted the air, where a normal weapon might have only whistled. I kicked the dead thing away to get it clear, then slammed the door closed and latched it. There were several heavy thuds as the creatures slammed against the barrier, but it was a siege door. It held.

Several minutes passed before either of us caught our breath.

"Alken . . ."

I turned. The hallway would have been pitch black, but my axe still glowed dimly to illuminate Catrin. Her brown hair was disheveled, her fine blue dress ruined with chimera blood.

Her eyes were fixed on my wounded left arm. They burned with a hungry red light.

CHAPTER THIRTY-SEVEN

CATRIN

You're wounded."

Normally, those words would have held a note of concern or panic. Catrin said them like it was something erotic.

She stepped forward on light feet, heedless of the chimera blood on the floor. She'd lost her fine shoes at some point, and left one purplish footprint on the stone as she advanced.

"I'm fine," I said, heart quickening in my chest. The young woman—was she truly young?—brushed my left arm with her fingers. The chimera had left two deep, ugly gouges just above my elbow.

The elven armor I'd received from the Oradyn wasn't a full set of plate, and there were parts of me it didn't protect. In this case, I only had metal covering my upper arm from the spaulders and short sleeves of the hauberk, then a gap until the vambrace strapped to my forearm. The monster had found that gap.

So did Catrin. Her fingers curled around my elbow, her red eyes fixing on the wound. They were unnaturally bright in the gloom, a feverish shade of crimson, the sclera darkened closer to yellow than white. She seemed to be breathing quicker.

Then, before I had even quite realized what was happening, she brought her face down to nuzzle the wound. Her tongue ran across the slashes and her whole body shivered.

I shoved her. Catrin slammed against the opposite wall of the hallway. She recovered instantly, glaring up at me. Her face had turned corpse pale, her eyes fever red and veined. She hissed like an animal, revealing teeth closer to wolf than human.

She lunged at me, or tried to. With a furnace growl I summoned my aura again, filling the passageway with dim amber flame. Catrin recoiled from it just as the chimera had, letting out a noise of frustration and fear.

I kept it up until she got her breathing under control. With it came her senses. She knelt against the wall, her corpse eyes unfocused, but I saw a hint of the mischievous spy I'd come to know over the past several days peek through the bloodlust. Her eyes, still empty, widened as she met mine.

"Alken . . ." She shuddered. "I'm so sorry. Bleeding Gates, I'm sorry, I didn't . . . I can't—"

"Are you in control?" I asked. I still burned my aura, not quite trusting she *was* in control of herself. This might be a trick, a vampire's ploy to make me let my guard down. I had no way to know how much influence that part of her had over her words as well as her actions.

Catrin considered a moment, then shook her head. "I haven't fed in too long, and that silver arrow made it worse. I think . . ." She shivered and gritted her sharp teeth, hissing the words through them. "I think you should go on. Leave me here."

I considered doing just that. I didn't much like the idea of heading into what came next with a hungry dhampir at my side, but having that same treacherous companion at my back wasn't any more appealing.

I could only think of one thing to do, and it was a goring stupid idea.

I let the flames fade. "Fine," I said, and held up my wounded left arm. "Take enough to keep your head. Not a drop more. I need to be able to fight."

She hesitated three quick heartbeats. No more. She darted forward, fast enough to make me flinch, and dug sharp nails into my arm. It took every ounce of my self-control not to hurl her away again.

She pressed her lips to the gashes. I feared for a moment she'd bite and make the injury worse, but she only suckled at the wounds. A soft, muffled moan escaped her throat.

It felt . . . strange. Not as bad as I would have thought, though even that realization disturbed me. I could feel my blood pumping through my arm, feel her warm tongue pressing against my damaged flesh, soaking it up like a sponge. I tried to relax, knowing clenching my arm would only make the blood loss worse.

I felt revulsion, and guilt at the revulsion. I felt pity for her, that she'd been born this way. And anger, at whatever creature had been responsible.

And I hated myself, because this hadn't been mercy or trust, but a test.

When I knew she shouldn't take anymore, I still didn't pull away or shove her. I needed to know I could trust this . . . not creature. This woman, this person who'd been born with this dark hunger. I needed to know she could make the *choice* to pull away.

If she couldn't . . .

My fingers tightened on the oaken handle of the axe in my right hand. I didn't want to do it, but I'd done worse.

"Catrin," I said. Then, softer, "Cat."

A moment came where I didn't think she'd pull away. Her yellowed sclera had slowly filled with red as she fed, her pale skin taking on a healthier tint, her fingers growing firmer, stronger. Her grip tightened on my arm . . .

I started to lift the axe.

Catrin dragged red lips away and stepped back. She clenched stained teeth, squeezed her eyes shut, and hugged herself. After shivering violently she said, "I'm all right. I'm . . ." She sighed in satisfaction. "I'm fine."

Her ruby eyes, wide with disbelief, met mine. "You really just let me do that?"

I tore off a strip of my cloak and started tying it around the wound, turning my gaze away from hers. I felt a subtle pull there I recognized from that night in the castle chamber. I didn't want to get mesmerized again.

"I need you in your right mind," I said. "We have work to do."

". . . Right."

Did I hear a note of disappointment in her voice?

"Well, anyway." She wiped at her mouth with one arm, smearing the blood more than cleaning it. "Thanks for that, then."

I passed her another strip of my cloak. She accepted it and dabbed at her face, though it still did little to clean the blood. *My blood,* I thought.

Then, shocking me, Catrin stood up on her toes and pecked me on the cheek. When she'd lowered herself, her fiendish eyes were warm as they looked up into mine.

"Thank you for that," she said, more genuinely this time. "For trusting me."

I hadn't trusted her. Swallowing my guilt, I just nodded, not sure what to say. "You ready to go?"

"I'll lead," she said. "I know the castle a bit better than you, big man." Then she turned and started down the hallway, moving with a touch too much haste. She seemed almost chipper.

I felt at the spot on my cheek where she'd kissed me. When I pulled my hand away, my fingertips were stained red.

The halls of Castle Cael were far too quiet.

"When I was last here," I said to Catrin, who padded along at my side, "I didn't see any guards besides the Mistwalkers. No servants either, besides that one in the green cloak. Priska."

A lord with a holding as large as the Falconer estate should have servants, guards, even a reservoir of lower-ranking knights in their service.

"Couldn't say," Catrin said, speaking just as quietly. The cavernous halls had a disconcerting way of echoing even small noises. "It was like this when I arrived. Empty."

"We need to find the Baron," I said. "And Olliard, if he's actually here."

"Something ahead," Catrin whispered. We both stopped.

I focused, but heard nothing. The changeling's hearing must have been sharper than mine. I tightened my grip on my axe and drew up power. It came fitfully, singeing me in several places as I struggled to assert control over it. I gritted my teeth against the pain and focused forward.

A figure stepped out into the hall ahead of us. I went on guard. Catrin did not. She'd known who approached the moment she'd gotten their scent.

"Quinn." The dhampir's bloodstained lips pressed into a thin line.

The Mistwalker stepped into the light of the wall sconces, which flickered moodily on their ancient metal hands. His right hand held a drawn gladius, and a neutral expression masked his handsome features.

He'd been injured. Viscous blood dripped from the fingers of his left hand from a long, ragged tear along the forearm. A claw wound.

"Cat," the mercenary said. "Where have you been?"

"About," Catrin said, taking a step forward.

Quinn's glassy eyes went to me. "What do you think you're doing? There's no reason for you to be here anymore."

"What I think's right," Catrin said, her own eyes narrowing.

Quinn let out a strange, choking laugh. "I never understood that. The people you hang around with, the *things* you do, the man you work for . . . and you have all these scruples?"

Catrin shrugged. "I don't care if you understand it or not, Quinn. Where's the Baron?"

In the distance, an inhuman cry echoed through the halls. Impossible to say how far in the depths of the castle. It could have been from another level, or two halls down. I tensed, but Quinn remained impassive.

"Around," the soldier said in answer to Catrin's question. "Bastard's making us work for it."

"Why did you turn on him?" I asked.

He didn't answer my question. Instead, twirling his blade in an idle flourish he said, "You have no idea what you're getting involved with, Cat. Ditch the vagabond, and I'll make sure you get out safe."

Catrin didn't answer. Quinn's corpse-blue eyes seemed to focus, and he noted the red on her lips. He saw my wrapped left arm too, and a sickly sort of smile spread across his lips.

"Ah. So that's how it is."

Catrin's expression wavered, a touch of worry splintering her confidence. "You bastard. This isn't like that."

Quinn ignored her and focused on me. "I told you who she worked for. I didn't tell you why."

"Quinn—"

The Mistwalker interrupted her. "She's a whore. Entertains the Keeper's guests. Gets them off while she's taking their blood like a dirty, desperate leech."

He canted his head to one side and shrugged, still smiling. "Trust me, I'd know. How many times have I paid your price, Cat?"

Catrin hissed at my side, closing her eyes. There was anger there, intense frustration. Perhaps shame as well.

I took the time for a long inhalation through my nostrils, then began walking forward.

Quinn took a guard. "Don't you step any—"

"Don't move," I said, hitting the ghoul with a lance of auratic command.

Compulsions aren't very effective on non-humans, or any human with an awakened soul who'd learned to guard their will. But Quinn was a worm. His soul barely clutched his tired form, his life extended by a gruesome appetite that had him sifting through grave dirt and gnawing on rancid, rotting bones.

He didn't have much control of his compulsions on the best of days. He froze for a moment, stunned in place by my command.

I punched him. Brittle yellow teeth shattered, brackish blood scattered, and the fop went down hard.

I flicked blood from my knuckles and glared down at the Mistwalker, who lay there in stunned disbelief. A boiling rage had risen up in me before I'd even realized it myself.

I had been a knight once. I might not have much of a claim to chivalry anymore, but those customs were something very much like instinct. Perhaps they *were* instinct, the core values of knighthood wrought into my aura same as my oaths were, compelling this response.

Or maybe the reason was more simple. Perhaps I'd just come to respect the changeling woman and felt genuine anger. At him, and at me for forgetting myself.

Maybe it was a bit of both.

Who can say?

I glanced back at Catrin, a thought striking me. She looked almost as stunned as Quinn. "I'm sorry for the names I called you before," I told her. "Vampire, bloodsucker . . . all those. It was unworthy of me. And I'm sorry for accusing you of being responsible for Micah."

Catrin just nodded, the motion a bit stiff. "It's fine. I'd already forgiven you."

I turned back to the ghoul. "Where is the Baron?"

"Go fuck a troll," Quinn snarled. He reached for his fallen sword.

My axe came down on his wrist, severing the hand. Amber-tinted flame erupted from both stump and hand, consuming the latter and scorching the mercenary's arm. He let out a wheezing, half-formed wail of pain and horror.

"I will not ask again," I said quietly, feeling a strange calm. The memory of the slaughtered villagers bled slowly through my thoughts. "Where is Orson Falconer?"

Quinn cursed again, this time less intelligibly. I showed him the burning edge of Faen Orgis and fear flickered in his too-pale eyes.

"Below!" he hissed. "In his lab."

I glanced at Catrin, and she nodded. "I think I can find it."

I turned back to Quinn. He clutched at his burnt wrist stub, breathing heavily. The breaths looked forced, almost theatrical, like a bad actor trying to mimic distress.

He's pretending to be more alive, I thought. It was a way he could keep his soul tethered. My weapon's hallowed bite could exorcise his ghost, but he kept it in his body through sheer will.

"Where are the others?" I asked. "The Baron's guests."

Quinn's eyes moved back to me, narrowing. "Gone," he said. "They have what they came for."

I frowned, not understanding. "What do you mean? When did they leave?"

"After," Quinn spat. "After the ritual. The captain left us behind to clean up."

I began to understand, in the same way I might begin to take note of a cut artery and realize, even as I felt very little pain, that it was a lethal wound.

Quinn saw my dawning realization and laughed, revealing macabre yellow teeth in a dry mouth. "You're too late, paladin."

"What?" Catrin asked from behind me. "What does he mean?"

Quinn and I both ignored her. The ghoul was too busy gloating, and I was too preoccupied with the coiling tendril of horror in my gut.

"What did you think this was going to be?" Quinn hissed, corpse eyes going wide with fury. "Some heroic tale where you'd slay the monster and stop the evil sorcerer? This was never about Orson Falconer."

He winced in pain, a shudder rippling through his body as the holy fire I'd struck him with scalded his spirit. "He was just an intermediary. No more than a merchant. He made the same mistake any caravanner does, thinking we wouldn't just *take* what he had to offer. What an arrogant fucking prick he was. We taught him good!"

"What are you babbling about!?" Catrin's voice had turned frustrated.

"The demon," I said. To my own ears my voice sounded more tired than angry. "I was wrong about all of this. I thought he was going to bind the spirit to him and use it as a weapon against the Church. Maybe that was his plan, but it didn't *need* him."

I should have killed the Baron that first night. I tried to be clever, but I'm a damned fool who can't tell a lie from a song. It was just like before. Just like ten years before. I was a gullible fool who couldn't look at the big picture.

The only thing I'd ever been good at was swinging a blade. I should have cut my way to my enemy from the start, my own life be damned.

"Look at you," Quinn said with a laugh. It was an ugly, wheezing sound, half pained and half maliciously cheerful. "Ah, that's a fine expression. Some hero you found yourself, Cat. Then again, you always did like the big, dumb ones."

He returned his attention to me and his voice turned conspiratorial. "She let you fuck her yet? She will. It's the blood, turns her into a loose—"

He never finished whatever ugly thing he'd been about to say. My axe came down on his skull, splitting it and sinking an inch into the stone beneath. There was a low rumble of fire, and the body immediately began to disintegrate as hallowed aura tore through it.

I stood, planting a boot on the dead mercenary's breastplate to rip my weapon from the floor. I spent a minute watching the body burn without really seeing it. My mind wasn't in that hall.

"Alken . . ." Catrin's voice drew me from my stupor. She had a sad look, though whether it was for our situation or for the death of the Mistwalker she'd formerly been acquainted with, I couldn't say. "I don't understand. What's going on?"

"Orson Falconer thought he had all the power here." I cursed savagely. "I should have seen it! A backwater sorcerer gathering so many dangerous allies. They used him. *Duped* him. That witch, Lillian, helped him prepare his ritual. When it was ready, she just went and did it herself."

I turned to the dhampir. "They're all gone. And they have one of the nightmares that helped destroy the elves for their own uses."

I'd failed to stop the calamity Lady Eanor had feared.

"Damn." Catrin bowed her head. "I'm sorry, Alken. Really. If I'd known . . . I swear if I'd known what they were really planning, I would have tried to stop it. I think Quinn played me too, letting me know where you'd gone so I'd go off and not be there to stall the ritual. He knew I wanted the villagers left out of all this."

I nodded. "I believe you."

Catrin shuffled, averting her eyes. They were still red, I noted, not having darkened to their usual soft brown. "You . . ." She licked her lips, wetting some of the drying blood still there. "What he said about me, it—"

"Doesn't matter," I told her.

"But it's true." Catrin squeezed her eyes shut and folded her arms. "The Backroad isn't just a traveler's inn. It's a brothel, and . . . that's how I get blood."

"I've no right to judge you, Catrin. I saw you weep for those villagers. I've seen real monsters many times in my life . . ." My voice hardened. "You are not one."

A tear fell from the dhampir's ruby eye.

"We don't have time to waste," I said. "I still have a job to do."

CHAPTER THIRTY-EIGHT

THE BARON'S MADNESS

We found more evidence of the falling-out between the Baron and his "guests" deeper into that house of darkness.

It started out as a corpse here and there. A Mistwalker ripped to shreds as though by some beast, rancid ghoul blood splattered like paint strokes across the rich tapestries and fine masonry of the halls.

The evidence grew as Catrin led me into the bowels of the castle. The men Issachar had left had met steep resistance from Orson's household, and here I finally got a look at the enigmatic servants who kept the place up.

They were all chimera, or perhaps homunculi. Twisted, warped things grown in glass and bubbling liquid, sickly and misshapen. They had been strong, ripping apart the mercenaries like dolls, beating them to a pulp, or eating them.

But the invading monsters had proved superior, in both tactic and number. Though the Mistwalkers had taken casualties, most of the corpses we found were the Baron's creatures.

We found a group of three soldiers plunging long spears into the tumorous mass of a hunchback big as three men. It wasn't dying no matter how many times they stabbed it, but it clearly felt pain.

The ghouls were *laughing* at it.

By the time I'd finished with them, my bloodstained axe smoldered with molten light. The little victory felt hollow, after what Quinn had revealed.

Catrin knelt by the hunchback's side, laying a hand on its twisted neck as it struggled to breathe. She gave me a pleading look, and I lifted my axe.

When I'd put the poor thing out of its misery, we took stock of the corridor ahead. More bodies. Most were twisted humanoids like the big brute, but some resembled the creatures we'd fought down in the flood tunnel. These lacked wings, looking more like big, leech-headed reptiles that crawled on all fours.

"Baron must have emptied out his kennels for this," Catrin noted. "You think he's still alive?"

"We'll find out," I said. I glanced down at the dead hunchback one more time and clenched my fist. "He has much to answer for. Creating sapient life with alchemy is forbidden."

"Nobles have been doing it for centuries," Catrin reminded me. "Not all of them Recusant."

". . . I know." Even still, this seemed *wrong*. These things were clearly slaves.

We carried on, meeting light resistance. Catrin, for her part, didn't slow me down so much as a beat. She was no fighter so far as I could tell, but her sharp senses and awareness of the massive castle's layout were indispensable. She'd warn me when danger approached, faster even than my powers could, then melt into the shadows to reappear by the time I'd dispatched the threat. More than once I managed to avoid a nasty ambush that way.

It felt strange, having a comrade backing me up. I'd fought alone for so many years. It reminded me of the old days. I'd had allies back then, too. Donnelly. Lias.

Donnelly would have liked Catrin. Her skills were much like his, as was her sense of humor.

And this was no time to be thinking about a different life. I put my mind on the task at hand, as loathsome as it may have been.

"Are we close?" I said with a grunt, pulling my axe from the skull of a lamprey head. We stood in a nexus chamber connecting several parts of the castle. Three branching hallways, all splitting from a cylindrical space guarded by time-worn statues. The stone faces watched us in sullen hostility.

Orson watched us. Or, his haunted castle did. Like many old halls, the entire edifice was an extension of his will. We'd found evidence some of the defenders had been empty suits of armor apparently come to life, a favorite trick among the aristocracy.

"We're getting close," Catrin said. "These stairs here, they lead down to the dungeons. The Baron keeps his laboratory down there, along with most of the chimera kennels."

Which might mean the fiercest resistance remained below. I hefted my axe and went ahead. Catrin kept behind me, ready to sink into a shadow at a moment's notice.

Catrin suddenly started sniffing. "Blood below. Not ghoul, or those other things. Smells . . . cleaner."

She gestured to the wall, where a small smear of blood had touched the stones. My heart skipped a beat. Was it Olliard down there? Or Lisette?

We descended the narrow, spiraling staircase. The air grew colder and damper.

When we reached the bottom, we *did* find a body sprawled there. It had fallen down nearly the entire flight of stairs, landing limbs akimbo.

Far too many limbs. I approached cautiously, taking in the strange sight.

It—she—had been some kind of changeling or homunculus. Her skin was a dark shade of gray-blue, and she was smoothly bald. Her body was small and skinny, almost childlike, with long, jointed appendages sprouting from behind the shoulders of more human arms. Each was tipped in barbed claws and was longer than the whole length of her body. She had too many eyes, all glassy green spheres on a face only vaguely human in shape.

Yet, she looked familiar.

Catrin stepped up next to me. "Priska. I never saw her under that cloak." She cursed suddenly.

"What is it?" I asked.

"It's his daughter. I saw her in some of the castle's paintings. Bleeding Gates, what did he *do* to her?"

I knelt by the small body. I remembered how she'd seemed to glide while clad in her concealing green cloak. I could imagine those spider legs scuttling beneath, hidden from sight.

"Or maybe just made to resemble his daughter," I suggested. Catrin didn't argue, and I suspect she had the same thought—that it wasn't any better.

She was dead, alien eyes unblinkingly fixed on one wall. It looked like she'd fallen down the stairs and broken her neck. Though, with those inhuman limbs, I somehow doubted that had been what truly killed her.

I closed the chimeric child's more human set of main eyes. As I did, I found a small, neat hole punched through her forehead, just above the eyebrows. Silver blood oozed from the wound.

"Olliard did this." I stood and fixed my attention on the corridor ahead.

We went farther, finding fewer bodies and no resistance. Catrin tensed at my back, but she didn't need to tell me she'd heard something this time. Noise echoed down the shaft. An angry shout, then furniture crashing.

I recognized the voice. It wasn't the Baron's.

We reached entry to a large chamber, sickly artificial light spilling from within. The door had been forced open. Looking inside, I saw furniture scattered about, complicated-looking equipment ranging from huge glass tanks to frames of brass and copper. A tank had been broken, leaving glowing green liquid pooling over the floor. It hissed like acid.

Mahogany desks and brass candelabras were scattered across the space, many upturned. Parchment, books, and precious materials were strewn everywhere.

Across the length of the spacious room, near a broken chair that'd been near fine as a throne, stood two figures. One was Orson Falconer. He was still clad in his kingly robes, precious gems glinting like little stars along the netted shoulders. He leaned against the wall, a hand pressed to one shoulder. Blood dripped through his fingers, dampening the expensive material of his overcoat.

The other was Olliard of Kell. He had his strange foreign weapon trained on the Baron, a terrible expression hardening his wizened face. He looked like he hadn't slept in days, but his hands were steady.

Alchemical light of green and too-pale blue lit the scene, casting it in an almost feverish sense of threat.

The doctor noted my arrival and bared his teeth. "Lisette!" he barked.

Movement in the corner of my vision, the hasty muttering of ritual words. The young cleric stood near one wall, out of sight from the door. Her fingers played with strings done cat's-cradle style, aura flickering like half-visible flame around them.

I was ready for the trick this time. Furrowing my brow in concentration, I made an effort of will and lifted my axe. A nearly invisible sphere of pale amber light appeared around me. Lisette's magic enwrapped the sphere and stopped inches from my actual body an instant before they would have ensnared me.

The strings, a paler gold than the more amber-tinted aureflame, strained with a sound like crackling lightning. I gritted my teeth at the effort.

Damn, but the kid was strong. "Cat." My voice came out as a strained growl.

"Got it," Catrin said. She stepped into a patch of shadow—there were plenty in the room to pick from—and melted into it as though sinking into water. She appeared a moment later beside the apprentice and, shocking me as much as the girl, rabbit-punched her in the back of the head.

Lisette crumpled to the ground. As her concentration broke, the golden tethers flickered from existence. I lowered my axe, sighing in relief.

Olliard lifted his crossbow higher, aiming at the Baron's skull. "Don't move!"

The Baron wheezed out a laugh. "Oh, this is a rich irony!"

The doctor glared at him, not understanding.

I hesitated. "Leave him, doctor."

I had questions for Orson Falconer, and his death was my responsibility.

Suspicion and confusion warred in the vampire hunter's features. He glanced at Catrin, and a look of revulsion formed on his face. "You've been enthralled. I know what she is. Snap out of it, man, or I'll have to kill you."

I exchanged a glance with Catrin. She shrugged and knelt to place her dagger to Lisette's neck. "This is a hostage situation, right?" She didn't quite keep the questioning note from her voice. "Listen, young lady, just don't try that trick again."

Lisette groaned, dazed.

"Get away from her!" Olliard snapped.

"Calm down, doctor." I took a step farther into the room, clearing the doorway. I didn't want anyone sneaking up behind me. "I just don't want to get snared by your apprentice's Art again. And I need *him* alive to answer some questions."

I turned my attention from the hunter and pointed at Orson with my axe. "Where did the others take that thing?"

Orson just smiled and spread his hands out. More blood spread across his rich garments in a growing stain, but it seemed to bother him little. He looked at peace.

Olliard hadn't given him that. There were dead Mistwalkers in the room, and some more of the Baron's creatures along with evidence of brutal violence. A bloodied short sword lay near the hem of the nobleman's robes.

I bared my teeth. "You smile, after what you've unleashed?"

"And what is it you think I have unleashed?" Orson asked tiredly. He'd lost a lot of blood. I didn't have much time.

"The villagers . . ." I took another step forward. "Your *own* people. Your duty was to protect them. You were their liege lord, and you served them up like sacrificial cattle. *You* brought the other Recusants here, gave them the tools and the reason."

I hissed my next words. "Would you have done it yourself? Sacrificed all of those innocents to complete your weapon?"

"Yes," Orson said, without hesitation or apology. "I would have done it."

I almost lunged forward to kill him right there. But I needed to know where the rest had gone, what they intended. He was my only lead.

Olliard stared at me, then turned his attention back to the lord. "What did you do, Orson? What is he talking about?" His aged features twisted with rage. "Micah . . . that man practically raised you! Why did you kill him?"

"Because he was in my way," Orson spat. "Because he served immortal tyrants who killed my homeland. Because, in our tired world, death has no meaning."

A sickly smile spread across his face. "Ask him." He nodded to me. "He knows of what I speak."

All eyes in the room turned to me. Even Lisette's, who had started to recover from Catrin's blow.

"What is he talking about?" the doctor asked me. "Speak, man."

I didn't have time for this. If Orson died before I learned where his treacherous allies had gone and what they planned, this entire sad tragedy has been for nothing.

"You are one of them, are you not?" Orson's eyes narrowed. "One of the Archon's champions? I suspected it when we spoke. I saw your eyes, and the demon seemed to fear you. Wasn't hard to do a bit of reading and put two and two together."

His thoughtful tone hardened. "You know *exactly* why I do this. Your order made the same choice!"

I glared at him and took another step forward. More aureflame crackled along my axe. It singed my hand, but I just clenched my fingers tighter and ignored the pain.

"I did not betray King Tuvon," I spat. "That was the captains. I had no part in their betrayal."

A half-truth is little better than a lie. The fact that my power scorched me was proof enough I wasn't guiltless.

Lisette's eyes widened. She hadn't tried to move with Catrin's silver blade at her throat, but I could tell I'd surprised her.

Orson took that in and looked disappointed. "I see. I had thought you were a kindred spirit, a disenfranchised knight seeking vengeance against the *blessed ones* who had so wronged you. But you are one of the loyal ones, aren't you?"

He sighed. "Just my damned luck. Ah, well."

He winced and began to slide down the wall, too weak to keep his feet.

I studied the nightmarish laboratory. One of the broken tanks had contained a shriveled, fetal thing with a beak and otherwise disturbingly human features.

Orson turned his head on a limp neck to regard the doctor. "I freed Micah of his slavery. He would have never listened to reason."

Olliard just shook his head. "You are mad."

"I am *awake*," Orson insisted. His face had become ashen. "Awake in a land full of sleepers. We are prisoners, Olliard. Prisoners in a cage of dreams and stories. I have *seen* it. I have crossed the veil and found iron walls."

Again his eyes moved to me. "That man is a paladin of the Alder. He knows. He is one of their wardens."

This time, when Olliard followed the lord's gaze, it lingered on me. "Explain," he said, cold. "And tell that creature to step away from my disciple."

"Fuck that," Catrin shot back. "She's a bloody sorceress."

"Let her go," I told Catrin, who startled. "But don't let her weave again."

Catrin complied reluctantly. Lisette started to rise, looking dazed.

"You won't save yourself talking about theology," I said to the dying noble. "Judgment has been passed, my lord. I am here to deliver it."

"Judgment?" Orson's face, ashy and weak, transformed with sudden rage. "They would judge *me*!? After all they have stolen from me?"

"You had more than many." I felt little pity for him.

I felt a shiver run through me and closed my eyes. Half-heard words whispered through my thoughts, my blood. *Heretic,* they murmured. *Bring him to the light.*

I shut them out. "I know the Onsolain aren't perfect. Believe me, I know. But the Adversary is worse. You gave one of the Abgrûdai flesh. There is no worse sin you can commit."

Lisette's already-pale face turned ghost white. Catrin winced, and Olliard blinked at me with owlish disbelief.

Orson Falconer just bowed his head, not a hint of shame on his face.

"A Demon of the Abyss," I almost whispered the words. "One of the same monsters who rampaged through Seydis ten years ago."

"At the command of mortal man," Orson muttered. "Let us not forget that."

I sneered. "You are no Reynard, Orson. Not even a shadow of him. Your *guests* taught you that. Had you been anyone, they wouldn't have turned on you so easily."

I stepped forward and lifted my axe, letting it burn with aureflame. "Where are the others, Orson?"

"You would panic at such a thing, wouldn't you?" The Baron laughed dryly. "You Alder Knights were practically engineered to fight them. But you are too late this day, Headsman. Yes!" He laughed again at the surprise on my face. "My sources are quite knowledgeable, and I got missives from Vinhithe. The Earl there is in my pocket. I know who you are, what your role is. You may deliver my sentence, but I am only a small part in all this."

His smile was nearly as wide as those macabre grins of the ghouls. "I . . . do not *know* where my benefactors have gone. How they intend to use the spirit, I cannot say. I only know they will use it to burn this rotten world, and I am satisfied."

There was a metallic pop, a thudding impact and the crack of cranial bone. The Baron's head jerked back, struck the wall, then he slumped limply to the ground.

Olliard lowered his crossbow and let out a weary breath. "Madness," he said to himself. "Madness. All of this, for . . ."

He shook his head, looking more tired than satisfied.

I glared at him. "His life was *mine*, Olliard."

The doctor's weary expression didn't fade as he loaded his crossbow with methodical indifference, then lifted it to aim halfway between me and Catrin, ready to swing to bear on either of us in a moment.

"Don't be a fool," I warned him. "I am not your enemy."

"Come over here, Lisette." The doctor didn't take his eyes off me.

Catrin threw me a questioning look. I lifted a hand, telling her to wait. Lisette shuffled over to the doctor and turned to face us. I noted that Catrin had confiscated her little finger strings, and felt a surge of gratitude for the changeling's quick thinking.

"Who are you?" Olliard demanded. "What do you have to do with any of this?"

"That's a long story," I said.

Olliard's lips tightened. "Summarize."

"I serve the Lords of Heavensreach," I said.

Lisette's eyes widened. The doctor only sighed, clearly believing I was being obstinate.

"It's true," I said. "I am an agent of the Choir Concilium. The Onsolain sent me to serve a sentence of execution on Orson Falconer."

I pointed at the dead nobleman with my axe. "You ended up delivering that, but it was my purpose since the night I arrived in Caelfall."

"You sound as mad as him," Olliard spat. "You serve the Choir of God? They are stories. He speaks of afterlives and demons, and you tell me you were sent by angels . . . this is all madness."

Lisette glanced uncertainly at her mentor. "Master . . ." she began.

"Not now," he snapped. The young cleric flinched.

"Then, that commotion in Vinhithe . . ." Olliard's expression went distant with thought. "That *was* you, wasn't it? He called you Headsman. I've heard that name."

I wasn't willing to give all my secrets to this man. "You came here to hunt monsters. I assure you, we're on the same side."

Catrin shifted at my side. I didn't want to take my eyes off the old physik and his alchecraft crossbow, but I sensed a subtle tension from the dhampir.

"And yet you keep their company," the doctor said, eyeing the changeling. "How do I know it has not enthralled you?"

"She was Micah's friend, same as you."

"Is that what it told you?" Olliard asked, amused. "You were his friend, were you? Catrin of Ergoth?"

Catrin drew in a sharp breath. I risked a glance at her. Her whole body seemed wire-taut with tension.

Ergoth . . . The name sounded familiar. But where had I—

I hadn't ever heard it, I realized. Not with my own ears. The strange, ghostly nostalgia of my Alder-given magic knew the name, not I.

It had been a small kingdom, long ago. It had fallen. Not to war, but to . . .

The ghost memory faded.

"He knew what I was," Catrin said with a quiet sadness. "He treated me well all the same."

"He was *addicted* to you, leech." Olliard's expression went almost imperious with disdain. "I warned him your nature ruled you, but he always turned a blind eye. I should have killed you when you were still young and human enough for it to stick."

His eyes narrowed. "Was it you who—"

Catrin didn't reply, only hugged herself and averted her red eyes. She still had some of my blood on her face, and her noble dress had been tattered and stained with muck over the last two days. It made her look like some vampire lord's maidenly victim, though I knew that was far from the truth.

"Orson already admitted to being responsible for the preoster's death," I cut in.

"But all those years you fed on him aged him past his time," the vampire hunter accused. "When I last saw him, he was weak. Ill. He should have been strong enough to stand up to the likes of Orson Falconer."

His eyes went to the corpse by the wall. Orson's violet eyes remained open and glassy in death. Olliard sniffed, no hint of regret on his face. The kindly old man I'd met beyond the woods of Caelfall seemed gone. I didn't recognize this bitter, accusatory hunter for that altruistic healer.

But I *did* recognize him.

"I've heard enough," I said. All eyes turned to me, and I waited a beat before continuing. "My work is done here. Are you going to push this, Olliard?"

The doctor glanced between me and Catrin. "She is a dangerous predator ruled by her hunger. I have seen it a thousand times. They can become true vampires, you know, these half-dead. The older she gets, the worse her hunger. If you are truly a warrior of the divine, you will heed me."

"If you try to slay her," I said, still surprising myself with how calm I sounded, "I will fight you. I owe her a debt, whatever she may become."

All of us in that room were a sort of monster already. Except Lisette, perhaps.

Olliard spoke an ugly oath. "On your head be it, then."

I nodded and glanced at Catrin, then jerked my head to the door. She looked shaken, but went ahead of me. I put my back between her and the hunters.

"Alken."

I turned toward the doctor. The old man had lowered his alchebow, and his posture had slumped with exhaustion. Even still, a steely resolve flickered to life in his eyes.

"Should we meet again, I will consider you an enemy. I have heard of you . . . The Headsman of Seydis." He lifted his chin. "You are a murderer. A butcher."

"And you aren't?" I asked, gesturing again to the dead lord.

"I hunt monsters," the doctor said. "I protect innocents. You are just a phantom left from the war."

What a sad mirror we made. I wonder if he understood the irony.

I just nodded. "Until next time, then. If there is a next time."

I turned and left.

CHAPTER THIRTY-NINE

DEPARTURE, DUTY, DREAM

"Ready?" Edgar asked. The monk breathed hard, his pudgy features covered in dirt and sweat, but his expression remained determined.

I nodded, and we both lifted the heavy corpse of Caelfall's innkeeper into the pit. It settled into place in the darkness below, half hidden in the failing light.

The mist had burned away, and the onset of dusk cast the marshes in a somber red light. I stood behind the village chapel with Edgar, and there were already many fresh graves. We were both filthy with gore and mud, and neither of us cared.

We'd survived. This was the least we could do for those who hadn't.

"You didn't know them," Edgar said suddenly, as we stared down into the most recent pit. "They were strangers."

Strange he asked me now, after we'd been at it most of two days. I shrugged and grabbed a spade off the ground, starting in on filling the grave. How could I explain it to him? That I was sworn to protect *everyone*, and I'd failed.

I owed far more than a few days of hard, dirty labor.

There was work I couldn't help with and didn't have time to remain for. The graves needed to be soaked in blessed water. Gravestones had to be carved and set over the mounds, each inscribed with lines of scripture and blessed to draw in the ghosts of the dead and hold them, so they wouldn't fade or be eaten in the wilderness. It was painstaking work, and the monk might not have the strength.

I didn't mention as much. I just helped, knowing it wasn't enough.

After we'd finished the most recent grave, the shuffling of cloth from the edge of the graveyard drew my attention. I turned to see Lisette standing there, clad in the same humble brown robes as usual, a heavy satchel tied to her back. She lingered by the gate.

I looked around, but saw no signs of the old doctor. I walked over to her.

"He isn't with me," Lisette said, having seen my survey. "He's waiting out on the road with the wagon and Brume." She waved off toward the village.

"Then why are you here?" I asked. I didn't mean to be unkind. I didn't blame the girl for anything, but her power made me wary. She'd been strong, and she had nearly gotten the better of me twice.

"I wanted to help," Lisette said. "I'm ordained. I can hallow the graves." She licked her lips and shuffled. "It's . . . the least I can do."

Her next words mirrored the bitterness I'd held within over the past two days. "We didn't help anyone here."

I nodded, not arguing, and let her go to the monk. They conversed for a while, then Lisette began to walk among the graves, her auremark in hand. Edgar marched behind her, having produced a jar of incense hanging from a long chain, which he swung back and forth. A pleasant scent, I imagined, to draw in the lost souls.

I didn't bother mentioning most of those ghosts would probably be too mutilated to go anywhere, and that the church would need to be abandoned. Oftentimes, such rituals are for the living as much as the dead.

If they did draw in the dead, it would be to bind them beneath stone and dirt so they couldn't do harm as much as to give them peace. Would the Shepherds of Draubard even wander through this accursed land, to lead the dead to where they needed to go?

"It was good of you," a voice behind me said. "To stay and help bury them."

I turned to see a shadowed shape lurking at the edge of a small copse of trees beyond the graveyard, leaning against a tree. There wasn't much daylight left, but Catrin still needed to be wary of it.

"I'd have helped," she said. "But . . ." She waved toward the setting sun with one hand. Though her expression remained nonchalant, I saw the tension in her shoulders. The frustration.

"You did help," I said. "We both noticed there were more graves dug this morning. That was you, wasn't it?"

Catrin shrugged, not meeting my eyes. "Maybe it was the elves?"

I just snorted and moved to stand next to her, folding my arms as I watched the young cleric work. I didn't mention that I'd spotted Catrin helping dig graves the night before. I didn't mention that I'd seen her conversing with some of the ghosts, either. They seemed more comfortable with her than with me. Kindred spirits.

One of them had worn amber preoster robes. Had either of them managed to find some closure, or was that just wishful thinking?

"This was a dark thing, big man." Catrin sighed. "I feel like we just watched a tragedy happen from the sidelines."

"That's how it often is," I said. "I wish . . ."

When I paused, Catrin stirred at my side. "What is it?"

I shook my head. "When I started on this path, it was to punish people like Orson. But, I thought, it was also to *stop* them. To prevent things like this. But almost every time, I feel like I'm just putting down a mad dog after they've already spread their sickness into the world. It's like trying to stop a river with my hands."

Catrin thought it over a moment, idly brushing the dagger at her belt. She wore the yellow peasant's dress she'd had the night I'd first met her now, rather than the ruined courtly gown she'd taken from the castle.

I liked this dress better. It suited her, and she seemed more comfortable in it.

That's a strange thought. Put that out of your head, Hewer.

"I'm not going to pretend like I understand all this stuff about elves and holy knights and angels," Catrin said. "Sounds like madness. But there *was* something about you. I saw it that first night when I took you to the castle. Like you'd just stepped out of a story."

"Sad story," I noted, eyeing the graves.

"So what's next for the mighty Headsman?" Catrin asked.

"Please don't call me that," I sighed. "It's just Alken."

Catrin nodded. "All right, then. What's next for you, Alken?"

I closed my eyes, breathing in the last of the fading daylight. "I wander. I wait for the Onsolain to send me some sign or messenger. Then I do this again." *Less badly next time,* I thought.

"And this demon?" Catrin asked. "All those other bastards who were part of this?"

I glanced toward the castle. "I don't know. I'm sworn by oath to my duty, and the consequences for ignoring it would be . . . unpleasant."

Catrin was quiet a moment. Then, as though tossing a leaf onto the wind she said, "Let me see what I can dig up. All types of strange people and stories pass through the Backroad. I'll keep an ear to the wind, see if something of your Council of Darkness comes up."

I winced. "That's a terrible name."

"Works though, doesn't it?" Catrin laughed, then shifted closer to me. I noted it and went on guard. Not because I thought I was in danger, but because I sensed something in the movement and didn't want to encourage her.

I had no room for it in my life.

If Catrin noted my distancing, she ignored it. She stepped in front of me and brushed my left arm with her hand, at the crook of the elbow where she'd fed from. I shivered at the feel of her cold skin, but she didn't take it further.

"When I tasted you . . ." Catrin looked up to meet my eyes. Even though my bangs half-concealed them, she squinted as though glancing into a sunbeam. "When I had your blood in me, I got a bit more too. I *felt* you, Alken."

She stepped closer, squeezing my elbow. "You're in so much pain. I saw it that first night, just from watching you, but I know it now. What happened to you? *Who* are you?"

A ghost, I thought. *A phantom, just like Olliard said.*

Melodramatic, and not an answer she'd accept.

"That's a long story," I told her, unsure if I'd say more.

Catrin recognized the deflection, and to my relief respected it. She drifted away, the movement casual as if she were just adjusting her balance. "I'll teach you how to find the inn. There's a trick to it, but once you know the way you can find it anytime, anyplace. I'm there most times."

She didn't quite keep the hopeful note from her next words. "You'll stop by sometime, right?"

I nodded. "Seems like it might be a useful place to gather information." *And maybe I'll even tell you my story,* I thought.

"That it is," Catrin agreed with a wry smile. "Just don't come in swinging that fancy cutter, all right? Hard for my like to find steady work."

The sun set, casting the land in shadow.

"Alken . . ." Catrin folded her arms as though cold. "It's strange to say it, but . . . I feel like the world got darker here. Like nothing's ever going to be the same again."

I knew what she meant. Only, that realization was ten years gone for me.

I tried returning to the Hall of Irn Bale, to return the elf's armor and perhaps find some answers. I gave up after two days of wandering the woods. Whatever paths had brought me to that house, they'd been closed.

As dusk approached at the end of the second day, a ghostly music lured me deep into the woods. I knew to be cautious, but followed it all the same.

The song, played on the strings of a lute, brought me to a stream fed by a short waterfall. On the smooth rocks along the brief cliff sat an elf. Dressed in a white gown of ancient design pinned at one shoulder, she strummed a lute of inhumanly fine craft.

I stood by the stream, listening to the song until it ended. "Your father's left these woods?"

The Oradyn's daughter smiled, opening just her left eye, the golden one. It gleamed like a freshly minted coin in the sun-dappled woods.

"Yes. He has pulled his hall deeper into the Wend. Why did you return?" She laughed girlishly. "I imagine it wasn't for my music."

I hesitated. The excuse about returning the Oradyn's gift seemed shallow now. "I'm not sure," I admitted. "I suppose . . . I'd hoped for more closure."

The elf maid leapt gracefully off her high rock, her dragonfly wings fluttering as she alighted lightly on the grass on sandaled feet. The wind from her wings kissed my face, tussling my hair.

She stared at me with her mismatched eyes, her expression unreadable. "I am Tzanith, daughter of Irn Bale and Irn Raya, heir to all their legacy. I say this, Alken Hewer—you will be hard-pressed to find closure in this war. It has endured for many an age."

"Do you have a message from them?" I asked.

Tzanith's smile turned sad. "From the Choir? I'm afraid not. That is not my role."

She tucked the beautiful lute under one arm and stepped forward. I remembered her attempt at seduction from before and kept very still, not wanting to invite a repeat performance. But this time, she didn't seem the flirtatious youth anymore. She seemed very much the immortal, seeing more than I could even with my blessings.

She reached out and ran her fingers over the black iron rings of the armor her father had given me. "My mother's mail," she spoke in a near-whisper.

"I am willing to return it," I said. "Now our enemy is dead."

She shook her head, causing her long blue braid to swing. "No. This was a gift, and it is yours. I do not wish to go as my mother did. I love music, and laughter. Perhaps, in some age far away, I will be the warrior. My people have time to be many things throughout our lives."

"About before," I blurted. "When I sent you away from the room, I—"

She laughed without ire. "I was very angry! I considered cursing you, but . . ."

She became serious again. "I am not so young that I do not recognize a broken heart when I see it. You did not reject me because I did not please you, Alken Hewer, but because you still see another in your dreams. Is that not so?"

I couldn't reply. My throat felt tight, and I didn't want to risk finding out what might spill from it if I opened my mouth.

"And yet . . ." Her eyes went down to my right hand, where my ring rested. "You deny yourself your dreams. Is it not better to remember, even if there is pain?"

I ran a thumb over the ivory band. "This is better. Safer."

Tzanith turned, her long braid swinging. Then, in a flurry of dragonfly wings, she returned to the rocks. After adjusting her dress and folding her legs, she placed her fingers to the strings of the lute.

"I think I will make a song for this thing. For the lord of Caelfall, for what he became, and what he might have been."

"And how many lives of men will pass before it's finished?" I asked, arching an eyebrow.

The bard only laughed.

Weeks passed before I received the message I'd been waiting for.

I'd strayed far from the dark woods and haunted marshes of Caelfall. I didn't know the name of the forest I'd found myself in, but it was depthless and dark, quiet as a grave.

I sat by a crackling fire within the ruins of an old temple. Some precursor to the Church, I imagined, back when many Onsolain did not have that name and were worshipped as gods without a celestial queen to lead them. The ancient edifice had worn down to little more than a few crumbling walls and sunken foundation.

But power remained in the patch of hallowed ground. Enough to let me rest.

The forest ghosts lurked in the darkness beyond my camp's light, pooling in murmuring schools like amorphous fish along the edges of the ruin walls. Some of them piled in the broken gaps just beyond the wall, staring at me with faces that seemed lit from no apparent source, eyes bloodshot and lidless as they glared at me.

It was a moonless night, overcast, but the dead seemed to produce an unearthly light all their own.

Faen Orgis lay at my side. I had not slept in some days. I ran a thumb over my ring. Red patterns like blood swam through its black stone.

"*Failed again,*" the forest ghosts whispered. "*Failed us. Didn't save us. Let that thing rise out of our corpses like a maggot.*"

Some of the ghosts were from the village I'd left behind weeks before, clinging to my shadow. Lisette and Edgar hadn't managed to bind all of them after all.

"*Perhaps you hoped it would be her?*"

My head shot up, looking for the source of that last voice. I didn't find it and settled back down.

"I did *not* want that," I hissed at the darkness.

The darkness only laughed.

"You shouldn't talk to them," a voice more tangible than the forest spirits said. "It only makes them stronger."

I looked up from the fire to see a figure leaning against one of the ruined walls, just outside the true radius of the firelight. A short man in his late thirties, with a homely face covered in dense brown stubble, a mop of hair loosely tied behind his head. He wore studded leathers over a lean frame.

I could almost see the stone wall *through* him.

"Donnelly," I greeted the ghost. "You can share my fire. Just you."

Donnelly lurched forward and sat cross-legged across the fire from me, holding his hands out. It wasn't a cold night—we were well into summer—but he shivered as violently as if he'd come out of a blizzard, shaking his hands in gratitude for the warmth. Immediately he began to grow more substantial, until he seemed the man he'd been in life. Below average in height, all wiry muscle and cocky attitude, his peasant's features tanned by sun.

He didn't much look like a hero of the Ardent Bough, or the herald of a divine court. And yet, he *was* both.

"Thanks," the rogue said. "Been a while since I got some flame in me. Thought I was starting to fade, like that lot." He jerked a thumb toward the shadows.

"Where've you been?" I asked, tossing a twig into the fire. Sparks danced into the air, and a few will-o'-the-wisps emerged with them to twirl playfully. They'd followed me from Caelfall, too, though most had wandered off into the wilds over the weeks.

A sour expression crossed the ghost's bony face. "Working. Feels like all Urn's bloody burning, some days. Parts of it still are, in truth . . ."

His gray eyes went distant, then snapped to me. "I heard you did a job for a member of the Choir."

I nodded and told him about what had happened in Caelfall. I left some details out, such as my alliance with a dhampir and confrontation with the itinerant monster hunter.

"Damn . . ." Donnelly folded his arms, rubbing warmth into them. "You really think it's one of the demons old Reynard had on his leash?"

I shrugged. "It felt like it. My powers aren't always reliable. Could have been a stray, or something lurking in the Wend. But I think . . . I think it *was* one of the monsters the Traitor released, yes."

I shook my head, setting my jaw. "We should have worked harder to seal them all."

"Without ol' Tuvon, it's a tall order." Donnelly shrugged, and I had to suppress a smile at his casual mention of the elven king.

"I want you to ask them to let me hunt those other Recusants," I told him.

Donnelly's expression fell into neutrality. "You know it doesn't work that way, Al."

"Tell them what happened," I insisted. "This is what I'm meant for. I need to follow through on what happened at that lake."

"You're not a knight anymore," Donnelly said bluntly. He ignored the angry look that passed over my face, holding up a hand to stall my next words. "You're the Headsman. Your job is to carry out sentences of execution when and where the Choir tells you to, just like my job is to be their courier."

He shrugged. "Neither of us have a fine gig, kid."

I scoffed at that. I was old as Donnelly had been when he'd died.

The ghost sighed. "I'll tell them what you've told me, but no promises. You know the Onsolain don't see everything. Besides . . ."

He hesitated. I leaned forward and clasped my hands, eyes on the fire to watch the wisps play. "You have another mark for me."

Donnelly spread out his hands in a *what can I do?* gesture. "Guilty."

A while passed before I replied. To his credit, Donnelly didn't try to make excuses or hurry me.

"Tell me," I said after several minutes.

"They want you to head west, to the Bannerlands," Donnelly said. "Can't say much more as of yet."

I nodded. It was often like this. I'd be given a direction, then either perform a rite of communion or wait for some other message to get the details. Sometimes it would take weeks of following vague signs and portents before I found myself in the right position to get the full picture.

"That's a populated country," I said after some thought. "Not the kind of place I'd think they would send me. Lot of towns. Lot of nobles." *Lot of soldiers,* I thought darkly. I wouldn't be able to vanish into the wilderness so easily in a realm that was so densely populated.

"Even still," Donnelly said unapologetically, "that's where you're bound. Once you've crossed the border, perform the rites. You know the drill."

His eyes went to the woods. "Too many ears here. No telling if any of these wild ghosts are reporting to some necromancer somewhere. Better to give you the rest of it in a church, or in a dream. Either way, head west."

Donnelly left not long after. Vanished like a mirage as was his wont. That suited my mood. The ghosts whispered in the shadows, wild chimera hooted in the deeper darkness beyond, and the silent clouds rolled above. The whole world seemed to be made of night and monsters.

Sometimes, it could be hard to remember there were other little islands of light beyond all that fang-filled black.

I sat by the fire for a long while, thinking. The wisps kept it warm. Handy little creatures. Part of me had been glad of their company, but they were fey. No telling when they'd wander off. Perhaps, when Irn Bale had closed the ways to his hall, they'd been stranded.

"You can stay with me long as you like," I said to them, not sure they understood. "Might see some nasty things, though."

One little mote of faerie-light danced toward my face, spun around my head once, then returned to the fire. I almost smiled. Almost.

Part of me regretted not asking Catrin to stick with me. I think she might have, had I asked. Of most anyone I'd met, she may not have minded my grim work.

But she'd also need to feed, and I wasn't willing to let her use me that way, or other innocents in my presence. Better for her to stay at her strange devil's inn, where she could get her blood from those who offered it freely.

It wouldn't have worked. We would have resented one another, eventually.

I tossed another twig into the fire, watching the tiny lights dance through the dark until they cooled. I lifted my right hand and ran the thumb of my left over my ring. The stone had gone almost entirely to red over the past weeks. It had fed well.

I slipped the ring off my finger, settled against the shattered temple wall at my back, and closed my eyes.

I let myself dream.

ABOUT THE AUTHOR

A. J. Drummond is the author of the Oathbreaker series, originally released on Royal Road. He is a lover of all things fantasy and science fiction, and his work also includes dashes of romance, horror, and action and adventure. Drummond lives just outside Kansas City with his family and has friends from all over the world.

JOIN THE FELLOWSHIP

follow us on our socials

 podiumentertainment.com

 @podiumentertainment

 /podiumentertainment

 @podium_ent

 @podiumentertainment